This novel is the first to portray
the spiritual development of an empath.
Read here about the author, an acclaimed intuitive.

"Rosetree seems most reasonable and convincing in her accessible descriptions of spiritual abilities and demonstrated sample readings [in her video *Thrill Your Soul*]. With spirituality a 'hot' topic in public library collections, this program is an enlightening choice for receptive viewers."
  Booklist

"It's like she's known you forever . . . but that's crazy, because you just met. Still, she has described you perfectly, and not just your surface traits."
  The Washington Post

"She doesn't immediately seek feedback on her accuracy. She sits back, confident that she's at least partly on target. When she does ask, it's with a flat sense of curiosity, like someone peering out of a rain-splattered window to check on a storm's progress."
  The Washington Times

"Rose Rosetree can spot a potential fibber a mile away. Or, in this case, 2,400 miles away."
  Las Vegas Sun

"I decided to send her a picture of myself . . . with the caveat that my wife would 'check' her report for accuracy. 'She's got your number,' was my wife's simple response."
  The Catholic Standard

"[Governor John Engler and Mayor Terry McKane] were highly skeptical . . . [but] both men said they found Rosetree's readings uncannily true."
  Lansing State Journal

"Most of the stories I write don't generate quite this much interest."
  USA Today reporter Cathy Hainer, e-mail to Rosetree

Praise for *Empowered by Empathy,*
a how-to by Rose Rosetree

Even for those of us who aren't New Agers, Rose Rosetree has written a fine, fascinating book: clear, insightful, and packed with easy-to-follow techniques.
  Marguerite Kelly, Author, *The Mother's Almanac*

This book embodies a wealth of wisdom, vision, and heart, and it is the fruit of deep experience. I especially like Rose's personal stories, guidelines for skill building, and practical questions and answers. I envision this book helping many people to connect with their spiritual gifts and expand them in service.
  Alan Cohen, Author, *Dare to Be Yourself*

Another multi-faceted miracle from Rose Rosetree: practical, simple, methodical, compassionate, funny, and absolutely thorough. You'll use it again and again.
  Susun S. Weed, Author, *Menopausal Years: The Wise Woman Way*

Rose Rosetree is a fountain of joyful spiritual wisdom. We can all benefit from her positive insight.
  David Lawson, Author, *A Company of Angels*

Rose Rosetree's book lovingly invites us to own our natural gifts, to rise to the awesome task of being who we are more consciously, and to accept our empathic nature as a powerful tool for living. Rose's teachings reflect her uncanny ability to jump start our own powerful empathic spirits.
  Bill Bauman, Ph.D., Author, *Oneness:*

Ms. Rosetree's easy way of putting into words concepts that I had been vaguely aware of—but never thought there was any way of quantifying or describing—is very refreshing. By sharing her own personal experiences with empathy she demonstrates that you, too, can recognize your own empathic gifts and learn to use them as tools to build a more balanced and joyful life.
  Fearless Reviews

Empowered by Empathy describes ethical ways to connect with others while maintaining your own boundaries and staying grounded. Miracles ensue.
  Pathways Magazine

THE ROAR OF THE HUNTIDS

Rose Rosetree

Copyright© 2002 by Rose Rosetree
Cover Design© 2002 by Mythic Design Studio, www.mythicstudio.com
Inside Design consulting by Eda Warren, Typesetting by Rose Rosetree
Editing by Catharine Rambeau, Copy Editing by Suzanne Wolfe
Author photo by Jan Kawamoto Jamil
Printed in Canada by Westcan Printing Group
10 9 8 7 6 5 4 3 2 1

Library of Congress Control Number: 2001097733
Publisher's Cataloging-in-Publication
  (Provided by Quality Books, Inc.)

Rosetree, Rose.
    The roar of the huntids / by Rose Rosetree — 1st ed.

    p. cm.
    ISBN 0-9651145-5-4

    1. Spiritual life—Fiction. 2. Self-realization—
Fiction. 3. Feminism—Fiction. I. Title.

PS3568.O84137R63 2002   813'.6
                      QBI01-701299

Please direct all correspondence and inquiries to:
Women's Intuition Worldwide, LLC
116 Hillsdale Drive
P.O. Box 1605, Sterling, VA 20167-1605
703-404-4357

Visit the author's website: www.Rose-Rosetree.com

Dedicated to those who believe
there could be higher praise for a woman
than to say, "Did you lose weight?"

Acknowledgments

Even a work of fiction, I've discovered, has its basis in truth. I'm grateful to all the friends and family members who have taught me by example about living fully in the moment, with humor and integrity. They were my role models as this novel shaped itself over the years and its characters presented themselves to my imagination.

The copyright page of a book may not be fascinating reading to most people but this one reveals the main people I have to acknowledge, and I'd like to give special thanks to Catharine Rambeau, the best writing teacher I've ever had as well as the finest editor.

Friends helped me at every phase of writing and production, be they spiritual teachers, students, librarians, writers whose work I admire or buddies I've met only over the Internet. Among the hundreds of people whom I gratefully acknowledge, heart to heart, for making this book possible, my best friend and husband, Mitch Weber, stands at the head of the line.

Chapter 1
Better Than Rotten George?

"Hurry up." Rachel ran toward the front door of her house, calling her son as she juggled purse, water bottles, and jog shoes... plus she threw in some good ab crunches, not that she necessarily needed them.

Brent opened the door from outside and came in to meet her, 52 pounds of irrepressible energy, dressed in bright green shorts and a T-shirt silk-screened with his own smiling picture.

"So that's where you were. Come on, we're late."

Brent seemed untouched by her grumpiness as his blond curls followed Rachel into the family's Honda Hybrid. Every scale on the car's no-wax alligator finish gleamed—not enough, however, to change Rachel's mood. With good traffic they'd be lucky to make it by six. She hated being late, especially now, when she needed so badly to talk to Heather.

Of all the stupid cars. How could it tell me to take Bush Parkway? Soon as they turned the corner, Rachel could see all eight lanes on her side of the road were pure crawl. And this was the best route her car could offer? She dug into her seat, preparing to sit, sit, sit. *Might as well do some Kegels to keep the time from being a total waste,* she thought.

How was Brent doing? She looked over her shoulder. Engrossed in re-reading *Globula High*, his favorite kid-sized vampire novel, Brent's eyes never left the page; he took a sip from his soft drink bottle, replaced it between his knees, then un-wrapped an extra stick of gum. All that product should keep him busy for a while.

Even if five-mile-an-hour traffic was a predictable nuisance in their part of Capitol City, Brent never seemed to mind. Rachel? She minded. Did the stress of her poky life show? That was the important question. She stared into the rear view mirror and didn't feel reassured by the fact that, of course, she was technically beautiful. What woman in the 20's wasn't? Rachel's best features were her perky angled eyebrows, naturally straight nose and sexy big cheeks. But who noticed?

And who cared that her shoulder-length brown curls were perfect or how her make-up flattered her eyes, which were an unusual shade of golden brown. She stared deeply into those eyes, searching for what her husband, Jeremy, had ever seen in her.

A nearby car beeped, making her jump. Traffic was so slow. Inside Rachel felt a grumble of disgust begin to gather force. What was it with her lately? Rage was starting to take on a life of its own, as though Rachel had pressed her own accelerator down to the floor.

"Swing your arms like this," Brent instructed as they marched from the parking lot. "See? I figured out how you can use your arms to speed up your legs. We don't want to be late, Mom."

They held hands, swinging them fast back and forth. Rachel loved the feel of Brent's miniature palm, fitting hers perfectly. And the flow of love between them. Sometimes it seemed to Rachel that she spent all her days loving people—not perfectly, maybe, but the best she could. Yet her son seemed to be the only one who loved her back.

How many more years would he be willing to hold hands with her in public? Some day that last bit of little-boy sweetness would go the way of his loony, liquid baby laugh. She'd miss the feel of his happy presence connected with hers, palm to palm.

"Look, Mom, other runners are coming, too. Maybe we'll make it on time."

Last July, they'd been late for the first meeting of Summer Runner's Club. Brent claimed it spoiled everything and refused to participate for the rest of the summer. No way would Rachel let that happen two years in a row! She and her best friend, Heather, had made a date to walk-and-talk here every Wednesday. And maybe, just maybe, Heather could help Rachel figure out what to do about her travesty of a marriage.

They joined the group in time for warm-ups. A spry looking 90-something volunteer in hot pink Air-Flopper shoes was having everyone fill out legal disclaimers. "I promise not to sue you" forms were so routine, you'd fill them out at the entrance to every store in the mall. Without being asked, Rachel showed the volunteer her Digitized Datamate. On the disclaimer, she stamped in the datamate's unflattering hologram of her family, plus the rest of the standard info:

Signature: Rachel Murphy, Date: July 8, 2020
Spouse: Jeremy Murphy, Children: Brent Murphy
Address: 618 Terrytown Lane, Sterling, VA 20189-1203-X3V
Skin-phone: 888-314-670-1444, Home Phone: 703-927-8640-672
E-mail: JerRachBren@SterlingVA.home, Website: Partygirl.com
Health Services ID: RMurphy-287-43-9733-0210
Do not rent or sell this information. Privacy offenses punishable by law.

Rachel joined Brent on the lawn. Seemingly he was doing warm-up stretches. Really he was busy looking backward between his legs, checking out the other kids. Rachel tried this, too. Just before toppling over, she managed to see Heather race to the warm-up area, dragging one daughter by the hand, while her older daughter sprinted ahead. Heather saw Rachel, too, tilting her head to one side and her hip to the other, as if to give Rachel a full-body wink.

"No matter what I do, somebody's going to get hurt." That's how Rachel wanted to start the conversation once she and Heather began to walk around the track. But Rachel always had to let Heather vent first. That was Heather's pattern, to Rachel's carefully hidden annoyance.

"Rachie, you look so pretty with those denim sunglasses. Did you buy them to match your jeans?"

"Just my first pick out of the family UV box." Rachel said, thinking, *Pathetic question! Every family has dozens of wraparound glasses. Who but Heather would care?*

Her friend, the clotheshorse, preened by patting her braided tower of blonde hair. It was framed by a hologram turtleneck with images of Marilyn Monroe against a soft yellow background. Heather looked better than Marilyn, though. In addition to Heather's long cheerleader legs below, were her fabulous dimples above.

They showed even when Heather didn't smile. Now, for instance. Several months into her separation from Rotten George, Heather still complained on a regular basis. Rachel was determined to listen with depth, like the good friend she was, but what a thankless chore! Whether you listened to her so hard your heart ached or you merely went through the motions, Heather didn't seem to be able to tell the difference.

At least Rachel was getting exercise walking the track. Unlike Heather, she needed it. In her natural state she'd plump out like microwaved tofu.

Continuing her tale of woe, Heather said, "The girls came back from visiting George last weekend. He took them out for ice cream. Ashley made the mistake of asking if he thought she was pretty."

Rachel smiled fondly. Though Ashley was five now, she still had a baby doll look, with an innocent face framed by bright blonde hair. By contrast, her big sister was wiry and smart. Close to Brent's age, Kayla had straight eyebrows that darted across her face and an equally direct way of speaking her mind. Little Ashley took after her mother instead, and was promising to be quite the little flirt.

"Oh, Heather, how could he mess that one up? Ashley's adorable."

"You think so? Not to good old Georgie. He told her, 'You're cute now but don't let yourself stay chubby when you grow up. Men prefer girls who are slim.'"

"What? He thinks your daughter's been wasting her first five years of life, not dieting?"

"The night Ashley came home, she cried herself to sleep. How could a father tell his daughter something like that?"

"Coming from George, I guess it makes sense," Rachel said. "Let's face it. All the man thinks about is sex, and he's been taught that thin equals sexy."

"Rotten George was always a no-brainer sex machine. I guess the difference is, he used to pretend he was more."

Rachel nodded sympathetically, glad she was helping Heather to gain closure. "Considering where his so-called mind is now, your fabulous Ex probably thought he was giving Ashley helpful advice. He doesn't want her to suffer the same fate as *his* rejects."

Heather turned her woeful face toward Rachel. "I guess so. But don't you see how George made it sound as if our only real problem in the marriage was my not being thin enough? Like he didn't want me any more because of a little cellulite?"

Huh? In that moment, Rachel wasn't sure which was worse, Rotten George or self-centered Heather, with her tendency to turn every conversation into a commentary on how she looked. How about the trauma to Ashley? How about the fact that her alleged friend, Rachel, was hurting now, too? Given how much pain Rachel was in today, wouldn't a real friend would have noticed as soon as Rachel opened her mouth? By now, wouldn't she have asked what was wrong? All Heather noticed was *her* pain, *her* sex life, and how much cellulite showed in *her* mirror.

Quickly Rachel corrected herself. *With all her faults, Heather has a good heart. She deserves better in a husband than this immature idiot.* Putting her arm around teary-eyed Heather, Rachel steered her over to pick up their water bottles.

Runners Club members left their bottles by a water fountain. Hundreds of bottles were there, everything from double economy-sized bottles of Bubbled Uppers ("Made with a kiss of ginseng," the latest soft-drink craze) to old-fashioned, self-cleaning sippy cups. Locating your particular bottle could take a while. Under the best of circumstances, Heather had trouble. Tonight? Forget it. Sighing, Rachel picked up her water bottle and offered to share it.

Inwardly she felt less generous than she seemed. Heather might be her best friend, but only by default, a friend of convenience. She wasn't a peer like Jeremy (even if these days he didn't give or receive love any better than Heather).

Seminar Slaves like Heather and Rachel had a hard time making friends. Their limited friendship of pretend closeness wasn't anyone's fault, merely the best they could manage. *Something is better than nothing,* as Rachel's mom, Helene, would say. Undoubtedly Heather found Rachel at least as frustrating deep down—assuming that Heather had a deep down, which was hard to tell.

The self-pitying way Heather sipped at the proffered water bottle pushed Rachel past her limit, however. Since she couldn't complain, within the rules of the friendship, she speed-walked ahead. When Heather caught up, Rachel was keeping pace with an angry inner refrain: *So when is it going to be my turn?*

"Thanks for listening, Rachie," Heather said, running up. Gently she dabbed a tissue near her eye make-up. "You're lucky to be with a good man, a man you can trust."

Heather's words seemed to hang in the air for a fraction of a second before Rachel said, "I'm beginning to wonder."

"What?" Heather squeaked.

"Jeremy's having an affair."

"What?" again, higher pitched.

"Seems like it, anyway. He's been staying late at the office, which he never used to."

"The bug place, right? He studies bugs."

"Yes, he still has that nice secure government job with the good family leave and no mandatory overtime. And normally I suppose there's nothing so fascinating about his job that he stays late after work. Until lately. Something's been changing, and I think it's his new secretary."

Rachel stopped walking. She turned to face Heather. "I'm so scared. If he's cheating, Brent will be hurt. I'll be hurt."

"Oh."

"And what if I leave him? Then Brent will be hurt. Jeremy, too—even though he's acting like a jerk."

"Oh, no."

"So I wonder, should I say nothing and wait? Or should I play tough and force him to give her up? No matter what I do, somebody's going to get hurt. What would you do, Heather?"

"I don't know, Rachie."

"Lately every single thing that man does makes me mad," Rachel said, holding back her tears.

The women walked faster now, swinging their arms, getting down to business. From a distance they looked like sisters: equal attractiveness, perfectly matched steps. Both were busty babes. Admittedly that was now standard for American females over the age of 14, when you'd get your starter set of implants if genetics wouldn't let you make C-cup on your own; then at 21 you'd upgrade to D and beyond.

Both these women, though, had come by their figures the old-fashioned way, which was one of the reasons they bonded as friends. Having grown up conspicuously curvy at a time when this was rare in high school gave both of them status—a memory they clung to, however fleeting. At this time in their lives, neither Heather nor Rachel felt herself busting out with status.

Yet they were beautiful. And staring at them close up, you might have seen a resemblance. Both were members of the Dimple Club. Both had huge eyelids—Heather's being decorated with a peach-frosted silicon polish that perfectly matched the sparkles on her silicon Glamour Face Make-up—where a sprinkling of sympathy tears was now beading up like water on a windshield.

Rachel's eyelids bore no make-up, high-tech or otherwise. Her red lipstick might not even show by now, considering that her whole face scrunched into a frown. Aggressive not-crying did that. Her story was muttered in shades of gray: how Rachel hated Jeremy's new secretary, Sally, right from the first time she heard her syrupy little voice; how a man as handsome as Jeremy always got passes from women; how lately he'd been acting more withdrawn than ever; how yesterday she'd heard him sneak into his den and frantically search through his papers. He must have found what he was looking for because afterwards she heard him slam his briefcase shut.

Was it lingerie receipts? Hotel receipts? Maybe it was entire restaurant menus for future rendezvous.

Heather asked, "How can you be sure he was looking for stuff like that? Your house doesn't have cameras, does it?

"The sound of shuffling papers isn't easy to mistake. Even though Jeremy keeps our home intercom off, we still have air vents, you know. All I had to do was put my ear next to the bedroom vent and listen."

"What did you do when things sounded suspicious, keep listening?"

"No way! I marched into his home-office and said, 'You want me to help you find something? After all, you're the neat one but I'm the organized one.'"

Heather gave her a look. "Are you sure that was feminine?"

"I said it lightly, like a joke."

"Yeah?"

"You should have seen him jump. The guy looked so guilty."

Heather looked concerned. "Do you blame him? I mean, that reminds me of something I saw on John Gray's Therapy Show about how we should let our men stay in their caves. Let's see, when was that? I know, last week, when the Bill Gates heir came on with his wife. You didn't happen to see that episode, did you?"

"No, Heather."

Volunteer counselors blew whistles to signal the end of the hour. Rachel jumped. "God, that's so loud," she complained, not that Heather gave any clue of sharing Rachel's super-sensitive hearing. Sighing, she followed Heather's lead to the area where parents of eight-year olds were collecting their kids. Kayla was playing with Brent, throwing pebbles at a tree. Rachel didn't have much time left, even to be heard on the most superficial level.

Quickly she whispered, "Heather, last night, Jeremy didn't come home 'till 10:30. Will the same thing happen tonight? What should I do?"

"You're asking me, the big expert on saving a marriage? You're the smart one." She gave a playful smile that popped out her dimples, then grabbed Kayla. "Byeeee. We gotta get Ashley."

Even before Heather and Kayla disappeared into the crowd, Brent walked towards her. He caught her eye, really saw her. What a relief it was to greet him and feel his energy respond to hers.

Having the inner part of a relationship be real is what I crave, Rachel thought, *I need that much more than having a person act nice on the surface.*

Nevertheless, when Brent compounded his good vibes with a huge smile, that scarcely went unnoticed. Rachel drank it in like a cactus being offered a raindrop.

Driving home in the car, Rachel thought about her sort-of-friend Heather. Some people were wired to experience the inner juice of life. Ones like Heather weren't, no matter how cleverly they might mimic the signals.

Probably Heather worked as hard at their relationship as Rachel did. Heather knew about Emotional IQ; she'd taken loads of relationship seminars. But she couldn't hear when Rachel sent out energy signals that went deeper than the mere names for emotions.

One part of Rachel always stayed awake, witnessing the energy signals between people. Heather's core self seemed to sleep in darkness, aloof as some faraway planet receiving radio waves. Rachel couldn't even guess what kind of planet Heather would be, when she came alive enough to transmit something back.

Once Rachel had tried to explain to Jeremy how frustrating it was that Heather, like most people she knew, seemed unaware of the flow of energy. The part about feeling people's signals wasn't foreign to him. But the need for exchange was—Jeremy being such a deep loner.

Heather needed friendship as much as Rachel did; the problem was, she couldn't do it with depth. Outwardly gorgeous, inwardly Heather functioned like a doll whose hinged eyelids were glued shut; the spectacle of her beautiful lashes was scant consolation. Rachel kept longing for a doll to play with who would open the eyes beneath her physical eyes and really see.

Giving *was* Rachel's favorite part of life. Only it didn't feel like giving when her husband was incommunicado and Heather, her only close friend, would let all that Rachel gave her slip away, apparently un-received. Brent was the only person Rachel knew right now who accepted her love. It consoled her, being able to give and take with a person who had depth. Still, she had to treat him like a child, not an adult friend. So now, for Brent's sake, Rachel hid her loneliness. Driving the Honda, she wore a brave mask, though it felt as slickly false as her Revlon 3-D Red Hot Babe lipstick.

Stuck in the traffic jam on Bush Parkway, Rachel felt a wordless song run through her head. It was a song of despair. Her only real adult friend was Jeremy. She'd always assumed that he was better than Heather's ex, Rotten George. But maybe not.

Chapter 2
Keep the Flame of Hope Alive

Jeremy didn't come home until Rachel was in bed. What time was it, midnight? She squinted at the Radio Pal on his night table. Eleven thirty was bad enough. She faked sleep while he tiptoed around the bedroom, padded fingertips searching his closet for an empty suit hanger.

If there was one thing she couldn't stand it was having him sneak around. "Jeremy, just put the light on. I'm awake." She tried to sound friendly, not annoyed.

"Sorry about the late night at the office, Sweetheart. Don't worry, I'll be in bed soon."

Don't worry, as if! Rachel rolled onto her side, turning away from him in advance. Tall and slim, with dazzling blue eyes set in a wide forehead, he was easy enough to imagine. Even without imagining, she could *feel* his presence—sexy enough to light up any room he walked into, though maddeningly unapproachable.

Once under the covers, though, Jeremy reached for her as usual. Angry though she felt, Rachel couldn't resist his kisses. The way he stroked her body moved her outdoors, into a big sky of hugeness and stars. It was their place of tenderness. Rachel snuggled into his armpit. She recognized a certain smell that would ripen as they made love.

She loved the progression of smells as much as all the ways he would please her. What if everything between them was really okay? What if she had only imagined...

But abruptly he moved away. "I'm tired, Sweetie. It was a tough day at work."

"I understand," Rachel said mechanically, turning back to her side of the bed. That's how their "sex life" was these days, a half life. Wasn't that a term from physics? Jeremy would know. He also knew if he was cheating on her, which gave him way too much power in their relationship right now.

After Rachel could hear from his breathing that he was asleep, she rolled onto her left side, watching him. Jeremy ran his hands down the sleeves of the blue silk pajamas she'd given him for their last anniversary. Was that a good sign, like he was symbolically thanking her for the gift? But sometimes arm gestures were supposed to mean a brush-off. Why, oh why, hadn't she paid better attention to that Body Language Seminar?

"Rachel," a man's voice called to her gently. "Wake up and start your new day, Thursday, July 9, 2020. Today is going to be wonderful."

The message sounded wonderful, anyhow. It should. Rachel had scripted the words herself when she bought the wake-up console. And she'd personally chosen that gorgeous voice from the company's selection of dubbers.

Would Jeremy like a console like this? She could have her own voice taped on the message, not this dubber's. Rachel visualized him from his voice: African bloodstream, deep-chested, idealistic and young. Jeremy, by contrast, sounded like bland old Boston-Irish bloodstream, intellectual, middle-aging, only poetic when in a good mood and, the rest of the time, what Rachel deserved as a match for her own sarcastic self.

Yet they knew each other so well after all these years. Watching him in the morning light, Rachel felt a special tenderness for the unexpected things about his face, quirks that had taken her years to discover—like the way his ears tilted back at a rakish angle. Maybe that's what made them musician's ears. Back in college, he used to play the harpsichord. When they met, his intensity made him stand out from all the other guys. Intense he had remained over the years, but lately it seemed that he'd walled himself off, acting distant even for him and—not that she quite dared admit this to herself—ordinary.

How Rachel wished she could break through his indifference and bring him back. As he lay next to her now, he snored contentedly through a part-open mouth. In profile, his nose stuck out way too far. It was the only imperfection in a drop-dead gorgeous face. Once she had hinted that he should let a cosmetic surgeon take a whack at that schnozz and bring it down to normal size. Jeremy just glared. Her Retro-Techie husband didn't believe in cosmetic surgery. Admittedly Rachel didn't need it herself, but she'd been tempted to send him just once, for that nose.

They'd been married 13 years now, so the rosy-fingered dawn of romance had long since morphed into the harsher, potbellied light of high noon. Flaws showed in full view, and even more glaring than his nose was the possibility that, at this very moment, Jeremy was in a form of post-fornication recharge. He could have been having this affair with Sally for weeks.

Uncertainty put Rachel in a horrible position. What if she asked him point blank about Sally? Rachel had no evidence other than his late homecomings and the fact that they hadn't made love in how long, two weeks? Asking might make her look pathetic. Yet if she didn't ask, how long could she live with the feeling that something between them was wrong?

Rachel's wake-up console stopped repeating its message and shut off with an abrupt click. *Earth to Rachel: Get going already.*

What would he do if she slipped on top of him, lissome and naked? She could wake him up by unbuttoning his pajamas.

Forget it. Surprise attacks hadn't worked even on their honeymoon. Jeremy was a true introvert, requiring solitude first thing in the morning or else he'd get a headache. Nothing personal, he claimed.

Now he breathed loudly, close to a snore. It was hard to believe that such a lusty breather could be so unsociable. Jeremy didn't need people the way Rachel did. Except, of course, that apparently he needed Sally, or whoever it was.

In many ways, Jeremy was a difficult man. His being Retro-Techie certainly didn't help because it contributed to one of Rachel's other major problems in life, the lack of friends. Most scientists were either among The Righteous or they were simply Techies; some were even Seminar Slaves like her. Who else at his office was such an old-fashioned skeptic?

She'd never forget his crack about the Inner Closet workshop. Last winter Jeremy mentioned how popular it was among some of the guys at work, and Rachel's ears perked up. Maybe this would be the seminar for him!

She replayed their conversation now against the background of Jeremy's snores. He had been taking his clothes off before bed.

"Want to hear something funny?" he said.

"If I have to. I'd rather *do* something funny."

"Come on, Rachel. Wayne told me he spent all last weekend deciding where he should hang his personal memories. According to this dopey Inner Closet seminar, every ten years you're supposed to clean out the memories that don't belong in 'a healthy subconscious.' Can you believe that a scientist like Wayne could be so gullible?"

"But you should approve of that seminar, Jeremy. You're neat."

"Not in my subconscious, thank you. Everyone needs a junk drawer. That's mine."

When he got into bed that night, she pretended to search his body for secret drawers. Of course, that was back in the days when they made love every night.

Sure he'd always wisecrack about seminars, but otherwise he showed her such tenderness, even quoting love poetry to her sometimes at odd moments. And how about the way he played music downstairs in his office? He made that cheap synthesizer sound like a million bucks, playing all those Bach organ pieces. Some days she learned more about Jeremy from overhearing how he played music than by anything he said to her directly.

What could you do with an introvert like Jeremy Murphy, especially when he turned off the sex?

Rachel was not going to cry beside him in the bed while he snored. Instead she did a couple of angry butt crunches. Some sexy men couldn't be monogamous. For breakfast, they craved Variety Pack. That's how it was.

You've got to keep the flame of hope alive, she thought. Even though this was one of her favorite songs, she didn't want to have the tune run through her head. To move it out, she poked him: "Jeremy, wake up."

His body jerked all over; then he started rubbing his sleeves again. What was going on with him? She decided not to kiss him good morning. Instead she gave him a playful Get out! shove, the classic gesture from "Seinfeld."

"You up?"

He grunted and tried to smile.

"Good. I'll race you to the shower."

She let Jeremy win, which was hard considering that he scampered out of the bed like a star from "Night of the Ancient Zombies." Sighing, Rachel went to wake up Brent.

He lay across his bed sideways, wrapped in the cocoon he had made of his sheet, which was printed with a colorful Spielberg-Stewart space design. Boys started out so frisky. How could they mature into lumps like Jeremy?

"Rise and shine, Brent. I'm going to get the timer. We'll start your bath in exactly two minutes."

As the tub filled, Brent chatted excitedly. While Rachel listened, she washed her face, an operation that involved using her scrubbie appliance with Ultra-penetration Lipid Cream, then layering on a series of three custom-made, genetically designed skin products. After she finished, Brent still hadn't washed his face. Or anything else. She threw him a second washcloth. He was so long now, his legs looked like stilts. Rachel paused to admire Brent's perfect little boy body.

He was saying, "Know what? When you come to Scout Camp today you'll see me do archery. Isn't that great? Can you sit with me, Mom, when we have lunch? Can we have our own table?"

His smile melted her, and it didn't hurt that his eyes were electric violet, the same shade as Jeremy's.

"No promises," she said, using her Tough Mom voice. "I don't know what it's like, volunteering at Scout Camp. But I'll do my best, okay?"

By seven Jeremy left for work, pressing his lips to hers without touching any other part of her body, as if she was an appliance with an on-off switch at the mouth. Whether this gesture meant that he was turning her on or off, it made her feel awful. But she wouldn't sit there and sulk. With Brent occupied out of earshot, she could call someone for moral support.

Rachel moved to the big-screen phone in her office and dialed up her mother. Helene looked happy to see her. As always, she also looked reassuringly well preserved. What was she, a Size Two? Of course, Rachel had inherited her physique from the other side of the family, the pudge side.

After some introductory chit-chat, Rachel asked, "Mom, you and Dad have been married so long. Were you ever worried that he might be having an affair?"

Helene's huge brown eyes widened. "Are you guessing or do you know?"

"Guessing, I suppose. Worrying."

"Honey, you look like you've been keeping yourself attractive. How about the house. Is it as clean as it should be?"

"Excuse me? I've come to like cleaning. Really."

Helene gave a barely audible snort.

"Mom, after you and Dad had been married this long, did he ever act like he found you boring?"

"Honey, do you really want my opinion?"

"Sure." Inwardly Rachel cringed.

"If anything, I think you care too much. You could be more involved elsewhere."

"What, go to Temple? We've had this conversation already. I'm not into Judaism like you are, okay?"

"Not that, then. But you could be more involved with your son."

"Like how? What that I'm not doing already?"

"Rachel, how should I put this? I know you're a good mother. You love your son...."

"What, then?"

"Remember all the activities I used to do for you and your brothers? The play dates I made, and the special parties?"

"You kept us very active, Mom. I guess I could do more. But what does that have to do with my marriage?"

"A man can tell, Rachel. You live in your own world. I think that today men want their wives to be committed as homemakers."

"Homemakers! I can't believe you'd use such a retro word. How about you? When you had young kids, you did things for us at home but you still worked at Dad's business, didn't you?"

"Well, Rachel, you asked what I think and I told you. So what if I don't take all your fancy seminars. I'm 61 years old. I've seen plenty of marriages come and go."

Her mother could be right, Rachel thought later, walking out to the car with Brent. Maybe Rachel did need more involvement. Easy for her mother to say! She never visited, and only checked in occasionally from a screen-phone. Running a thriving catering business in Manhattan, how could Helene begin to understand how lonely life could be for Rachel, stuck in the suburbs in the 20's—especially considering that, for Helene, a major act of imagination would be adding extra sauerkraut to a hot dog.

By spending today volunteering at Scout Camp, maybe Rachel and Brent might meet some real friends, kindred spirits. Soon she'd picked up her first Cub Scout from the neighborhood. *Another squirmy eight-year-old,* she laughed to herself. Tom Smith had been in Brent's class last year. Now, like Brent, he wore blue jeans and a silly Scout Camp shirt with cartoon characters on it.

"Good morning, Mrs. Murphy," he said. Smiling he revealed the big, rabbity front teeth of an eight-year-old. This wholesome kid's mother was what Helene would call "involved." Jessica Smith volunteered actively in three classrooms, one for each kid. She coached Tom's baseball team. No doubt Jessica was a pillar of her church, too. She was an All American—not one of those zealot Traditionals or (even worse) one of The Righteous. What really impressed Rachel was how, with the countless chores Jessica did to hold their neighborhood together, she worked with such apparent enjoyment.

Rachel would have loved to spend more time with Jessica. But Rachel would never qualify as friend material. All Americans like Jessica were clean-cut people with neat hair, normal folks. Just look at Tom. His face looked like deep dish apple pie, wide open and jovial. You wanted to hug him, wishing that some of that effortless good-heartedness might rub off on you. But of course you did nothing of the sort. You said, "Hey, Tom, having a good time at camp this summer?" You expected a grunt for an answer. And when you got it, you thought it was one of the nicer kid grunts you'd heard in a while.

When they picked up their second passenger, Harrison Austin, Brent was showing off, reading out loud from a kid-sized consumer magazine aimed at teenagers. Instead of saying hello, he shouted, "Hey, want to hear about what's wrong with toys?"

"Toys? What kind of toys?" yelled Harrison, as the car buckled him up in the back seat. Although she'd never met him before, he didn't look hard to size up. Obviously, he was one of the Virtual People. These were families where parents and kids spent most of their waking hours hooked up to V-R games, playing one hour-long round after another. They called it entertainment. Outsiders called it addiction.

According to *The Washington Post-Times*, V-R addiction was a typical techno-problem. Millions of Americans had been raised on unlimited TV. When Virtual Reality came out with a cheap price tag, they turned to it, assuming the product was safe. Only years later did psychologists discover the addictive powers of "the Electronic Companion."

In hindsight, it should have been obvious that V-R could be even more addictive than television. Didn't it come with whopper screens, full Sensaround Sound and Life-Tone Color? Plus you had that great selection of interactive story lines. Rachel envied V-R addicts sometimes. What wouldn't she give right now for the sense that her life had a story line!

Luckily Jeremy had been adamant about banning V-R from their home. Addiction started so easily. Both she and Jeremy agreed that V-R addiction was barely one step up from being hooked on drugs like heroin. Just because drugs were legal didn't make them right.

Virtual People didn't make Rachel want to throw up, the way addicts did, with their hollowed-out eyes and contagious spaciness. All the same, Rachel's gut told her to keep Virtual People at a distance. Conveniently that was just what they wanted. You could easily tell V-Rs because their faces seldom moved. Harrison, here, was loudly demanding that Brent give him toys, yet the kid barely moved his lips.

Being in charge of Harrison for a day would, at least, be interesting. How could a boy this peculiar not help Rachel take her mind off Jeremy? Decorating his head with attitude, Harrison's little ears jutted out at an impossible angle. Was that natural? Nah, it had to be surgery.

Rachel smiled at him pleasantly through the rear view mirror.

He ignored her friendly look. "Hi, could you give me some backseat screen?"

By now they were inching along Leesburg Lane, headed toward Holiday Lakes Scout Campground. "Sorry, but we don't allow TV in our car."

"A CD is okay, so long as I get my entertainment."

"Are all you boys comfortable?" Rachel asked, trying to ignore him. "We sure have a beautiful day for camp."

"I need my entertainment," Harrison whined, refusing to let the matter drop. "Do you have rap music by the Hornets?"

Through the rear view mirror, Rachel gave him the lite version of a smile. "No, dear."

Since he rolled his eyes, she explained, "Our family spends so many hours on the road, we like to save it for quality time together. You know, driving can be a great chance to talk."

"Booooring," Harrison said. "Okay, kid, you might as well read."

Soon, though, all three boys were talking away, interrupting each other like old friends. It was easy for them to bond, Rachel thought. The shared the goofy, off-the-wall energy peculiar to eight-year-olds. Who cared if one was V-R, another destined for well-adjusted life as an All American, and her own son a hybrid whose dad was nothing at all while his mom was a Seminar Slave? The boys bragged about how they liked to pull the heads off Barbies and fling the rest of the doll around, playing catch. Rachel glided through the light traffic at 35 m.p.h. Not bad! She started to feel optimistic about today. Reaching out for friends would help her keep the flame of hope alive.

Chapter 3
Scouting for Friends

In the crowded parking lot at scout camp, Rachel resolved to comport herself like a professional mom—whatever that might be. When Mark McDonald and LeShawn Green were put in her charge, she mustered up her most welcoming smile.

In response, LeShawn's close-set eyes narrowed.

"Hi, boys," she said, and turned toward him first. "I'm Brent's mother, Ms. Murphy."

He scuffed the toe of his new Hikestrides into the wood chips on the path.

"Well, LeShawn, your laces need tying. I suppose I'll be tying plenty of shoes today." Rachel's smile stiffened imperceptibly as she touched his straggling shoe-laces. They felt like they'd been chewed by a dog. Meanwhile LeShawn gave her a killer sneer.

After Rachel pulled the laces tight, she yanked the boy's ankle a bit to get his attention. No use. Far as he was concerned, she was invisible.

"My laces need help, too," Mark said. Rachel's fifth scout had wide shoes with big floppy double knots, obviously the work of an adult. The kid reminded her of a basset hound, Rachel thought, humoring him by retying the laces. On impulse, she gave him a quick hug. He clung for a minute. Hah! This child might be willing to connect with her. The others acted as distant as Jeremy.

Rachel looked more closely at Mark, noting his full, pale lips and dull brown hair. Dull but neat—he seemed like an All-American, though not a prime specimen like Tom. As for LeShawn, Rachel guessed that he was Traditional, or else one of The Righteous. Undoubtedly he'd find a way to let her know. Regardless, Rachel would show all these boys how loving a volunteer mom could be. She wasn't volunteering just because each scout's family had to put in a day at Holiday Lakes. If only Helene could see her now—she was involved!

As Rachel led her scouts out of the parking lot, they began poking each other with sticks. Because they'd been in Scout Camp since Monday, by Thursday they knew the path cold. Apparently Rachel was more of a novelty because they put considerable gusto into correcting the way she was "leading" them. This was not as inappropriate as it might seem. Rachel could get lost in a closet.

Eventually something in the distance distracted them, leaving Rachel to continue at her own pace. Ancient trees lifted her eyes upward, awakening memories of childhood vacations: Untouched land with no blacktop, just huge trees and green, green grass.

Her whole life, countryside had meant freedom, but these days it meant so much more. Every year, green spaces became harder to find. The track at Runner's Club, for instance, was dirt set off by some kind of green "miracle" plastic that substituted for grass. Back when Rachel was young, median strips bordered the highways with real grass and trees, but that had long since been paved over to make extra lanes. Now sound walls were the only vertical when you drove major highways. Right behind the concrete wedges, you'd see rows of look-alike townhomes. Entire suburbs stretched like that—townhomes, houses and condos, with tiny gardens at best, for the entire length of Capitol City (formerly called Baltimore, Washington, and Richmond).

This campground came from another time. Hidden behind a thicket of roads, Holiday Lakes was loaded with trees, hills and more than its share of clear blue sky. Forgetting the boys, Rachel stopped to relish it. The smells! The under-smells! Landscapes seen on TV couldn't come close. Maybe that was an ungrateful way to think, since almost every country scene in Rachel's memory had arrived courtesy of home entertainment. Still, real live country was different.

Standing here Rachel felt Nature drop into her as if she were a cup of hot water brewing the most delicious teabag in the world: juicy, fragrant, silent, satisfied...she couldn't begin to name all the flavors—which was amazing right there, because Rachel was one hell of a namer.

If Jeremy could be here to share this, maybe he'd find the words to describe it. If only they could be together here, how could everything between them *not* be all right again?

A call from Rachel's scouts, now far off, made her pop back inside her skin. *Look normal,* she scolded herself, but she had no control over the tears. When she wiped them away, more came—a slow, cold trickle over the apples of her cheeks.

Crybaby, get real! Rachel blinked hard. When that didn't work, she took deep breaths. But that only made her notice the air more, how it was breath-givingly fresh. Conditioned air in the smartest of smart homes couldn't compare. This un-chemicaled air set off a longing deep in Rachel's chest.

Luckily the bobbing orange caps of her scouts in the distance meant the boys were too far away to see her cry. Rachel watched them follow a path up to a huge grassy area crammed with scouts and blue plastic pop-up tents.

At the Volunteer Check-in Station, near the tents, Rachel stamped her datamate. All the parent volunteers had to leave behind their beepers, filmers, vid-phone slings and all other "indispensable" equipment they were used to carting around. Fortunately Rachel had traveled light; all she had to do was let a staffer deactivate her skin-phone.

Rachel glanced down at the array of plastic buttons and holes over her left forearm, at the inside of her elbow. The phone had been embedded so many years ago that by now it seemed more like a part of her body than a machine. This phone+calculator+memo-pad+money manager+appointment book was only the size of an old-fashioned credit card. Well, just so long as the prune-faced guy who turned it off would be able to turn it on later....

Rachel caught up with her five scouts. They found their home tent and flung down their backpacks; bag lunches were placed in a yellow plastic lunch bin that camp staff would soon transfer to the irradiator. When her den joined the others from Sterling, Rachel surveyed the complete scout pack in all its glory. Four other adult volunteers stood around awkwardly; luckily they'd been promised one Professional Scout Camp Leader. Altogether Rachel counted 26 squirmy eight-year olds for them to supervise.

Enter Arnold Dunn, dressed in a tan Scout uniform, much decorated. He seemed to know his stuff; Rachel could tell from the way he greeted the adult volunteers, then the kids. On command, they straggled into line and marched to a part of the field where other packs of scouts were lined up, too.

I can handle today, Rachel thought. *Nobody's here but little kids and volunteers. They might even turn out to be nice. Why shouldn't I be able to find some friends for Brent and me? That would be such a triumph to tell Jeremy.*

The boys teased each other, waiting for the Morning Ceremony, when a chubby Scout approached Rachel.

"I'm sick. I want to go home."

He did look green around the gills. "Where does it hurt?" she asked.

"My stomach."

Rachel brought him to Arnold, who whisked him off to First Aid.

Minutes later Arnold returned. "All set," he said with a wink. His shiny black hair positively twinkled with exuberance. Now here was a man who fit in. Enviously Rachel watched him lead the color ceremony, starting with the Pledge of Allegiance.

"One nation, under God …."

As if! Rachel snorted, watching Brent and the others. In 2020, being one nation in any meaningful sense was a joke, since the ones who talked about it incessantly were either The Righteous or the Traditionals. Once again she mourned how much your social life depended on your affiliation—or lack thereof.

Even friendship with All-Americans, who practiced non-Fundamentalist religion, was hard to come by. Observant Jews like Rachel's parents, or Catholics like Tom's mother, were quick to sniff out those who were different. You couldn't belong if you were too introspective or artistic, too intellectual or mystical. Given her perpetual habit of groping for life's deepest insights, Rachel was destined for the group known as Seminar Slaves. Back when she was in her twenties, the war against terrorism had begun. Psychotherapy went out; seminars came in. And charismatic teachers, flashy as Oprah, developed huge followings that the media dubbed "Seminar Slaves."

Ten years later, it was a fringe group. To stay a Seminar Slave for long, you had to be motivated. Nothing about it was dependable, except for the hope that this week's class or tape would be The One, and you'd improve enough to stop feeling like a secret (or not so secret) collection of sorrows, flaws, phobias, misdirected sensitivities and other worrisome imperfections.

No doubt it was easier to be a Celebrity Watcher. Not into self-improvement or religion, members of this group kept busy by following the lives of actors, musicians, models, and other celebrities who were mostly famous for being famous.

Rachel wished making friends could be as simple for her as it must be for Celebrity Watchers. They could make friends in loads of places: concerts, raves, interactive movie theaters, karaoke bars, Internet fan clubs and kiosks for Media on Demand. Besides, wasn't entertainment America's most lucrative export worldwide? Buying clothes or household stuff with celebrity images was almost a patriotic duty.

Patriotic as saluting the flag, Rachel thought. Her eyes ranged over the hundreds of scouts, standing more or less obediently at attention, directing scout salutes toward the flag. At a glance you could tell which kid fit into which pigeonhole… and envy him, if you didn't catch yourself.

Perfectly groomed All-Americans had their socially useful projects. Wholesome young scout Traditionals, easy to spot with their crosses, had their missionary cause. Fidgety members of The Righteous clung together, as if congratulating themselves for being among the saved. Celebrity Watchers had their surrogate families and trendy clothes. But isolation was your fate as a Seminar Slave.

You couldn't make friends in front of a seminar tape, not unless you counted the folks you met online. And grateful though Rachel was for *any* kind of friendship these days, virtual friendships had too high a likelihood of being fake. The kind of rapport she shared with Jeremy and Brent, knowing for sure who was at the other end of the conversation, didn't happen with a virtual friend.

Without Jeremy, Rachel wouldn't have a single quality adult relationship. And where would she find new ones? With the V-R addicts in her neighborhood or among the drug addicts? Both groups relished their social unconnectedness. Techies like Jeremy were the same way. Their best friends were computers—or other people with dry wits and rumpled clothing.

The only group members Rachel found harder to comprehend were the Jocks, who started heavy athletic training by the age of five. By her age, gymnasts, runners, football stars, ballerinas and the rest were collections of artificial joints, specialized hormones, and memories.

Let's face it, Rachel thought, as the Scouts finished pledging allegiance. *In 2020, America was "one nation under God" only politically. And most of these kids had been raised to expect that their version of God would soon triumph over everyone else's. With each social group so isolated, it took uncommon courage to reach out to anyone with a different affiliation.* Maybe, for these scouts, some miracle would happen and America could come together in their lifetime. But Rachel doubted it.

Fishing was scheduled next for the scouts from Sterling. When Arnold marched them to the lake, a sullen LeShawn pushed ahead to the front of the line. He grabbed the pack's flag and started marching off to the left.

"Excuse me? Is that where we're supposed to go?" Rachel shouted ineffectually at the rapidly disappearing line of scouts.

Arnold's voice boomed: "Not into the woods, boys. You know where the lake is. Pack Leader, surrender your flag and come to the end of the line."

But LeShawn kept going, straight into the woods. Once Rachel caught up with him, she asked, "What's with you, LeShawn? Come back."

He wouldn't meet her eyes.

"Don't you think we should be joining the others?"

"Holiday Lakes is for turkeys. I wouldn't be here except my Mom made me."

Rachel led the little stinker to the lake, grabbing his elbow like a rudder. When they rejoined the pack, they were sitting nicely in a circle around Earl, the Fishing Counselor. He was using colorful ID holograms to teach the boys about different types of fish. Soon, he said enthusiastically, they'd do some real fishing. Each adult volunteer was given a plastic bucket of bait for her boys. Rachel's was filled with corn kernels, frankfurter pieces and worms. How boyish!

"What would you like to use for bait?" she asked Harrison.

"Worms," grunted the half-dead V-R boy, looking animated for once.

He baited the hook to his fishing pole, flattening the worm's bloody red underside, then jabbing with the hook. Twice more he jabbed, rolling the worm into a spiral. *Better it than me*, Rachel thought.

Tom wanted hot dogs plus corn, as did Mark. LeShawn wanted corn plus worm, which he called "a sandwich." Rachel called it revolting. He asked her to bait his hook, which she did clumsily, chasing the worm around with one finger, reluctant to touch something so slimy.

Hey, you're a mother, she told herself. *You've cleaned up vomit, changed a thousand diapers, you kept nursing through that breast infection—even when it hurt so much you wished you could cut the thing off. You're a mother. Are you going to let a little worm stop you now?*

Rachel jabbed. She conquered. Meanwhile LeShawn observed her with contempt, narrowing his close-set eyes. "Man, you're slow," was his only comment.

"Archery next," Arnold said with a grin. His once crisp scout shirt had begun to wrinkle near his cutely old-fashioned—surgically unaltered—mid-life belly. By now, every one of her boys was driving Rachel nuts. Mark, it turned out, wanted to hold her hand as they walked toward the targets. "Wait," he said, gesturing that he needed to whisper into her ear. She bent down, seduced by his confiding expression. While she puzzled over what he kept saying (it sounded like "Moo"), the little darling licked her ear.

And wholesome All American Tom, it turned out, loved spitting.

"What's with the spitting, Mr. Tom?" she asked, draping a supportive arm around his shoulder.

"I like it, " he said, letting out a lengthy piece of drool just to the side of Rachel's knee.

Meanwhile, her pride and joy, Brent, was sulking because he hadn't caught a fish.

Several times, LeShawn wandered away from everyone else and Rachel had to herd him back like a reluctant sheep. Personally, she would have preferred to have the wolves get him. But this was not an option. For one thing, wolves had been extinct for years.

Eventually the wayward Pack made it to Archery, where the first seven scouts lined up for target practice.

"Men," said the Archery Counselor, in the manner of a drill sergeant, "What you have here are dangerous weapons. Use them carefully."

The boys perked right up. Their arrows were made of sticks, with green plastic tips. Targets were printed designs on Styrofoam sheets. *How traditional,* Rachel thought. *But how can they pierce Styrofoam with round-tipped arrowheads?* None of her aspiring Robin Hoods seemed to notice this, fortunately.

Oh brother, she thought. *Even my Mom couldn't make a triumph out of this.*

"Stop throwing the mulch" Arnold was shouting. It was Nature Crafts. "Counselor Wendy has prepared a project. Unless you complete it, you will not get the green bead for this activity. Repeat, you will *not* receive your bead."

Wendy brightened visibly. Boys were crazy for their scout beads, which they were handed upon completion of every official deed at Holiday Lakes .

Wendy showed the boys how to cut out and color a paper butterfly, then weight it by taping pinto beans to the bottom. Properly completed, your butterfly could balance on your fingertip. After Wendy demonstrated this, she told the boys to begin.

What's with these kids? Rachel wondered. Mark cut out a blob instead of a butterfly. Maybe that wasn't surprising. But most of the other boys weren't making anything at all. They sat tapping their feet, wiggling, jiggling. What was *their* problem?

Harrison yelled, "Get me my music. You can't expect me to concentrate without my tape."

"Yeah, where's my CD?" another boy chimed in.

Another boy hollered, "I need my V-R."

Rachel panicked. What would she do if they started a riot? Without a working skin-phone, she felt so vulnerable. Arnold, however, rose to the emergency:

"Boys, tell me how many of you brought along your Prayer Beads?"

"Me." "Me." Most of the boys were shouting a response.

"Then use 'em," Arnold said, smiling. "The rest of you, just imagine you're doing your scout craft on TV."

"Doesn't that pull at your heartstrings? They're so young, yet so eager to walk in the Way." Rachel overheard one of the adult Volunteers say this to the woman standing next to her.

"Surely it will hasten the presence of the Lord," answered the other, as if by rote. Pulling beads out of their pockets, they moved their fingers rhythmically.

If you wanted to tell who was a member of The Righteous, Rachel reflected, *all you needed to see was those Prayer Beads.* Over the last decade, she had witnessed the growth of their Movement. Even though she'd seen it coming, part of her still couldn't believe it.

During Rachel's childhood, Christian Fundamentalists became America's loudest voice for religion. At the turn of the millennium, members expected a Rapture to send God's people straight to Heaven, plucked directly from their cars, if need be. Jeremy once told Rachel how, when he first learned to drive, he saw bumper stickers that read, "Warning: In case of Rapture this car will be unmanned."

No Rapture came, though, and by 2005, millions of faithful were growing restless when a leader arose to meet their need. The Rev. Hickory Helms began to prophesy about what had caused the Rapture to be postponed.

It wasn't enough to be religious, he explained. Piety pleased God but in these wicked times, when sinners abounded, extra righteous believers were needed. And they must *multiply* themselves.

How could this be accomplished? Simple, Helms said. Multi-tasking was the way. Perpetual prayer became the proudest ornament of spiritual life. Millions traded in their crosses for rosaries—except that these prayer aids weren't called rosaries, which would have been too Catholic. These beads were for doing prayers of The Righteous.

Like LeShawn, who seemed relieved to have taken his beads from his pocket, Righteous children learned prayers with "real God power." Although converting others could also win you points as one of The Righteous, multi-tasking was considered vital: The more prayers you did simultaneously, the bigger impression you could make on the Lord. Therefore, kids like LeShawn were brought up multitasking. When they learned to color, for instance, they were also expected to sing gospel songs. While they ate meals, they had to dance one of the rhythms of the saints. Brushing teeth, at the sink or the toilet, members of The Righteous were not supposed to pause in their incessant pleading on behalf of the wicked.

Finally, there was one further duty, at least if you were an adult member of The Righteous—like some of Rachel's co-volunteers here at Holiday Lakes. If you really loved your Lord, you must raise progeny and the more, the better. As Rev. Helms explained on his daily TV show, there was an urgent need for more souls raised in Righteousness or their equivalent, as shown in multi-tasked prayer. To bring on The Rapture at least 10 billion Righteous were needed, 10 to the 10th power.

Rachel remembered watching TV when Helms announced this during a press conference, shortly before Brent was born. She had never been so angry. Nor had she been the only one with a strong reaction to Helms and the growing social visibility of The Righteous, counting their beads and occasionally twitching out of sheer fervor. Something about having a rival sect became terribly embarrassing to the rest of America's Christian Fundamentalists. Through no fault of their own, except contrast, their group now seemed distressingly bland. Many of their members were lost to Helms' highly visible new faith. Those who remained were recharged by an evangelical preacher who stepped forth with attitude, the Rev. Stacey Pilgrim.

A strapping, big-boned woman from Texas, she sprang from a long line of cowboys, and whether or not you chose to pray with her, you had to admit she looked as if she could punch cows with the best of them. If you were in her herd, you sure wouldn't want to pull a LeShawn.

To reposition her Movement, Rev. Pilgrim held a dramatic press conference on the Fourth of July, 2013, proclaiming the Second Dying of Christ. Jeremy and Rachel watched that historic newscast together.

"Instead of the Second Coming, we have the second dying." she said. "Jesus has been practically crucified all over again, and why? The problem is not lack of belief. But way too many who call themselves Christians believe things that are *wrong*... and say them too often."

Pilgrim asserted that the Rapture was coming, just not in the way preached by Rev. Helms. She explained that she'd made a careful study of the Book of Revelations. It proved that everything about the Rapture had been prophesied, down to an obvious foreseeing of the sadly misguided Rev. Helms.

He was the Anti-Christ. (Ironically, the man hinted the same about her.)

Pilgrim's research into the Bible, meanwhile, revealed that what the Lord really needed was no more of this unseemly babbling with beads. Steadfast faith was required, a wholesome and single-minded devotion. To distinguish her Movement from The Righteous, her spiritual flock would be called "the Traditionals." They, and they alone, were the real Christians from Biblical times.

"Reincarnated, surely," Jeremy joked, when he and Rachel watched Pilgrim's speech.

Even if Jeremy wasn't impressed by Pilgrim, her historic speech convinced millions. To show their allegiance—perhaps also to make it easier for God to spot them—Traditionals began wearing extra-large crosses, suspended by strap-like leather chains or more elaborate ergonomic harnesses.

Traditional crosses for adults weighed three pounds or more. "Strong" Traditionals would flaunt these proudly for all the world to see, in the manner of Rev. Pilgrim, whose cross must have been at least a ten-pounder. Among youngsters (especially sexy young teenage girls from Traditional homes) the current fad was to wear lightweight crosses on gold filigree chains, stuffing them inside their blouses so that just the dainty chains would show, rising up out of their cleavage.

Other ways to express one's Traditional faith abounded. Anything was okay, so long as it was duly reverent... and couldn't be confused with those tacky Righteous beads. Many Traditionals wore T-shirts proclaiming messages about Jesus, or faith, or the Second Coming. Others wore buttons with quotations from scripture.

However they dressed, members of the Traditionals were avid missionaries, home schoolers, and political activists. Among all America's social groups they were the most militant, always trying to extend their reach into the media, Congress, or even the White House. It seemed to Rachel that they lived on perpetual religious red alert, ever watchful for the moment when God would come again, with a Second Coming like a Trade Center destroyer, but come to heal rather than kill. As Rev. Pilgrim explained on her daily TV show, this would happen when everyone expected it least. "And then the howls of the unrepentant will sound across our wicked land like a cleansing wind."

Arnold was grinning as the boys prayed with their beads. Plump jowls made his grin look repulsive rather than boyish, unfortunately. "Spirit is an important part of scouting," he whispered to Rachel. "See how they quieted right down?"

"I thought Boy Scouts aren't supposed to favor any religion." she said.

"Oh, we welcome all. Scouts receive belt loops for each and every faith."

She glowered at him.

"Righteous boys will be boys," he said with a wink.

Rachel turned this over in her head while Arnold led the boys to lunch. A yellow lunch bin contained the pack's assortment of disposable lunch boxes. Scouts scrambled to get their food first, and a few pushing contests broke out. Arnold missed the chance for discipline, though. After grabbing his own plastic sack, he headed for a faraway table. Rachel could see him, working his Beads fast and smiling dreamily.

Now other Righteous parents pushed forward; after pulling out their lunches they raced with their children to lunch benches. As they ate, they swayed in their seats; they must be doing Rapture Dances, Rachel thought.

Only one other adult volunteer remained by their group's lunch bin. She and Rachel were left standing alone, like the cheese in the old song "The Farmer in the Dell." Catching each others' eyes, they understood they were moms with a job to do. Together they hoisted the lunch bin onto a table, so scouts could clamber around it from all four sides. Then all the moms had to do was keep the boys from beating each other up as they rooted around for their lunches.

After the frenzy, the other woman and Rachel shared victorious smiles. *Might they become friends?* Rachel felt hopeful. They exchanged names. Diane wore blonde curls and huge cheek implants—a dated look, but still flattering. Ruefully she rubbed her throat with the palm of her hand. Only then did Rachel notice a chain around her neck, a wad of metal half-hidden, half-protruding beneath her blouse.

Reflexively Rachel's hand went to her own throat. Diane smiled at her. "You're so good. I know we're not supposed to wear our crosses while we help out with Scout Camp. I just couldn't bear to go out without wearing even a little one. It would be like taking off your wedding ring, you know?"

Rachel smiled back, kind of. Making friends at Scout Camp sure was harder than she'd expected.

Chapter 4
On to Greater Glory

Brent grabbed Rachel by the hand and led her to a far-away table. The scouts already sitting there didn't even look up at the new arrivals, which suited Rachel just fine. The lunches she'd packed were tasty: virtuous low-fat salad for her but Brent had homemade coleslaw, rice with almonds and leftover Teriyaki chicken, plus dried papaya sticks for dessert.

As he ate, her eyes wandered around the huge mess hall. Table upon table was filled with the lively faces of young boys eating. Wearing their camp uniforms with the jaunty orange caps, they looked so wholesome. Scout Camp was important, Rachel decided. These boys had no idea how lucky they were to be in the great outdoors. By the time they were fathers, parks like this might well be extinct. Even National Forests had been sold recently, by special acts of Congress.

Between bites of salad, Rachel looked more closely at the other boys at her table. Nobody talked. Three rocked as they chewed, doing the Rapture Dance. Two others stared vacantly into space, craning their necks upward. Of course—that would be their usual position for watching family-style V-R. Though her table was full, none of the boys made eye contact. It was parallel play at age eight.

Golly! Rachel took another look at the mess hall. Those happy faces in their orange caps weren't, maybe, so happy after all. Few talked, except for boys who appeared to be either pinching or punching their neighbors. Although volunteers like Rachel seemed interested in their children, nobody else seemed connected to anybody.

But wasn't today the scouts' fourth day at Holiday Lakes ? Hadn't they been with their fellow den members all year? You'd expect more of them to be friends by now. Were they aloof just because they were boys? Or could they suffer from the same social isolation that drove Rachel crazy? *If my marriage fails, that isolation will matter even more, to Brent and to me,* she worried.

Well, Rachel resolved. She'd spend the rest of her volunteer day connecting with these boys every chance she had, in a meaningful way. If only they'd let her.

"On to greater glory," Arnold proclaimed to the group. He slapped his thigh, apparently to signify a hearty and contagious enjoyment. "See where we're walking? The sports field. Fellas, it's time for kickball!!"

Despite Arnold's glee, what followed was a poor excuse for a game. Boys didn't want to kick or field. A tired-looking Sports Counselor did robot-like pitching, and when a boy scored the first run, he ran home so slowly, it looked like he was wearing mud in his Nike-Reeboks.

Rachel sidled over to Arnold, sitting near her on the bench. "No team spirit at all!" she said in a lightly flirtatious voice that she thought would appeal to him. "Can't you think of any way to get this game going?"

He had been slumped over, fingering his beads with an absent expression. Now he sprang to attention, as if Rachel had rammed a coat hanger down the back of his shirt. "Of course," he said, grinning broadly. "We're scouts! We've got a big bag of tricks."

"Guys, listen up," he shouted. "I have an important announcement. Our teams need better definition. So you know what we're gonna do to make that happen?"

Brent and the others looked curious.

"We're renaming our teams. We're calling them The Shirts and The Skins.

"You in the field, peel off your shirts. Place them on this rock carefully. Carefully."

Squeals of joy came from the fortunate Skins. Brent was one. With their shirts off, they preened in the sun, stretching like the fauns in "Fantasia." Adorable hairless chests—the boys pounded on them with their fists.

The new strategy worked for a full 10 minutes. Then the boys fingered their beads, or simply looked bored.

No, Rachel couldn't stand it. This was supposed to be camp! Again, she sidled over to Arnold. "Can't we do anything more? I feel like the game is dying."

He jumped, then removed his hand from his beads. "What is your problem, exactly?"

"You've had so much experience with scouting, Mr. Dunn. Doesn't it disturb you to see such a lack of interest among the boys?"

A secret smile suffused his face, and he cocked his head to the left. "It isn't working well, is it?"

"Am I wrong in thinking that eight-year-old boys should have more spunk than this? Brent does, at home. Nobody here's connecting."

Arnold nodded.

"And watching some of these kids, I wonder if some of them even know *how* to connect. You know what I mean?"

"Look, Ma'am—"

"My name's Rachel."

"Rachel, then. I think I know exactly what you mean. May I speak frankly?

"I just did. Why shouldn't you?"

"In the words of Rev. Helms, these are broken times."

Rachel felt like she'd just been punched in the gut. But she let him continue.

"Broken times, during the last days, show in boys like these who have lost their spirit. I believe the only thing that can fix broken times is full participation in prayer. You know, practicing the Presence of God during all your waking hours. If you truly want to help, you won't find the answer in pep talks or cheers.

"I can't help noticing, dear. You aren't wearing your beads. Tell me, how long is it since you've been to church?"

Gently he touched his hand to Rachel's chin and lifted up her face. "Will you join us in raising up these broken times?"

She flinched. "Wait a minute, Arnold. Isn't this supposed to be Scout Camp? I didn't come here for religious training. And neither did these boys."

"Well, of course. But so many these days are newly open to the call of the Lord. In moments of frustration or boredom, I believe we have a need to turn to prayer—a need and even a duty."

Rachel tried to smile diplomatically but it felt more like a sneer. She cleared her throat. "Scouting is what I came here for. The tradition is a hundred years old, isn't it?"

Arnold nodded. "In America, 110 years, to be precise."

"Don't you have books full of things to interest these scouts? Tips and cheers and things. Don't you?"

"Absolutely."

"Then why can't we turn around this poor excuse for a camp? I'm willing. The other volunteers are willing. Let's make something out of this day."

Arnold stood back a step and composed himself, standing more stiffly than ever. While he paused, Rachel saw him as if for the first time. His forehead looked strained, his eyes set. The chubby cheeks that puffed out above his lips were rigidly held in a tight little smile.

Arnold seemed shrunken within his skin as if he, like some of these boys, was hanging onto reality by a thread. Rachel automatically compared him with Jeremy. Yes, Jeremy seemed moody these days. And absent minded. Maybe he was being unfaithful to her at this very moment. But at least his lights were on. Jeremy knew how to be himself, and Rachel wouldn't trade Jeremy for a hundred wind-up toys like Arnold.

"Look, Ruth, I'll do every trick in the book. But I've been head Camp Leader year after year, and every year it's harder to motivate these boys.

"You see," he confided, "Scouting doesn't work in broken times. As for what we can do about it, I've already given you my opinion."

"Excuse me?" She crossed her arms to hold in her anger.

"Ruth, I'm glad you shared your concerns with me. And I can at least promise you this. Starting today, I'll add you to my personal list."

"What list?"

"In broken times, many express the need for us to pray for their souls. You will be remembered in my prayers."

"No thank you," Rachel said. She turned on her heel.

But when she looked back, she saw that Arnold was still smiling at her, a sweet martyrish smile. His hand rested lightly on his beads.

She stomped back over to him. "I mean it, Arnold. My name is Rachel, not Ruth. And keep your prayer list for people who ask. My religion is none of your business."

Arnold shrugged, turning his palms upward.

Whew! Rachel couldn't wait for the next activity of the day, which would also be her *last* activity at this lousy Scout Camp. She'd had it up to here.

As they hiked back to the lake, she reached out to hold Brent's hand. For once she wasn't trying to give strength. She was *taking*, trying to divert her rage about Arnold, plus her worry about these boys.

"Hold *my* hand, okay?" whispered Mark, who was walking directly in back of Brent.

"The cute one," Rachel thought. Detaching from her son's hand she fluffed up his curls, then stood next to Mark.

"Here I am, kid." She gave his fat, moist hand a little squeeze, then took a deep breath of the gorgeous, green-tinted air. "It sure is beautiful today, isn't it Mark? We're lucky to be here, don't you think?"

"Can I tell you something, Brent's Mom?"

"Well, if it's fast. We don't want to slow down the other scouts." She bent down until her head was level with Mark's pale eyes and fast-blinking, sparse eyelashes. She turned her head to let him whisper into her ear.

"I can't quite hear you, Mark."

"Oink, oink, oink" he snorted at the top of his lungs. Then he licked her ear.

"Paddle boats? At Holiday Lakes?" Rachel and fellow volunteer Diane stood near the lake, limply watching boys head over to the big box of life jackets.

"Leave it to scouts to have the latest motorized life vests," Diane said, "They sure keep up with the times."

Rachel said, "I wouldn't put it past our little dears to tip over 10-ton rowboats."

"Today has been way too long, hasn't it?"

Rachel smiled back at Diane. "I'm enjoying the paddleboats, though. Never seen anything like 'em."

Each boat was so large it could seat two adults and eight pedalling kids.

"Aerodynamic wonders," Arnold said greasily as he paraded by.

In the distance, Rachel saw Harrison and some other boys, including Brent, at a part of the shoreline far from the life jacket bucket. She told Diane she'd bring the boys back, plus get life jackets for the two of them.

The boys had sticks. They were digging into the soft mud. For once, they looked fascinated.

Coming closer, she saw that they'd made holes just below the mud's surface. Something was coming out of them. Flies. Their bodies were the color of green Jell-O, their wings were purple—like jelly beans. Prettier than your average insect, for sure. Rachel stopped to stare at them with a kind of awe.

"We were poking around for worms. But this is better isn't it?" Brent told her.

The flies started to swarm around the boys, buzzing like bees.

Brent stood very still. Quietly he announced, "I can get one to balance on my finger, just like the butterflies we made with the Nature Counselor." A slow smile lit up his face.

"I can, too" Tom said. A few other boys followed their example.

Rachel blinked hard, then shook her head. Brent and the others were standing with their palms turned upward, index fingers pointing out straight. On their fingertips, each boy had one of the flies vibrating gently.

"Yuck, how weird. I'm gonna squash one," said Harrison. He clapped his hands.

to squash his unsuspecting fly. "See, guys?" he bragged. "I'm a fly swatter machine."

"Let me try," several said, following his example.

"We have to tell the other guys. The bugs just sit there and let you do whatever you want. This is too cool." The squashers ran off laughing.

"You guys need to go back," Rachel said. "It's time to do paddleboats. Grab your life vests."

Brent still had a fly on his finger. He blew it away. Rachel grabbed jackets for herself and Diane.

"Get going" she told him.

Once home, Rachel felt exhausted. Although she cooked a good dinner just in case Jeremy came home, he didn't. Nor did he call. So she sat with Brent at the dining nook in the kitchen, with its raised geometric pattern and built-in place mats. She felt so depressed she never even pushed the button to choose a color overlay: The entire table stayed in its default version, plain yellow acrylic with faint outlines of place mats but nothing filled in.

Brent chatted away, full of stories, until Rachel put him to bed. Then she plucked up her courage and called Jeremy at work. It was eight o'clock, for crying out loud. If he had to work that late, the least he could do was talk a few minutes. And she wanted to tell him about her how upset she felt after that day at Holiday Lakes.

Nothing came up on the phone-screen except for Jeremy's pre-recorded message face.

Nothing? Should she call his skin-phone? No, that would be stupid. It would show insecurity, just what drives a man away—as she'd heard from a dozen seminars. Rachel couldn't remember a time when she had felt more alone.

Chapter 5
Project Jeremy

Morning dawned fresh and new, with air quality in the acceptable range. Before Rachel was halfway through her breakfast bowl of Crisp 'n Trim (the non-fat snackin' cereal with the taste of real bacon and eggs), she had figured out exactly how she'd spend her day. Forget the bead thumpers, the cross wearers, the V-R and other addicts in their so-called "community" who would never be friends for her or Brent. Rachel had a project.

That project was getting Jeremy back 100 percent. Whether or not her husband was dallying with that creep from his office, Rachel wasn't going to sit around like a victim. Instead she would make herself into a new and improved Rachel. . . an even more perfect body, more thoughtful behavior, perfect in every way and, therefore, irresistible.

Rachel stirred honey into her licorice tea and took a dainty sip. Having no job but homemaking, day after day, blew things out of proportion—like her little worries yesterday about the scouts' inability to connect. Or that pushy Arnold. No big deal, for heaven's sake!

Yes, Rachel had managed a good night's sleep, despite her husband's late return home, and now she sat reinvigorated at the dining nook, a jaunty gingham place mat beneath her breakfast. She was banging her right foot against the pine-finished leg of her chair, tapping in time to James Taylor's latest CD, *Geezers Parked in My Lot*.

Ooh, her favorite song was coming on, "Don't Call Me a Codger." Over the years, James' voice had become more compassionate than ever (if possible). Often this song brought tears to her eyes:

> And don't think that you know me
> Simply because I'm old.
> Don't take one look and walk away.
> My story, my story is still untold.

Well, thank goodness her case wasn't that bad yet. She wasn't even 40—no flab on her upper arms or liver spots on her face. Men's heads still swiveled when she entered a room. At the rate she was going, it could be decades before she became socially invisible. Nonetheless, people could be misunderstood at any age, as Rachel well knew, which is why she loved that song. She sang to herself: "And don't think that you know me, simply because I'm cute. Don't take one look and walk away."

How would her story turn out? Maybe Jeremy would star, maybe not. Brent would be in it for keeps, anyhow.

Her son had no idea what she'd sacrificed for him. Before he was born, Rachel had a great life as a party planner, with phones ringing off the hook all day long. Every night she'd go out to events that were exotic, creative, fascinating, or at least outrageously expensive. Sometimes she'd work as a walk-around character, wearing a fabulous costume. Like one fun job for MCI-Sprint-Bell, where she dressed as the Statue of Liberty, an old-fashioned cell-phone sticking out of her hand instead of a torch.

Back in those days, even the parties where she didn't wear special costumes were fun. She loved how competent she felt, squeezed into in a sexy but tasteful black dress, overseeing her musicians, fortunetellers, dancers, game-table operators and so forth. Though her clients were often nervous, on the job (at least) Rachel was totally self-assured.

The caterers lusted after her business and would do anything to please her during the economic rebound after the Bush presidency. And as the daughter of a New York caterer, did she know her job or what? Companies couldn't put a thing over on her. Nothing but the best for her and her clients.

Her employees, the party entertainers, worked hard to please her, since her company, Party Girl, was the best in Capitol City. She hired everything but strippers, and hired the best. By the age of 26, Rachel was clearing $150,000 a year. After marrying Jeremy, her business continued to grow, and she kept putting off motherhood because she didn't think it could beat the thrill of walking into one of her parties, like the Online Lobbyists Consortium's New Year's bash in '11, with that huge buffet of gourmet meats and cheeses; a two-foot-tall ice sculpture, shaped like an elephant, looking down from the top of the three-tiered buffet table; salad-bar stations heaped with asparagus, orange peppers, and miniature eggplants, roasted together like something out of the vegetable version of the Kama Sutra.

At parties like this, there'd be a roomful of sequin-dressed women, all perfect bodies except for the obligatory grandparents and such. Guys of all ages looked dapper in their perfectly tailored tuxedoes. For the Online party, she had harpists stationed on pedestals in each corner of the ballroom, creating quadraphonic sound that fell on the ears like rain, each harpist wearing a sequined baby-blue gown from Lopez couture, playing the same Chopin mazurka. And that was just the entertainment in the dining room . . . .

Rachel sighed, pouring herself a second bowl of cereal. She wasn't hungry any more and the CD had played itself out, but she didn't want to halt the flow of her memories. So she stayed where she was and kept on spooning in more bacon-and-egg-flavored soy glop. How confident and successful she'd been, until that lousy law of President Rinaldo's. More than the birth of Brent, that law had changed her life. Otherwise motherhood itself might not have been such a big deal.

She and Jeremy had planned her pregnancy, expected her to work part-time until their baby was old enough for day care. Then she would go back to her job as queen of the DC party circuit. Unfortunately, childcare had become a hot topic. Cybernews stories gushed about the formative childhood years and how lack of personal attention could wreck the kiddies' lives forever. Then economists got into the act, filling talk shows with their worries about recession. Republican Trickle-up economists argued that Americans needed to cut employment, which would turn the remaining jobs over to real wage earners, as had occurred during the Era of Family Values. By creating a 1950's-style economy, the values would follow, causing strife and crime to disappear faster than a downsized worker.

President Rinaldo, a Democrat, deftly co-opted the argument by pushing for an ingenious program of tax incentives that would keep families married, keep mothers at home, close down most daycare centers, and solve a host of other economic and social problems. His humongous tax credit would reward couples for marrying, rather than living together. So much money would pour into each family that one spouse wouldn't have to work. Afterwards a second colossal tax cut would reward all families with children who kept one caregiver home. Families were tempted with a tax cut so huge it made no sense, even for someone as successful as Rachel, to work once she became a parent.

Technically, a family could have refused the financial windfall. In practice nobody did. And technically the man of the house could have stayed home. But Jeremy never would have stood for that. Not with his Ph.D.-glorified need to fuss with the bug kingdom. Rattling around the house all day, as the only adult, he might have gone bonkers over teensy tiny pets—maybe a theme park for ants in the back yard? Besides, Rachel wasn't about to leave a handsome man like him at home all day, where he'd be the only house-husband in a neighborhood full of bored housewives.

The upshot was that a brilliant businesswoman like Rachel was reduced to eating fake bacon and cheese for an endless breakfast. When Brent turned 10, and his parent's tax credit went down to a mere $200,000 per year, maybe she could get Jeremy to okay her going back to work. Maybe. Otherwise Rachel's perpetual job would be to fill up her days, like this one. No Scout Camp volunteering today? Then she'd find something. She had to.

First order of business was, of course, Brent. He woke up moping, prematurely mourning the end of scout camp.

"Camp isn't over yet. Don't ruin today just because it won't last."

His scowl deepened, and he stomped toward the bathroom, shoulders hunched over. When he got mad, Brent looked just like his father. Cute.

"Today could be wonderful," Rachel persisted. "For heaven's sake, Brent, don't act like a grumpus. Can't you let yourself live in the moment?"

He glared back at her, then slammed the bathroom door.

By the time Rachel dropped him off at Tom's house, however, Brent had returned to his usual fun-loving self.

"Mrs. Smith," he told Tom's mother in his super-considerate voice, "I've been thinking about all the carpooling you do, with three kids and all. What if today you stay home and leave the driving to me? You know how easy it is to drive. I can take Tom and LeShawn to Holiday Lakes. Wouldn't that be nice for you?"

Jessica Smith and Rachel exchanged looks. "So thoughtful," said Rachel.

Jessica said, "I'll have to think about that, Mr. Murphy. I didn't realize you had your driver's license yet."

She and Rachel exchanged smiles that made Rachel hope that maybe today she would succeed at connecting with people after all.

Back home, she proceeded to make her bed. Ugh! Jeremy had come home late again last night, long after she had fallen asleep, and had left his gray socks on the floor. Jeremy, missing the hamper? Jeremy was usually so neat that he *folded* his socks and underwear before putting them in the hamper.

Something was definitely going on.

Jeremy was Rachel's project today. She must make him fall in love with her all over again. Suddenly she had an idea.

Years ago, back in college, when they were first courting—they called it "hanging out together after music class"—she and Jeremy exchanged life stories. One of his greatest experiences was a concert performance of an Eric Satie piece called

"Vengeance." This was a simple piano piece, repeated some mind-boggling number of times. The pianists played in two-hour shifts for 24 hours straight. He told her that being lost in the sound was practically a religious experience.

Rachel did a quick Internet search and downloaded the score of that very piece, transcribed for violin. She would learn to play it, then make Jeremy a CD. Wow! First advantage, the piece was only four lines long, so it should be easy to learn. Second, she'd only need to record it once, and then use replays to fill up a 90-minute CD. Third, due to the very nature of the piece, he'd play it for hours at a time, rekindling their love. Brilliant!

She'd better warm up.

Damn, it was hard, getting her violin fingers back.

Okay, enough for perfecting her sound, which seemed to come from an instrument of torture rather than music.

Time to count out the rhythms in the Satie. Ouch! Rachel didn't have a recording to listen to. Usually, that was her lazy way to avoid the math part of music. She learned by listening, not counting— unlike Jeremy. Sight-reading was such a snap for him, he was too snobbish to have a music-reader program on their computer.

Rachel was in a bind, she realized. Sure she could pick up the phone and order a CDD (CD on Demand) with the Satie played by a real musician. Then she'd be able to learn the piece by ear. But in that case, why struggle to give Jeremy her homemade recording? They'd already have a machine-perfect version.

The alternative was for Rachel to teach herself the piece like a purist by reading the music. She could count it out, measure by measure.

Or not. Soon she wanted to scream. No matter how hard she tried, her rhythms wouldn't fit the measures. And Jeremy was such a perfectionist with his rhythms. She thought, *Music won't help me win back Jeremy if I work myself into a state. Rage is unattractive.*

What if he called while she was bent out of shape due to making him a present whose very purpose was to make herself more desirable?

Okay, she'd play something she already knew, the slow movement of Mendelssohn's violin concerto. And if she messed up in all the usual places? Tough.

Gradually the music inside the music won her over. Rachel began to feel herself coming awake inside—her inner self buzzing in perfect harmony—like the strings of her self-tuning fiddle. Playing music could turn into magic for her, even if she was sitting in front of a funky old metal music stand—an "heirloom" from Jeremy's childhood that probably cost under $50 in today's currency.

Dreamily, Rachel shifted to a world where people like her were the norm—people of passion and sensuality, people who called out with great yearning, people who heard (and responded to) the yearnings of others.

If only Jeremy would call her right now! Rachel was positively glowing, which was the most alluring way to intrigue a man. She should call him—not his skinphone but his work number, so she could leave a sight bite if she had to.

No answer.

Why wasn't he at work? She left a message anyway, capturing an image of herself with the fiddle propped on her shoulder at a flattering angle. "Just thinking of you, Jeremy. Sending you music." She waved her bow flirtatiously.

Wayne Smith poked his head through the door to Jeremy's office at the Department of Health and Human Services. "Hey, Jeremy. Your phone didn't pick up but I had a hunch you were here anyhow."

Only then did Jeremy realize that he was sitting hunched over, clenching the edge of his desk. His mind had been a million miles away, circling a familiar orbit: worry, consequences, strategies and yet more worry.

Usually Wayne's presence cheered him. The guy didn't just stand at the door, he planted himself like a tree. Solid as a football player, Wayne's broad shoulders tapered to a trim waist, with muscular toughness everywhere up to the big contradiction, his face.

Above his thick neck, Wayne looked like a kid—a big, open puppy dog face with a bunch of baby fat near his jaws, and round brown eyes that smiled a lot.

Meeting his gaze, Jeremy felt like he was 100 years old. He loosened his grip on the desk and pushed back the straight blond hair that tumbled over his face. "You think we should talk before the meeting?"

"Yeah, to go over our strategy. Let's psych ourselves up."

The sickening feeling in Jeremy's stomach reminded him how much would be at stake in this meeting—and how unequal he felt to it. Sociable types like Wayne always had an advantage in meetings. Even more so with Rich Davis, the White House PR guy they'd be seeing. The bigger the group, the higher the stakes, the more Rich puffed up with self-importance. Jeremy hated the man.

Stavros Menelakos, Jeremy's boss's boss at HHS, wasn't a performer like Rich, merely calculating. In his first term, President Tucker had brought in Stavros as a political appointee. That was more than four years ago; he still gave the creeps to everyone, even easygoing Wayne.

Cooper was the other one to watch. A big muckety-muck over at the Central Intelligence Agency, Cooper's visit was a rare "honor." Cooper Hackenworth, Ph.D., was the only one in today's meeting who could qualify as an intellectual. Theoretically, therefore, he was someone Jeremy might have related to. Yes, Hackenworth had a brain— unlike Jeremy's immediate boss, Marty Hiyakawa. Hackenworth, however, was a slimeball.

Just thinking about this cast of characters was all the psyching up—or down— Jeremy could bear. Curving his long, thin lips into a rueful smile he said, "I think we're sufficiently aware of what we're up against, Wayne. How long do we have before this meeting anyway, 20 minutes?"

"Well, I thought maybe we could go over our strategy with Cooper and Stavros."

"Strategy? Let's not feel compelled to imitate Rich Davis, for crying out loud. Why should we need strategy when we have facts? You did prepare the vid-show and handouts, by the way?"

Wayne nodded.

"I'll see you in the conference room, then."

Soon as the door closed, Jeremy's fingers began to fidget and he reached in his desk drawer for the tube of Eucalypt-all. It was the only thing that could stop the itching.

Carefully he rolled up his right sleeve and began to rub in the thick, soothing cream. Man, how it itched. Eczema often erupted when Jeremy was under stress. For years he had joked to himself about how lucky he was that all hell could be breaking out under his shirt, but so long as hell kept to its place, they had a bargain.

His fingers were spared, for instance, which was great. Nothing showed beneath the elbows. All he had to do, Jeremy thought as he rubbed in the cream, was to find a stronger brand that didn't stain. Also, you had to learn how to handle a sleeve when you rolled it up past the elbow, avoiding wrinkles. You did that by moving slowly, deliberately and gently.

Although, technically, Jeremy's office had a door, the privacy it afforded was nil. One cubicle next to another, a rat's maze of little cubicles connected by halls, the whole agency had been designed in strict government mode. No room was allocated for personal egos here in the public sector. No, the place had been built so that political types might bring in the cameras and brag all over TV that no money was being wasted on pampering those lazy government workers. Consequently, a fully qualified entomologist like Jeremy could work his butt off with fewer perks than if he'd been an untenured college professor. Knocking on the door to his office? It was a mere formality.

Jeremy could just imagine what would happen if he pulled off his shirt, to really cream himself up, soothing the chronic itches by his shoulder blades. The very minute he began basking in the cooling vapors, a knock would sound and two seconds later, in would march Wayne or their new idiot secretary with the hungry eyes, Sally. And there would be Jeremy, standing in all his glory, rubbing creamy globs of Eucalypt-all on his serviceable but modest biceps.

Okay, so he didn't sport the trendy faux-weightlifter look, even though the new Muscle-Gro chemicals were supposedly safe. Jeremy Murphy didn't go with the latest body fads. This wasn't news.

It did bother Jeremy somewhat that over the last few weeks how he'd been graduating to stronger creams, from Vaseline to Nivea to AD&E and now this minty-green, eucalyptus-based but odorless crap. It was supposedly odorless, anyhow.

Stavros and the other guys who'd show up at their meeting today weren't noted for their nasal refinement, so Jeremy wasn't worried about their noticing. The main thing was that he could handle this little problem all by himself, without going to Health Services. Even Rachel didn't know.

Insomnia was part of it, too. His whole adult life he'd suffered from mild sleep problems. But lately it was worse. He'd wake up scratching in the middle of the night, or before dawn. He'd itch uncontrollably at odd hours, at work or at home. In the privacy of the night, as his wife slept—or sneaking around in his work cubicle—Jeremy would rub in more and more cream, especially around his elbows, where the scaly patches felt like running sores even though there was no blood, just layer after layer where the skin cracked. He had become a walking desert.

Rachel was creaming her neck with Skin Sauna Rejuvex before putting on her neon-orange unitard. A workout would boost her self-confidence, she decided.

Brookside Health Spa was the ultimate in luxury, open 24 hours a day. From 9 a.m. to 9 p.m., the Spa filled up three sound stages at once, featuring every possible type of calisthenics class. All the instructors were women with flawless bodies and the low, masterful voices that had been considered ideal since Jane Fonda, the exercise guru, had been a big fad. As a kid, Rachel and her Grandma used to "do Jane" with old tapes. Just one more piece of evidence that she was a heck of a lot older than your typical Brookside member.

Looking around at the trophy wives changing their clothes in the locker room, Rachel tried not to be jealous. She checked out her thighs in the mirror. Not bad for an old lady of 39. She was, however, a good 10 years older than most of the housewives who worked out at the Club. Usually a woman her age let Health Services take care of her shape, having surgery like clockwork once a year. Rachel, however, was determined to stay shapely on the inside, not just the outside—which meant doing the work.

Admittedly, it was discouraging to see the competition. Young things at the spa wore the latest in hair and contact lenses, which meant purple, red, and orange... and that was just their eyes. All the curls and spikes, the triple-twirl waves and yard-long hair extensions—being in the locker room with them could make a woman of Rachel's age feel passé.

Was it a mistake that she still kept her naturally golden-brown eyes and dark hair? Most women Rachel's age wore surgically enhanced body accessories, just not ones as wildly artificial as those favored by women under 25. One reason, in fact, why Rachel felt so comfortable with Heather was that her friend dressed sedately, keeping one long, straight blonde braid that reached to her knees. Usually she'd coil it around itself, exactly the style made popular when Madonna had reinvented herself a few years ago. Heather had copied the "Blonde Snake" when it first became a fad, and it flattered her so well that she made it her signature look.

By contrast, the few women Rachel recognized at Spa classes would change their look every three months.

If Rachel didn't want to take cardio classes with these Brookside darlings, she could at least work out in the Techno Room, which offered the latest cardio-vascular equipment. She could choose from hovercraft-based ski machines that were thrilling as well as effective, or rowers with adjustable stress-points that shifted their angle of thrust every 14 seconds, or mountain-climbers that came with screens and earphones, so you could watch an image of yourself take a simulated hike up the Himalayas while you burned off your cals.

Exercise bikes could take you cycling through a Reebok Adventure, and the journeys were mini-televised with special effects. Most of the bikes—like the treadmills—were set up to function with computers, so you could use your exercise time to catch up on your e-mail. In 50 minutes you'd get all your mail and, simultaneously, fabulous body tone.

Rachel loved the machines. Problem was, she hated all the other junk in the room. Even when you wore the complimentary pistol range headphones, you'd hear Muzak blaring from audio speakers. And the suspended wide-screen TVs constantly broadcast depressing news from around the world. What got to her most were the sprayed-in aromatherapy scents—violent hues of peppermint and fake cherry. Rachel liked to choose her own sensory overload, thank you very much.

You never made friends here, either, Rachel thought. Strapped into a rower, she kept thinking of Jeremy. And the competition, Sally. How lonely it was in the midst of the crowd at Brookside.

Forget it! She was getting out of here.

Before Rachel had time to reconsider, she had grabbed her things from the locker. Without changing out of her unitard, she put on her street sneakers and drove home, where she immediately picked up a screen phone to call Jeremy.

Nothing appeared but his message. Well, she'd leave a message then.

"Jeremy," she said. "I'm fed up. You come home late for the second time in a row and never tell me what's going on. What am I supposed to think?"

Jeremy's live image popped into view. "Sweetie, what's—"

"Well, a big thank-you to *you* for picking up the phone! Did you hear what I was just saying?"

"That's why I picked up, actually. You sounded upset."

"Gee, why would I be upset? No sex for how long, a month? And you're hardly ever home, and…

"Obviously in an ideal world I'd have abundant time at my command, but—"

"Oh, come off it."

"Please, I don't have time to talk now. I'm going into a meeting." He was crossing his arms and rubbing them up and down.

Rachel wanted to roll her eyes in the worst way, but this would set Jeremy off, so instead she looked away from him and grabbed herself by the arms, folding them across her chest, and tried to contain her annoyance.

He said, "There's a lot going on here. I'll call you as soon as I can, I assure you. Come on, Rachel, would you just *look* at me?"

His eyes were fierce. His lips pressed together, thinner than ever. As for what this expression meant about their relationship, it baffled her. Rachel's own eyes teared up with frustration. She leaned in toward the screen to make sure he'd see a close-up before she slammed off the phone.

Chapter 6
Becoming Pinkness

Her cards were on the table, at least. While Rachel waited to hear back from Jeremy, she'd do a video class to make up for her aborted workout. Unbelievable that she had driven all the way to Brookside only to leave after what, 14 minutes?

Anyway with a TV workout, she'd feel more connected to people than if she stayed at Brookside. Thank goodness for those new interactive programs! After the broadcast, she could go to her computer and sign on for after-class chat. All those hard-bodied fellow viewers made great company, and she'd seen how becoming the images were of her own sweat-glistening arms and chest. Seeing and being seen online after a workout, everyone became more glamorous than in real life, and friendlier, too. Chat sessions made you feel as if… you were in a beer commercial.

So yes, absolutely, Rachel was psyched to turn on "Dancin' with Roger" from The Fitness Channel.

Roger was fun, kind of a cross between Richard Simmons and Julia Child. Costume changes happened as he moved, thanks to some kind of animation overlay, and Roger sported a different partner each workout, which added to the fun. Today it was Daisy, a thin woman even taller than he. She wore a Carmen Miranda headdress of fruit, two feet of pure fantasy culminating in a pineapple.

That outfit would have been a good party concept, Rachel thought, as she copied their warm-up pelvic gyrations. Daisy was pretending to be cold and snooty—Roger's show always had a subtext of romance, in a tasteful way.

The phone rang. Rachel used her skin-phone without missing a beat. Not Jeremy. Heather.

"Busy, Rachie?"

It felt nice to be needed. "I am, but no problem. Just let me just switch to a headset so I can keep up with my workout."

Quickly she negotiated the switch, then commanded the TV to mute. The workout was picking up in pace—and flirtatious looks. Rachel copied Roger's twist-

and-flex torso stretches while Heather said, "I called to tell you about the hottest seminar. It could solve all our problems."

"Yeah? How much does it cost, a million bucks?"

"Don't be such a skeptic. It's called 'Becoming Pinkness.' Isn't that cute? It's a play on words."

"I don't get it." Floor exercises now, on your back. Knees bent, feet on the floor, you began butt crunches. By the 50th rep., you'd start sweating. By rep. 200, you might also need a chiropractor, but hey, that came free from Health Services.

Heather's voice bubbled with enthusiasm. "Mainly you learn to become the essence of Womanhood, which is Pinkness. But also you learn techniques to make you really alluring, as if you were wearing a becoming shade of pinkness. Get it?"

Roger's method was really very effective. Tomorrow Rachel's butt would hurt like crazy. Yet the show's romance was so entertaining, you hardly felt a thing while you followed the movements.

Meanwhile Heather was going on about how much this new seminar meant for her self-respect. "For the first time in my life, I feel—blah, blah, blah."

Familiar stuff. Roger's show, however? Brilliant. His outfit was now a plumed purple hat atop a Three Musketeers getup. And Daisy was wearing some kind of vintage French ballgown; as she coyly lay next to him on the floor, her red-stockinged knees poked out from a hoop skirt.

"I just saw the tape for the third time. Hey, you don't sound enthusiastic. But I'm telling you, Rachel, this seminar is magic. Everyone's doing it; all your competition, for one thing. Sadie or whoever at your husband's office has probably seen it a hundred times."

Rachel grunted, mostly unintentionally. Roger had shifted to ab crunches. Man, they were hard.

"Just a tip from a friend, Rachie. It's for rent at Costco Supreme. Or you could buy it for keeps, just $249.99." Heather zoomed herself in, showing her face to Rachel in a tight close-up. She confided, "I'd buy it myself except I don't think I need it any more. Like I'm—the last time I saw it?—it went deep into my entire being."

"Look, Heather," Rachel said, once the cool-down phase of the workout began. Roger was doing slow-motion circles with his arms. If you looked carefully you could tell that in quick gestures, at near-subliminal speed, he was blowing kisses at Daisy. She was now wearing a sequined evening gown so tight that it was fascinating to watch her try to move, copying his gestures. Still, the thought of a man's blowing kisses to someone as trashy as Daisy jeopardized Rachel's hard-earned state of contentment.

"Tell me one good reason why I should try this seminar after all the others."

Confidently, Heather said, "One word."

"Pinkness?"

"No, Jeremy."

What else did Rachel have to do except sit by the phone all day, waiting for her husband to call? After a tiny, virtuous lunch she drove to Costco Supreme. She stood in line in the Video Dept., where at least three other women in front of her were clutching the same "Becoming Pinkness" box as they waited for service. Cheap chain: They never used more than one robot during non-peak times. Still, Rachel felt her petty grumbles fade away as she beheld the promise of this shiny new "Cure for an Aching Love Life." Her first act on arriving home was to turn it on.

"Hello, I'm Tanya Willoughby," began the sultry-voiced Seminar Star. "This is a seminar I developed to help women just like you. Unfold the power of Pinkness, your key to success as a Real Woman."

A close-up showed Tanya's famously flawless face, a creamy complexion with every feature in perfect proportion and eye-poppingly lustrous teeth. On her, even pink eyes looked good. For a second, Rachel considered breaking her policy about cosmetically enhanced eye color. Maybe if she experimented she—and Jeremy—would like it.

"I've suffered," Tanya was telling the viewers in her Southern accent. "Suffered grievously! Until I learned to control men instead of having them control me." A few light pink tears welled up as a tribute to Tanya's sorrowful past.

In came the music, violins and oboes. Very classy. "But, girls, we're going to change all that aren't we? Here's what we're about to learn." She winked, and suddenly the tears lifted off her face and turned into typographical dingbats that swirled onto the screen, growing brighter by the second. Words appeared after each dingbat as Tanya summarized the topics to come:

* Turn a man into your personal love slave.
* Ten reasons a woman's true feelings turn men off.
* Pinkness means more than just being pretty.
* How to show a man you're sponanteous and vulnerable.
* Be as irresistible as a chocolate chip cookie. YOU CAN DO IT.

The hours whizzed by. Soon Tanya was drying her eyes, and Rachel was too, except that she used a tissue whereas Tanya used a white lace handkerchief—just

$42.50, if Rachel wanted it. Other selections from the Pink Toybox Catalog were also available *now* with no obligation, if she'd call her local Kiosk.

Rachel felt so inspired, she headed straight for the kitchen, where she whipped up a bowl of one of Tanya's irresistible recipes, "Chocolate Soup Supreme," easy to make with just five symbolic ingredients:

* One can of chicken soup for comfort, blended with
* One quarter cup of cocoa, for sexiness
* Half a can of coconut milk, to add that exotic touch, plus the thickness (as in your man's saying after he ate it, "I'll be with you, my darling, through thick and thin"—admittedly hard to imagine coming from Jeremy's unsentimental lips, nonetheless something to aim for)
* A discreet sprinkling of sugar, symbolizing feminine control, and
* That pinch of salt to keep a man *respectful*.

Many of Tanya's recipes involved chocolate. *I think I'm going to like this program*, Rachel thought dreamily, letting the thick creamy soup linger over her tongue. She remembered her first kiss with Jeremy, back at Crooner State College, in upstate New York. They met her freshman year in music theory class; it was a senior elective for him, trying out a major for her.

Before her first college course in music, Rachel had prided herself on musical ability. She got a good sound out of her fiddle and could convey the underlying mood of any piece of music. Unfortunately, in college she learned that her teachers were more interested in whether she could read notes off a page or demonstrate respect for someone else's rhythm. Rachel preferred her own.

Aspiring world-class violinist or not, Rachel barely passed "Introduction to Theory." She did manage to meet Jeremy, though. They got into a routine of walking together after class to the campus coffee shop: Talking, gazing into each others' eyes, talking some more.

Then, one magical afternoon in early spring, Rachel did something outrageous, something more like her party planner self than the plodding housewife she would later become. Throwing off her shoes, she picked up a soprano recorder and climbed a tree in her quadrangle. Sitting provocatively in the crotch of the tree, she played an assortment of trills and imagined Jeremy flying by like a bird. Eventually, he arrived in human form.

Laughing, he called her name. She came down from the tree, her heart pounding because she could feel It coming, their First Kiss. Jeremy wrapped his arms around her and brought his lips to meet hers. As if they were magnets, those long thin lips pulled her into him, until Rachel's searching lips made contact. Automatically, the rest of her fell through those lips, magnetically pulled into the mystery of Who He Was.

There she was, part of him. After the kiss, she tumbled back out, into her own body, and she felt inebriated by that strong, clean male fragrance Jeremy always had when you were up close to him.

He pulled her to him again, pulling decisively, as if claiming her forever. She'd never forget that decisiveness.

Nor would she forget the magnificence—yes magnificence wasn't too strong a word—the perfect fit when they stumbled down from the tree and had their first full-body embrace; she put her ear to his heart and heard its delicious bass solo, one steady beat after another. The man *was* music. He could hear, really hear, the depth of life. Then and there, Rachel decided to major in *him*.

Tanya's advice came back to interrupt Rachel's chocolate-induced reverie. "Remember," she'd said on the tape, "If you can capture the memory of your first kiss, you're halfway there. Clues are in that memory, ladies. Remember all you can about exactly *who* you were and *what* drew him to you. Discover the most distinctive secrets of attraction from your past. Then apply them now. You will become a truly complete, sought-after, feminine woman. That's the magic of Becoming Pinkness."

Exactly what were Rachel's most distinctive secrets of attraction? Being 18 again? The tree? The recorder, long since lost? What was Rachel supposed to use as a clue for the tough times now?

It was so. . . vexing. How could Rachel feel at once so romantic (moist, even, in her special place), so secure in her memory and, at the same time, so frantic, so desperate, so clueless and insecure?

Here came another horrifying realization: Didn't that rapid switching of mood, from one to the opposite and then to a totally unconnected other, constitute the real Rachel more than anything else? Personally, she despised it. What charm did her perpetual roller coaster ride offer a stable, sane guy like Jeremy?

Would Rachel succeed at "Becoming Pinkness" any more than she had with a dozen other relationship seminars, all of which promised the moon?

The phone rang. Good! Maybe it was Jeremy.

Chapter 7
The Threat

Stavros Menelakos, Secretary of Health and Human Services, stood behind his chair at the head of the conference table. "Bluebeard" was his unofficial name around the office, thanks to a heavy beard set off by blue-black hair and bushy eyebrows, plus a notorious "take no prisoners" attitude. Although Jeremy hadn't seen Stavros for months and didn't especially like him, for once he was glad to have the man around. As Jeremy's boss's boss, Stavros was a member of President Stevie Tucker's Cabinet, so he brought clout to Jeremy's team.

Cooper Hackenworth, Director of the CIA, was coming to this meeting, and Jeremy trusted him even less than Stavros.

Jeremy lined up next to Stavros and imitated his position, standing behind his own chair. To Jeremy's right, Wayne stood tensely, clutching a fat pile of handouts. Next to arrive was Marty Hiyakawa, Jeremy's immediate boss. Jeremy caught his eye and Marty peered out from under his bushy, hinged eyebrows, telegraphing his usual calm smile. This contagious air of serenity couldn't have been more different from how Jeremy felt. Was it too much to expect that Hackenworth would catch Marty's mood and turn affable for once in his life?

"Welcome, Rich, welcome ladies," Stavros was saying in his booming baritone to the three who came through the door. "Rich, why don't you sit next to me?"

Rich Davis, at 27, was a kid compared to Stavros at 62 or, for that matter, Marty, pushing retirement at a well preserved 73.

Rich was a perpetually angry but charming young man: good looking, athletic and muscular. His chiseled jaws caught Jeremy's eye—along, of course, with his coloring. For political reasons, Rich had darkened his skin to a heart-of-Africa gloss. The guy's parentage, it was rumored, was lily-white—mentally Jeremy corrected that to the PC term now in use, "Nordic bloodstream." Now that Nordics no longer constituted a majority in the U.S., an ambitious upstart like Rich could benefit from a darker skin color.

Whatever it took to have clout, Rich would do. The White House Press Liaison wouldn't deign to stand behind his chair like everyone else. He sat. Everyone followed suit, including the ladies.

"Brenda Chen, PR for the Environmental Protection Agency, Pesticide Approval Division," announced the slim, attractive woman next to Rich. Her low voice sliced the air like a well sharpened knife.She wore a magenta suit and a low-cut white blouse with nice cleavage out of which peeked a small, tailored cross.

What was she? Jeremy couldn't help wondering, which showed how old-fashioned he was, because nobody was supposed to think about ethnicity these days. Besides, who could tell? With a name like Chen, you'd think Asian bloodstream, but this beautiful blonde had a double fold to her eyelids, whether naturally or surgically. If she were in Brent's generation, odds would be high that genetically she was a mixture of several bloodlines. Even in her age group, few Americans were pure WASP bloodstream, pedigreed poodles like Rich Davis.

The other woman announced, "I'm Juanita McCracken, Special Investigator for the U.S. Department of Agriculture, Plant Protection and Quarantine."

"Excuse me," Stavros said pleasantly, "But would you mind sitting next to Ms. Chen instead? We're saving the end of the table for Dr. Hackenworth, the C.I.A. Director.

"Certainly. I didn't realize that Cooper was going to be here." Juanita wore a blue pantsuit with a ruffled blouse, woven with varied hues of sea-foam green. Jeremy wondered if she purposely dressed to convey the illusion that slow breaking ocean waves were splashing into her upper torso… probably not. Humor didn't seem to be her strong point—or she wouldn't wear that cross—so big, dangling from its leather harness, it must have been a five-pounder.

Cooper Hackenworth, Ph.D., Director of the Central Intelligence Agency, paraded into the room. His gray suit was impeccably tailored, perfectly pressed. The tie riveted Jeremy's attention. It was beautiful: geometric shapes, slightly darker than pastel, with colors that shimmered as only silk can. Underneath the jacket, in the same elegant print, were Hackenworth's trademark suspenders. Nothing else in the conference room was beautiful; there were only a few nondescript paintings and, on a side table, the TV monitor to be used later for showing vid-clips.

"Greetings," Hackenworth said, taking his seat at the end of the table. "Haven't kept you long, I trust?" He spoke with what passed for statesmanlike authority, but to Jeremy (and probably everyone else at the table) Hackenworth's exquisite diction was mostly irritating. "Slow down, you fools, and stop to hear a gentleman speak," was the subtext as miniature pauses framed each golden word.

Loathe him or not, however, this pompous, middle-aged blueblood was the man Jeremy hoped to get on his side. He wanted Hackenworth's clout for pacing what did and didn't go public. The question was, how would Hackenworth position himself?

"Cooper, we were just getting started," Stavros said. "You know Juanita from USDA, right?" Briskly they nodded to each other.

"And here are our two communication specialists," Stavros continued. "Rich Davis is the new White House Liaison and Brenda Chen does spin for the EPA."

"Forget the spin. Just call me Brenda," she said.

Hackenworth did one of his slimy smiles, stretching his near-invisible upper lip sideways while his huge lower lip protruded more than ever.

"And you must be Rich," he said, nodding.

"Don't believe I've had the pleasure," Mr. White House, Jr. said grandly. Impressive voice, Jeremy had to admit. The man could have been a broadcaster.

Stavros leaned back slightly and clasped his hands over his considerable belly. "And may I introduce our stars for this meeting? Meet the cream of Health and Human Services: Marty Hiyakawa, my Deputy Assistant Secretary; under him, here's Jeremy Murphy, Division Director, Technical Research; and that's Wayne Kinsella, Senior Research Specialist."

"What is the specialty there, exactly, Wayne?" Hackenworth asked.

"Control and Containment." Stavros, Jeremy and Wayne all answered together. Nervous laughter sounded from Wayne, to Jeremy's embarrassment.

Stavros continued, "As you all know, our purpose in meeting today is to receive technical updates from these fellows to help us shape our strategy for dealing with this latest problem. But first, here's a background report from Investigator McCracken, who has flown in today for our meeting—from where in the Midwest, exactly?"

"Chicago, the Champagne-Urbana suburb," she said.

"Might I add a comment?" Hackenworth said. "We may as well be clear from the outset that background is neither here nor there. Our true agenda today is damage control."

"Well, yes, I'd agree with you, Cooper," said Juanita, rising to her feet. "Forgive me if I talk standing up. It will keep me from falling asleep. I have this new hobby, flying back and forth between time zones."

Juanita's eyes were darkly shadowed. She continued, "What we're discussing today are the huntids. Our first warning about them came from the company that may be responsible for their existence.

"Hunsforth, Tidwell & Bacon is a low-profile, mid-sized conglomerate specializing in bio-engineered products. This spring they started testing a new designer vegetable called Macro Corn 219, a bug-resistant, drought-resistant corn with big kernels. Major selling point is that, when ripe, the kernels are supposed to turn a vivid shade of Popsicle green. I understand the company was planning to market it as a green vegetable, because of the color—nothing to do with Vitamin A or any other nutritional factors, more like a nicely engineered coloring insert, but the hype still might impress the public. Ask me again in a year, when Macro Corn hits the market."

"Hold on," Hackenworth interrupted. "Tell us more about the players in this conglomerate. I've never heard of it before."

"With good reason," she said. "The CEO's are three mega-millionaires from a suburb of New York called East Orange. None of them are a day over 25. Their real names are Jill and Fred Kim, a brother-and-sister team, and Carmen Castaneda. They took different names for their company because which would you rather do business with, someone who sounds like he grew up with Cooper Hackenworth here, or what these kids really are, second generation immigrants from third world countries? They call their company Hunsforth, Tidwell & Bacon."

"The Bacon's a nice touch, I think." Hackenworth smiled, angling his left eyebrow upwards. "So tell me, how did kids like that wind up owning a conglomerate? They didn't inherit it, did they? Do the parents have ties that could link to organized crime or terrorism?"

"We checked that out, Cooper. The parents are of no importance; their kids just have juice. A generation ago, they would have been hackers. You know—smart, go-getters and, let us say, not entirely respectful of the establishment. In high school they developed a little hobby, day trading. Made a bundle. Then they built up capital by working as commodities brokers. By 2015, they had made enough cash to form Hunsforth, Tidwell & Bacon and the real fun began. They started developing products of their own."

"Such as?" asked Stavros.

"Everyone here knows them, just not as products of Hunsforth, Tidwell & Bacon," Juanita said. "Put on your thinking caps, guys."

Jeremy drew a blank. He looked around the table. Everyone else seemed to be looking around, too.

Brenda's face lit up. "I think I may be wearing one. It's that hairdo product, Ravioli Curls. Doesn't Hunsforth own Pasta Perfect?"

Everyone stared at Brenda's hairstyle, a fad Jeremy had seen around but not known the name for. When you looked closely you saw that each fat blonde "Ravioli Curl" folded over to enclose a pink gel. The result was to create a kind of under-hair halo. It gave Brenda's face a soft glow. She posed at her seat, one hand framing her hair, while her other hand rested provocatively on her hips. "Try me," she said, mimicking a well-known TV commercial. "I'm Pasta Perfect."

Shifting back to a businesslike posture, Brenda explained, "It's a hobby of mine, watching commercials and following the trends. I like to see how big companies advertise their range of products. If I'm not mistaken, Hunsforth, Tidwell & Bacon owns all the Pasta Perfect products.

"Which are what?" Stavros said impatiently.

"They're colorful hair gels that make hair do anything pasta can do—spaghetti, spirals, seashells, ravioli. They're quick and easy, which makes them popular with the Generation Qs and anyone else who likes to dress trendy...." Brenda stopped talking, as if she suddenly realized that nobody in the room besides her appeared to be even remotely trendy. Her spontaneity reminded Jeremy of Rachel, a thought that brought him a second of happiness before Stavros' grating voice broke the mood.

"What else does the company make?" he asked Juanita, pointedly ignoring Brenda.

Juanita paced back and forth as she answered, "High-tech candy, soft drinks with the latest 'health' ingredients like macadamia nuts—and increasingly, their revenues come from agricultural products, which brings us back to the corn." She stood still, facing Hackenworth. "Hunsforth, Tidwell & Bacon owns a bunch of scientists, for research purposes."

"The old foundation ploy, right?" Hackenworth said. "First they buy a professor at a state-funded college. They interest him in conducting a research study, which coincidentally relates to matters of interest to them. Professor applies for grants to a particular research foundation, which just happens to be owned by Hunsforth, Tidwell & Bacon. Surprise! Scientific philanthropy buys the company a $2 million tax write-off, instead of an in-house bill for R&D." With a patronizing smile toward Wayne, obviously the junior player at the table, Hackenworth explained, "That, of course, means their own free Research and Development team."

Juanita nodded knowingly whereas, Jeremy noticed, his assistant Wayne looked shocked, even indignant.

Juanita continued, "So you can picture the professor and his research assistants out in some university cornfield. On June 19th, they're digging for seedlings to bring back to the lab when they come upon a bunch of weird little bugs, Popsicle green with wings the color of lilacs. So they take them back to the lab, along with the corn. Researchers go on to name the bugs Hunsforth-Tids, figuring it will please the company to give them credit for a new species. They register it with the International Code of Zoological Nomenclature; the Latin name is *Musca Viola*, but in plain English, they're Hunsforth-Tids.

"Not a great PR move in the long run, I gather," Hackenworth said dryly.

Juanita smiled. "Ever since hell broke loose, Hunsforth, Tidwell & Bacon has been working almost as hard as we have to keep the flies—and especially their name—hush hush."

"Evidently the science guys didn't know much about the PR side of their R&D," Brenda observed.

"What happened, exactly?" asked Hackenworth.

Juanita said, "Other farmers started to dig up huntids—"

"Huntids?" Hackenworth asked. "I thought you said Hunsforth-Tids."

"Hey, you try saying it fast. Oprah Winfrey was supposed to be named Orpah, remember? Anyhow, reports over the last two weeks have come from farmers as far away as Springfield—the one in Missouri, not Illinois." Juanita paused. "But so far we've contained word of mouth pretty well."

Brenda said, "For that you can thank Juanita's hardworking team in the Quarantine Division. What she really quarantines is chat, not flies or corn."

"Good point," Stavros said. "And now I think we need to move to the heart of the matter which is, after all, the substance, not the PR. Let's hear the HHS technical report on these strange flies and the kind of threat they pose."

"Excuse me, but I disagree," Rich said, impatiently tapping his Palmster Notetaker with well-manicured fingers. "We'd better clarify the PR threat first, because that exists regardless of what the bugs do or don't do."

But Hackenworth said, "Hold your horses, cowboy. Mostly we need to know what we're talking about." Jeremy noted with some amusement, this annoyed Stavros. Undoubtedly he'd been ready to say the same thing himself and didn't like being pre-empted.

Now Stavros said, "Marty, are your boys ready?" And Marty gestured to Jeremy, who wiped his forehead and stood up slowly (at 6'2" he was easily the tallest person present). "Show time," he thought. Deliberately he picked up the remote for the vid-slides and turned on the set.

"My assignment was to supply you with background on the huntids. We have an abundance of that, I assure you. Since not all of you are fascinated by entomology, I'll spare you the minor details and go straight to what you'll find practical.

"First shot shows you what they look like, *Musca Viola*.

"If not for their color, huntids would appear identical to ordinary house flies. At first we suspected their color was just a mutation related to the color of Macro Corn 219 and nothing else about them was unusual. Since then, we've discovered otherwise. Although we haven't had time to research all possible factors related to color, we're reasonably sure that their color isn't especially significant, except that it helps you to spot them. Now—"

"Excuse me," Rich Davis interrupted. "If you're talking about the public, color is *very* significant. Even with modern advances in cosmetic coloring, color is the first thing people notice in each other, or in animals. I don't care whether you use the PC term "bloodstream" or good old-fashioned labels like White, Black and Yellow. People notice color. So the shock value of green-and-purple flies is something we'll have to handle very carefully."

"Good point," Jeremy said. "And now may I continue with what *is* unusual about these insects? As Juanita has told us, huntids were first discovered in soil. They were in mud, actually.

"Think about that. It's not unusual for some flies to *mate* in mud, though that's normally found with deer flies, not houseflies. But pay attention to the fact that the huntids *return* to mud, going there to rest on a regular basis, as you can see from this next video sequence.

"Because of behavior like this, we conclude that huntids appear to be the first truly amphibious insect.

Click. "They swim."

Stavros said, "Hardly unusual for flies to light on water, is it?"

Jeremy said, "But how about swimming underwater? Huntids can do that for hours. There's some kind of breathing mechanism related to their oddly colored wings."

Click. "They fly, of course."

Click. "And they crawl."

"What, this doesn't quite shock you? Let me add two words, then: In *formation*."

Hackenworth snickered. "Information? You mean I might consider hiring these bugs."

Jeremy ignored him. *Click.* "Fly in formation, too. See the line? Now let's pause this image a few times. Notice the wing positions?"

"I leave it to you to calculate the odds that these movements are random. What you're seeing here are a dozen flies with synchronized wing beats. *Click.* Up at the same time. *Click.* Down at the same time.

"And there's more."

Click. "Huntids crawl in formation. You see that, or you want me to pause that one for you, too?"

Hackenworth nodded. In slow motion, and magnified ten-fold, the insects made a sinister march across the TV monitor. Even Jeremy shuddered inwardly. Hackenworth grinned. "Powerful image, there," he told the group. "We'll find some way to use that."

"Amphibious capabilities and movement in formation are both unusual to the degree we see them developed in the huntids. This will have implications in terms of control," Jeremy said, "should we consider a program of extermination."

"Should?" Hackenworth sputtered. "I think you'll find an easy consensus about that. The *issue* is not IF we should exterminate these mutants, but HOW. (For emphasis, Hackenworth pronounced the word British-style, ISSSS-euw.)

Stavros glared at him. "Mutants is an interesting choice of words. Perhaps you're already familiar with entomological mutation phenomena, Cooper?"

The C.I.A. Director gave a smug smile.

Stavros continued, "Although we confine our research to personnel with top security clearances, like Director Hiyakawa and Dr. Murphy, we know that our friends in Central Intelligence have great powers. So perhaps, Dr. Hackenworth, you'd like to explain to the group what Dr. Murphy's lab research has found about the huntids' specialized talents in the area of mutation.

"No? Then I hope you and everyone here will listen with the closest possible attention." Stavros gave a tiny triumphant look, and Jeremy felt the group's attention shift back to him.

Jeremy continued, "Insect intelligence is one of those things that we humans don't like to think about, even in the best of times. Insects make us uncomfortable, period. For starters, they out-number us. Perhaps you already know that for every pound of human flesh there are 300 pounds of insects, most of them so small they can't be seen.

"Another disconcerting fact is that, beyond all forms of animal life on this planet, including our own, insects are the best equipped to survive."

Click. Jeremy showed an image of cockroaches magnified ten-fold, then he right-clicked to split the screen. Six images came into view. "Cockroaches are shown crawling in kitchens based, respectively, in the El Paso suburb of Texas-West, in Miami, Reno, LA, Boston—your home town, I believe, Cooper?—and Sioux City—Stavros, that's your part of Iowa-West, isn't it?

Well, what do all these cities have in common? A well-contained cockroach problem, of course."

Click. The six kitchens re-appeared. Now, thanks to a little cut-and-paste from the Graphics Dept., each roach had been replaced by a miniature dinosaur.

Jeremy's voice took on a note of urgency. "Gentlemen and ladies, we want you to think about this image before you decide what to do about the huntids.

"Flies and roaches have been with us this since the days of the dinosaurs. Dinosaurs did not survive, as you know. They weren't bright enough. Bugs were. Survival doesn't always go to the largest—or the prettiest."

Click to a montage of flies, mosquitoes, cockroaches, bees, spiders, centipedes and ants.

"What do these creatures have in common?" Jeremy asked.

Click and the screen refreshed itself, showing each animal magnified ten-fold. "Insects and related species are *not* glamorous, except for butterflies and, maybe, moths.

"I like to think of them as creatures of intelligence. They wear their brains on the outside, unadorned by personality or charm. Insects are built as survivors. And make no mistake. Unlike dinosaurs, these creatures are likely to survive."

"Come on," said Rich Davis. "America couldn't have built the Panama Canal without solving the problem of mosquitoes spreading yellow fever. And I'll bet everyone here learned in school about tsetse flies, the carriers of sleeping sickness. They were stamped out, weren't they?"

Jeremy answered, "In both these cases, stamping out disease depended on eliminating breeding grounds and developing a vaccine. It was relatively simple to learn each specie's reproduction cycles and habitats. Therefore, eliminating them was simple, by today's standards. All you had to do was spray insecticides, no genetic tinkering needed.

"With the huntids, however, reproduction patterns and behavior may not be so predictable, which could make them a lot harder to deal with. Still, we're fortunate because, insofar as we know, the huntids do not carry any disease.

"Did you hear that?" Jeremy stared pointedly at Rich Davis and Cooper Hackenworth. "Huntids don't carry any disease, so let's not react to them with fear.

"They don't appear to endanger crops, either. Granted, we've had them under observation for only two weeks now, but well-controlled tests have shown they eat only leaves, grass and crumbs of food; no greater amounts are ingested than with ordinary houseflies, and huntids show no preference for any agricultural crops. The danger to farmers is zip."

Juanita interrupted, sounding angry. "With all respect, Jeremy, it's easy for you to say there's no danger to crops. You're not an agribusiness owner, fighting the commodities brokers on one side, the pests on the others. At the USDA, our clients *are* agribusiness owners, remember?

"Tell me, everyone, you think *you* have a lot of headaches to deal with?" Juanita indignantly eyeballed everyone at the table, starting with Rich and ending up with Brenda, as she reeled off the list of headaches for farmers: seed brokers, pesticide suppliers, soil technicians, equipment designers, mechanics.

"And let's not forget loan officers, high-tech designers of the latest produce, migrant worker unions, employment policy advisors and insurance companies. Agribusinesses even have to keep attorneys on retainer—sure, you'd love to pay them every month if you were a farmer. Then let's not forget Old Man Winter or the environmental fanatics.

"In my opinion, American farmers top the list of endangered species. Generations ago, America was a land of farmers, including your own ancestors if you go back far enough.

"Farmers gambled and most of them lost. Their descendants today may seem tough and their businesses impressive but, I'm telling you, they're unbelievably fragile. When you add mutants, or whatever these horrible insects are, they could be the straw that broke the camel's back. React with fear? You'd better believe it. It's been hell for Brenda, trying to keep a lid on this thing."

"And just how have you kept the lid down?" Hackenworth asked her.

"Well," Brenda said, "The first guys in the Chicago suburbs weren't much of a problem because discretion is a way of life for them. They publish only what they want the public to see.

"Farmers were the next group to discover the huntids; just seeing that weird color flying around in their fields, farmers panicked. But most came straight to us, because they figured we had the bucks for a pesticide bailout. Remember before Tucker's first term, the crisis over Burmese mosquitoes?

"Oh, the Democrats' cute little $3 billion handout?" said Stavros sarcastically.

"Pardon me, that was $2.7 billion and it bought us significant goodwill." Hackenworth smiled at him condescendingly. "The boys on the farms thought their screaming got our attention, while all along we were pulling the strings. President Rinaldo, 'The man of the people,' was delighted to help. Now your *very* Republican President Tucker has likewise seen the value of pacifying America's farmers. They've become some of our strongest supporters."

Brenda Chen continued, "The Federal presence has certainly been a visible presence for farmers this time. As soon as they complained, we offered to tackle their problem with our experts in Washington." Here she bestowed a courteous nod that swept from Marty to Jeremy. Wayne puffed up visibly at receiving even a glance of recognition.

"Why turn to us?" Stavros asked.

Brenda said, chuckling. "You think farmers want the public to get wind of something new like huntids? Even the hint of a problem in America's heartland could send a signal abroad and change the balance of trade. Look, our farmers are plenty worried about competing with aggressive marketers from China, India, Argentina, Mexico, New Zealand—even Poland, for heaven's sake. Foreign growers are just looking for an opening to approach the biggest conglomerates and take over long-standing contracts. Asians can grow rice and soybeans, too, in case you hadn't noticed."

Stavros pounded the table lightly with his right fist. "Back to the main topic, if you don't mind. That was, I believe, mutation. Correct, Dr. Murphy?"

Stavros' power gesture had, inadvertently, called attention to his other hand. Jeremy noticed for the first time that Stavros' left hand was in his pocket. He was fingering what, beads? Had Stavros become one of The Righteous? Jeremy wasn't the only one to notice. He saw Brenda and Juanita exchange looks. And Hackenworth seemed to be sneering a tad more than usual.

Jeremy said, "Frankly, the intelligence of the huntids worries us more than anything else."

"What's the problem?" said Hackenworth. "You think they're coming after your job?"

"Careful," Stavros told the CIA Director. "If intelligence is the issue" (a word Stavros made rhyme with 'tissue'), if I were you I'd worry more about the bugs exposing the relative size of everyone's power base. Couldn't *that* be upsetting."

Hackenworth shot him a look that could have come from a laser gun.

"I'm sure you're going to want to hear what Dr. Murphy has to tell us," Wayne said, flashing his most conciliatory smile. Jeremy knew his assistant was trying to help him win back the group; as usual, Techies stood at the bottom of the pecking order.

Jeremy showed the next vid-clip: A monkey banging two coconuts together. "Intelligence, as I was saying, is a matter of vital importance to us all. Can any of you visitors guess why I'm showing you this animal, obviously not an insect, in the context of animal intelligence?"

"Don't tell us the bugs are going to steal coconut milk from monkeys. Hey, that's like taking candy from a baby," Rich quipped.

"Some intelligence," Brenda joined in. "Everyone knows that coconuts are high in saturated fat. You call animals that eat that stuff intelligent?"

Jeremy said, "Okay, coconut experts. Any of you ever hear of the Hundredth Monkey Effect? Intra-species intelligence is well documented. People have it, monkeys have it, and huntids seem to have it—only an *inter*-species version. Wayne, come out here to the front of the room. You were the first to observe these distinctive phenomena. Why don't you explain them to our guests here?"

Wayne smiled modestly as he walked over toward Jeremy and took the remote. *Click.* The screen showed a glass tank half-filled with mud. Out flew a few green flies. "Note their phosphorescent lilac wings? You could call that their trademark."

Wayne clicked onto the profile view of one fly, magnified 500 times. The screen showed a plump green body, translucent wings with light purple veins, and an eye that was red. Wayne said, "The network of veins, like the irrigation pattern in a leaf, gives that ethereal lilac effect."

Jeremy was fascinated to watch the group respond to the image of a huge huntid. Brenda and Juanita's hands flew to their crosses. Stavros fiddled with his beads, double time. Cooper Hackenworth's eyes opened wide, a refreshing change from their usual calculating blue and white slits. Rich's gold-lensed eyes grew huge and round; his tense jaws twitched. By contrast, Marty stared with admiration, revealing the scientists' delight that allied him with Jeremy and Wayne.

Wayne's voice rang out clearly. "Since we first started observing the huntids, they've learned to swim.

Click. "A week later, the whole population learned to swim *underwater*."

Click. "Ten days later, they all learned to fly in formation. What will they learn next? We don't know."

Hackenworth gave a sly little smile. "And how much else about these little buggers don't you know?"

Jeremy felt his hackles rise. There was something ominous in Hackenworth's voice, something more than his usual contempt.

Marty gave a slight bow in Hackenworth's direction, "You tell me who's a bigger expert, Cooper."

Hackenworth turned away, but Jeremy could almost see steam rising from his face.

"Look," Rich interrupted. "It's time we talked PR, not just bugs. We've taken our sweet time with this meeting but I'm due back to the White House in half an hour.

"I've seen enough here today to know one thing. What I tell my staff will give 'em the creeps. Whatever else these huntids may be, with their little red eyes and weird wings, they're political poison."

"Oh, come on," Stavros glared.

Rich pointed a long index finger at him. "You think our President wants to go on TV and tell the American people about these disgusting mutants? But he's got to. It's his job as the most powerful man on earth."

"Why the rush?" asked Stavros.

"What, let his authority crumble when a public announcement comes from some loudmouth from the Midwest? What's to stop any fool from getting on the Internet to tell the whole world about the huntids? I'm amazed it hasn't happened already."

"That means you're thanking us, right?" said Brenda.

"I'm telling you all, this insect is gonna scare people. President Tucker has to announce a plan to get rid of 'em."

"Extermination *is* the obvious recourse." Hackenworth said softly. "So the question for our experts here is what Dr. Murphy previously referred to as 'practical.' What justification can we give President Tucker to exterminate the huntids?"

"Not so fast, please," Marty said. "For technical reasons we're about to explain, extermination may not be the answer."

"Definitely not," said Jeremy. "Listen, Rich, we've been working on this research day and night. Hear us out." To Wayne he telegraphed, "Our strategy! What the hell happened to our strategy?" His arms were itching like crazy.

"Quick version, then, boys," muttered Stavros. The comment sounded anything but paternal. Jeremy could hear Rachel inside his head—*These guys are making you feel so like shit; it would serve them right if you gave up trying.* But the stakes here were far too important for Jeremy to give up. Stavros was right. He needed to score his points and score them fast.

Rich looked at his watch as if to say, "What a bunch of ineffectual losers." Aloud he said, "Five minutes until I go meet my White House 'copter. And the countdown starts now."

Wayne sprang into action, striding back to the table. He grabbed his stack of handouts and passed the packets around, beginning with Hackenworth.

Jeremy clicked on the remote. He said, "The intelligence of these insects is really extraordinary. Far from being pests, they might turn out to be useful."

"For what?" said Hackenworth.

"We don't know yet. That's why we need time for research. The worst thing we could do is make a hasty decision. Our technical panel from HHS includes Director Hiyakawa, my assistant Wayne Smith, a dozen research specialists, plus robots, consultants and myself. Speaking on behalf of us all, I definitely do not recommend extermination and—"

Rich interrupted: "I'm telling you, Jeremy. Extermination is not a matter of *if*, not with this President. Our people want answers fast, not some bunch of nerds going on and on."

"If you're concerned about the time," Stavros snarled. "I suggest you listen without interrupting. You might even learn something."

"Should extermination procedures occur," Jeremy said, pushing to keep the rage out of his voice, "they would have to be high-intensity, simultaneous, and probably sprayed from low-flying planes, all over our country, very precisely coordinated."

"And the cost?" asked Brenda Chen.

"You'll find it on Page Five, along with our analysis of deployment in the event of mass extermination of huntids. But this is not as important—"

"Sure is to our public," chuckled Brenda.

Stavros rose to his feet, both hands clenched. "We're talking policy here, not PR. You and your colleague at the White House don't make policy yet. Where's your mandate to go off half-cocked? This isn't some shoot-out in the old West. Will you listen?"

Jeremy was itching like crazy. Yet he felt oddly detached from his body. It was as if he was caught in a nightmare, where he kept trying to talk but, instead, his body was sinking into quicksand. "Extermination could poison the environment beyond our ability to sustain human life. We don't know enough yet."

Marty said, staring at Hackenworth, "That's why we attempted to invite some technical specialists from EPA to this meeting."

"Yes, I vetoed that." Hackenworth retorted. "Just look at the mess this meeting is already, with only the eight of us here. You really wanted to add another bunch of players to bumble around this conference table? Given how much trouble your boys have keeping control of your agenda, I think not, Mr. Hiyakawa. Take Dr. Murphy, here, in charge of Pest Control. Let just hope, Stavros, he's better at controlling bugs than an audience."

Stavros glowered. "Cooper, would you let the man speak?"

"Two minutes," warned Rich, "And I'm out of here. God, I can't tell you what snoozers your meetings are over here."

"The last page," Jeremy gasped. "Take it with you. We've summarized all the experiments. They show *no* threat from these flies. Do your own cost-benefit analysis. Extermination doesn't make sense."

"Sure," said Rich, throwing the handout into his overstuffed briefcase. "It's been such a pleasure. By the way, if I were you, I'd get a report to President Tucker right away about all the reasons you found to exterminate. Do yourselves a favor— make it look good."

Chapter 8
Practically Nothing

Wayne shook his head. Jeremy heard him mutter disgustedly, "I don't get it. Kill first, think later." Everyone outside HHS had gone, leaving Jeremy, Wayne, Marty, and Stavros alone in the Conference room.

"Great job, boys," Stavros said, ignoring Wayne's comment. "You'd better have a compelling report on my screen one week from today."

Wayne walked over to Stavros. Even though the younger man only came up to Stavros' glistening black beard, he stared upwards and locked eyes with his boss' boss' boss, the Federal Director of Health and Human Services. Wayne asked, "Would you please explain something? Why didn't you go to bat for us? What's so wrong with giving us more time to study these flies before we get rid of them?"

Stavros seemed about to answer abruptly when a look of inner reflection crossed his face. If Jeremy didn't know better, he would have said the man looked thoughtful. Certainly Jeremy was unprepared for the gentleness in Stavros' voice as he answered, "Politics, son. If I know our president, when he holds his press conference this week, he'll score points by playing The Great Protector. The polls will show America loves having a new enemy to fight."

Wayne's stare intensified.

"Look," Stavros said, "we can protest and logic and pray our hearts out, but media is where the power is today. Earthly power, that is."

He waved goodbye absent-mindedly, doing some kind of complicated footwork on the way out.

Marty, Wayne, and Jeremy stared at each other in disbelief.

Marty broke the silence with an impish smile. "What do you think that man was doing with his feet?"

"They call it 'Footwork of The Righteous,'" Wayne said.

Marty stood up, bemused. "So that's what it looks like. I'd heard about it before, never saw it, though."

Clumsily he worked to imitate Stavros' sequence of toe taps followed by double heel taps. Though lean-bodied and well preserved for his age, Marty wasn't much of a dancer. "Harder to do than it looks," he observed.

"Footwork of The Righteous, alright," Wayne sneered. "Did you guys notice how Stavros was into his beads for most of the meeting?

"And he fought so hard for HHS," said Marty. "Poor guy, he's only a Cabinet Secretary. What can he do?"

Quietly Jeremy said, "He's only the one man in America, except for President Tucker, who has the clout to set national policy when it comes to the huntids."

"No big deal, it's only mass extermination," Marty said, looking disgusted. "Then he accuses *us* of not doing our job. Where I grew up in Iowa, people would talk to you straight. Even if they disagreed with you, at least you knew where they stood."

"Well, what can we expect from a man like Stavros?" Jeremy said. "Did you like him any better as Bluebeard, when he earned that reputation for being ruthless? You knew him back then, didn't you Marty?"

"Stavros in the old days? He was utterly ruthless. Then, a few months ago, I heard that he had fallen in with that strange group of religious fanatics—what are they called, the Righteous? This was the first time I've seen him since he's become so Righteous."

"And now, I take it," Wayne said, "you don't plan on converting any time soon."

Marty laughed. "All our employees at HHS are Techies, wouldn't you say? Techies I can deal with. But with these Righteous...."

Wayne and Jeremy shrugged.

"I don't know any followers of Rev. Helms. Do either of you understand them?"

Wayne reddened. "My wife, Marnie, became a follower of Rev. Pilgrim after our last child was born. Confidentially, it seems weird to me, but at least she's not as extreme as the bead thumpers--hope you don't mind my saying this, Jeremy. It's hard to tell what anyone is anymore." Wayne put his arm around him for a quick sideways squeeze. (He was, like Rachel, a hugger.)

For once, Jeremy almost hugged him back. "After the beating I've taken today, you're worried about offending me? Wayne, without you there, I would have drowned, man. Thanks for your support. You too, Marty. Guys, we've always known where the power was, and it wasn't in science—not unless science had money."

"Is money really the problem?" Wayne asked. "Maybe it's more a matter of personality."

"What, you're saying we ought to model ourselves after the charming Mr. Davis?"

Marty nodded. "Wayne has a point, Jeremy. Why would anyone listen to a bunch of no-personality Techies?"

"So what should we do, Marty, take personality seminars?"

Both men laughed.

"That's it," Wayne said. "We can turn into Seminar Slaves. Think we could hire Rich Davis to give us a little personality coaching on the side?"

"Actually, Wayne, I think you're the exception," said Marty. "You do have personality. No offense meant, Jeremy."

"Hey, that's how it is," Jeremy said. "Maybe we should give up trying to make the White House or CIA listen to us. Let them invent their own science fiction, along with all their phony news angles. America has come to be the land of sizzle, not steak. "

Marty said, "Isn't that the mysterious benefit of being a nerd? When pop culture dominates, those of us who speak in sentences with more than a few simple words, can become invisible."

"Unless we manage to become celebrities." Wayne said. "Think there's any chance we'll get the Nobel Prize for being the first to study the huntids?"

"For what it's worth," said Jeremy, "I think your experiments were brilliant. Especially the one we took to the meeting for them to not look at. Magnificent!"

"A thousand years hence, it'll all be the same," Marty said. "Let's go home, get a good rest and come back fresh on Monday."

"Then do what?" Jeremy said. "Dream up extermination procedures?"

"Well, we'll continue to monitor the huntids and see what more we can learn about them. You go ahead, Wayne, write a report about possible hazards from huntids. Jeremy, maybe you should come up with an extermination plan in case we need it. Have both ready a week from today to humor our friends Davis, Hackenworth and Menelakos. Since I have a load of projects to monitor, overseeing these reports will be your baby, Jeremy."

Wayne nudged Marty. "For the Extermination part of it, maybe we can tell them we're working so carefully because we're impressed with their fabulous concept. Tell Rich it's not about bugs any more. It's about protecting the nation as a whole."

"We'll work the Extermination plans so carefully and deliberately that it can't be called stalling, huh?" Jeremy gave a limp smile. Wayne grinned.

"Whatever gave you that idea?" Marty said.

Jeremy and Wayne knew him well enough to know that meant, "Do it."

Marty asked, "Anyone want to share a heli-taxi to the Metro?"

Jeremy and Wayne fell into step with him. Secretly Jeremy felt so weary, he could hardly stand. No itches, anyway; that was the good news. The bad news was that he didn't have the strength to scratch. As he headed for the rooftop 'copter taxi pad, some lines from Yeats kept running through his head, "Things fall apart. The center cannot hold. Mere anarchy is loosed upon the world."

"Rachel, it's Jessica."

Not Jeremy? How disappointing! Rachel said, "Hi, Jessica. I can hear you. All I have is my skin-phone, though."

Definitely the equipment of choice, Rachel thought, since she planned to change clothes while talking. This would be her first outfit geared to the principles of "Becoming Pinkness." Her new pink wardrobe to be was heaped on the bed.

Yes, during one of the seminar exercises, Tanya had talked Rachel through doing a Pinkness Inventory. This involved identifying every stitch she owned that had even a hint of pink and flinging it onto the emperor-sized bed she shared with Jeremy. Every jumpsuit or dress, blouse or skirt, slacks or leggings! Every accessory! All underwear! Anything with even so much as a pink polka dot!!!

That gave Rachel maybe 300 items to choose from. Now she'd dress while Jessica talked.

"I'm calling from my husband's car, the one with a video implant, so if you want, you can take a look at the boys. They're in the back seat."

"Sounds good, Jessica, but I'll just go with your voice." She buttoned up a paisley blouse—clingy, silky, and dripping with femininity to the tune of at least five different shades of pink. "Where are you? Crawling along Nancy Reagan Freeway?"

"Rachel, I don't want to worry you but we had to end Scout Camp early."

"Yeah, how come?" On went the adorable peach-fuzz textured, super-velour pants with rose trim at the ankles. Nice. Maybe Tanya was right about the sex appeal of wearing a toe ring.

"After lunch, some of the boys came down with colds, including Brent."

"Well, that's quite some coincidence. Was this some new nose-blowing competition from the archery counselor?" On went the first of her circus-pink patent leather shoes with the trendy tap dancer's heels.

"We're not sure what started it." Jessica sounded worried, Rachel suddenly realized.

"Oh, Jessica. I'm sure it's not anything you did. Kids get colds. Even at Tom's age, they swap around their ice cream bars and such."

"Well, we're a little concerned. If you would step over to your phone console, I think you'd see why."

Luckily Rachel was decent by now. She crossed the hall to the nearest phone screen. "You're coming into focus now, Jessica, and my face should be popping up for you."

Jessica's face appeared in stages: first the straight brown bangs, then the wide, compassionate mouth and broad, curved chin. Jessica was wearing a yellow T-shirt. And what was that on her chest, Tweety Bird? No question, she was the perfect Mom.

Now her jaw dropped. "You're so funny, Rachel. Are you going to some special kind of party?"

"You noticed my pinks, huh?"

"I guess I'm not used to seeing so many shades all in the same outfit."

"Yes, I suppose I'm wearing about seven shades altogether. But pinks cannot clash. That's something I learned today."

"Uh-huh. And I can't see you all that clearly while I'm in traffic here, but is that a hair ribbon you have on, tied in a bow?"

Rachel thought back to Tanya's voice. "Hair ribbons are such a girlish touch. No red-blooded man can resist the trace of a little girl on his woman." Jessica, however, wasn't a Seminar Slave, so Rachel would spare her the explanation. "You got it, buddy."

Jessica rubbed her cheek with her left hand, then cupped her chin. "Goodness, I needed that. Thank you. I've been a little tense."

"Tense at camp?" Rachel rolled her eyes. "Jessica, I'd say you deserve a medal if you're anything less than wacko after a day with the little dears—by the way, your headset doesn't have speakers, does it?"

Jessica shot her a look. Unintentional, no doubt. (Jessica had flawless, All-American caliber manners—well, Holiday Lakes Scout Camp could get to anyone sane.) "Rachel, can you see the boys in the back seat?"

"Hmm. Tom is on the side opposite you. Brent's in the middle and our *dear* little friend Harrison is sitting directly in back of you."

"Good. Can you see clearly enough to tell that they have some tissues back there?"

"Sure. Leave it to you, Jessica, to keep plenty of supplies in your car."

"Rachel, can you see them blowing their noses?"

Rachel squinted at the blurry images flickering on the console. "Playing as usual, huh?"

"Not really," Jessica said grimly. "It isn't exactly blowing their noses, either. Brent's mucus is coming out of his ears. Tom's is coming out of his mouth. Harrison's is coming out of his eyes. And Rachel, it's a pretty unusual shade of green."

Inwardly, Rachel started to tremble. She made contact with Brent by feeling, and when he seemed okay she sighed with relief. But a bunch of worries popped in with her next breath: Doubt about her own inner message; worry about Brent and the other boys; envy of Jessica, being so calm. If Jessica hadn't given Rachel advance warning, she might have gone bonkers when her baby came through the door leaking bright green mucus. Revulsion came next in Rachel's parade of emotions—imagine how it would feel to have that weird stuff dripping out of your ears.

To her shame, however, Rachel noticed that all these feelings paled in comparison with one central secret emotion, which was excitement. Now she had a great excuse to call her husband and show him what she was made of. Practicing, she said, "Weird-colored mucus is pretty gross, Jessica. But you know our doctors can cure anything and they've probably seen a million cases like this."

"Really? I'm not so sure, Rachel. Lime green mucus is a new one to me. If it were common, wouldn't we have seen it by now on the news?"

"Oh, it's probably just some exotic kind of flu. You know how it's the fashion to color your hair, your eyes, even your skin. Jessica, you and I don't do it, but most of the women in Capital City do. Haven't you noticed? Maybe those artificial colors are rubbing off on our diseases or something."

"You think that's it?" Jessica looked hopeful.

"Anyway, Brent is scheduled for his monthly Health Screening at 4:30 today. Isn't that a lucky coincidence?"

Jessica nodded yes.

"So it's perfect timing for me to ask the docs about this weird cold goo. Want me to call you after we get home? I can tell you what they say."

"Would you please? I'm worried. Oh, and could you do me a favor, Rachel? Call Harrison's mother now so she has some advance warning. He'll be home in less than an hour."

"Sure, right away. I've got her number."

Rachel winked comfortingly, but Jessica probably couldn't see. Screen resolution in car-phones wasn't that high. Besides, what was Rachel doing, winking at another woman? Must be getting her media mixed. What she meant to do was e-mail Jessica an emoticon: ;-)

Over the car console, her expression probably looked more like a twitch than a wink. Too bad.

Jeremy hadn't called. Now, though, Rachel had a perfectly legitimate reason to call him.

She would turn up the heat, in every sense of the word. Just a little extra make-up first.

"Lipliner can work wonders," Tanya had said. "Becoming Pinkness means never letting him forget that your lips... are for kissing."

It did look good.

Omigod, was he actually picking up her phone call? The first time since when, the Dark Ages? This week, anyway.

"Rachel." He sat at his desk looking worried. Her noble husband was rubbing a pencil back and forth between his palms. A pencil, for crying out loud? How archaic! And he didn't seem to notice her pinks.

"What's up? I know I was supposed to call you earlier, but I had this urgent meeting and then I had to get with Wayne and Marty..."

"Jeremy," Rachel smiled dazzlingly. "Don't worry. Great to see you. You're looking rugged, in spite of your meeting and all." (This word, "rugged," came from Tanya's list of approved compliments designed to magnetize your mate by appealing to his manly pride.)

He grunted.

"Scout camp ended early today. I thought you'd want to know. A little emergency. But I'm taking care of it." There, she'd said just enough to tantalize him.

"Good. You take care of it, then, because I've got a lot going on here."

"You want me to handle everything?"

A furrow of frown was building across Jeremy's forehead. Right now it consisted of three long wrinkles. This was a danger sign. Rachel didn't need Tanya to tell her. Jeremy could, and occasionally did, build all the way to a full five-layer forehead wrinkle, which would mean that he had worked himself into such a state, he'd need several days to pull himself back together. Jeremy incommunicado, with nothing but monosyllables and grunts for conversation, was one of Rachel's worst nightmares.

"Sure," he said. "You can handle the scout stuff great."

His tone of voice (cheerily non-sexual) made Rachel feel like a big, fat, pink nothing. Specifically, she felt cheated. Wasn't the whole point of this conversation to smooth Jeremy over and make act like the man of her dreams? Wasn't she was doing her part, dropping hints? He was supposed to ask her for more details.

He would pull, she would give a little, then stop and look down at her shoes. They would do this again and again, until he was crazy for her. Tanya had demonstrated how this dance was meant to work. In her video, she had used the cutest pink-tinted rope to symbolize a couple's bond. Rachel could still remember Tanya's manicure tugging on that rope—scalloped nail extensions with swirls of hot pink against a clear background.

In real life, over the screen, Jeremy looked guilty, if anything. Definitely not fascinated.

"Rachel, I want to tell you what's been going on with work lately. But it won't be a short conversation and now isn't a good time for me."

She pouted visibly.

"Sweetheart, did Brent have a good day at Scout Camp before the early dismissal?"

"You can ask him yourself, at dinner. What would you like for dinner, anyway?"

"I won't be home. Sorry, I meant to call and tell you."

Rachel worked on her pout. Nagging was NOT going to escape from her pretty pink lips. "No problem," she said. "I can handle everything. See you 'round."

Even before she hung up the phone, her lower lip quivered. In the old days, Jeremy would have seen this. He would have called back to process her feelings on the spot.

Now he seemed a million miles away. And Rachel didn't believe for a minute that this was about his job. Everyone knew that government workers like Jeremy did practically nothing.

Chapter 9
Golden Opportunity

"Brent doesn't feel too bad, does he?" Heather asked Rachel. They were waiting for their appointments at their friendly neighborhood Medical Center VLS-3017. Both women watched Brent bend his head to one side, holding a tissue up to one ear. He gave it a rub, then crumpled up the tissue and stuffed it into the pouch compartment of his Kleenex Kangaroo dispenser.

The brown plastic container popped up a new tissue between fake kangaroo ears. This jolly dispenser was too young for Brent but at least it looked less institutional than Rachel's other choices, adult boxes that offered clean tissues from one end and, at the other, locked up the dangerous germ-ridden ones.

"Can I look at your next Kleenex?," Kayla asked, chewing gum vigorously. "I've never seen ear mucus before."

Heather silenced her with a look. Ashley was pretending to be engrossed in her custom-made Barbie, a doll computer-designed to look "Just Like Me." Only it was built like Barbie instead of a five-year-old. This one had dimples, fair hair, brown eyes under very curved brows, a little rosebud mouth—altogether a pretty good imitation, except that it lacked Ashley's expression of sneaky, suppressed curiosity.

Brent wore a worried face. "You want to know what it feels like?" Both girls nodded. Even Heather stared, lips parted in rapt attention. "Somebody stuck a bunch of peanut butter in your ears, and it dribbles out when it's good and ready. When you look at your tissues and see that what came out of your body looks like a Popsicle, it makes you want to hurl."

"But there's no pain, only congestion. Right, Brent?"

"Mom?" Precocious Brent sounded for all the world like a teenager saying something like, "Mom, you totally pathetic idiot." With a look he must have learned from TV commercials, he added, "How about the pain of worry? Mucus like this isn't normal."

Brent didn't feel sick to Rachel, though, only scared. She refused to let him wallow. "Look at me. Do I look worried? When I look worried, you can worry. All you have is some new kind of cold. The doctors will fix you right up."

Heather squeaked, "Your Mom and me, we're gonna take great care of you. Isn't that right, Rachie?" Heather put her arm around Brent, looking like reassurance personified.

Rachel put her arm around her son from the other side and gave him a little squeeze, saying, "Kid, your turn will come any minute. Once you get your medicine, you'll feel great. Trust me."

"Brent Murphy," announced the intake robot.

"See?" Rachel sent him off with a little pat on the rear. "When we're done, we'll meet you in the TV room."

Soon Ashley and Kayla were summoned, too, and were bustled off to their exams by perky, short robots with colorful gingham aprons. Kids always had priority at Health Services, and anyone over age five was expected to go alone.

Their children in good hands, now Rachel and Heather had a precious half hour or more before their turns would be called. Usually they started by discussing their choices for this month's Health Elective. Each checkup was a golden opportunity, as TV commercials proclaimed on a regular basis.

For once there was truth behind the hype. Monthly checkups combined the thrill of shopping with the virtuous feeling that you were doing something good for your health. Besides, being in a waiting room with hundreds of people was a rare treat in today's electronic society.

It was hard to remember a time before Health Services. President Stilton signed it into law back when Brent was a toddler, changing medical care as America knew it. The Social Security Health Card gave each citizen a monthly tax credit big enough to meet most medical needs. If you were healthy, you'd have surplus credits you could use to pay for electives chosen from a huge grab-bag of optional goodies.

Democrats promoted this plan as a means to give health insurance to every American. Republicans bragged that it expanded health care, which was (after entertainment) America's biggest industry. Medical pundits touted the Health Card as a fantastic opportunity to sample world's most advanced medical technology.

Of course, Jeremy snorted whenever politicians came on TV to talk up the Health Card. He told Rachel the legislation was mainly a triumph for the American Medical Association, enabling doctors to simultaneously enlarge their businesses and trump alternative medicine, which had grown exponentially since he and Rachel were young. First, MDs scoffed at techniques like acupuncture and Healing Touch. Then they tried to debunk them. When people continued flocking to alternative practitioners in ever-greater numbers, some genius doctor remembered the old saying, "If you can't beat 'em, join 'em."

So maybe it was more than coincidence that, concurrent with Stilton's announcement of the new Health Card plan, the AMA rolled out its first government-approved program of Official Holistic Medicine. OHM included certification programs for doctors in everything from aromatherapy to X-ray viewing without a machine—each course graduate a fully qualified medical intuitive. Supposedly the AMA had taken the best from herbal medicine, chiropractic, homeopathy, you name it, making it all modern and safe.

AMA-sanctioned trainings had been developed to the point where it became routine for MDs to pick up certifications the way Cub Scouts picked up belt loops. Practically overnight, internists were qualified to do traditional Chinese acupuncture or give a deep-tissue massage. Moreover, their skills were rated superior by the government. So, although technically you still were free to see the other practitioners, who bothered? You'd have to pay out of pocket. You'd waste your free health electives. Besides, Americans had an abiding trust in their white-uniformed medics. Like the bio-engineered burgers at McDonald-Revlon-Times-Warner, OHM was a brand name.

What fascinated women most, of course, were the cosmetic options. Breast implant surgery was routine; liposuction and tummy tucks were popular, as was the procedure known as cellulite relief. Faces could be reconfigured, skin color changed, and eye color altered.

Now that everyone could be flawlessly beautiful, did that make women like Rachel and Heather feel more secure? No such luck. Discriminating men and women, alike, developed an eye for what was natural in a woman. Her body might be slender, for instance, but was her muscle tone what the movie critics called "compelling"?

All the surgery in the world couldn't give you a truly shapely calf. Only exercise could do that. Of course, some people tried to make a kind of mysterious social statement by going "natural." They let their flab accumulate, walked around wearing eyeglasses, you name it. Rachel would have laughed at them more... except that her own husband was one of these counter-culture weirdoes. Retros—that was the media called them. For Jeremy's sake, Rachel made it a point not to criticize Retros, not in front of him, at least.

Personally, she preferred to improve herself the hard-working, natural way. She exercised off-and-on all day long. She ate right, at least as right as she could. Then had Health Services supply the holistic extras. Media were always giving you plenty of ideas for improving your image, and seminars supplied deeper ways to strive for beauty.

It was a golden age of medicine, and Rachel certainly didn't mean to be ungrateful. Yet nothing at Health Services answered the question that meant most to Rachel: What could she do about her yearning to connect to people? If only her deep self could communicate with the deep self of others.

Heather laughed the one time Rachel mentioned this to her. "Health Services takes care of that stuff automatically, Silly," she said. "Because every visit reminds us to lighten up and pay attention to what really matters. If you look good, your life will look good. Your first duty is to your bod."

Not everyone used their Health Credits for beauty enhancements, of course. Some credits were routinely allocated for safety procedures. Each month, as a matter of course, every American had to get a sunscreen application. Smokers received a mandatory lung drip. (Nicotine showed up in one of the blood scans, confirming the popular saying, "Don't even try to hide from Health Services.") As a precaution against heart disease, anyone seriously overweight received a coating of the digestive tract, thick enough to last for a month, minimizing absorption of fat. The complete list of Health Service tests and procedures seemed impossibly long to Rachel, but then she wasn't one of the robots keeping track of it all.

Anyway, provided that you were healthy, like Rachel and Heather, the exciting part about monthly jaunts to Health Services was the opportunity to upgrade your look: Semi-permanent colors could be placed on your lips, eyeliner could enhance your eyes, electrolysis would remove hair anywhere you didn't want it, and hair implants could add it, where desired, with surgical-quality precision. Just punch it in as your Monthly Elective!

Then came the range of skin tones, all FDA approved. A color choice display, with life-like swatches and floodlights, took up half a nearby wall. This season's line had names related to food: Hot Fudge, Nutmeg, Milk Chocolate, Café au Lait, Double Latte, Vanilla Custard, Shortbread, Eggnog, Gourmet Toffee, Golden Butterscotch, Just Peachy, Apricot Nougat.

Every one of these trendy shades came in several variations, with undertones that were yellow, red, or blue, and doctors could lighten or darken you to any shade you wanted. Altogether, you could pretty much custom design your complexion. The procedure took just a few hours. Then it lasted until you chose something else. Rachel thought there was wisdom in the slogan beneath the skin electives display: "Stay colorful. Stay interesting."

Families or steady couples usually did a color job together, so they would match. Thus far, Rachel had never had any luck persuading Jeremy to be adventurous in that way, so she remained her usual pale Gourmet Toffee, pretty but predictable.

Now she and Heather sat side by side on yellow plastic chairs, as they always did, waiting in the lobby of Health Services. Much of their friendship was built on people-watching—hair performances, make-up scrutiny, judging when facelifts were falling. When you added that to clothes and perfume, each woman had countless ways to project her image. Therefore,monthlies at Health Services combined the gossipy thrill of people-watching with gathering exciting ideas for using your electives. Plus, once kids were disposed of, the wait in the lobby was a great chance to dish the dirt.

"Notice my pinks?" Rachel said.

"Of course," Heather replied. "I like the feathers."

"Really?" The feathers in question were scarlet and pink, added onto her hair via cosmetic grade Super Glue and red plastic barrettes. This reflected one of Tanya's slogan's, "Tickle their desires with feathers. No real man can resist the sensuous weight of a feather."

Heather scanned the crowd in the waiting room, uncharacteristically silent.

Rachel sighed. Their conversation always had to start with Heather.

"Well," Rachel offered, correcting herself. "Have you decided yet? How are you planning to use your elective Health Credits this month?"

Heather turned to look her full in the face, "Psychological counseling."

"Heather, what's wrong? Are those tears in your eyes?"

Heather's face crumpled like an umbrella in a hurricane. "Last night, Rotten George came back to the house to pick up something. I never found out exactly what. After he sweet talked me a while, one thing led to another...."

"No! You know what the advice columnists say about sex with your ex. How could you?"

"Well, we didn't." She broke down again. "Georgie took off his clothes. He turned around to dim the lights and I happened to see his left butt. Right there, under his Health Services ID tattoo, he had the H."

"The H?"

"The H. You know, the mark they stamp on your backside when they check you for one of the HIVs every month. The mark that means your test has come back positive.

Heather's voice started to rise in pitch. She went on, "Why do they have to do that for every sex partner to see? I'll tell you why. So rats like George won't conveniently forget to mention it when they try to seduce you."

Rachel grabbed her friend by the shoulders. "Heather, did you kiss him before you saw the tattoo? Did you engage in other, um, risky behaviors?"

"No," sniffled Heather. "We always start getting mushy by having me take off his clothes. Then he takes off mine. I used to think it was cute. Don't you and Jeremy warm up that way sometimes?" She looked embarrassed.

Rachel switched to another seat, to Heather's left. That way, Heather could blow her nose while Rachel held her other hand. Which amounted to the most comforting thing she could think of to do.

Being there for her friend, feelings started to move through Rachel, feelings that surprised her. They must come from Heather. Waves of emotion had to do with loneliness. The whole nature of emotions seemed unexpectedly physical, as if her body had turned into a haunted house. Nobody wanted it any more.

Rachel rubbed the back of her neck with her free hand. *Come in Rachel. Come back. Heather's way is not your way.* Rachel could return to being herself and she was going to do it right now. With a push, she popped back inside her own skin. *What a relief*, she thought, rubbing her palms together briskly.

"You're such a great friend," Heather was saying, her voice as flat as the brainwaves of a dead person on "ER."

In response, Rachel heard herself send back some comforting clichés. Inwardly, though, something else clicked. *Heather doesn't know how to show deep emotions. She may not even know when she's having them. That's why, half the time, she comes across so plastic.*

Rachel felt an entirely unexpected degree of compassion for her old friend. Heather might be ditzy—*was* definitely ditzy—but she still could know a woman's pain. As Rachel turned to make eye contact, Heather's face even *looked* different. For the first time ever, Rachel saw the pain beneath the beauty.

She patted Heather's hand. "One of the things I love about you is your loyalty. You still care about George, don't you? Underneath it all."

Heather nodded. Her cheeks and mouth turned hard. "Stupid of me. Check Jeremy tonight, won't you? If he's been cheating on you, it could be a matter of life and death."

The Health Center had cures for just about any ailment you could imagine, even some you might make up just for fun. But there were still some things the medics couldn't cure, and 15 of them were forms of AIDS.

Chapter 10
In the Know

"Dad, you're home!" Brent said, practically knocking Jeremy down with puppy-like leaps.

"Rachel, Sunflower, I'll get back to you later." Jeremy waved and made a goofy face at her while Brent pulled him backwards toward the playroom downstairs.

Was Rachel tired from the excitement of going to her Monthly? She sure couldn't relate to her husband and son's joyous reunion. Nah, what she felt wasn't fatigue, it was resentment. All the times he hadn't been home for her lately, and now she was supposed to welcome the man back like a conquering hero?

"Sweeten up," she could hear Tanya saying. "Don't drive him farther away. Rein him in, like a dog on a rhinestone-covered leash."

Admittedly, cooking dinner should help. That was it, she'd make her guys a perfect little pink meal!

What would it be? Rachel's dimples began to pop out for real as she settled on six cubes of Swifties Portion Minders. Her choices were Flavor Burst Burger, Chicken Teriyaki, Tempeh Joy, Creamy Spinach, Rum Raisin Casserole, and Shish Kebabs 'n Salad.

According to their labels, the six packages should total 36 servings. In reality, 13 servings each would make a pretty lite meal. Most families ate about 20 servings per person—along with a generous helping of guilt—because, frankly, most families ran to fat. They probably spent half their Health Electives on Surgical Fat Reduction.

Not Rachel's family, though. Smiling, she ripped off the cardboard containers and set them cooking in the microwaves.

Things weren't so bad. Hadn't she received a terrific massage at Health Services? And who knew what further body work might await her tonight. Meanwhile Brent had come through his checkup in fine spirits, with a shot of Superbiotics in his sweet little rump. The ear goo had dried up while he sat watching his Monthly

Socialization Video. What did he say it was, a baseball adventure? Undoubtedly it had been designed to counter the nation's epidemic of youthful inactivity.

Alas, there were so many epidemics, according to the media. Rachel was peeling mandarin oranges and grapefruits for an appetizer plate when an image of Brent's muscular butt collided with the thought of the disgusting rear end belonging to Rotten George. With its new tattoo for HIV. Out of habit, Rachel started a series of butt contractions and ab pulls. Got to keep firm!

As for Jeremy's butt, who knew? When was the last time she had seen anything of interest beneath that man's underwear? It was high time they made love. What was it with him? Rachel started ripping the grapefruit sections apart, limb from limb, thinking of Sally and what she might have made poor Jeremy do.

The husband in question sat at the computer console in his den, Brent in his lap, and Space Age Whacker Boffins cavorting about the screen. "Thank God, or whatever it is, for this little bundle of joy," Jeremy thought. Brent's energy was contagious. Whenever he wasn't whacking the 3-D critters on the screen, he was chattering away:

"Dad, do you think we'll score more than half a million points?"

"Want me to tell you something, Dad? Griseldo's theme song is great, isn't it? I can sing it without the computer. Want to hear me do that, Dad?

"Hey, Dad, which do you want me to go after first, the Combheads or the Hairy Elephants?"

Jeremy turned his participation onto automatic pilot as though he, too, were a programmed game, animated with Scrumptu-tropic Sound—exhausted, itchy, but grateful to be home.

His thoughts drifted to Rachel, puttering in the kitchen: Her beautiful body. Her cute ways in the kitchen, where you never knew what she'd bring to the table. Would it be burned? So strangely concocted as to be nearly inedible? At least you knew she'd never make the same meal twice. Her creativity made Jeremy smile, even at a grim time like this.

His wife was so different from him. As colorful Boffins raced across the screen, dozens at a time, Jeremy thought of her peculiarities—maybe not as numerous as the Boffins (at this moment, anyway) but consistently endearing. Unlike Jeremy, or other normal people, Rachel had a strange need to commune with dozens of friends on a daily basis. She had an insatiable enthusiasm for seminars, a funny tendency to clutter the house with unfinished projects—funny because she'd hide each pile in a large, neat cardboard box, a housekeeping method which was tantamount to a baby covering his eyes so that you couldn't see the rest of him.

Her visual clutter was simple, however, compared to all her emotional ups and downs. Still, that was Rachel, larger than life in everything, including the endearing degree to which she needed him and how much she cared about being a good wife. You knew you could depend on Rachel.

"Well, here we are," Rachel announced as they pulled up to the table. "Do you realize this is our first dinner together since Monday? No, last weekend. Isn't it great having the family together again?"

Brent was playing with his chair, seeing how far backwards he could tilt it before it fell over.

"Rachel, my amazing morning glory, it's obvious that you went to a lot of trouble over us." Jeremy smiled affectionately. Privately he wondered what was going on. She had set each place with a large crystal bowl containing bits of grapefruit, orange, and coconut, topped with a maraschino cherry. A new paper cloth was on the table, the color of red Virginia soil. And planted at random positions were little pink paper bowls; how many plates for the three of them, 100?

He looked closer. The nearest bowl contained a soybean hamburger throbbing with rich, meat-like gravy. This pitiful frozen fake burger had been sliced as though it were a rich cake; this particular plate contained three small slices. Next to it, a bowl contained a shish kebab stick threading a few mushrooms, carrots, and one limp shrimp. But the gap between each morsel of food was like the spaces between some of Brent's teeth. Evidently Rachel had slid off about half the original items and arranged them onto a different plate.

He said, "Have you been missing your party work, Sweetheart?"

"No, I guess I'm just in a good mood. Brent and I went for our Monthlies today, remember? Well, my elective was a Himalayan massage. Ever have one?"

"Not that I've noticed," he said dryly. Sometimes it was a sore point between them that Jeremy didn't take advantage of his precious Health Electives—fuss and feathers and affectation, so far as he was concerned.

Speaking of which, what on earth was his wife wearing? She looked like a box of Crayolas, all the pink ones. Better not to ask.

Meanwhile, Brent was running around his chair, capering like some kind of small feral animal.

"Brent," he said, "Would you consider using your chair as a place to sit while you eat?"

"Oh, Jeremy," Rachel said, "I think his moving around is a good thing. Look at all the calories he burns.

She leaned over and showed him her big brown eyes and her cleavage. "So, how was work?"

Jeremy gave back the nicest smile he had in him. "You know me," he said, "I'd rather leave the office back at the office."

What's wrong with Jeremy? Rachel wondered. *Is he racked with guilt? Where's his sense of fun?* The man was picking at his food like an archeologist at an unpromising dig. Meanwhile Brent was doing his usual mealtime workout, interrupting it for occasional mouthfuls of the sweetest items he could find at the table. The kid had radar for sugar. Tonight he went straight for the Rum Raisin entree, scattered though it was at four different quadrants of the table.

Maybe it was just as well that Rachel had decided against the long, pink tapering candles. Brent could have knocked them over. For a full five minutes (which seemed an eternity), Rachel waited for Jeremy to say something romantic. She'd settle for his saying anything, actually.

"Pinkness means being a graceful listener," she kept repeating to herself. Heck, she couldn't stand the silence another minute, Tanya or no Tanya.

It would be up to her to keep the conversation going. As usual.

"Brent, would you like to talk about Scout Camp?"

Silence as Brent played with his food.

Rachel tried again: "Tell Dad about all your belt loops."

"Oh, Dad, archery was fun. I won a belt loop for that. You know what? My favorite activity was the games at the end of the day."

"What games?"

"Just stuff like Sharks and Minnows. While we play, the counselors throw buckets of water at us through the fence. We get really wet. I'm mad that we missed it today."

Jeremy smiled at him sympathetically. "That's right, camp ended early, according to your Mom. How come?"

"Oh, because of weird green mucus," Brent grinned.

Jeremy put down his fork and stared, first at Brent, then at Rachel. "Oh?" he said, in a faux casual tone. Uh oh. Rachel knew what was coming next. Jeremy had a thing about Brent's health. He was always getting on her case about not worrying enough. Of course, Jeremy didn't put it that way. He would complain that he wanted to be informed.

She said, "You want to tell him about it, Cookie?"

"No, you, Mom."

Rachel explained that camp had gotten out early because a few of the boys had a *little* problem with mucus coming out of their faces. Brent's happened to be coming out of his ears. Tom's mother was a bit concerned, but Rachel had called back to reassure her after Brent's checkup.

"I took him to the Health Center right way." she said, emphasizing her competence. "It was no big deal, really. They gave him Superbiotics and then the whole thing dried up."

"Dad, you should have seen my tissues. Maybe I could find you one from the garbage. Know what? It was a weird shade of green, like the Combheads in our game. And it came right out of my ear, like peanut butter. Really gross, Dad." Brent started jiggling with delight.

Jeremy pushed his chair away from the table. "Rachel, how many times have I told you that I expect to be informed of things like this? Unlike you, I don't believe that Superbiotics are the solution to all of life's ills. Next time I want to be consulted. Tell the people at Health Services you are signing up for Right of Consultation before they administer drugs."

Rachel felt squashed like a bug under her husband's heel.

He turned to Brent. "This mucus was lime green?"

"Yeah, Dad. It was really gross."

Jeremy started pacing around the living room, his legs stiff and his butt stuck out a little. This particular kind of stomp was done by Jeremy only when he was really, really mad.

Rachel's gut felt like she'd just been punched. Was he upset because his real loyalties lay elsewhere, with Sally? Was he picking a fight so that he'd have an excuse to walk out on them?

"Brent, go to your room," Rachel said shakily.

"What did I do?" His face looked stricken.

"Nothing," Jeremy said. "Your mother's right. Go."

Soon as Brent closed his bedroom door, Rachel turned to face him.

"What's all this about, Jeremy? You don't come home all week and now you criticize me? How dare you?"

"Frankly, I'm concerned about health issues, Rachel. This is the first I've heard of this new disease."

"Oh, fuss and feathers. Who says it's a disease? All Brent had was some kind of cold."

"Coming out his ears?"

"Hey, I remember the first time I slept over at my grandparents' house. It freaked me out so bad that when I woke up in the morning, my eyes were glued shut with a weird kind of cold. They soaked the stuff off with a warm washcloth. If you can get a cold in your eye, why not a cold in your ear?"

"Times are different now, Rachel. I've told you before. Immunological weakness is the great disease of our time. When a new type of cold comes up, or a brand new kind of mucus, it just might be serious!"

"How can you say that, Jeremy? You worry too much."

"Doctors prescribe Superbiotics as though they were candy. I'm telling you, soon they won't work any more, just like the old antibiotics.

"Oooh," Rachel muttered, head down. She started to clear the table, stacking the now-grungy pink paper bowls on top of each other, as if she was piling failure upon failure. She mumbled, "You're such a worry wart. Why would I want to tell you a thing? You would have freaked if I told you about the candy-colored flies at Scout Camp."

"The what?" Jeremy wheeled around to stare straight at her. His bony face paled, making it look positively craggy.

"See? There you go again. Yes, there happened to be some strange looking bugs at Scout Camp yesterday. The boys were digging them up at the fishing hole."

"The same boys who got sick?"

Rachel thought for a minute. "I guess."

"And you didn't consider that any of this might be worth mentioning?" Jeremy faced her, hands on hips.

She stared back, arms folded just above her magenta patent leather belt.

He continued, "Didn't it occur to you that this could be of interest to me? I'm Jeremy Murphy, the entomologist, remember?"

As if you could ever let me forget, you boring, boring man. Rachel didn't say that, of course. Her jaws twitched. She remembered Tanya saying, "If you can't act coy, you might as well be a boy." Mentally she blasted the image of Tanya away with a cannon. A pink one.

"What's the big deal, Jeremy?" she said. "They come out with new-colored things every time you turn around: computer games, foods, hair products...."

"Diseases?" Jeremy rubbed his hand across his broad forehead as if to say that Rachel was some kind of idiot. But she wouldn't sink to his level. She forced herself to smile, which had the advantage of pushing out both her dimples and her chest.

"Jeremy, if I were you, I'd be grateful that at least our pee stays the same color." He didn't smile. *What could you do with a man like that?* Rachel walked out of the room to wash the dishes, hoping he'd follow her.

But he didn't. Very aware of being alone in the kitchen, Rachel threw the plates away and shoved the silverware into the dishwasher. Still no Jeremy. She couldn't stand this another minute. She marched out to the dining room. He was upstairs, on the phone.

She peeked in at the office doorway several more times. When he'd finally turned off the phone, she let him have it.

"Listen, Jeremy. You don't come home for a week. You don't tell me what's going on. You have this slinky new secretary, whatever her name is. I just found out today my friend Heather's husband George got the H stamp from sleeping around. She's going to get a divorce. What's going to happen to us?" She turned and stomped back into the kitchen.

Jeremy followed her, rubbing his elbow. He looked apologetic. "Rachel, you know there's a lot I don't tell you because of my high-security clearance. But I think I'm going to have to explain about what's been going on. Can I trust you to keep this totally private?"

Rachel nodded solemnly, masking her relief. They went into the bedroom. Jeremy explained about the new insects. And, as usual, he told Rachel bitterly, his job wasn't really about science. It was politics, much as that disgusted him. He could spent hours working with Wayne and their assistants, putting together research about huntids, but what did it matter? And research at the lab is what he'd been doing all those nights he came home late, he said. They'd worked like crazy, only today his big meeting turned out all wrong, and his presentation was virtually ignored by the president's PR guy and slimy Cooper Hackenworth.

Brent interrupted this explanation several times with calls for water to drink, new music to listen to… the usual stalling tactics. Finally, he went down for the night.

Relieved, Rachel felt amused that Jeremy thought the colored flies could be such a big high-security deal. Hadn't she just seen them at Holiday Lakes Scout Camp? It's not as though anyone could keep flies a top secret.

She locked the bedroom door and lay down in bed next to Jeremy. "Well, what do you think? Are you going to have to exterminate the flies?" She was lying on her stomach, face propped up on her elbows. She wished he would stop worrying and stroke her.

"I hope not," Jeremy said. "Wayne and I are investigating every possible alternative." Jeremy started rubbing her back, miracle of miracles!

She rolled over, feeling the heat of his body tantalizingly near. "You want a turn now?"

"Are you kidding? I was just getting started, Sunflower." Jeremy smiled down at her. Gently, he ran his palms down the length of her breasts. Then he did it again, slower. Shivers, then heat moved through Rachel's body. She pulled him closer, for a long, slow kiss.

"Jeremy, I feel so much better. How about you?" It wasn't just the sex that relaxed her, either. She finally believed her husband was telling her the truth about work.

He laughed. Even though they had been making love in the dark, she could feel him looking at her. He said, "Well, you finally got my mind off those flies."

She laughed. So did he. To Rachel, this sound was more powerful than any prayer from The Righteous or the Traditionals. Jeremy's laughter made her feel that all was right with the world.

He'd even kissed the arches on her feet, which was new. Rachel liked it. In a way, Jeremy still was acting peculiar. Not just all the attention to her feet—he'd insisted on wearing his shirt while they made love. If she didn't know him better, she would have sworn *he* was the one taking seminars.

"I'm glad you told me what was going on," Rachel said to him now. At her request, they'd reverted to their normal style of lovemaking for the after play, where he meticulously stroked her body, out from her center, spreading energy all the way through her hands and feet. In addition to Jeremy's physical attentions, his touch covered Rachel with his mood. Unmistakably, he was painting her with peace.

Usually Jeremy's silences were about a racing mind, not tranquility. To share his transitions through indifference to lust, love, tenderness, closeness and, now, peace—nothing in life brought Rachel more joy.

Not that Jeremy needed to hear her tell him the mushy version. All she said was, "It gives me a great feeling to be in the know."

He answered, "Everyone's going to know about the huntids. Once the media get started, it will be 'All Huntids, All the Time.'"

"Is that so bad?" Rachel hoped to coax the worry out of his voice.

"No," Jeremy said. "What bothers me is the pressure to kill them off. Killing the huntids would be a major mistake. I don't know why, but I'm sure of it."

II. Taking Life Seriously

Chapter 11
The Powers That Be

Sure they'd had a nice weekend, Rachel thought, vacuuming away. But did that mean her marriage was saved? She was sweating like crazy. Man, she couldn't need a stronger deodorant. As if such a product was even available! What was going on with her then? *Stage fright.* Golly, she was only getting the house ready for when Jeremy came home after work.

Maybe I miss Brent, she thought. (He had a play date at Heather's.)

No, it's not Brent, Rachel thought, feeling her silky poly-fiber jumpsuit turn tacky under her armpits. *I'm sweating because I'm nervous about tonight; I feel more like a date than a wife.*

Well, let that energy motivate you to work those thighs, she told herself sternly, and started squeezing her inner thighs together, hard, the way she had learned in some seminar years ago.

Suddenly her Supervac made a sound as if it were trying to sneeze. What the heck was that? Rachel wondered if she should check the Supervac's manual; she hadn't had to use the appliance since last winter.

"Snort" went the Supervac, louder this time and more like a horse. Suddenly Rachel remembered what these escalating noises were supposed to mean: "Pay strict attention and keep up with your Supervac—or else."

There was no time for isometrics when the appliance at the end of your hand had the fierce hunger of a Clairol Supervac. Great for suctioning out dust to a depth of five inches, it would, as advertised, make her beige high-fluff carpet look new. Not so great, as the TV commercials showed in a comical way, this turbo-charged appliance would send out three warning whinnies if you didn't move fast enough. By then you'd better have picked up your pace moving it; otherwise your darling Supervac would proceed to eat holes in your rug.

No exercise, Rachel, and no worrying about Jeremy, either. Just concentrate, Glamour-puss.

Although it was only Monday afternoon, Jeremy already felt like he'd put in a week of overtime. At the computer station in Research Lab One, he sat waiting for Wayne to finish inputting data. Jeremy looked around the room and thought, "Just look at this place—HHS had no clout at all."

Admittedly, when this lab was first built 15 years ago, it had been state of the art. Craning his neck, Jeremy could see the room's Arrow Security System cameras. Beneath them were piled row upon row of DVD boxes containing research, plus a ladder for reaching the highest shelves, some 20 feet high. Jeremy raised his eyes toward the dingy ceiling with its geometric pattern of ventilation holes. Stainless steel cabinets for equipment and supplies rose up to meet it, row upon row. The metal was dull; the lower shelves, scratched.

Although the latest form of eye-friendly Spectrum-Soother lighting had been installed a couple of years ago, the drabness seemed overwhelming. "This place is so thick with government gloom," Jeremy thought, "It's like the taste in your mouth when you have a hangover."

Since Wayne still wasn't finished, Jeremy twirled around in his chair to survey the room from a different angle: The computer stations had pathetically old-fashioned 3-D imaging capability, the microscope console wasn't as good as what you'd find in an affluent neighborhood's high school and the lab sink was so ancient it had built-in soap dispensers (a more modern Steri-zap box had been installed above it). Supply cartons were stacked off to one side, near an old, wall-mounted Graph-o-Matic data synthesizer that did pretty decent 3-D data imaging. The ancient-looking mesh lab vat contained huntids; Jeremy stared at them, fascinated.

Since when did you see insects—or any other animals—fly in a spiral? What was the meaning of that twirling, twisting formation? The huntids made a lilac-tinted blur; evidently a fly's brightly-veined wings could outshine its fluorescent green-colored thorax and abdomen. Jeremy sighed at the beauty of these mysterious animals. If huntids were as smart as *Musca Domestica* (common house flies), each of them could see a mosaic of 6,000 moving images at one time. If *Musca Viola* were smarter, how much more they could see?

"Jeremy?" Wayne's voice made him jump. Jeremy spun around to face his research assistant. Arms crossed, Wayne looked uncharacteristically uptight; he was, in fact, pounding one fist into the other arm's massive biceps.

"Marty isn't going to like this. Stavros *really* isn't going to like this."

"What did you find?"

"Nothing. I worked like crazy all weekend, compiling dozens of research studies. We looked at the effects of huntids on corn, algae, beans, cattle, flowering clover, alfalfa sprouts—you name it. And compared with ordinary houseflies, the huntids seem to do no damage whatsoever."

"The pest that wasn't—no wonder my Extermination Plan's progressing so slowly."

Wayne nodded. "If agriculture were really in trouble from our little purple flies, that would be a real problem. This big fat nothing should come as a relief, right?"

"Relief, I suppose is a relative term. How many techs did you bring in over the weekend?"

"Don't worry, we kept the place rockin' round the clock: Eight technicians in the various labs and a load of robots. We worked with more than 1,000 flies, testing as many scenarios as we could. I figure we plowed through enough data to give our main robot a headache, if he had a head. But for what? Jeremy, you read the latest printout this morning. We haven't found a thing."

"Well, who could realistically expect us to, with a one-week deadline?"

"If we call Stavros, do you think he could get Davis and Hackenworth to give us more time? Maybe we could actually get from Square One to Square Two."

Jeremy grunted sympathetically.

Wayne continued, "What really gripes me is that they aren't giving us enough time to research several complete life cycles. Following a few generations might be interesting, and if Stavros would just give us time to do our job, maybe we'd find that huntids continue to mutate in a way that really does pose some significant danger."

"It's also conceivable," Jeremy said, "that we'd find they do something beneficial. Hackenworth and his boys have no curiosity, only a load of pre-conceived opinions to match their unnecessary deadlines."

Wayne jumped off his lab stool and started pacing up and down. "You know, it tears me apart," he said. "You get into this kind of work because of curiosity, not to back up other people's power plays. I wish they had told me back in school that I'd be using Science, the holy grail of Science with a capital S, to do hack work like this. The nerve of Davis telling us to find a good public reason for extermination! I swear—"

"I know, man. The enemy here isn't bugs, it's politics. If it's any consolation, I'm the one whose job is on the line. Which reminds me—survival compels me to ask how soon you can deliver a pretty little vid-slide show of data—trivial but pretty—something I can show Marty, and then he can give it to Stavros."

"Realistically? No sooner than Friday, because I've gotta tell you, I'll keep looking for something until the very end. My wife will think I'm nuts, not to mention the techs. But I can't help it, okay." At that moment, Jeremy thought, his assistant looked as ragged as Brent's well worn stuffed puppy. "You'll get it by Friday, don't worry," Wayne concluded.

Jeremy Murphy, Division Director, Technical Research for Health and Human Services, said encouragingly, "Good enough, guy. But just to cut us both some slack, how about you bring it to me no later than Thursday at noon? Meanwhile I'll go back to my office to crunch the numbers on the data we already have. Since you'll be working, too, don't be surprised if I send urgent requests for new tests at three in the morning." Jeremy tried to smile, but it came out more like a twist of his mouth. As he stood up, he had a weird feeling that the huntids were witnessing him and his grim attempt at geniality.

As he walked to the door, a series of pictures flashed through Jeremy's mind like a vid-slide show. One minute he was gripped with worry that failure to produce the required research would cost him his job; the next minute a quiet part of him saw himself altogether differently:

Click. In a detached way, Jeremy saw his body morph into a tower of swirling energy. A dark mix of fear, worry and anger cascaded through the cells of his body, which seemed to be made out of moving lights. The dark, throbbing light particles formed their densest pattern at his shoulders and arms, their pulsation matched with the familiar throb of his eczema.

Click. The point of view turned physical as Jeremy's light body took on flesh, then clothes. He saw himself take one slow-motion step towards the door to Research Lab One.

Click. Another view came, halfway between the physical level and the dancing light: Jeremy's body was naked flesh, but in very faint outline form. In slow motion, a thin gold line pulsated, then lit up his spine from the back, making his sacrum look like the bulb of an old-fashioned mercury thermometer. And the gold began to rise upwards.

What was that? Jeremy wondered, and instantly the view magnified to show a tiny flicker of golden light spiraling up his back as two tubes of light, not one. The second gossamer line of gold twirled in a downward direction, forming a double helix along his spine.

Click. A top view showed that white light, of a different quality, steady and gentle, was coming in through the top of his head; this light merged with the spirals of gold moving up from his sacrum.

This must be a dream, Jeremy thought, yet it gave him comfort. Even though the HHS powers that be had put him in an impossible position, he was being shown that, on some level, he was okay. No, to be honest, the word wasn't merely "okay." In the small part of himself that was noticing this strange and delicate vision, Jeremy had to admit, what the light inside called him was "blessed."

Marty gestured for Jeremy to sit on the blue plush sofa in the corner of the office, far from the sight of his computer station which, typical for upper management, was an intimidating expanse of imitation mahogany. The HHS Assistant Secretary preferred holding his meetings here, in this cozy corner where a soft sculpture lamp was centered on a round end table. Short, slim, and looking decades younger than his 70-something years, Marty settled into a well-padded armchair. Neatly folding his hands in his lap, he smiled.

"Jeremy, it's good to see you. What do you have to report?"

"Over the last few days, Wayne plus 8 techs and 12 robots have compiled a fair amount of data, which we've summarized in this vid-slide show." As Jeremy handed his boss the box, he added, "Marty, there's nothing in this."

"But this morning didn't you say that Wayne was exploring a genetic mutation on corn that was altered by contact with the huntids.

"A *possible* mutation, is what I should have said. It was a mutation on one corn plant out of hundreds that our lab analyzed. When we scanned other ears, they showed no mutation at all."

"If you have more time, more samples of corn, don't you think it might show up again?"

"It might. Or it might not."

Marty sighed and his dark-circled eyes looked up at Jeremy. "You think it's a joke, don't you, that we have so little time to conduct this research."

"Not a joke, Marty, more like a professional tragedy. Since when are research scientists ordered to produce a threat on demand? This isn't science. They're asking us to do Public Relations. Why don't you tell Davis to make up his own damn research?"

"The pressure *is* intense, isn't it?"

"Marty, we've worked together for so many years, now, we've seen our Department bullied before—

"That's an understatement. You know very well, we're bullied so often, I'm surprised it isn't in our job description."

"Exactly," Jeremy said, trying to keep his voice even in front of his boss. "The difference now, as I perceive it, is that never before have they out-and-out told us what to say."

"And in this case, they're telling us, if we can't find anything legitimate, we must make it up." Marty sighed. "I know, our professional integrity flies out the window."

"Frankly, Marty, I wonder why you're not fighting more, why Stavros isn't fighting."

"Well, Stavros is sold out to his Footwork of the Righteous. His inaction is understandable, at least—pitiable but understandable. As for me, I've never been a fighter, you know that."

"But Marty, you have a better weapon than fighting: Charm. I've seen you charm people into getting along. You can do it so well that people like Stavros and Hackenworth don't even know what hit them."

Marty's expression went blankly non-committal. Just how far out of his way would he go to back up Jeremy? Evidently not very—Marty came from tough stock, part Iowa farmer, part Japanese entrepreneur; he was foremost a survivor. Jeremy head hung low for a second; then he caught himself and pushed back his forehead by pretending to rub it with his hand.

"You have a headache?" Marty asked sympathetically.

Jeremy shook his head.

The men debated what to tell the powers that be. After half an hour, they drafted a statement about ecological balance and its vulnerabilities, highlighting the dangers posed by mutation. They took Wayne's video footage about the one mutant ear of corn, added a voice-over saying that this was an example of what *could* happen if nature were left to take its own course.

Jeremy insisted that they include a disclaimer telling more of the truth—how research was needed, that this one ear of corn was the only problem spotted so far and how sometimes mutations happened on their own. Marty, however, made sure the disclaimer ran in rolling text next to a close-up that slowly magnified the corn, then freeze-framed on an ugly-looking brown spot.

Even the pores on your skin would look scary magnified that big, Jeremy thought. Marty was a pro at shading the truth: Watching the vid-clip, most people would react to the scary visual and wouldn't even notice the disclaimer.

Very carefully Marty and he recorded an extra sight bite for the media to pick up for the news: Marty in front of his mahogany desk looking straight into the camera. Turning up his palms to convey sincerity, he said, "No danger has occurred and the public needs to remember that."

It took five takes to get Marty to sound just the right degree of defensive. This was what Stavros would want. He, Marty and Jeremy had watched news shows long enough to know how the broadcasters would play a clip like this. Immediately afterward they'd show some frantic expert proclaiming that government must be engaged in a cover-up. Action must be taken *now*, before everyone's life was in danger.

Marty duplicated the report, so he could file copies the standard three ways. Meanwhile Jeremy thought bitterly what a practiced team they were: his job was to circulate Cover-Your-Ass reports within HHS, whereas Marty's job was to present the shaded truths, refine them, and sell them to the other department heads.

Some scientists! Marty spent only a small fraction of his time in this cozy little office. More often he was meeting with press liaisons like the insufferable Rich Davis. Higher up, Stavros crisscrossed the country, representing all of HHS in meetings; he also set policy with President Tucker, who generally had scant interest in either Health or Human Services. Unlike Marty and Jeremy, Stavros never pretended to be a scientist or even an administrator; he was pure politician, and proud of it.

"Good enough," Marty concluded, packing the DVD in its sleeve. "It looks very professional."

"Under the circumstances," Jeremy said dryly. "Listen, will you answer one question for me?"

"I'll try. For you, at least, I won't have to fake an answer." They were sitting at Marty's computer station; inquiringly Marty turned his wise old face towards him.

Jeremy said, "Epidemiology seems to me like the real place to look for problems with the huntids. My kid got sick from contact with them, and so did his friends. Admittedly, they didn't get very sick, but they did develop infections. How come? And why didn't Wayne get sick from working with them, or any of the other lab techs? Do Huntids manufacture some kind of virus that could only endanger kids?"

Marty shrugged. "The problem is, we don't know who gets it, apart from anecdotal evidence."

"Well, Marty, we don't know here at HHS, but aren't they researching it at the Center for Disease Control in Atlanta? Why can't we get access to their research? If we could meet with them it might even help us put something together for Davis— you know, something legitimate."

"Believe me, I wish I had access to that research." Marty sighed. " At least I can tell you the part about that."

Jeremy clenched his jaw and listened as Marty told him. Apparently CDC had come up with a name for the ailment linked to contact with the insects: Huntid

Disease. Marty said, "First I heard that the head of CDC told President Tucker about it on Tuesday; then I heard that Rich Davis is planning to make Huntid Disease a big part of the PR conference on Friday, along with whatever else we can come up with. So I called my counterpart at CDC and asked if he could meet with me; I also asked to meet with counterparts at USDA, Plant Protection and Quarantine, and the pesticide unit at EPA.

"Well, that sounds like the first intelligent idea I've heard since we were ordered to do this phony research," Jeremy said. "What happened?"

"Zip. I was told that all these guys are reporting directly to Hackenworth, and only to him."

"What gives Hackenworth the right to do this?"

"Security risk, according to my source at Disease Control."

Jeremy frowned. "All these guys have a top security clearance. They're just steps away from the President's cabinet. How could they be considered security risks to each other?"

"Good question." Marty lowered his eyes.

"Go on," prodded Jeremy. "Tell me what you think."

"Two possibilities, not mutually exclusive, have occurred to me."

A knock on the door made both men jump. "Come in," Marty said."

"It's me," said Wayne. "Am I barging in? You guys have been in here so long, the suspense is killing me."

Marty motioned for him to come join them. They moved to the corner of Marty's office with the couch and armchair.

"Fill me in, won't you?" said Wayne. Jeremy did, up to the idea that Marty had a couple of hunches.

Marty said, "Remember, guys, these are theories, not to go outside this room."

Wayne nodded vigorously. Jeremy merely lifted his eyebrows.

Marty took a deep breath. "One possibility is that the huntids have been bred as an act of terrorism, which would make them Hackenworth's legitimate business."

"Like chemical warfare, you mean? Bug warfare?" Wayne asked.

"Come on," Jeremy said. "America's fighting terrorism is hardly new, but are we supposed to believe that some foreign political zealot carried these flies through customs and set them breeding under a cornfield in a quiet college town?"

"I agree with you," said Marty. "The likelihood isn't enormous. Remember, I said there are *two* possibilities."

"So what's the real one?" Wayne asked.

Marty said, "A power play by Hackenworth—he wants to split the power so he has more."

"I still don't get it," Wayne told him.

"Let's see if I can figure this out," Jeremy said, eyeing Marty. "Hackenworth claims there can't be direct discussions because of the possible threat to security. What he doesn't say is that talking terrorism also happens to be a great way to pander to America's fear of another World Trade Center disaster; with each terrorist threat on our soil, fear grows until we'll do whatever our leaders say is in our national interest. Wayne, surely you've noticed—this kind of thing has been happening ever since you were a kid."

"Hold on, buddy," Wayne said. "Isn't the CIA too accountable to make things up?"

The older men laughed and looked at each other. "You're saying that government agencies don't twist things to suit their convenience?"

"Well?" Wayne asked, looking disgusted.

"Hey, we do it," Jeremy said.

"What?"

"We just did it to *your research*, as a matter of fact," Jeremy said.

"Any government job involves politics," Marty told Wayne. "You invent what you have to. It's a matter of saving your skin. When you have security clearance as deep as Hackenworth's. . . . "

"What, he can tell even bigger whoppers than we do, and get away with it?" Wayne was yelling by now.

Marty overlooked it. "Jeremy's right, Wayne. And I agree with his suspicion that Hackenworth is using the threat of terrorism to separate our three departments, weakening us all. If he doesn't let any of us know what the others are doing, he can use whatever we have to strengthen his own position. Hackenworth is an ambitious man; he knows that President Tucker is very security conscious."

Wayne looked rattled. "Politics wasn't my thing in college," he said. "When I wasn't in science classes, I did sports. But I guess I've landed in politics now, right up to my neck."

Chapter 12
Use Imagination

"Coffee, anyone?" Marty said, leading the way to the vending station down the hall. Jeremy picked mocha; Wayne pushed the button for cherry.

"You really like that stuff?" Jeremy asked.

"Sure," Wayne answered. "The flavor makes it so sweet, you can hardly taste it's coffee. You ought to try it some time. Hey, what'll it be, boss?"

"Breathless."

"I don't see the button for that," Wayne said.

"Push black, no cream or sugar. I'll mix it back in the office," said Marty.

When they took their steaming cups of coffee back to Marty's cozy corner, he walked over to his faux mahogany desk. From the bottom drawer, he pulled out a bottle of vodka and poured a generous shot into his drink.

Wayne grinned. "Breathless coffee. I get it."

"Would you like some? It goes with any of the flavored coffees. Believe me, I've tried them all."

Jeremy looked down. He could practically hear Rachel's voice in his ear. "You big worrier. Just because a man likes a drink once in a while, that doesn't make him a problem drinker. Lighten up!" At least Jeremy's own coffee tasted pretty darned good—without the liquor.

"Would you guys explain something to me?" Wayne said. "Both of you suspect Hackenworth isn't playing things straight, correct?"

"Understatement of the millennium," Jeremy said.

"Well, he's the one who called our meeting," Wayne said. "If he wanted to keep things separate and not let HHS know what the other agencies were doing, why did he hold a meeting at all? Wouldn't it make more sense to hush up the whole huntid thing?"

"It's difficult to fathom a mind like his," Marty said. "I'd rather not try. I am, nevertheless, convinced that the man knew what he was doing."

Jeremy rolled his empty cup back and forth between his palms. "I agree with Marty," he said. "I wouldn't put it past Hackenworth to come to our meeting as a kind of spy—to find out what we know so that he can make us dance. If he held similar meetings at Ag., EPA and Disease Control, he could have found out what they knew, too, all the better to jerk us around like puppets.

"Listen, Marty, did your contact at Disease Control at least tell you if Hackenworth called a meeting with them and Davis?"

Marty bobbed his shoulders, making one of those casual bows that must come from the Japanese side of his bloodstream. "Well, Jeremy, I did take the precaution of asking. The answer, I'm afraid, is yes."

"That means Hackenworth holds all the cards and there isn't a darned thing we can do about it." Wayne looked indignant.

Marty said, "Let's look on the bright side. None of our jobs is at stake. Why not sit back and watch Hackenworth's little game? Eventually the time will come when we can thwart him."

Silence hung grimly in the air. Wayne put down his empty cup and started walking up and down in the narrow space between the sofa, the armchair, and the door to Marty's office. It was a long, thin stretch, paralleling the hallway. Wayne paced like a caged animal. "Guys, I can't tell you how much this bothers me," he said.

Jeremy avoided comment. He stopped rolling his cup between his hands and started picking pieces off the top. The vending machine cup was made of light blue Styrogel—bio-degradable Styrofoam, government regulation. A small piece came off, imprinted with Jeremy's thumbnail. Marty diluted his coffee dregs with more vodka.

Wayne turned and faced both men. "Don't things like this bother you?"

"Sure," said Jeremy. "But you've got to pick your battles."

"Jeremy's right," Marty added, sipping his latest cup of Breathless. "Corruption is, in some measure, a fact of life."

"Well, I'll fight it 'till the day I die," Wayne said fiercely.

"Surely the best way to fight it," Marty said, "is to keep your job. Then you can do something, however small."

"For us, unfortunately, 'something' is precious little." Jeremy said grimly. "Here we are, being forced to kill the huntids. Four days from now, we're supposed to come out with alleged 'research' for Tucker's pathetic Presidential Press conference. If Socrates lived now, I don't think he could cope any better than we are. I mean, what else can we do?"

Silence filled the room like the gray smell of the lab.

"Say, Marty," Wayne asked, finally. "How much of this can I tell Marnie? With my level of Security Clearance, I usually figure it's safest not to say anything about work at home. But I feel like I'm gonna explode if I can't talk about this to someone."

"After the White House Press Conference on Friday, I suppose anything goes." said Marty.

Suddenly a rare smile lit up his face. "Wait a minute," he continued. "Didn't you mention once that your wife is a member of the—what's the name of that religious group? Not The Righteous, the one that's second biggest, where they wear the huge crosses."

"They're called Traditionals. Yeah, they're the quiet talkers instead of the loud, cheerful types." Wayne cleared his throat and began to imitate their characteristic up-talk. 'Traditionals always seem very peaceful? Nothing much bothers them? Except that they're certain everyone's going to Hell?"

"So I gather you're not exactly thrilled that your wife is a follower of the famous Rev. Stacey Pilgrim," Jeremy said, relieved. Until now he hadn't dared broach the subject with Wayne.

"You have no idea," Wayne told both men. "When I first met Marnie, she wore one of those little inside-the-blouse jobs, but it was no big deal. After the kids came along, and she stayed home with them, she started out hanging out with other mothers who were Traditionals. Now she's so far gone, she harnesses up with one of the big metal things that pokes you in the chest any time you try to give her a hug."

Marty smiled. "Between you and me, and Jeremy here, I wonder what's the worst that could happen if the Traditionals heard about what was going on—before the Press Conference."

"You mean a leak?" Jeremy asked.

"Maybe some talk about a minor government conspiracy. Don't they all love to hate the government? You could call it a government plot to destroy the huntids."

"When actually the huntids have right to life?" Wayne said, his face brightening.

"Very good," Marty said.

"How about this?" Jeremy gave a crooked smile. "What if Rev. Pilgrim finds some kind of religious connection to the huntids? She could make up some reason that it's important for them to be here now."

"What kind of connection?" Marty asked.

"I don't know. With those exotic colors, huntids are very attractive. Maybe the Traditionals can put them on flags and start waving 'em. Traditionals make a big show of their patriotism, don't they?"

"That's for sure," Wayne said disgustedly. "Marnie makes the kids say the Pledge of Allegiance every morning. . . after all the other prayers. Our daughter Melanie's four and Tyrone's only two, but Marnie sticks them in front of the TV every morning to pray along with Rev. Pilgrim. Can you believe it?"

"So you think that's a little much, do you?" said Marty. "Well, so are Hackenworth and Davis. How appropriate that an anonymous source might bypass them and leak this story to Rev. Pilgrim! As for what would happen next, let's leave that to Rev. Pilgrim's imagination."

Chapter 13
Watch Out!

That night, Rachel made sure there were candles at dinner. Long, tapering, pink candles. They went with a swirl-patterned magenta tablecloth to set off fresh pasta with white clam sauce. Brent detracted from the meal's romantic potential, however; the kid wanted to turn dinner into a slurping contest.

Or maybe he just wanted attention. She was putting most of her focus on Jeremy, trying to twinkle at him. As in, "Brent, we see how long you can make your spaghetti last; how about showing us how fast you can put one piece in your mouth?" Saying this she sent a big-eyed twinkle, verging on wink, to Jeremy.

Silently he sat there. God knew what he was thinking.

Rachel fluffed her hair and gave him a coquettish sideways look. Where was the man, on Mars? Brent started talking about how he wanted to start Kid Olympics with food, to see who could set records eating spaghetti. "You mean like the Guinness Book of World Records?" she said, finally.

As if she wanted to talk about that! Wouldn't Jeremy ever say a word? Rachel felt so discouraged, she didn't want to eat, except that pulling those succulent strands of comfort food into her mouth at least gave her something to do while little chatterbox was blabbing away.

Was it her job to hold the family together? If Brent wanted to do all the talking, maybe she should let him. Jeremy never noticed. Silently grumbling, Rachel kept her mouth busy with pasta; before she gave a thought to the calories, a second plateful disappeared, too.

Yet she still didn't realize fully how frustrated and angry she felt—not until she was halfway through putting Brent to bed. He was asking her his favorite riddles... from kindergarten. "Quit stalling," she yelled at him.

Brent cowered, looking so small in his "big boy bed" that Rachel felt guilty and kissed him. Unfortunately this made him think she wanted to play, so he started asking more riddles. Wearily, Rachel shook her head. "Goodnight," she said firmly.

Jeremy was down in his office. She knocked on the door. "Hi, guy."

His briefcase was open; papers all over his desk were stacked in neat little piles. (Jeremy called himself a "horizontal filer.") "How about you come up and visit me, sailor?" she persisted.

"I don't know, Rachel. I'm kind of busy."

"Oh." She let herself look disappointed. He was wearing his glasses, ancient metal-framed things that Jeremy had started to need a couple of years ago. They still gave her a delicious shock of surprise, they made him look adorably brainy in an old-fashioned way. Jeremy had a way of concentrating over his computer that definitely turned her on.

Why couldn't she go over to him and distract him? Because he'd hate her for it, that's why. And Jeremy was the one who didn't understand why she was a Seminar Slave! The man had driven her to it.

"Okay," she said, finally. "Guess I'll go upstairs and watch TV or something. Do you think we could connect before I go to bed?"

"You got it, Sunflower." That tantalizing long mouth sent her a smile.

Rachel went directly to her computer and started responding to e-mails. Unfortunately Internet friendships didn't really satisfy you, no matter how many hours you spent on them. Visuals and voice bites notwithstanding, you still couldn't connect with a live person's presence. All you knew was a sliver, and maybe you didn't even know that.

Well, here was a letter from Karen at least. Karen hailed from some Ohio suburb and she was one of Rachel's hottest e-friends these days, through a listserv at Moms-at-Home-Support.com. Lately Rachel had given Karen a lot of support, several weeks' worth of lengthy e-mails, over her son's recent diagnosis as developmentally delayed. It had been a great feeling, knowing she made a difference to someone. Opening the e-mail, Rachel felt a little thrill of excitement, like watching the curtain go up in an old-fashioned theater.

"Thanks to all my List-Buds," it began. Rachel felt a sinking sensation as it became clear that this was a group letter. Karen wrote several grateful paragraphs, thanking her "Best friends in all the world" who had showered her with advice through her crisis. Rachel found her name all right, after scrolling through about 150 other e-mail addresses. Her name was third from the end; these names weren't in alphabetical order, either.

Rachel resisted the urge to flame Karen back, "You're so welcome, dear, precious, intimate friend." Jeremy would have told her not to take things so personally. And Rachel's mom would have said, "Don't throw a friendship away so fast. Something is better than nothing." All Rachel knew was that her feelings were hurt, whether she had the right to feel that way or not.

Suddenly Brent burst into the room, ran over to her, and gave her a hug. Then, just as spontaneously, he turned to go back to bed.

"Everything okay, kid?"

He turned around to give her a beaming smile. "I just wanted you to know."

Know what, that children are so affectionate at bedtime? "Well, thanks. I'll think about it," Rachel said, blowing him a kiss. "Now back to bed."

Returning to her e-mail screen, Rachel's loneliness deepened. *No sulking allowed! Reach out to someone,* she told herself sternly. So she called up Heather.

"Hey, you" she said, cheerily. "How do you like your new aromatherapy potion from Health Services?"

"What a waste of my monthly elective!" Heather whined. "The bottle just sits on my bureau. You know what it says on the label?"

"Health Services Aromatherapy, probably. I had one a couple of years ago. Their logo's still a big red cross on a white background, right?"

"Not the logo, Rachel, the label. It says, 'Grief.' How can the smells inside a bottle cheer you up when every time you walk by it, you see the stupid label that says 'Grief'?"

"Well, do you at least like how it smells? Aromatherapy is supposed to bypass your conscious mind. What does it have in there, anyway, lavender, sandalwood?"

"Who fucking cares, Rachel?"

"Oh, come on, Heather. This will pass. At least George is getting what he deserves, with his HIV. And you tested safe, right?"

"Yeah, but that's beside the point." Heather paused to hunch closer to the video screen. She cupped one hand over her mouth, as if to make what she was about to say a big secret. It flickered across Rachel's mind that Heather was utterly transparent about technology—the woman could seriously think she was whispering, as though pushing your face in for a close-up on a computer screen 3-feet-square or bigger wasn't the least bit public.

"You know, because life as I know it is over."

"Oh, Heather," said Rachel. "Is it really that bad? Don't you think that maybe you can work out a new relationship with George? Maybe you can become buddies now, since the physical stuff is finally out of the question."

"You think the high point of my week is supposed to be when he stops by to pick up the girls every Saturday?"

" I mean patience and love, even if the relationship's very limited. You realize, Heather, you practically see George more often than I see my own husband these days."

"Patience?" shrieked Heather, backing away from the phone. "He has no patience with me, I can tell you that. Just yesterday, when he brought back the girls, I made him coffee so we could talk. I asked him to hear my feelings. You know what he said?"

Rachel shrugged expectantly.

"Rotten George says, 'Go feel your own fucking feelings. I've had enough of them to last me until the next millennium.'"

"He should live so long," Rachel said. "That would be fit punishment."

Heather's pink-cheeked, picture-perfect face crumpled into a sob. Her shoulders heaved as she said, "Without George, my life feels so empty."

"So that's why you need to plan lots of activities to fill up your day. Get a grip, Heather. Tell me what you're going to do tomorrow"

Heather wiped her eyes gently with a tissue. "Honey, you can string together a hundred activities. But having a special relationship is what makes it a life."

Rachel was about to say something about how Heather still had the girls. In fact, she had two children, not just an only child like Rachel would have, if she and Jeremy split. But over the screen, Rachel saw the expression in Heather's eyes. Clear as day it showed that Heather wasn't just suffering from love hunger. It was man hunger—the kind only a man could fill. Rachel knew that kind of hunger all too well.

She said, "I wish I could hug you right now."

Heather looked up, sniffling. "Well, how are you doing, Rachie? Did Jeremy explain everything yet? Maybe he's a rat, too. Maybe all men are."

"I suppose he explained. Stuff at work has him coming and going."

"You believe him?"

"I guess. We did the big one on Saturday. I was kind of hoping we might score another shot tonight, but no such luck."

Rachel started pacing around the room. It was her turn now, according to tradition. "Did you ever worry about George when it made no sense whatsoever?"

"You're still worrying?"

"Jeremy told me there's nothing going on between him and Sally."

"Did he explain about all the papers that had you suspicious?"

"I didn't bother to ask him, Heather. This morning, while he was at work, I went through his papers —the top of his desk, his drawers, everything. I figured anything weird would show up but nothing did. So I think he was telling the truth, but I'm still wondering if another woman could be in the picture. Jeremy isn't acting normal. How can I trust him?"

Rachel's circles around the room got smaller and smaller. When she looked up toward the screen, to catch Heather's expression, her eyes swept across her desk. And there was Jeremy, standing outside the half-open door to her office. How much had he overheard?

"Got to go, Heather. Stay busy."

"Stay busy," she said. The screen went dark but Rachel didn't stick around to watch. She was already running to catch up with Jeremy.

He was staring out their bedroom window, muttering to himself.

"Well?" Rachel said finally.

"You're exasperating, you know that?"

Rachel pouted, questioningly. Or maybe it was more that she looked questioning, plus a pout. In any event, Rachel knew that she looked beautiful, trembling on the verge of anger. She was starting to enjoy this. She and Jeremy didn't fight enough. True, he had probably overheard her telling Heather that she'd been snooping in his office, but why should that make her feel guilty? At least now he was paying attention.

"You want the honest truth?" Jeremy asked.

She nodded, pretending to look stern. She decided to fold her arms under her chest; this probably made her bust look a little bigger

"Rachel, you make things up."

"How can you say that?"

"Maybe you can explain to me why you make things up—not just this infidelity scare. Remember your pregnancy scare? Your gallbladder surgery scare? Your house-being-gobbled-up-by-termites scare? Rachel, my love, whenever things get too calm around here, you start up some rip-snorting drama."

"Jeremy, are you insinuating that I make everything up? The termites for instance?"

"The termites were real, just not the crisis. All it took to fix was one simple treatment from the exterminator. Then a carpenter had to replace some boards that were damaged. How many boards, three? That was a problem, Rachel, not a crisis. Can't you tell the difference?"

Rachel had to calm down. The rage she felt wasn't feminine. *I'm becoming Pinkness*, she repeated inwardly. Oh hell, she was too mad to act sweet.

"Jeremy, I'll tell you something, too, okay. It has always bothered me that, with your so-called not-real-crisis, I had to hire an outside exterminator. You're supposed to be the big expert on bugs. Why didn't you see what was right in front of your nose? It's like the old saying, doctor's families run around sick and all shrinks' children are wackos."

Jeremy smiled patronizingly. That's when she really got mad. "So you think that's funny? Guess you're the big expert when it's theory, not real life. Next time you're tempted to say that I live in a fantasy world, think again. I'd say we're pretty well matched."

Right after the anger, which felt so cleansing and good, came a horrible feeling, like a dent in her gut. Rachel uncrossed her arms and sat on his side of the bed.

In the minute of silence that followed, Rachel felt scared. Sounded like Jeremy didn't respect her. Could she stay married to someone who didn't respect her?

He walked over and sat next to her. He took her hands in his. "Rachel, Sunflower, I think it's sweet you were jealous. It's a way of showing you care. As for snooping around my office, that's different. Don't do it again. Understand?"

She nodded meekly. He stroked her cheek, then cupped her chin to raise her face up to look him in the eye. Those laser-bright eyes of his looked so tender, he was going to try to get to her again, wasn't he?

In that deep voice that melted her heart, he said, "Now, regarding the other things, like the gallbladder scare and the pregnancy scare, I can understand why you've been tempted to blow things out of proportion. You're bored. If I were stuck at home, like you, know what? I'd exaggerate things, too."

Rachel moved across the bed to her side, stretching like a cat. "You know what's really bothering me?"

He shook his head. He was listening, for once.

"I'm lonely, in the most horrible kind of way. Here I am, 39 years old, and I still haven't met my real friends. Except for an occasional kindred soul. And you, of course." She felt her face grow hot with embarrassment.

"Exactly how would you recognize a real friend?"

"Well, there's this thing that happens, where I look into people's eyes and go through one layer after another, until I find the real person inside, like a baby. That's one of my favorite things in the world. It's like riding in an elevator and changing floors, you know?"

His wide brow furrowed in concentration.

She continued, "Or I'll be with someone like Heather and one minute I'm me, feeling my feelings, and the next minute I'm inside *her* feelings. That's precious to me, Jeremy, like gold. Only mysterious."

"So what's the problem?"

"Not one person I know talks about that kind of stuff. Not seminar gurus or anyone. And I want friends who have the same kind of thing happen to them. Is that too much to ask?"

Jeremy's long lips stretched into a rueful smile. He reached out one hand to stroke her hair. "You've got such an imagination. Not everybody's built that way."

"Don't you know what I'm talking about?"

For a moment, he flashed on what happened in the lab yesterday, watching himself from far away, with that golden light. That was wild, but probably not what she meant. Anyway, there was no point in confusing his wife any further. He cleared his throat. "I'm looking for more in life, sure. I don't think I look the same way as you. Do any two people? When chemistry happens, resulting in what you call 'real friends,' I'm not sure it's the consequence of effort. If anything, you could call it the grace of God."

"Even Techies like you can't explain that one, huh?" Rachel sat back and put her right leg into a half lotus. Gently she tried to push her upper leg into full-lotus position on top of it. "Speaking of mysterious, how come you can do a full lotus and not me? Who's the one who works out every day of her life?"

As he looked back at her admiringly, she felt the love. She continued, "You know what people expect of women in the '20's? I've thought about this, a lot."

"What?"

"We're prized for our beauty, our faith, and our accomplishments. Nothing about who we are on the inside."

"Accomplishments?"

"Like if we can play a musical instrument or keep a perfect house."

"Rachel, you know I don't expect that. Don't be so hard on yourself."

"Sometimes I feel like I'm in prison, that's all. Where are my people? People who are deep, like you. And Brent."

Jeremy rubbed his shoulders. "Couldn't that be just because you know us? I'm not so deep, to an outsider. Ask the people who work with me. They wouldn't win prizes for depth, either. I hate to break this to you, Rachel, but maybe you're looking for something that doesn't exist."

He paused, as if hesitant to say something unpleasant.

"Go on. I can take it."

"Watch out, that's all."

"For what?"

"Cults can be very attractive to people who feel the way you do now."

"What, you think I'm gonna go join The Righteous?"

"It could be any religion, any seminar. Lots of the joiners come because of, well, their unmet longings. They trade in their uncertainty and suffering for being saved, one way or another. Happened to the wife of a guy I work with. He told me his wife, Marnie, has graduated to a five-pounder with good old Rev. Pilgrim. Bet Marnie won't even talk to him any more, except for trying to convert him. That's how people act when they're in cults."

"Hey, don't underestimate me. You think I married a cynic for nothing?" Gently she gave him a little Get out! shove. Defensively, his arms flew up to his shoulders.

"Hey," Rachel said, "Why do you keep rubbing yourself like that, Jeremy?"

He looked down. What was that funny look on his face? Shame? Was it sexual?

"Tell me already." She tried to sound playful, not scared. She felt scared, though, as if something traumatic might happen.

Slowly he unbuttoned his light blue Oxford cloth shirt and took it off. Red scaly patches ran from his shoulders to his elbows, and across his back. His forearms were layered with pale skin, like the edges of a very stale croissant. Still, Rachel felt relieved. Rashes weren't that big a deal, though his looked kind of disgusting.

"God, Jeremy. What is this?"

"Eczema—brought on by stress, I suppose. Those huntids!"

"How does Health Services let you get away with it? Didn't they diagnose you at your last Monthly?"

"No, Rachel. I don't go to Health Services the way you do. They give me the creeps."

"But you've got to go, don't you, once a month?"

"Or what? They haven't caught up with me yet." He grinned. "Presumably they're busy with the more enthusiastic clients—like you."

"Promise me you'll go, Jeremy. They'll clear it up in a minute. You may not like them but they do good work."

"Do they?" he asked. "I'm not so sure."

"You know, your skin breaking out like that could be your body's way of complaining about the same thing that bothers me. I think you're lonely, too. We live in a neighborhood that isn't a neighborhood, and virtual friends are practically the only people you can meet. Unless you're a religious wacko. The way The Righteous are taking over scouts! I never had time to tell you what it was like when I volunteered at scout camp. Those poor innocent kids. And those V-R addicts. Ooh, don't get me started."

Jeremy frowned. "Come on, with me it's just a little stress over work. With you, I don't know what to say, except maybe you have to cut your expectations way down. We'd all like to live in the hallowed 1950's, but it ain't gonna happen."

"Well, that's unfair!" Her smile was teasing.

Jeremy got up, walked over to his dresser, and pulled out a pair of blue cotton pajamas. He started changing into the top. Rachel got into action, tugging it off with the kind of playfulness she used to have in the good old days. Next she liberated him from his underwear.

"Clothes are so nasty," she complained. "We absolutely *must* become nudists!"

Soon she was telling him all about their future life at the nudist colony, drawing cave paintings on his chest with her finger. Sidelong glances showed that he was beginning to smile, fascinated. She'd win this time. Her competitive spirit had switched on.

Sure enough, his lips found hers. His body began to glow with that mysterious fragrance that turned her on, bringing a tingle to the muscles of her inner thighs. Soon she was clambering over him. Soon after that, he was hard enough to forget all his worries and she could forget about everything but him.

Chapter 14
Gravitas

"Lighten up to attract your man. Be like the fluffy pink frosting on a birthday cake."
Tanya's words came up on Rachel first thing in the morning like a sugar hangover.
Beside her Jeremy was snoring lightly, unmindful of the world and oblivious to his
wife's glorious sexiness.

"Ridiculous," she thought. "I'm going to stop all the silly stuff my Jeremy says
doesn't make sense, like expecting to find friends who are just like me."

But that would leave a huge hole in her heart. What could she put there? Rachel
still needed a project. In the shower, she positioned her hair directly under a
delicious cascade of cooling water. *Worrying again. Just relax, kid.*

Suddenly *gravitas* popped into her mind. That was a word she had learned in
an English class back in college. *GRAH-vih-tahss*: a presence in the world that
people take seriously, a persona with substance and weight. Wow, wouldn't that be
a worthwhile project!

Not that she'd let her body go to undue substance and weight. She could still
look attractive and feminine, only for once in her life she'd be well adjusted to
reality. Rachel was drying herself vigorously now, with an oversized rainbow-cov-
ered towel.

Would it help to redecorate? Maybe earth tones in the towels, and a new wardrobe for herself in mature shades like taupe and brown?

No. *Gravitas* had nothing to do with color or lack of color. That would be her
assignment today, to find it. *God*, Rachel prayed (and she really meant it, which
she'd been told in one seminar was very important), *merciful God, bring me a
teacher. Or let life, itself, be my teacher in a more powerful way.*

Since it was Tuesday, Brent had a play date at Tom's. By 9:00, Rachel was back
alone in the house, free as a bird. Free to find *gravitas*. She decided to flip on TV.
Sometimes it gave you ideas.

Good old TV, she thought, clearing her throat before giving voice commands to the console. Rachel's grandmother had been born a few years before TV started. Hard to imagine living that way. Now people still called it TV, but Grandma wouldn't have recognized it: fully three-dimensional and layered, a life-sized screen that wrapped around to fill a whole wall of their living room, plus an edge on either side wall for when they clicked on close-ups or made home videos.

Rachel dimly remembered Grandma's old-fashioned color television from her childhood. Then came DVDs, satellite wars, the ban on cable, the new QRC technology that they had now. TV let you play games, show V-Rs with plug-in headsets, balance your checkbook, you name it. And even though one dinky set could do everything, the average American household had three or more. In Rachel's house, the living room console was the major one. Her home office had a second TV for close-vision games, Internet keyboarding, and voice mail. Jeremy's den had a TV like hers, only smaller.

When it came to home entertainment, everything was network these days. According to President Tucker when he passed his TV reform package, this was supposed to pull the culture of America back together again. It didn't, but at least you spent fewer hours daily drowning in channel surf.

Ordinarily Rachel favored Channel 17, *Oprah's TV Network*, featuring seminars and talk shows. Today she was in the mood for something different. Maybe Channel 8, *History Tragedy Network*. This was filled with tearjerkers about discrimination and racism. Actors would talk about the history of their bloodstream—Latino, African, Chinese, etc.—and then the individual's story would turn into a drama about being victimized. Shows like that might be good for *gravitas*.

What was on now? *Kossovo*. This series had the same plot each episode, replaying the late-20th century war. The twist was that each week a different ethnic groups re-enacted the theme of ethnic cleansing. When the show first came out, she thought it sounded hokey, a kind of musical chairs with rotating victims, but the show was pretty good.

Still, did she want to watch? By the end of the episode, peace would be declared and the stars of the week would work their way back to their bombed-out village. Rachel would feel their courage; her human spirit would be renewed. Sure, but if her own personal History Tragedy was any guideline, afterwards she'd go on an eating binge, triggered by all that crying. Forget it.

Maybe Channel 10, for fun? *The Gay Parade Network* offered love stories and light comedies, mostly about married gays and silly sidekick characters who were rigidly, outrageously straight. A couple of shows re-shot TV classics with role reversals. Sure enough, here was *The Jacquie Gleason Show.* It starred a tough-looking woman who played Ralph while a cringing nerdy-guy played her long-suffering spouse, akin to Alice in the original show. Today's gender-bending version could make you think about social oppression. For TV, it had a lot of depth, Rachel thought.

Unfortunately, three jokes in a row weren't nearly as funny as they were cracked up to be, and today's laugh tracks tended to give Rachel the creeps when she wasn't laughing along. Quadriphonic sound made it seem as though her whole living room was filled with invisible cacklers, gigglers, and other assorted hysterics. Well, click them away!

At Channel 16, she found *Fogeys Anonymous*, now broadcasting *Senior Moments,* where the plot revolved around characters forgetting things, finding them again, and then reassuring each other that, despite appearances, they were really as sharp as tacks. Maybe the typical plot didn't sound terribly clever when summarized like that, but sometimes Rachel found these shows surprisingly uplifting. The cleverness was in the perfectly timed comedies of errors.

Nah, Rachel wasn't in the mood for that, either. Her job was to get depth *before* retirement age. So she found herself commanding her set to turn to *Channel 31, National Public TV.*

What was this, Reverend Pilgrim? Couldn't be. Rachel never chose Channel 6, which belonged to Pilgrim and the Traditionals, any more than she would voluntarily brainwash herself by turning on Channel 5, the propaganda station for The Righteous. Both networks competed, broadcasting their version of sermons, Bible quiz shows, and hymn sing-alongs.

"What the hell is *she* doing on National Public TV?" Rachel tried switching to other news channels: Channel 28 (*News of the Republic*), then Channel 29 (*Democracy TV News*), then 30 (*Independent Rebel News*), then 32 (*Radical Chic Update*). It was the same on every live network, nothing but the Reverend Stacey Pilgrim. Why?

Rachel commanded her set to go back to her favorite of all the news stations, National Public TV.

"I have had a dream," proclaimed the Rev. Stacey Pilgrim. The camera showed her, stalwart and solemn, dressed in a brown silk shirtwaist that brought out the richness of her milk chocolate complexion. Big brown Texas-style hair, thickly curved eyebrows and a large-boned frame all contributed to the impression she made of granite-hard solidity.

Pilgrim was speaking live at a press conference. A long shot showed the TV studio filled with reporters and a big collection of portable spotlights. On screen, Pilgrim had the heft of a woman who was fully six feet tall and couldn't weigh a pound under 250. Naturally, the cross dangling from her neck and shoulders by a thick leather harness was her trademark ten-pounder.

"Hear this, my children. I have had a dream."

Modestly Pilgrim cast her eyes downward; then she looked straight at Rachel (or whoever else was watching). "Yes, I suppose, you could call it a gift of prophecy. Let me share my message with you, because it concerns you in a very personal way. It concerns us all.

"Those of us who worship the Lord in the *Traditional* way are blessed with a certain. . . tenderness. You could call it a feeling of protection for those who are innocent and uncared for, the vulnerable and the weak."

Pilgrim's voice grew louder and more sing-song: "Maybe that's what first brought you to the Traditional way. Maybe someone once reached out to you at a moment when *you* were vulnerable."

Her voice fell to a whisper. "You see, my children, we are in the business of blessing the weak. It's the Traditional way. But last night, I had a prophetic dream about vulnerability, and it came in a way I never would have imagined.

"I dreamed about tiny creatures."

Pilgrim had a performer's voice, Rachel thought in disgust. She mimicked, "Taaahny creeeechurs."

No doubt Pilgrim's faithful audience was hanging on every word. "These flies had shimmering wings and their color was a vibrant green, like new grass in spring. What a sign of God's love! Their tiny wings were the shade of Easter lilacs. These creatures were tiny but so beautiful when they came to me in this dream.

"At the time, I did not have a name for them. Since my dream I have spoken to others who have actually seen them. Yes, some members of the Traditionals who are pure of heart have physically seen these creatures. Huntids is their name.

"Huntids," she repeated tenderly. "During my dream, I saw along with the huntids certain men in power, political men." Her voice dropped an octave. "Godless men."

The camera zoomed in for a close-up, and Rachel felt herself drawn towards Pilgrim's lips, which were fairly thin and narrow. Her vivid magenta-toned lipstick was actually flattering. How odd!

That was Rachel's first reaction, anyway.

But as the close-up of Pilgrim continued, Rachel kept staring at the preacher's huge Cupid's Bows, large triangles beneath the strong ridges that linked her nose to her mouth. Somehow Pilgrim thrust her Cupid's Bows forward for emphasis as she talked. Rhythmically, the Bows moved back again and flattened. Then her uncanny lip movements would start again. The magenta triangles began to mesmerize Rachel, along with Pilgrim's comforting, motherly voice.

"We might call these politicians deluded instead of Godless. That would be the Christian thing to do, wouldn't it? Yet I must be honest with you, my children, and tell you what happened in my dream. When I saw these great men of power, my first reaction was fear. Next, as I saw what they were about to do to the huntids, my fear turned to hatred. How dare they harm these humble defenseless creatures who had never hurt them, not even the tiniest bit?"

Pilgrim straightened up and glanced to the side. You had a view of her rather noble-looking profile. Then a long shot of the TV studio showed that she swung back to glare at the reporters who stood directly before her. Her look was scathing until Pilgrim rearranged her face into a smile for the cameras.

"Of course, the habit of faith serves us well at times like this, even during our dreams. Immediately, I heard the old hymn, 'Hate them not.' You see, as a child I was blessed to receive a solid foundation of Christian faith. Thus, it was second nature for me to remember that these were merely men with a frailty. Many good men and women today have the misfortune of believing the wrong message.

"No matter, brothers and sisters. Sinners can always come to us for forgiveness. If you have been to even *one* of our Revival Gatherings, you will have witnessed that no one who repents is ever turned away—ever. We would welcome any mis-believing, hypocritical wretch on the face of this earth. Our arms are wide open."

The camera pulled back to show that Pilgrim's arms had, in fact, opened like the petals of a blossoming flower. Then she gave an exquisitely feminine shrug. "Yet in my dream, my Beloveds, a large group of these deluded men in power were saying, 'We must kill the huntids.'

"Kill," she repeated. "They were saying, 'These flies are strange. And because our hearts are full of hatred, we will call them pests. And we will put these strange creatures to death.'"

Pilgrim's voice softened to a whisper. "In my dream, a man appeared who holds the greatest of worldly power. You know this man. It was President Tucker, head of the free world. In the palm of his hand he held one of these creatures. Yet, I tell you, even in his hand of hatred, the huntid shimmered and glowed."

She held out her upturned palm and thundered, "Then Tucker said, 'We must kill this.'"

Rachel felt a jolt of electricity rush through her spine.

Rev. Pilgrim's voice regained its softness. "The tiny creature, the huntid, buzzed in this man's hand, bzzzz, the way insects do. And as surely as I stand before you bearing witness, I could hear a voice within its voice. And let me tell you what that voice said—to President Tucker and to every single American with a conscience.

"It said, 'Thou shalt not kill. Listen to the messengers of The Lord. We testify that the Last Days are at hand.'

"It said, 'Children, we come here in God's holy name. We are what you would call *missionaries*. Do not be fooled by the fact that we are come in humble disguise."

Pilgrim turned her head, and her wide, chiseled jaws caught the light. "Perhaps you remember a certain stable in Bethlehem where another representative of the Lord came in humble disguise. Only a few Prophets of that time had the vision to greet his coming. Do you happen to remember that Bible story?

"Back in my dream, the head of our country today was deaf to the truth. He wouldn't listen at all. In fact, he was giving a speech—a press conference like the one I decided to bring you today. President Tucker was talking, my children, with numbers and facts, with *technical words*. He made it all sound so important, as if killing was the responsible thing to do.

"Yet all the while, in my dream, the tiny creature sang out. It was radiant, I tell you, like an angel clad in an Easter robe. Then I saw Tucker's hand close around it, squashing the life away." Pilgrim squeezed her palm shut. She looked up to the camera and one tender tear fell from each large, brown eye. She opened up her hand again and let it fall, dramatically, to her side.

"Beloved ones, let us not mock the Lord this time. Let's be clear about this: I am not saying that these huntids are God. No, that would be blasphemy. But huntids are missionaries, just like you and me, like all of us who are called to be Traditionals. We must not kill them.

"If I dreamed truth, these huntids are coming to save us before it is too late."

The preacher stepped back, opening up both palms, and began to sing:

> "Let us make ourselves ready.
> Let us come to His call."

She moved her hands to prayer position:

> "Let us be judged blameless."

She knelt.

> "In ourselves, we are nothing.
> Let us kneel before the Mercy
> Of Him who is All in all."

Pilgrim must be singing a chant from the Traditional worship service. Rachel had never gone to one, but sometimes she'd bump into them while channel surfing.

"Let us pray," Pilgrim said. Then cameras cut away to the station's news team.

Dave and Donna were Rachel's favorite pundits. They seemed more intellectual than the other news broadcasters. Plus Donna was actually older than her partner, the opposite of most female broadcasters, who looked like the third wives of middle-aged men.

Donna Swenson was statuesque, thin and busty and blonde. She seemed like your typical TV pundit until you looked closer and saw that all her cosmetic surgery couldn't alter the papery skin and delicate hair of a woman well over 60. Donna spoke with a measured, steady voice. What dignity! A great role model for *gravitas*, come to think of it!

Dave Nguyen was short, chubby and wry. Even without the bloodstream give-away in his last name, the man seemed Asian, with eyelids that went straight down from the brow bone. His short black hair stuck straight up, giving him a slightly comical look. Unlike Donna, he talked fast.

"A prophesy, Donna," he said. "Do you buy it?"

"Pilgrim does make you wonder," Donna replied, arching one eyebrow. "Can the woman really need more publicity? As you may remember, Rev. Stacey broke upon the American scene just seven years ago. Yet she's already the star of her own TV network, for those of you who somehow missed that…

"Yeah, because you're in ET astronaut training school, right? As if anyone from the 'hood who watches TV could have missed Stacey Pilgrim!"

Donna silenced Dave with a look and continued, "The Reverend Pilgrim gives sermons daily. Her words are broadcast all over the world from pulpits as well as household entertainment centers."

"Donna, let's not forget her famous Revival Meetings, either. What is her schedule like, this week, L.A., Tuesday; Capetown, Wednesday?"

"Here's the point." Donna said, ignoring Dave as usual. "Never before has the Reverend Stacey Pilgrim gone on record with prophesy. Unless we're prepared to take her words at face value, we must ask ourselves, why has she chosen to speak up now?"

"And, Donna, why set a precedent with bugs? I mean, the woman already has a multi-billion dollar franchise on religion. Now she needs to form a strategic alliance with huntids?"

"Well it does seem a strange choice, doesn't it? Most Americans have never heard of these new lilac-winged flies with bodies the color of green Popsicles. Honestly, Dave, did you hear of them before today?"

"What, in my nightmares? Seriously, Donna, you think maybe Pilgrim is worried her franchise is too small?"

"Well," Donna said. "When the Reverend puts her first prophecy on record since she started the Traditionals religion, you've got to wonder. Why would she go to such lengths to link her name with the huntids?"

"Well, what do you think?" Dave said, turning to address Rachel and other viewers. "Could Pilgrim's speech today signal more aggressive in-fighting between Traditionals and The Righteous? Anyone else who speaks in public, like Hickory Helms, has no choice now but to come out as Anti-Bug-Life. When you set the terms of the debate, you own the debate. That's historical fact."

"So cynical, Dave," Donna said, smiling into the camera. "Maybe the prophecy we heard today was simply the courageous speech of a visionary. I think Pilgrim has guts, and she's just proven it by coming out in public to telling two billion Americans about her dream about the flies."

Dave nodded. "So you think her speech was religious, not political? As Freud might have said, sometimes a prophesy is just a prophesy. Maybe you're right, Donna, and there's nothing here to analyze at all. Think we could be out of a job?"

"Whatever," Donna said, ignoring Dave as if he was *her* third spouse. "Anyway, I'm going to follow up by analyzing some real-live footage of huntids, just in case some of you don't know what they look like. Are they bugs or missionaries? Stay tuned."

Rachel didn't. She'd seen huntids before at Scout Camp and, frankly, except for being the prettiest flies she'd ever seen, they didn't seem like such fascinating or "blessed" creatures. Political garbage!

"Next station," Rachel told her TV. Channel 32 was re-running a close-up of Pilgrim in slow motion, with a Truth Expert commenting on every micro-expression. Rachel turned off the sound and marveled. What charisma that woman had! Yet she made Rachel's flesh creep.

Jeremy didn't react the way Rachel thought he would, when she called up to tell him about Pilgrim's prophesy. He looked interested, all right. But instead of sharing her revulsion at Pilgrim, he gave a strange little chuckle.

Jeremy wasn't a chuckler. Clearly this was a sign that Rachel had even less *gravitas* than she thought.

"Well," she said, mustering up her full self-importance (which at the moment was nearly zero). "I've got to go now. I have a project to get back to, you know."

"What project?"

"I'll tell you about it when you get home," she replied with a fetching smile. This sounded better than admitting the truth. In the looming wasteland of Rachel's Tuesday afternoon, there was no project.

Chapter 15
Seriously Cooking

At Runner's Club on Wednesday, Rachel tried explaining to Heather that *gravitas* was her new project, but Heather didn't get it and kept talking as though gravitas meant making a fashion statement. *Maybe if I succeed at* gravitas, *that will bring out depth in my friends,* Rachel thought.

It had better. Heather's rapt attention right now was pure airhead. And later that night, when she was with Jeremy, he treated her like a glass of fluffy, no-cal, Whammo Guaranteed Weightloss Shake.

Thursday, Rachel resolved to look deep inside for a stronger sense of self. "Who am I?" she asked, as if making a phone call. The universe seemed to be putting her on hold. Should she take another seminar? Maybe there was one about *gravitas*.

She'd check later. Now her job was to act like a homemaker, which meant making a haven for her son and hard-working husband, Jeremy, the man who felt as if he was a hundred miles away. If only tonight he'd wrap his arms around her—physically or emotionally—she'd settle for either one. Emotional connection with anyone was hard to come by these days.

Maybe she should start with Brent, who was upstairs playing with Tom. She could show her new image— correction, her new *self*—by listening better. Now, should she also pitch her squeaky soprano voice lower? No, that hurt. She'd just talk less. And talk slower.

"Boys, how ya doing?" she asked. They were building elaborate monsters or something from Robo-Kits, the kid-friendly cyborg blocks. When Brent didn't answer, she picked up one of the creatures they were making. It had three arms and two heads. "Very creative! Want to show me what it does when you turn it on?"

"Mom, you're embarrassing me. Can't I play alone with my friend? Come on, Tom. Let's turn on pinball."

Downstairs went Rachel again, this time to Jeremy's office to do e-mail. Geesh, she'd only received 46 letters over the past 24 hours. The old Rachel would have worried that this meant she was a social failure. This time, though, the new Rachel forced herself to see the best in each correspondent, and when she noticed how faddish or badly groomed some of their images looked over the computer screen, she refused to make fun of them. Instead she resolved to write to their deep inner selves, which proved to be such a struggle of imagination that she gave up after the first two tries. She deleted the rest of her e-mails, making a bold executive decision about time management.

Is this the new you or what? Rachel bragged to herself. And heaven forbid she was going to peek at Jeremy's private files, just because they were nearby. Rachel didn't need to snoop. She stood up, proud and tall, all 62 inches of pure, regal *gravitas* woman. Now what? It was 2:00 p.m. The rest of the afternoon stretched before her unattractively, like a yawn from a mouth with uncapped teeth.

Cooking, she thought, might be the answer. She wasn't a caterer's daughter for nothing. Cooking a glorious meal could *prove* her to be a woman of substance.

When Jeremy married her, Rachel had insisted on an old-fashioned house. Many of their friends seemed like prisoners of their smart houses, filled with video screens and cameras, buzzing with electricity and beeping with new programs. Before bed, those exhausting houses would change the mattress texture for you, heat your blanket to a precise temperature, show your tooth plaque buildup in the mirror before you brushed your teeth and pester you everywhere you went, like an over-zealous housemaid.

And these obnoxious programs were so hard to learn, most smart-house owners hired a part-time tech consultant, like a maid of yore, only the job of today's servants was to service your machines. Techs would coach you on using the updates that came out every month. This was way too much trouble, Rachel thought, for coffee that poured out from the tap with just the right number of sugar cals.

Besides, programming would never work for Rachel. She had no one favorite way she liked her coffee. It changed from day to day, like her outfits or how she wanted to make love to her husband. Even when she was filled to the brim with *gravitas*, Rachel would always be wildly creative; no smart house was smart enough to keep up with her.

When purchasing their un-smart house, back when she and Jeremy were newlyweds, Rachel had insisted that they keep the old-fashioned kitchen. It came with an oven and microwave, built-in water filter, self-cleaning countertops, and glitter-finish cabinets—old fashioned stuff, but it worked just fine.

Carefully, Rachel extricated her antique roaster pan from the crammed storage shelf. She rinsed it, dried it, and oiled it lightly to facilitate cleanup later. These days, disinfectant procedures with a chicken were more elaborate than the actual cooking, which is why few people cooked from scratch any more. Rachel was prepared, however, and plied her spray bottle of Doctor's Disinfectant Solution. Next she applied a jerk spice rub and popped the roaster pan into the oven. Then she had to scrub under her fingernails and scour every utensil that came in contact with the germy little bird. Only after that did Rachel realize that, all the time she'd been cooking, she hadn't played any music or book on tape, nothing. She must be in some ripe state of contentment.

Which entertainment should she reach for now? Buzz went her skin-phone. Wonder if you could ever use your husband's skin-phone for a vibrator; get it to redial as a kind of foreplay…. Rachel smiled to herself, but straightened her face right away when she heard the voice of her mother. Even though it wasn't a screen phone, mothers were mothers.

"Rachel, honey, where are you?"

"I'm home, Ma. But I'm cooking. I need both my hands free. Listen—"

"So I called at a bad time?"

"Not that. I'm always happy to talk to my mother. But let me pick up the phone with the headset and call you back. Then we can have a nice long visit, okay?"

"Whatever you say, darling."

Now was as good a time as any to keep in touch with her mother, a chore Rachel tended to avoid. Many of her guilt buttons tied into Ma, as she'd learned from taking the "Mom is Your Lifelong Seminar" seminar; with practice, she had improved at handling Helene. Now Rachel thought, *Bring on the chance for more gravitas!*

Headset in place, Rachel voiced Helene's phone number, then pulled the gorgeous potatoes out of the fridge. These would be transformed into garlic mashed potatoes; Rachel began to scrub their lustrous brown skins. "Ma, I'm here. How are you?"

"First tell me about you—you and my grandson and Jeremy. Are you and Jeremy still having problems?"

"No, we're fine. It was a false alarm. Hey, Ma, I'm cooking us an old-fashioned chicken dinner. What are you and Dad having?"

"It's a terrible thing getting old, Rachel. We ate, we ate. But your father's not well, darling. I didn't mention any of this the other day but I'm afraid we're going to have to put him in a home."

"That bad? Is it Alzheimer's?"

"Hardening of the arteries, Rachel. Your father is losing his mind."

"Does Eric think so, too?"

Eric, her older brother, had taken over the family catering business since Dad's retirement.

Eric was Mr. Insensitive. Thinking of him brought up anger, but thanks to an "Anger Button" seminar Rachel had learned that her feelings could be used constructively. Vigorously she shoved potato scraps down the disposal.

Helene said, "Eric was the first to notice. Your Dad kept wandering away from the store. One minute he'd be nudging Eric, driving him crazy, next thing, your father would disappear."

"To where?"

"Usually he'd be at a donut shop down the street."

"All this must be incredibly hard on you, Ma."

"You have no idea. Seeing Benny Frischwasser this way, the man I married straight out of cooking school, it seems like just yesterday—and your other brother, Stefan, is no help at all. Half the time he's drunk, of course. Oh, don't get me started."

Stefan, the hotshot lawyer. Rachel rolled her eyes. She let Helene talk, talk, talk. Meanwhile Rachel ground cumin, pepper, and fenugreek for *palak panir*, Brent's favorite vegetable recipe. Soon the spices, ghee, onions, and spinach were simmering fragrantly.

Helene's complaints turned to her health, while Rachel continued to make sympathetic noises.

Inside, she wondered, *Why didn't Ma ask about how I felt? Didn't she think I'd have any reaction to this news about Daddy?* Easy enough to explain— Helene never wanted to know about Rachel's feelings. As for Rachel's reaction to this horrible news about Benny, more guilt. She felt nothing. He hadn't been much of a father to any of his three children, and Rachel had always come last. In the part of her heart where love and sympathy should have been, there was only a dead space.

Didn't you learn anything from that Mom seminar? Rachel thought. She shouldn't keep scolding herself. Instead she focused on putting together a Moroccan carrot raisin salad. Jeremy loved it. For Rachel the highlight of the conversation with Helene came as she mixed the dressing: Ground cumin, fresh lemon juice, honey, and the secret ingredient, orange flower water that came in an indigo glass bottle. Smelling the highest note of the orange perfume helped Rachel to remember the sweetness of life, something Helene had forgotten long ago.

"Well, Ma," Rachel said cheerfully. Her mother's lamentations had come to a pause, if not an end. "Dinner calls, but I'm so glad you filled me in on everything."

"Rachel, baby, I just want to see you, okay?"

"What?" Rachel felt a whine come into her voice. She couldn't help it. "You want me to come all the way to New York?"

"No, baby. Just go over to your telescreen. Maybe I'm no kid anymore but I still know how to use a full-spectrum telephone."

Rachel raced upstairs two steps at a time. "Guys, put your game on hold, okay? I've got to flip on Ma for a minute."

Back in the kitchen, Rachel wandered around. It was as though she had gone into a room to get something, then forgotten what on earth she had come for. The meal? Enough already. She didn't really need to make the frosted zucchini or the Ethiopian bread or the Instant Pastry Napoleons. It was a simple Thursday night dinner, and nobody in the family really needed to plump up.

How depressing about Dad! Poor Mom, too, and there wasn't a single thing Rachel could do about it, except to let Mom vent by describing her troubles.

It was terrible that she felt nothing about this news about Benny. Where, for crying out loud, was her *gravitas*? Brent and Tom saw her as someone not especially bright. Jeremy saw her as what, convenient? Rachel flipped on the TV. This time she went straight to Channel 31. Maybe Pilgrim was back for another weird lesson in *gravitas*.

Golly, the other one was on this time—Hickory Helms. Rachel hadn't seen him much, but who could fail to recognize the leader of The Righteous? Movie star handsome, he had an athletic build and massive forearms, which showed to advantage now under the rolled-up sleeves of his denim shirt. "Let's get to work" seemed to be his message. But there was something else, too. What?

"White." That was it. Somehow the man projected an image that Hickory Helms was the product of pure-bred Nordic-white bloodstream. And proud of it.

Rachel stared. How did he do that? True, his skin was the kind of alabaster that goes with ash brown hair, and the Press Conference lighting showed off his hair to perfection—thick, straight hair that gleamed like cornsilk. His cheeks had a schoolboy glow. But other people had coloring like that and they didn't send out a message, "I'm white and proud of it."

Strange. Anyhow, all of this registered in seconds, and then Rachel felt his rich, deep voice wrap around her mind.

"Tests are what we are really talking about here, my friends. Make no mistake, those little green huntids are a test, which is why it's so important how we handle them.

"As always when I speak, I'm assuming that you viewers are among The Righteous. As your spiritual leader, I bear witness to how well you do with your tests: Tests of idleness and sloth, tests of conformity. Are you a winner or a wimp? This is what you must ask yourself every day.

"When a test comes, will you let down your guard and become like *them*? Or will you fight like one of The Righteous and become a winner? I must tell you, the end days are near. Do your habits of service bring glory to The Lord? Then you will be among those who rejoice for all eternity. Helms's voice thundered so loud, Rachel covered her ears.

He continued, "Let me bring you some joyful news before I turn to the unpleasant subject that has brought us together today.

"The good news has to do with a number that you and I have long been dreaming of."

"Huh?" Rachel thought.

"Ten billion," thundered back Helms. "Yes, my friends. We are rapidly approaching the population size that will trigger the Second Coming. This is exciting news for which *you* can take credit, my friends throughout the world. And I'll tell you why.

"According to population experts, the latest calculation shows world population reaching 10 billion in less than two years time. Wonderful, isn't it?

"Back in the year 1800, humanity was primitive. Our population barely grew. It took more than a century to add just a billion people. Eventually birth rates gathered momentum. By 1999, we were up to six billion. By 2000, up to nine billion. Afterwards we lost some numbers because of A.I.D.S. and the War Against Terrorism. The year I founded The Righteous—you remember, that happened in 2005— by then, global population was back up to eight billion. Since then, my friends, population growth began to *accelerate*."

Helms gave a lusty smile. Rachel hated to admit this, but the man was sexy. The way he said *accelerate* sent a thrill of electricity straight down to her crotch.

"Strange, isn't it, how our forefathers worried about birth control? My friends, they tried to slow down the miracle of procreation and bring the size of families *down*. As late as the year 2010, experts predicted that it could take us all the way to 2050 before humanity would approach nine billion. Supposedly we wouldn't reach our full portion, 10 billion, for a hundred years or more.

"Now, you and I do not want to wait that long, do we? Do we?" The rich voice thundered.

"Not when it has been foretold that the Second Coming depends on our reaching that long-awaited number. No," Helms said. "We won't wait. We will not wait for even two more years. After all, are we wimps or are we winners?"

Rachel found herself Kegeling in self-defense. No, that was too sexual to do in front of Helms, who had such a spark he could make two sticks catch fire across a room. She would do biceps isometrics instead, pushing palm against palm.

Helms was saying, "So we have been doing our share, growing our families, sending the message all over the world to be fruitful and multiply.

"Nor have we stopped there. We can multiply ourselves, moving our minds in ceaseless prayer, dances of spirit, and ritual movements. Many among us are doing the spiritual work of two or three people. Indeed, we committed Christians do this every waking hour of every day. Some of us have perfected the use of our bodies to such a degree that it is nothing, nothing, for one of us to do the work of four or more people."

Helms bent down to the Blessed Bottle around his neck, a small yellow flask with a protruding straw. He took a small sip, then cast a sweet look heavenward before he swallowed. The camera captured this. Then a series of shots displayed different parts of the Reverend in slow motion:

Click. Helms' soft leather shoes were tapping a ritual dance.

Click. A rosary draped over the fingers of Helms' right hand. One thumb caressed a blue plastic bead; then his other fingers moved the necklace along so he could start to work a new bead.

Click. On Helms' left hand, the index finger stretched out, did seven small circles, paused. After a few seconds, the motion repeated. "Christian Mudra #5" is what that particular pattern was called. (Even an unbeliever like Rachel could recognize the more popular Christian Mudras; this one was supposed to bring total surrender of the mind to God.)

Click. Helms angled his head downwards, breaking his eye-lock on the camera. He finished a silent prayer, swallowed another helping of Holy Water from his

Blessed Bottle, and curved his lips into a dreamy smile. Drinking a prayer, this was called, as Rachel knew.

She thought, *At least you have to admit the man is coordinated.* Having practiced these movements for years must help. Helms was concentrating hard, despite (or maybe because of) being under the lights at a press conference. However he did it, no question but that right now Hickory Helms was multiplying himself fourfold. And with no apparent effort. No wonder he had followers who practically worshipped him as God!

"Do the math, friends," Helms said. "Then you'll understand why our news is so exciting. Close to one billion souls worldwide are members of The Righteous. What happens if the average believer does the work of two people? That's not three or four, only two. All that would take is adding one simple Beadwork or Footwork on a daily basis. Well, don't you see? That would give us the extra billion we need."

A close-up showed Helms' confident expression as he said, "We can reach our goal and reach it soon, barring any calamities."

For the second time in two days, Rachel realized, she was being mesmerized by a preacher's mouth. Helms' lips were cherry red, very long, with almost no upper lip at all, while his juicy, big lower lip seemed like a pool, where part of Rachel's mind wanted to dive in and go for a beautiful, long swim.

As if she was going to let herself fall into the trap of this demagogue's mouth! Next thing, she'd be dialing up The Righteous Hotline and sobbing onto Helms' TV show that she was born again and called to live as one of The Righteous. On his network, Channel 6, you could see scenes like that all day long. Forget it!

Helms was still speaking. "Now, back to the little green flies. A certain misguided preacher has recently called them harbingers of our Lord. 'Do not harm a wing of their precious little bodies,'" He mimicked Stacey Pilgrim's slow, Texas drawl.

"Consider the source of these comments! Shucks, let me come right out and say it. These huntids may come from the same source as she does. Anti-Christ flies. Yes, I'm a plain-speaking man, not a wimp. I am a winner, and proud of it.

"Friends, you've already heard my opinion of the so-called "Reverend" Stacey Pilgrim, the Anti-Christ of our day. No wonder she, of all people, is asking us to treat huntids like precious tahny creechurs.

"Coddle them while they what? Bring down famine upon our heads, causing millions of innocent Christians to starve? I think not." Helms was whispering now. It made Rachel's stomach feel numb with a nameless fear.

"Just say no," he bellowed suddenly. "Kill them. Kill them whenever you can."

While he leaned in for a tight close-up, Rachel seized upon the opportunity to focus on Hickory's stuck-out ears. She wouldn't let herself be intimidated by someone with ears like that!

"Let me tell you a new way to prove that you are among The Righteous. You can be a winner and pass this new test sent to us by God. Continue to do your Movements each day but also take a stand. Insist that the huntids be stopped. Call your Congressman. E-mail your President. This plague must be controlled before it grows any worse. Are you a wimp or a winner? Let's make 10 billion this year. With your help, my fellow Americans, it *can* be done."

"Rev. Helms?" "Rev. Helms?" shouted reporters from the press. He waved their questions aside.

"When the Lord comes to judge the quick from the dead, He will know which of you have helped in this great Cause. Stick together and be winners," Helms said.

Then with a sidelong glance at the cameras and press corps, he folded his massive forearms. "That's all. For those of you who are called, my message should be very simple. If you need me to explain it, you wouldn't understand anyway."

Pundits Donna and Dave came on next. But Rachel knew what she'd just seen without anyone explaining it to her. Already she was moving to turn off the set and call Jeremy.

Chapter 16
The Field Effect

Jeremy and Wayne stared in horror at the mesh cage. The largest cage in Research Lab One, it looked like a mesh aquarium built into the wall, with air circulating instead of water.

"I see what you mean," Jeremy said. "How could we let something like this catch us by surprise?"

Supposedly, the cage contained just a moderate quantity of huntids. Both men vaguely remembered the sight of them, streaking across the eight-foot cube of the cage, their bright lilac wings reminiscent of fireflies. Seemingly overnight the cage had become thick with the flies, a blur of shining, pulsating energy.

"I don't know. I just don't know." Wayne folded his arms across his chest and turned around, pushing his back against the cage door. "I've had so much to keep track of, testing how huntids could threaten crops plus doing our quantitative experiments with insecticides. I've had extra robots to program and dozens of temps to train as we go."

Jeremy tried to keep his voice even. "With your temps, when they came to this cage to get their specimens, who was keeping track of the numbers?"

"Me, except I wasn't. I mean, who expects reproduction patterns to change? I clocked the numbers when our first sample came in, June 26. We've had almost a month to observe the huntids, studying their life cycle, measuring how they ate, standard stuff. They seemed just like regular flies."

"So?"

"So you'd expect them to take 10 days to reproduce, give or take a couple days. Who would expect this big population explosion? The lab techs were handling so many other details."

Jeremy glared at him.

Wayne squirmed. "Look, I didn't want to bother you with all the small stuff, but I may as well tell you, all along the researchers have been acting real jumpy. I've caught them having conversations about coming down with Huntid Disease."

Jeremy said, "Since Hackenworth won't let us talk to anyone outside HHS, we can't tell staff much to reassure them, either."

"Really! I didn't want to add to your frustrations by complaining about my researchers' little gossip sessions. Besides, I've been handling it. The only thing is, being spooked means the techs have been changing lab gloves a dozen times a day, and some have even demanded to wear gas masks."

"Come now, do they think the huntids are a form of chemical warfare?"

"We've got a great team here, Jeremy, even the temps. But right or wrong, they're scared. And I guess I've been less sharp than usual too, trying to keep them together." Wayne shrugged apologetically.

Jeremy took another look at the swarming flies in the cage. "Let me get this straight," he said. "You and your guys are pussyfooting around, testing insecticide types and doses, taking out the standard experimental number for each trial—what, 25 huntids for each preliminary test? "

"Ten," Wayne said. "We wanted to be parsimonious with our samples, since all of them so far had to be flown in from Illinois."

"Ten, then."

"That's out of 10,000 we had originally. After a couple of weeks, though, I let the sample sizes go back to our default of 25. You know, it looked like we had plenty to go around." Catching Jeremy's frown, Wayne added, "Don't worry, I made records. I can look up when I started. A couple weeks ago, more or less."

"So you and your techs take the huntids out of this cage in Lab One."

"I do it, nobody else."

"You take huntids out for them then, how often? Ten times a day?"

"Yeah. I deal with their whining—"

"Come on, Wayne." Jeremy said, trying not to let his annoyance get out of control. "With all this, you never stop to see the number of huntids is fucking exploding? Today you suddenly notice the numbers are way over a million?"

"That's about the size of it." Wayne smiled apologetically. "We knew they didn't have natural enemies here, except for our experiments. The average housefly can reproduce after a week and it lives for a month. So we'd expect this population to go up, but if huntids were like houseflies that would be maybe 300,000 flies, minus the ones we removed."

"Apparently we wound up with more than you bargained for, Wayne."

"Soon as we finish talking, I'll take video footage. Then I can use software to work out a more exact total. I'll try to figure out what's happening."

"You do that." Jeremy said, and turned on his heel. Then he turned back, "Hey, Wayne, I apologize for exploding at you. I could have noticed this, too, but I didn't. You should get credit for being the first to think that the huntids could have abnormal reproduction patterns."

"Thanks. We'll find out why this is happening. There has to be a reason."

"At least we know one thing now. Remember when you showed me the data on all those insecticide studies? You said that huntids were no different from ordinary houseflies?"

"Yeah."

"I think we can now assume they're different."

Back in his office, Jeremy paced the worn gray carpet in front of his desk. Something was bothering him, an idea that teased his mind like a vague itch. What was it that he and Wayne were overlooking about that swirling mass of huntids in Cage One?

Jeremy seemed distant when Rachel called to tell him about Helms' press conference. "I saw it earlier this morning," he said, then pulled his lips into a friendlyish sort of smile.

"Why didn't you call me then?" Rachel said. "Shouldn't it work both ways? You expect me to call you."

"A lot was going on around here." Jeremy sounded weary. "Just had a meeting with my head researcher. Before that, Marty and I had to modem our finalized video to the White House PR guy. We saw the Helms press conference long before that, but I was too busy to call you. Since it had political ramifications for our department, all the managers watched."

"Why political ramifications?"

"Because we have to second-guess how Stavros is going to react—especially since he's now apparently one of The Righteous. We discussed whether Helms was making a grab for political power when he positioned himself as anti-huntid. And we're trying to forecast whether President Tucker is going to change his position, the one we thought he was going to take tomorrow."

"President Tucker, letting himself be pushed around by someone like Helms? Why, because Ol' Hickory Helms looks like a wrestler?"

"Rachel, it's a matter of strategy. Traditionals have staked out the pro-huntid side and The Righteous have pre-empted President Tucker by coming out as anti-huntid. What position is left for him? You know the man doesn't have a principle in his personal software, so we doubt that he's going to follow the country's leading political demagogue by sounding off with a meek little Amen."

"That's why you're worried?"

"Partly. There's also a very disturbing numbers problem I won't go into."

"I didn't know you'd already seen the Helms speech. I thought you'd want me to let you know," Rachel said in a small voice.

"Well, thanks," Jeremy said. "I just don't have time to chat right now. And, by the way, would you please stop examining my every utterance? I feel like you're sitting at that phone-screen with your hand on the close-up button."

Rachel took a deep breath. She switched her automatic reaction (fury) into a more Tanya-like pink pout. Maybe it wasn't gravitas but it worked. Her grump of a husband actually started to smile.

He said, "Why don't you tell me your version of what you noticed with Helms? If you don't mind my cleaning out some e-mails while we talk...."

He must have switched on "Transcript," because she could see him scroll through the print-only versions, opening up one icon after another.

Rachel pushed herself forward for a close-up, and angled her face to show off her eyelashes. "First of all, that Helms is so greasy. He has way too much personality. It rubs off on me after I see him, like I was draining fries and he was the grease that got left behind—kind of sexy but gross at the same time, if you know what I mean."

"So he bothers you more than Pilgrim?" Jeremy said. "She's the one who repulses me. With that fake-peaceful smirk on her face, she hardly looks human—no grease left behind after you touch her, no anything. For all we know, the woman has no bodily fluids."

Rachel laughed. "You've got a point. Pilgrim is so together, it's frightening. Jeremy, the whole thing is starting to scare me."

"Which whole thing do you mean?"

"The idea of Righteous sticking together and breeding like rabbits, feeling so sanctimonious and safe while their hands twirl around like pinwheels. Why shouldn't I worry? Maybe that's healthy. Don't you think that Helms and his loonies are way too secure, like what you said the other day about cults? The way they stick together reminds me of *The Godfather*. Remember—"

"Rachel, that's it! The sticking together." Jeremy looked as if he'd been struck by lightning. "You just gave me an idea. I've got to tell Wayne."

"Ooh, can't you tell me first?"

"Well, I'll try. When Wayne and I looked at a cage of huntids a while back, there were no interference patterns."

"What's interference patterns?"

"Usually, with a large number flies swarming in a confined area, they'll start moving in random directions, bumping into the sides of their cage and swerving to miss each other."

"But the huntids weren't?"

"No. As a matter of fact they swarmed in a very unusual way, all together. Picture one solid mass of huntids swirling in the same direction."

"Ooh," Rachel said. "Like synchronized swimming? Sounds like it could be beautiful."

"Beautiful like a tornado! Look, I don't know what to make of it yet. But I've got to go. Okay, my hothouse petunia?"

Well, that was progress, Rachel thought after he hung up the phone. If we can keep talking together, maybe our marriage can be saved.

Jeremy told Marty about the strange reproductive powers of Huntids, up from ten thousand to a million or more in less than a month.

Afterwards Wayne brought in an official estimate: 4,067,000. Jeremy pointed out the peculiar swirling pattern. "It's as if they're all linked in some mysterious way, focused like a plague of locusts. I want permission to stop extermination research for a day."

"Now that their population explodes, you're not worried about them any more?" Marty asked sarcastically, his black eyes impenetrable as ever.

"I have a theory that the huntids' population growth might be linked to this field effect we observe in their flight patterns. Maybe they're reacting collectively to our extermination procedures."

Marty leaned forward and gestured for him to continue. He didn't seem tipsy, but then he never did. Still, right now Marty's alcoholism was the least of Jeremy's problems.

"When I watch the huntids swirl together, it reminds me of physics on the level of quantum mechanics, as though the huntids have consciousness like a field. You know, if you kill them here, they pop up there. Only with the huntids, their numbers increase when they pop back up."

"Why?" Marty said. "To make up for the lack? They're pretty, Jeremy. But let's not get sentimental over some little purple flies."

"Well, I know this sounds crazy, but I think their shift in reproduction is a response to their slaughter."

"And what's supposed to account for that? Some kind of protest march, hmm? Let's see. To show their disapproval, the flies threw away their birth control pills?"

"Not a protest." Jeremy fought the urge to scratch his arms. "Marty, I'm not into anthropomorphism, if that's what you're implying. The huntid population's exploding; that's a statistical fact."

"It does bear watching, obviously."

"Look, Marty, I asked Wayne to do a retrospective analysis using the video monitoring of Lab One. Only the default security camera was used, not the three we have going now. Still, even if his results aren't 100 percent accurate, they're still pretty shocking."

"Well?"

"He's correlated their population bursts in Lab One with the approximate times when Lab Two was doing insecticide trials."

"And?"

"Shortly after each batch is killed, the number of huntids in Lab One has grown in a consistent manner. When research techs took out 10 at a time, about 100 huntids appeared in the cage. That's 10 times 10. When researchers took out 25, then 625 appeared, which happens to be 25 squared. It's exponential, see?"

"What I'd like from you," Marty said, "is fewer theories and more monitoring."

"I'm with you all the way," Jeremy said. "We'll keep counting on the hour, around the clock. Then we'll exterminate a batch of 10 and see what happens in Lab One over the next 24 hours. If my theory proves correct, the extermination process itself is what makes these insects multiply abnormally." His arms were itching like crazy. To keep from scratching, Jeremy jumped up and paced in front of Marty's desk.

"Don't you see? If that's true, Rich's plan for extermination is the most dangerous thing we could do."

Marty said, "Perhaps we should call Rich and ask that he put off President Tucker's press conference in the light of our findings."

"Good luck!" said Jeremy. "How interested do you think he'll be in anything we could say? Or Tucker?"

"Well let's see what Hackenworth thinks. I'll call him now. Stick around—I want you in on this."

When the call went through, Hackenworth had such an enormous smile plastered all over his face, Marty and Jeremy exchanged a quick questioning glance. Otherwise, his image over the phone looked normal, pretentious but normal. The CIA director sat on his state-of-the-art suspension sofa, which made him appear to hover halfway up the 10-foot phone screen. Hackenworth's suspenders and bow tie were an attractive shade of periwinkle, but Jeremy thought his smile made him look more sinister than ever.

Marty deftly summarized the research, using a practiced deference that Jeremy found sickening. "Cooper," Marty concluded. "Should we tell President Tucker, or Rich? What's your opinion?"

In an ice-cold voice, Hackenworth answered, "Whatever happens with your research makes little difference to us, frankly, so long as you work to destroy the huntids. This crisis is our President's chance to tell the American people that he'll keep them safe. Incidentally, we've named your baby for you. We're calling it Project Exterminate. You might even make the news with it. Congratulations."

Marty gave one of his tiny bows.

Jeremy couldn't stand it. "What about these new facts?" he said. "Don't you see the danger if President Tucker goes on record in favor of extermination? Later he may have to back down."

Hackenworth gave a little snort of disapproval. Jeremy continued, "However inconvenient it may be to you, we've discovered some startling new facts about huntid reproduction. If you take even a few minutes to examine them, you'll find them extremely troubling."

Marty cleared his throat. "You do give the impression of being in a considerable hurry over this project. Is there something you're not telling us?"

"Gentlemen, it has all been decided and there's nothing further to discuss. Of course we expect you to continue keeping us informed of any new developments. And did we mention how very much President Tucker and I appreciate that you took the time to report to us today?" Hackenworth hung up.

Marty and Jeremy stared at each other. "To report to us?" Marty asked.

"I heard that, too." Jeremy said. "Since when is the CIA director so buddy-buddy with President Tucker?"

Chapter 17
Averting a Crisis

Like Jeremy, Rachel planned to watch President Tucker's Friday morning press conference. Because she planned to do a ballet workout at the same time, she positioned herself at the side of the living room sofa, holding the crimson leather like a barre. A glance at the wall mirror confirmed that she was picture perfect in her Size Four pink leotard and white tights. Smiling, Rachel voice-commanded the TV to turn on.

Weekly press conferences with the President, as mandated by law, must include a 30-minute Q&A at the end. Unlike Helms or Pilgrim, President Tucker couldn't get away with a quick speech that ignored unrehearsed questions. All this would take time, during which Rachel wasn't going to sit like a couch potato; she chose a tummy-toning, leg-firming routine from one of her favorite workout seminars, "Ballet Body." Even her timing was perfect this morning—when the show came into focus Rachel saw that Tucker's speech had just begun.

"Ladies and gentlemen of the press, viewers across this great nation of ours, it is my pleasure to meet with you personally on this historic day. Do not expect a routine press conference. Today I have exciting news. . . with a surprise at the end." Saying that, Tucker beamed his charming smile into homes across America. Pundits, at least, called his smile charming; Rachel called it sleazy.

So was his white hair, far as Rachel was concerned. It looked utterly fake, besides being out of style. White hair had once been a fad, but when, ten years ago? Well, on to her Ballet-Robics with some good, thigh-toning plies.

Tucker was burbling away. "My friends, I am here to tell you that a crisis has threatened this great and good land of ours—but we have found a solution."

The camera zoomed in for a close-up. "Terrorists have bred a dangerous new insect and brought it to American soil. This biological weapon against our nation is called huntids." Tucker's deep voice made the name sound sinister.

"The bugs appear like ordinary houseflies, but make no mistake. They have been genetically altered. Their wings are colored a sickly purple, their bodies a completely unnatural shade of green." Tucker gestured to technicians to show a vid-clip while he kept talking. Footage showed a field where huntids rose out of the mud, then swarmed over the corn.

"Thanks to CIA reports, we know that huntids are part of a stealth campaign of biological warfare. Who is responsible? Are they fundamentalist Muslims, Chinese communists, African radicals, a South American drug cartel? I will not publicize you by naming you publicly, but we know who you are and I'll warn you not to try this again. Next time, America's retaliation on you will be swift and deadly. This time, we'll just foil your plan by wiping out these insects." Tucker snapped his fingers dismissively.

Oh brother, Rachel thought as she held a deep plié for the full three-minute count, *the man sure plays it cool for such a fear monger. Like the huntids are really a terrorist threat!*

As if responding to her skepticism, the camera zoomed in for a close-up. The President's habitual expression of concern deepened to an extra-grim severity. "Maybe you wonder what the huntids have done since first spotted by our investigators. I'll show you footage from the United States Department of Health and Human Services. Research from these scientists proves that huntids were designed to cause pestilence."

The next vid-clip showed a close-up of an ear of corn, peeled back to reveal mostly yellow kernels. *That's the worst example they could find?* Rachel thought. *Ooh, a nasty brown spot.*

Tucker's voice rose. "If we let these disease-carrying pests live among us, entire cornfields will be devastated, like this one."

The telescreen showed a field of healthy, normal corn. One by one, the ears unwrapped themselves, each one showing the same kind of blemish. Obviously the image was supposed to scare you. But these days animation could do anything. *Since when did ears of corn in a field do a striptease, for crying out loud?*

Tucker returned to the screen, his sleek white hair gleaming. "Yes, this infestation amounts to a serious attack on our national security. If we leave these pests to themselves, they will swarm over America's farmland like a plague of locusts.

"But there's more. Terrorists have genetically altered these flies to hurt America in two different ways. Besides the threat of famine, these living weapons of destruction cause something called Huntid Disease. The first stage creates secretions... of a very unconventional color." Here Tucker looked repulsed. *Easy for him to do*, Rachel thought, as she thrust her leg into a glorious, painful arabesque. *"Repulsive" could be his middle name.*

"Regarding the second stage of Huntid Disease, we're not yet certain how serious it is."

On came a vid-clip of a hospital ward. Each bed contained a sleeping patient. *Could be mumps, for all we know,* thought Rachel.

"Bear in mind, no deaths have been reported yet, and the seriousness of this Huntid Disease won't matter for long because we *will* destroy them."

Tucker smiled reassuringly, like a strict but loving father. "Huntids, clearly, must be destroyed. Under my administration, we have built up strong defense capabilities. I'm calling for a program called Project Exterminate, with a team headed by Stavros Menelakos, Secretary of Health and Human Services."

Tucker pointed to a stern-looking man with a heavy beard. Then cameras shifted to show an image of three huntids. It filled the screen, and the huntids were blown up so big you could see their eyes. Their eyes were red.

The sight gave Rachel the creeps. She'd have to ask Jeremy if that was their real eye color or another special effect courtesy of presidential propaganda. Fortunately for her state of mind, a dopey jingle came on in the background and the visuals switched to a colorful banner, like something you might see on the Internet. Individual words lit up while animated letters appeared to sing their slogan to a catchy tune:

> August 29, 2020.
> Project Exterminate.
> While your country protects you
> Stay indoors and play it safe.

After the singing stopped, President Tucker cleared his throat and announced, "My fellow Americans, today is the official start of a bold new campaign of public education. Labor Day Week, one of our most treasured national holidays, will take place as always this year, on August 29 to September 4, but on the first day, we will take care of this little extermination project. All you citizens need to do is stay home. While you're safe indoors, planes flown by the National Guard will spray enough insecticide to crush the huntids forever.

"My friends, this is a designer insecticide," Tucker added reassuringly. "It will not, repeat *not*, harm our crops. Nor will it damage our water. This special formula is safe for people, only we prefer not to put it to the test.

"Just five weeks from today, America can enjoy a day of quiet reflection and prayer. When we go back outside, all danger will be gone." As he smiled paternally, Rachel switched sides on the couch, using the armrest to position herself for the second half of her Ballet-robics.

That wasn't so bad, she thought, except that she and Jeremy weren't wild about pesticides. There could be side effects for the environment, even though a greed-based guy like Turner wouldn't notice anything wrong until CEO's dropped dead in the streets.

Meanwhile, Tucker turned to face the camera for another close-up. His white hair glowed in the spotlight as he gave a self-satisfied chuckle. "Call it the crisis that wasn't. Another administration might have solved the problem and left it there. But, as you know, our administration is famous for anticipating problems, too. So I'm proud to announce an exciting new initiative.

"As you may have heard from recent media reports, our nation's two leading ministers have publicly taken positions about the huntids. The Rev. Stacey Pilgrim has told the American people that we need to coddle her precious tiny creatures. Well, with all respect, I must point out that her approach runs totally counter to science, not to mention common sense. Here's my advice, folks. If you see one of these pests, swat it like a common mosquito. Unless you want to show the world that you worship terrorists. In that case, by all means, get down on your knees, bow down and pray.

"Really, now, all you Traditionals, I sympathize with the desire to spread your religion, even if you're so desperate that you find allies among disease-carrying pests. And, of course, like every other God-fearing Christian, I sympathize with your desire to seek signs of the Lord. Nothing could be more American. 'In God we trust.' That's right on the money!

"As for Rev. Hickory Helms, I couldn't agree with him more that the huntids must be destroyed. Our great nation is vastly superior to any military force on the face of the earth, but America has spent this century fighting terrorism and the battle ain't over yet."

Tucker paused. Rachel stood still. Something big was coming, she could feel it.

"My fellow Americans, earlier today I promised to share a surprise with you. Here it is. Look at what I'm holding in my hand." He unfolded his left palm. Rachel gasped. President Steven D. Tucker was holding pink beads of The Righteous.

Slowly he put on the necklace, then said, "I am proud to tell you that I am one of The Righteous. Have been. Will continue to be."

"And now, members of the press, I invite your questions."

Following a stunned silence, reporters began to wave their hands and scream out, "Mr. President," "Mr. President." Rachel sat on the couch, curling her legs against her, nearly in fetal position. Numbly she listened to the Q&A.

A reporter asked, "How long, President Tucker, have you been among The Righteous?"

"Long before I took office my first term, I reckon," he said casually.

"Why didn't you make this public before?"

"Wasn't the time. But it has always been my plan to prepare America for the Second Coming." With a confiding smile, he added, "For as long as I've lived in the White House, I've found an hour each day to pray and multiply myself. Usually I work with the beads you see here." He started working them with his right hand.

A second frenzied reporter was recognized. "Mr. President, now that you've come out as one of The Righteous, do you plan to wear your beads in public?"

"Hadn't thought about it," he said. "I'm a simple man. Don't think much about image. You're right, though. Might as well." He grinned into the camera. "In fact, I invite all my fellow Americans to do the same. Let's show our true strength throughout the land."

From another reporter: "Just how many in your administration share your beliefs, President Tucker?"

"Let's see, Vice President Quinn, of course. When we ran for office, it was our little secret that we'd try to make America more like what's in the Bible."

Reporters were screaming their questions now. Rachel needed a drink. She ran to the kitchen and poured one of Jeremy's Coca Colas into a tall glass. Full-sugar Coke was all they had in the house—who cared? She needed something strong. And some chocolate chip cookies. Forget a plate; she took the whole bag in with her to the living room, ripped it open, and started shoving whole cookies into her mouth.

When she looked up from the couch, a reporter was asking a new question, something about Tucker's presidential cabinet.

"Funny you should ask," Tucker was saying. "As part of our decisive action against the huntids, we're taking measures to bring America's cabinet up to date. Yes, I have some new appointments to announce."

"But Mr. President—" sputtered the reporter.

"You know the existing positions," Tucker said, a stern note creeping into his voice. "Well, Vice President Quinn and I have decided to make some changes."

"But Mr. President—"

"Do you want me to tell you or not?"

"Yes, of course, Mr. President."

"We're keeping all the old 15 cabinet seats but one. That old position, Secretary of the Environment, is no longer needed. As you may recall, it was developed by President Stilton when he split up the former Department of the Interior into three seats: Minorities, Intellectual Property, and Environment. Last term, I cut out those first two. Since our problems with pollution and such are a thing of the past, I don't think we need to waste a cabinet seat on Environment any more, so I've asked for the resignation, effective today, of Secretary Habib. And he has offered it. Imram Habib will be taking a position in the private sector, I believe.

Tucker gestured to a side wall of the auditorium. Habib, wearing a cheesy smile, waved to the crowd.

"Today I am proud to announce the appointment of three new cabinet members. First, meet our new Secretary of Communication. Although I'm no missionary, I share Rev. Pilgrim's idea that when you have the truth, it comes with an obligation to share it. In my humble way, I'm doing that by example with this appointment.

"Historically, The Righteous have drawn their membership from those who have heard the call. Yet, I believe that people across this great land of ours who search their souls will hear that call now, even if you've never heard it before. My fellow Americans, with your help, we can actively add to our numbers. And so I am pleased to introduce to you a Righteous man who needs no introduction. His past job performance confirms that he is both articulate and committed to spreading the truth. His name is Rich Davis; he's my former Press Secretary."

A surprisingly young man, African-bloodstream (and with very sexy jaws, Rachel noted) smiled at the reporters. Dexterously he pulled a blue rosary out from the trousers of his three-piece suit. With a gesture that mingled humility and pride, he smoothed the beads around his neck.

Several members of the press corps, who seemed to know him, applauded loudly.

"Second," continued President Tucker, "Meet our new Secretary of Intelligence. As foreign invaders scheme to overtake our land, it behooves us to have a seasoned member of the intelligence community in our cabinet. Meet Cooper Hackenworth, my long-time friend and director of the Central Intelligence Agency. I'm also pleased to count him among The Righteous."

Hackenworth wore matching suspenders and belt, both made of a soft red calfskin. The quirky outfit looked strange, Rachel thought, when accessorized by the ruby-red beads of his necklace. Hackenworth caressed it with long, bony fingers as he posed for the cameras.

"Last but definitely not least," President Tucker said, "I am honored to appoint our first Secretary of Religion. Yes, America remains a country of total religious freedom, with clear separation of Church and State. Yet the line between them blurs, especially during these End Days on earth. We need a voice to speak for the devout to represent *all* Americans of faith.

"This representative would, of course, have to personally follow a religion. His religion would not be the official religion of our great nation, like a pope. Friends, our country already has more religions than you could shake a stick at—some Americans even exercise their freedom of religion by following none at all. And that is their choice in this great nation of ours.

"Given our situation, I thought long and hard about who would be the best person for this essential new leadership position. Let me share my reasoning with you. We live in a democratic nation. Well, The Righteous are America's majority religion. So my choice was clear. I am only grateful that Rev. Hickory Helms has graciously agreed to lead us."

Sure enough, the camera showed Rev. Helms entering the side of the room. Both hands moved separately, in prayer, but he recognized the cameras with a winning smile and a bow.

"No further questions for today," President Tucker said. "We have much to celebrate." As he turned away from the podium, Rachel saw him work his beads.

Chapter 18
Perfect Timing

"That's rich!" Jeremy gasped. Marty, Wayne and he were watching in the conference room. "Hackenworth doesn't have a religious bone in his body."

"Do any of them?" Marty said serenely. "It's all for show."

He stood up, offering to bring everyone coffee. Wayne and Jeremy declined, exchanging looks. While he was out of the room, undoubtedly pouring himself a Breathless cocktail, Wayne said to Jeremy, "This looks bad."

Jeremy rubbed his shoulders, more out of habit than genuine itch; his entire body felt numb. "Now we know why they needed to take their official positions by today. Project Exterminate is mostly an excuse for Tucker's version of a religious coup d'etat. Guess being President isn't enough. "No Pope" my eye! Through Helms, isn't that exactly what Tucker's doing, crowning himself as Pope?"

"Hold on," Wayne protested. "We still have Republicans and Democrats, don't we?"

"What difference does that make? If The Righteous can claim a political majority, they can do anything they want—shut down our lab, turn all of HHS into a giant extermination company, you name it."

"I can't help feeling a little responsible," Wayne muttered.

"You? Come on."

"Well, if I hadn't passed along the leak to Marnie and Rev. Pilgrim, maybe the religious part of this mess wouldn't have happened."

Jeremy shook his head. "Not enough for Helms and Pilgrim to have their own TV networks and theme parks and God knows what else—now they have to appropriate politics, too. But don't blame yourself, Wayne. Stevie Tucker just admitted he's been planning this religious takeover long before he announced it publicly.

Wayne said, "How can it be legal for all the members of his cabinet to belong to The Righteous?"

Jeremy shrugged. "I know. And it's hard to get over Tucker's new buddies, Stavros and Hackenworth—plus Rich Davis, Mr. Religiosity himself."

"Do you think the Secretary of the Environment had to resign for religious reasons?" Wayne asked.

"Is the Pope Catholic?—Unless Tucker made him convert, too."

"Between you and me," Wayne said, "I liked my wife a lot better before she started wearing a five-pounder."

Marty came into the room carrying a steaming mug. "So how do you think our fine colleague from the CIA looks in a necklace?"

"Spare me." Jeremy said. "I think I may have to go and vomit for several hours. Seriously, is it alright with you if I take sick leave for the rest of today?"

"Me, too," Wayne said. He did look terrible.

"Certainly," Marty said. "Still I hope that otherwise you fellows will stay cool and bide your time. Politically astute men have had to do this in ages far worse than this. Strive for equanimity, or at least the appearance of equanimity."

Easy for you to say, you do-nothing coward. Besides, you're drunk. Jeremy took care to keep his lips firmly shut. "Thank you for the advice," he said.

Ironically, he thought, as he opened the door for Wayne, Marty didn't look a bit stewed. Whereas Wayne and Jeremy were so shaken, they practically wobbled as they walked out the door.

"It stinks," Rachel muttered into the phone. She was wearing a very flattering violet silk unitard... and a scowl. On this sunny Monday morning, Brent was off in his bedroom playing Triple Decker Monopoly with Tom. She was out of earshot, in her computer room.

"It really stinks," she repeated, waiting for Heather to ask for details.

After a long silence, Heather giggled, "You're so funny. What are you complaining about now, some big smelly old cheese?" Heather was wearing fuzzy yellow pajamas and a sleepy smile.

"I've just had the most horrible weekend."

"Oh," said Heather, reaching for a hairbrush. "Isn't it annoying about all the political stuff? It ruined my TV, too. I hate those urgent news bulletins. And those pundits! Like who cares if President Tucker wants to become part of The Righteous? He's entitled, isn't he?" She started stroking her long blonde hair with the brush.

"Well, I think it's a pretty hideous situation, actually. But I figured that Jeremy and I could use it to turn things around for us."

Heather looked interested. "What do you mean?"

"You know, in war movies, how the sexual tension heats up?"

"We're not at war, are we?"

"No, we're just in Project Exterminate, which my husband's in charge of, and who knows if he's going to be pressured to pretend to become one of The Righteous now, like his boss's boss? Besides that, Jeremy's worried about Tucker. I am, too. As many thinking people are, Heather. Anyway, over the weekend I figured . . . in all the old classic World War II movies, people who are really in love became very, you know, passionate.

"So what happened at your house?" Heather brushed her hair faster.

"Nothing, I can assure you. Plus Jeremy made a new rule, no TV while he's home. He said that from now on he wants to rest until this huntid thing is history."

"That's annoying. But I wouldn't take the sex thing personally. Some people just lose their appetite under stress. It's like eating. When life looks ugly, some people want to eat like pigs. Others can't stomach a thing. You know," Heather said, popping out a dimple. "That's how you can tell the naturally slender people from the natural chubbos."

Rachel had expected sympathy from her friend, not some smug reminder of how different from her Heather was, with her effortless perpetual Size Two. Neither did Rachel want to think about all the cookies and ice cream she had gulped down this weekend. Of course, she couldn't argue with Heather. Rachel needed a friend, especially now. To her horror, though, she heard herself say:

"Heather, sometimes I wish you'd grow up. Is looking good all you think matters in life? Can't you ever think about something else? This political stuff could be very serious. Nothing like it has ever happened before in the history of our country. Plus bugs in weird colors are flying around—personally I don't think they're poisonous or anything, but aren't you even a little bit concerned?"

"I'm concerned when someone I thought was a friend starts yelling at me first thing in the morning. You start off complaining that your life stinks? Well, how about mine? You don't even wait to hear about me and my problems. Who do you think I am, your Health Services worker?"

"No, but I thought I could talk with you as an adult, not to mention my friend. Like, you might have some intelligent thoughts about our current situation. For instance, you're a mom, too. What do you think is going to happen when school starts in September, assuming we're not all blown up by Project Exterminate?"

"President Tucker didn't say anything about doing exterminations in the schools."

"Come on, Heather. Think. Tucker just took his whole presidential cabinet and stacked it with people from his same group of religious fanatics. What's to keep him from doing the same thing to our schools? What's in store for our kids, a new curriculum based on Hickory Helms' annotated Bible?"

"Oh, can't you lighten up just for once?"

"What if, come September, Ashley asks you to buy her school supplies and right on the top of the list, Bam!, beads of The Righteous. Your whole life could change right under your nose. What's wrong with you, girl? You'd pay more attention to a pimple."

Heather's eyes narrowed. "Don't call me 'Girl.'"

Rachel felt sick inside. She couldn't afford to lose her only friend. Heather looked really steamed, too. She blurted out, "Admit it, Rachel. This is all about sex. Maybe instead of complaining to me, you should buy yourself a vibrator. You know what? If you can't be more fun as a friend, don't bother to call."

The phone screen went blank.

For the next hour or two, Rachel walked around numbly. When the phone rang, she was curled up on the living room couch, watching TV while she could—before her husband came home to pull his tyrant routine and turn off the set.

Maybe this new call was Heather, apologizing. Or maybe Jeremy had something unexpectedly hot on his mind. Wouldn't that be great! She'd settle for his saying anything that she didn't have to pry out of him.

"Marguerite, of all people!" Rachel recognized her old friend's diamond-shaped face as soon as it popped up on the screen.

"How wonderful that you called," Rachel continued. "We haven't talked in years. Let's see, you left when Brent was three, right?" Marguerite's eyebrows were so distinctive, just like Spock's in the legendary "Star Trek" show—straight and thick and slanted upward. Rachel was so busy trying not to stare at those stubborn-looking unwaxed brows, she forgot to return Marguerite's friendly grin.

"OK, Rachel, what's going on? Why have you been on my mind all morning?"

Leave it to Marguerite to dispense with the small talk. Suddenly Rachel remembered that her feelings about this old friend were pretty mixed.

Marguerite was incredibly smart. Despite her vast intellectual prowess and her gazillion accomplishments, Rachel's one-time best buddy was a rotten correspondent. After moving away from Capitol City, Marguerite had dropped Rachel like a hot potato—unless you counted one brag e-mail family newsletter every Christmas as keeping in touch, which Rachel didn't.

On the other hand, there was a warm loving feeling because, years ago, Marguerite had been Rachel's best friend. They met in a neighborhood playgroup when Brent was just a baby. Eight mothers had been in that group, including Heather. By the time Brent was four, all the moms except Heather had either moved away or dropped the friendship. Marguerite had been the first to move; in fact, she had moved several times since then, all places out west like the exclusive Sedona neighborhood in Greater Tucson, and now Washington West.

You bond in a deep way when you race after your babies together, half asleep and snacking like maniacs, since breastfeeding make you so hungry. What wonderful talks the mom group used to have, all first-time mothers who were idealistic about doing the job *right*. What was the best way to feed, to potty train, to put kids to bed? There were a thousand things to do right or wrong, and like all the other women in her playgroup, Rachel had no help from her own mother or mother-in-law, both of whom lived far away. So the playgroup moms had become mothers to each other, mothers to their own children and (Rachel had expected) friends for life.

Beyond that, Marguerite had been Rachel's only friend from the group who had more going for her than her expected beauty, faith, and domestic accomplishments. In the eight years since Rachel had left the workplace to take care of her son, the only friend she'd made who was intellectually challenging was Marguerite. Now her small hazel eyes twinkled like little lasers; the woman was almost too bright to be human.

Rachel popped out a dimple and said, lightly as possible, "You called because I was on your mind?"

Marguerite laughed, her quicksilver effortless laugh. "That's right, your face kept appearing in my mind. After the third time I said, 'OK, I got the message. I'm supposed to call Rachel.'"

Rachel couldn't imagine what Marguerite meant about her face appearing, without the benefit of a telescreen. Maybe she didn't want to know. Marguerite freaked her out, sometimes. Still, her old friend's call couldn't have been better timed.

Rachel poured our her heart: Stuck in a marriage in which her husband became more distant every day, whether he was having an affair or not. Stuck in the dead-end non-job of being a housewife in the 2020's. Now this stuff about President Tucker's helping The Righteous take over America made Rachel feel more powerless than ever. She talked at length, and it was incredibly therapeutic because she could feel that, for once, the person at the other end of the conversation was actually listening. "I feel so stuck," she concluded.

"Why don't you get unstuck?"

"You think that's easy? What are you doing with *your* life?"

Marguerite said she was busy teaching camping skills to her son Gilavael.

"Does your husband still travel a lot?"

"Oh, Gregory? Sure, he's still doing urban planning with a vengeance. Not that I'm complaining. He makes good money, I invest it. And he comes home about every three months and stays a couple of weeks before going away again—to So. America, mostly. You can see why I've got to make sure I keep plenty going on."

"Like what? Anything else besides the camping?"

"Well, I'm involved in making art, as usual. Since the last time we talked—when, a couple of Christmases ago?—I went through a glass-blowing phase. Then I learned to do a little carpentry and some dried flower arrangements. What else? Oh yes, I tried Plastiglow sculptures. Hilarious! Remember when that new sculpting medium came out years ago, so you could make funny statues with the look of a life-sized cartoon? And I've met a spiritual teacher named John Wilcox, whom I've studied with for about two years, which has been very interesting. Then there was the whole job of setting up a garden for this house. When we moved here, a couple of years ago, there was no landscaping at all, can you believe it?

"Speaking of gardening," Rachel asked, "there's been a lot of talk around here about a pesky new bug. Have you been seeing them?

"What, the huntids? Gil and his friends dug a couple of them up last week. I found them interesting."

"Scary? Sinister?"

"Not in the least. I think the huntid scare may be some kind of media ploy."

"It sure seems real enough here."

"You know, Rachel, when you live in Capitol City, life is a little more media-ish."

"True. What do you think about President Tucker's newfound faith. And that cabinet?"

"Not much. John wasn't surprised by it at all. Rachel, people think differently outside Capitol City. If you come out here, maybe you'll find that you can get away from it all."

"Come out there? Is that why you called, to invite me to visit you?" Rachel's face lit up with amazement.

"That was my guidance. Maybe it would be fun for you—and Brent. Gil still asks about him, you know."

Rachel's heart beat wildly. "What a coincidence. Lately I've been so disgusted with Jeremy. Just this morning I was thinking, when Brent turns 10, in a year and a half, I just might do something wild and spontaneous—like pack him into the car with me and go off on an adventure somewhere--anywhere.

Marguerite laughed.

"What's so funny?"

"Did you hear yourself, Rachel? That word 'spontaneous.'"

"Well, I think I'm a very spontaneous person."

"In a year and a half? What, exactly, to the day?"

"Oh, I see what you mean."

"Why don't you just do it? Jump in your car. Do it now."

Maybe absence would make Jeremy's heart grow fonder—and perhaps Rachel wasn't as successful as she wished at hiding her dependence on him. Back in the "Becoming Pinkness" seminar, Tanya had said, "When you're distant, it's as attractive as a rosy pink glow in a sunset. Don't be afraid to go far away and draw your man to you. Distance will fill his heart with yearning."

So Rachel called Marguerite an angel and expressed her hope that an extended visit could help her and Jeremy to become closer in the long run.

They worked out a plan for a month-long trip; Rachel would check with Jeremy and get back to Marguerite in a couple of days.

"This is so exciting!" Rachel said. "And the timing is perfect."

"Your color looks better, that's for sure," Marguerite said. "When you first switched on the phone, I thought I was seeing a ghost. The Wild West will do you good." In that moment, Rachel felt as though they were sisters. To hang up, she made the extra effort to reach for the "Fade" setting. Their smiles met as their telescreen images turned to pastels, then blackness.

Chapter 19
Professional Advancement

Rachel was so excited, she could hardly keep from calling Jeremy on the spot, but prudently she decided to set a scene. She'd dress up, then time her announcement until after Brent went to bed. You never knew what might strike Jeremy as romantic. If only they could get back to the habit of making love more often, he could become her One-a-Day Vitamin. Wouldn't that be something!

As she put in her Mist Diffusion rollers, Rachel examined her face in the mirror alcove. Their master bedroom had cute double sinks with ultra- vanities, plus glam lighting. It made her look larger than life and (if she dared say so herself) drop-dead gorgeous. Rachel's best feature was her eyes, with their rare shade of golden brown enhanced by full, sensuous lids. But looking at herself again critically, she stopped at her funny little angled eyebrows. *Gravitas may not be your thing, girl. You look like Meg Ryan, not Greta Garbo.*

Putting the rollers at the back of her head was tricky; it took at least seven of them, placed just so, to create the proper degree of lift. Even if her brows were skimpy, at least they were high, and her cheeks were spectacular. Women paid good Health Credits for implants so they could make their cheeks look like hers—not that they knew they were aiming for a Rachel Murphy look.

Her nose was wide; at least in profile it tilted up nicely. Unfortunately, the mirror alcove also revealed how much Rachel's chin stuck out. When a chin was as small as hers, and pointy, at least it could have the decency not to stick out so much. The only thing about her face that embarrassed Rachel more was how much her gums showed when she smiled. Sighing, Rachel began to spray her hair with its final coating of Flexi-Hold Womanly Lacquer. Brent came to the door.

"Mom, where's my magnifying glass? And could I have a juice glass from the kitchen?"

A real glass, made of the breakable stuff, was what he wanted. Luckily Rachel had one. What did he and Tom want this for? Better not ask, she decided.

She took her fiddle from its case and played part of a pretty Vivaldi concerto that she remembered from years before. Maybe her only way to be a half-decent violinist was to play music she knew by heart, and never again try to figure out puzzles like that impossible Satie.

By the time she called the kids for lunch, Rachel was so much better that she felt up to her usual self-imposed task of giving Brent and his playdate an extra activity—some age-appropriate treat to make them feel special. Inventing them was one of life's great pleasures for Rachel, just like the hour of "King Time" she gave Brent every day, where he'd get to choose what the two of them played.

What would today's special treat be? Rachel decided to make the boys a waffle game: After cooking the waffles, she'd set out small dishes of goodies for them to put in the little compartments: peanut butter, honey butter, different shades of jelly, and ketchup—almost as sweet as jelly but with better shock value.

The boys being nowhere in the house, she looked for them in the yard and found them on the driveway, huddled over something. "Okay, big shots, what are you doing?"

"Frying bugs," Tom told her, cheerfully.

"What?"

Brent explained, "You take one of the ants from the garden and trap it under this juice glass. I'm holding the glass down, see? Then Tom takes the magnifying glass. He concentrates it and concentrates it until it starts to burn—

"So we can fry anything. Isn't that great?" Tom said.

Rachel put her hands on her hips. "You know, in this family, Thomas, we don't kill things just for fun. How many ants have you boys been roasting?"

Gleefully the boys counted, scrunching up their foreheads and wiggling their fingers. "Seven," Brent said finally. "And now we're heating up one, just to let it store energy. We'll let it go before it burns—it's one of those green flies."

"What?" shrieked Rachel. She grabbed the glass from Brent and lifted it up. The huntid flew upwards. It was okay, whew!

"He landed on your head, Mom," Brent said, swatting. Fast as a humming bird, its lilac wings hovered near the back of his hand. When Brent held his wrist still, the huntid perched. Tom reached for it, steadying his own hand, and the shiny fly alighted right on Tom's extended fingertip. The three of them watched silently, as if under a spell.

Rachel spoke first, trying to keep the fear out of her voice. "How can you get him off you, Tom?"

Instantly he started jiggling around like the frantic little eight-year-old he was—and acted like most of the time. The huntid flew away.

Rachel must have looked confused because Brent offered her an explanation: "It's easy, Mom. Soon as you start moving, they fly off. I've known that about that forever."

"Forever," she said. "Uh-huh."

On her way back to the house, Rachel turned around and asked, "Where did you boys find that huntid?"

"We have a zillion in our back yard. Come, I'll show you, " Brent said, leading her to a plot of purple impatiens.

"I'll be darned! There are loads of them just in this one flower bed."

"Our garden has always been great for insects, Mom. It has all the earthworms and ants you could want. I think the huntids fit right in."

"I'm not so sure, guys." Rachel realized that she was shaking inside. "Tom, it's time to go home."

Lunch with Brent was demoted to plain peanut butter and jelly sandwiches. As she put them together, Rachel psyched herself up for a serious talk, which she started as soon as they sat down to eat. "Brent, you are not to fry ants on the pavement—ever. Since when did you get the idea it was okay to torture animals?"

He returned her stare with his turned-off look and started breaking the crusts off his sandwich.

Rachel warned, "Don't touch huntids, either. People say they cause a disease." Infuriated by Brent's indifference Rachel lectured on, using her Official Parent Voice. Inwardly she realized that she had a strange feeling about the huntids, that they weren't dangerous at all but holy—whatever that meant.

That afternoon, Jeremy had a senior staff meeting with the two proud new Cabinet appointees, Rich Davis and Cooper Hackenworth. False compliments were being passed back and forth like a cold, and Jeremy noticed with some amusement that Stavros had developed an interesting new way of glowering at Hackenworth. At one point, Davis and Hackenworth held a bragging contest—in the guise of feigned vexation over the Senate confirmation process.

"Taking more than a week would be uncalled for," Davis concluded.

"It shouldn't take that long," Hackenworth told him. "I have it on good authority that some 82 of the Senators—across the aisle—have begun wearing their beads publicly."

Jeremy and Marty exchanged looks. Never had they seen Hackenworth look so happy before; the man positively beamed.

"Let's get down to business, gentlemen," said Stavros.

"That's true," Wayne blurted out. "We are all guys this time. Whatever happened to Brenda Chen? I thought she was going to be here."

"Oh," Rich said. "Nice kid but I think she . . . ."

"Chose to resign." Hackenworth said, giving Rich Davis a wink. "Investigator McCracken, too. Rumor has it, a lot of Traditionals are moving out of government now. Presumably they don't feel comfortable among all The Righteous."

Stavros cleared his throat. "If I may continue, gentlemen, our goal for today is to rethink Project Exterminate. Dr. Murphy has more research to report, I believe."

"I've been doing my own research," Hackenworth said. "I'm beginning to think those little buggers are everywhere. Have you noticed?"

Rich said, "I have, Cooper. I think it's like what happens when you learn the meaning of a new word and suddenly it seems like everybody's using it. Huntids are just on everyone's mind these days. I think all that tune-in should give Tucker high approval ratings after Project Exterminate."

Jeremy cleared his throat. "Thanks for giving me your attention, everyone." He walked toward the light dimmer at Stavros' end of the table. "The phenomenon you've noticed, about the growing prevalence of huntids, relates to an interesting scientific fact." That was Wayne's cue to click on the TV; Jeremy turned off the conference room lights.

A complex set of equations showed on the screen, chartreuse numbers on a light purple screen. "To put the matter simply, we've discovered an important relationship between killing huntids and accelerated reproductive activity. Here's another way to look at it."

After Wayne clicked, the screen showed an image of one huntid turning into 20.

"And here's another view, our lab cage that once held 3,000 huntids and now contains more than 4 million."

Click. Cage One in Research Lab One showed huntids flying so thickly, they looked like one huge buzzing spiral, moving up and down from the mud at the bottom of the mesh box.

"Fascinating—the swarm is so thick, they almost look as if they have hair," Hackenworth said.

"Love the camera work," said Rich. "You guys definitely have a knack. Could I have a copy? This could scare the shit out of viewers if we build it up right."

"Certainly you may have a copy, but . . . ."

Stavros pounded his fist lightly on the table (the hand that wasn't in a pocket, working his beads). "Cooper and Rich, would you listen, please? Jeremy's trying to make an important point."

Jeremy said, "I'm urging you to call off Project Exterminate, at least until we can gather more data. The implication so far is that when you slaughter one huntid, the survivors multiply exponentially. Unquestionably we've established that the huntids are highly intelligent creatures, surpassing bees or any other kind of insect I've studied before. In keeping with the field property of matter, as established by physics, they seem to have a flow-through consciousness."

"What's that?" Hackenworth asked.

"Quantum Field theory suggests that we can predict a defensive mechanism that transcends the ability of a single huntid to protect itself. Although we can't prove it yet, our preliminary model works like this: You kill huntid A and he puts up no fight at all. But then his fellow huntids B and C get busy and replicate A—by A times A. Our research so far shows that when you exterminate 10 of them, 100 new ones will appear nearby. Do you really want to risk the sudden appearance of 10 trillion?"

"Fascinating theory," Hackenworth said, "Like a starfish regenerating itself, presumably, only this way the job is delegated over a whole convention of starfish in another locale. I suppose you can prove all this? No, wait, you just admitted you can't." The sneer in his voice took on a deeper tone of menace. "If we wanted pure speculation, Dr. Murphy, I assure you we're sufficiently adept to construct our own."

"May I add something?" Wayne asked. "The practical point here, the really major point, to me, is that if we try this big extermination and don't do it 100 percent completely, our problem could become worse instead of better. Picture the air in this room as thick with huntids as the image you're seeing right now on TV. How would that make President Tucker look, Mr. Davis?"

"What, you scared you're gonna to choke to death?" Rich snickered.

Jeremy said, "Wayne is just trying to communicate the very real danger involved in a hasty PR venture called Project Exterminate. Without time to think through a viable strategy for controlling the huntids, we're acting like lesser animals, using brute force to overcome a lack of intelligence, and—

"So what?" said Hackenworth.

Jeremy tried to keep his voice even. "We'd have to kill off the whole population of huntids at once. If our timing is off, or we miss just one little cowpatch in South Dakota, the huntids could come back stronger."

Hackenworth asked, "So you're saying the Project will only be successful if we spray, and other nations spray, simultaneously throughout the world?"

Both Jeremy and Wayne nodded.

Hackenworth continued, "We could arrange something, I suppose. But it might be more advantageous not to let the other nations officially join us. That way, huntids would become *their* problem, wouldn't they?" He smiled.

Wayne swept his hair out of his eyes. "That stuff President Tucker was saying on TV about biological warfare. You just made that up, didn't you."

Hackenworth laughed.

"Well?" Wayne said, leaning forward in Hackenworth's direction.

"Stick to your job, kid." Hackenworth said, not unpleasantly.

Jeremy tried to sound casual as he said, "I really think we're better off letting the huntids go through their life cycle, die a natural death, and have done with it. Locusts show a similar growth pattern; they arise, proliferate, die; then it's over for a very long while. Why should we risk poisoning our country, our entire planet? There's still no hard evidence that huntids pose a serious threat."

"'Poisoning' is a strong word. I hope all of you heard Jeremy use it." Marty observed.

"So what, Mr. Hiyakawa?" sneered Hackenworth. "Let me see if I appreciate the full thrust of your use of the word 'poisoning.' It signifies your fears about using sufficient insecticide to eliminate the huntids. Your reasoning? Oh yes, you're worried about some hypothetical damage to the environment?"

"You got it," Marty said pleasantly.

"At the risk of calling my esteemed colleague squeamish, pardon me for asking your entire department, are you gentlemen certain that you're in the right profession? Have you any compelling, legitimate reason to fear that illness would result from this program?

"Illness? Interesting how you, of all people, should bring that up," Stavros said, glaring at Hackenworth. "All along we've been trying to contact the Center for Disease Control to discuss the epidemiological dangers of an extermination project. And every time, we run into a wall—a wall, we're told, erected by you."

"Only for security reasons," Hackenworth said, giving a paternal nod. "That's correct. We've placed consultation with CDC off limits. Just do *your* job, gentlemen, if you can."

Jeremy crossed his arms in front of his chest. "Okay, back at my job, Secretary Hackenworth, I've been wondering about something. Have you wondered why the huntid population started exploding in the first place?"

"What, you're going to announce that huntids are like rabbits? Give us your answer without the 20 questions, okay?" Rich sneered.

Jeremy kept his appearance polite. "We've contacted our counterparts on other continents. Their reproduction patterns for huntids are the same as our initial patterns, dating from when we first began to estimate population nationwide. Yet the rate of foreign huntid reproduction has stayed the same, whereas ours has started to skyrocket. And the big jump in America's numbers dates precisely from President Tucker's press conference. Don't you remember that he advocated killing the huntids?"

Rich said, "I believe his exact words were, 'If you see one of these pests, swat it like a common mosquito. Unless you want to show the world that you worship terrorists. In that case, by all means, get down on your knees, bow down and pray.' Frankly, I'm proud of that part of his speech, wrote it myself. Tucker has positioned himself, you see, so that anyone who feels aligned with him politically will swat at the huntids. It's a very visible political gesture."

"No more self-quotes, please, "said Stavros grimly. "And spare us the bragging. I'm on the side of The Righteous, too, but let's make some effort to act like responsible professionals."

Jeremy said, "Rich, I'd like to suggest that you ask President Tucker to make some kind of announcement that people stop killing the huntids. Leave the extermination to us."

Rich shrugged. "Maybe the one who needs to make the announcement is Rev. Helms. And we know who has his ear. What do you think, Cooper?"

Before Hackenworth could answer, Stavros jumped to his feet. "And while you're at it, Cooper, why don't you ask him why people like you get away with pretending to be members of The Righteous? For sheer hypocrisy you really take the cake. When have you said an honest prayer in your life?"

"Ah!" said Hackenworth so quietly it made Jeremy's skin crawl. "So the bond between religious belief and political ambition isn't familiar to you, Mr. Menelakos? I wonder if your problem isn't so much a comparison of our relative degrees of faith as it is our current equality in position."

"No," Stavros said, pulling the beads from his pocket and holding them between his hands in prayer position. "My rejuvenation was real. How dare you suggest that

I might taint my soul with hypocrisy? When the Day of Reckoning comes. . ." He replaced his beads and muttered, "Would that it may come soon."

Wayne walked over to the light switch and turned it on. "Well, we've had a lot to talk about today," he said in a chipper voice. "Before we're done, I'd like to make one final request that we wait until we've projected the environmental damage from a widespread pesticide program."

"Well, it's just a risk we'll have to take, I'm afraid," Hackenworth said. "Over hill, over dale—call out the boys in the planes. Stavros, do you have the jurisdiction and the budget or do you need anything extra from me?"

"We'll do it," Stavros announced flatly.

Hackenworth smiled, "Spray away, then." He rose to go.

Jeremy tried to block the door, "Don't you care?" He stared Hackenworth in the eye. If felt like looking down a long empty hallway. Hackenworth blinked a few times. "Excuse me," he mumbled absently on his way out.

Stavros got up, one hand moving continuously inside his pocket. He muttered, "Rev. Helms says the earth will be ending anyway, one way or another. Jeremy, do as you're told. All of us must."

Jeremy started to speak but Stavros stared him down. "Remember, Marty put you in charge of this project. It's a great honor."

"And what if I decline this great honor?"

"Then you're out on your sanctimonious little ear."

Jeremy extended a smile. "I'll ignore that comment, then, Mr. Menelakos. Instead, permit me to thank you and Dr. Hackenworth. What an extraordinary opportunity you've given me for professional advancement!"

Chapter 20
A Good Change of Scene

All day Rachel held in her secret about the visit to Washington West—except for a quick phone call around 5:00, telling Jeremy she had hired a sitter so tonight the two of them could go out to the movies.

"You funny little daisy, this may sound horribly decadent, but what I'm really looking forward to tonight is a very early bedtime," he said.

After a brief quizzical look, Rachel realized he didn't mean this as a romantic invitation. She sighed, tossing her curls.

"If only you had married a party animal, huh?" he said, sympathetically.

How could a man be so charming yet so frustrating? Rachel pretended to be a good sport, blowing him a flirtatious kiss before she hung up. Whereupon she shook her curls and stomped around the room, yelling "Jeremy, why do you have to act like an old fart?"

But would she complain to him? Noooo. That night Rachel kept out of his way, doing virtuous little chores like polishing her jewelry, all the while working on her composure as a *gravitas* woman. Just a little after 9:00, Jeremy came into the kitchen to give her a hug before going to bed. He felt warm and rumpled, more like a man halfway through a good night's sleep than someone about to hit the pillow for the first time. Relaxing into his lean chest made Rachel feel as though she was rocking in a hammock, making her so comfortable she couldn't hold onto her secret a minute longer.

"Guess who called me today."

"I won't even try," he said. He smiled in an affectionate way, reminiscent of Desi indulging his screwball wife Lucy in the old "I Love Lucy" reruns.

Taking a deep breath, Rachel explained that a friend from her old playgroup had called and invited her and Brent to come to visit them in Washington West.

"For how long?" he said, ending their embrace with a startled expression.

"Till after Labor Day Week, assuming we don't turn catty or anything." There, that had just the right touch of feminine irreverence. Rachel complimented herself. It sounded as though her heart wasn't breaking at the thought of being apart from her husband for a whole month.

"Which friend are we talking about, Sweetheart?"

"Marguerite."

"Doesn't ring a bell."

"Remember back when Brent was little and I was in a playgroup with a bunch of other new moms I met through Health Services? Marguerite was the short one with the naturally auburn hair, the oldest one."

"Marguerite—is she the one who fixes refrigerators and cars?"

"Well, yes."

"One time, you told me, she jumped up on the roof right before a big thunderstorm."

"To clean the gutters. Her smart house wasn't as smart as it was cracked up to be."

"Isn't she a little strange?" Jeremy's eyes looked wide open now, as he propped his head up, chin in hand, elbow on table.

"Well, you know. She had to fix the gutters," Rachel cupped her own chin in her hand and grinned sideways over to Jeremy. "Marguerite's husband travels a lot. The time with the gutters, he was out of town. I think it was brave of her, don't you?"

Jeremy shook his head. "She was into everything, that Marguerite. From what you told me about her, she seemed strange. With all respect, could she be gay?"

"How prejudiced! Just because a woman's capable doesn't make her gay. Besides, sex-orientation data's in everyone's genetic printout, you know, and we looked at the mom and pop ones together when we got the ones for our kids. We shared *everything* in that playgroup, Jeremy. It wasn't just serious stuff, like seeing which socialization tracks our kids would need, based on their printouts. We watched our babies grow up. And it was so *funny* sometimes, like when the kids played hide and seek and their idea of hiding was to keep coming back underneath the same table, 10 times in a row."

Rachel sighed. "Marguerite was my favorite out of all the moms in that group. In fact, we'd be best friends now if she hadn't moved."

Jeremy's forehead wrinkled, "You know, I do remember Marguerite. For some reason I never trusted her."

Rachel gave him a Get out! shove. "You're just jealous that she's so smart. As if *you* needed to be jealous of anyone, Mr. Mighty Brain."

"You're just buttering me up so I'll agree to let you and Brent go."

"I don't have to butter you up. I know you're crazy about me; you'll give me anything I want." Rachel tried to sound more confident than she felt.

Side by side, they brushed their teeth at the double sink in the master bathroom. Then Jeremy muttered something about a second wind. He went down to his office to play a Bach organ something-or-other on his synthesizer. She lay in bed, hearing the brains in the music and wondering where was Jeremy's heart? How could he not protest her leaving with Brent for an entire month? In his place, Rachel would have flung his arms around his spouse and said, "Darling, don't leave me, not for a single day."

Interrupting her fantasy, the real Jeremy plonked himself into bed. He squished down his three pillows just the way he liked them—how romantic! When his feet entered the covers, he grunted. Only then did he give Rachel a quick goodnight kiss, mumbling, "Maybe your trip isn't a bad idea, Sunflower. Things are going to heat up around here, with Project Exterminate. I'll be under lots of pressure."

Rachel felt him smile through the darkness, no doubt it was his rueful Fred Astaire-like grin. "I might be even worse company than I am now. By the way, did Marguerite mention anything about the huntids or President Tucker?"

"No, only she said we're a little weird in Capital City. Like our being over-sexed, except that we're fixated on politics—that's just my version of what she said, anyhow." Rachel gave a long, catlike stretch culminating in a playful kick to his shin (which was as far down his leg as her foot could reach).

"Well, what does Brent think about making the trip?"

"Jeremy, I wouldn't dare tell him about the visit before speaking with you! But I guarantee he'll love it. A play date with Gilavael—"

"Who?"

Rachel giggled. "Marguerite named her son after an angel, gil-AHH-vay-el."

Jeremy shook his head; Rachel could hear it in the dark. She continued, "For Brent to have a play date with Gilavael every day for a month, are you kidding? Nothing could be better for Brent."

"Good idea, then. Do it." Jeremy said. It reminded Rachel of his being at work, Mr. Executive. Rachel's world crashed in around her, reminiscent of childhood nightmares about being squashed to death, like in Edgar Allen Poe's story, "The Pit and the Pendulum." Jeremy's reaction was so what, *relieved*? Understatement! Try *perky*.

Rachel sighed. Then, like the trouper she was, she started talking as though nothing was wrong. "Well, that's great! I'll arrange everything tomorrow. Bet we can leave the day after, which would be Wednesday. Hey, how about you take me out to dinner tomorrow to celebrate?"

"You bet," Jeremy said. "You and Brent can come back right after Project Exterminate—sounds perfect." He nuzzled her lush brown curls. In the dark, he never saw the sorrow.

Yes, Rachel was wearing her grieving face, formed by habit and usually hidden from view. If only he could feel it!

So, what did people wear out West, anyway? Packing Brent's suitcase had been easy for Rachel. Computer-customized jeans fit his perfect little body beautifully. To go with them she packed a large assortment of colorful shirts, a few swimshorts, about seven pairs of shoes, and plenty of socks to lose in Marguerite's wash-and-dry-cleaning machine. But for her? First she packed a modest jewelry collection— a dozen necklaces, ear studs, and rings. Next she filled the suitcase halfway with pretty dresses and unitards, then added a mini-wardrobe of casual wear—custom-made jeans and flirty tops.

Afterwards Rachel packed her shoe-carryall, cramming underwear, sun-visors, and socks inside the toes of her 12 pairs of shoes. Seeing her sexy undergarments among the shoes brought a grim kind of satisfaction, as if she was going into a kind of sexual exile—though it wasn't really fair to blame Jeremy for that.

Picking her outfits had been relatively easy, now came the tough part: packing her entertainment chest. First came several pieces of violin music—but she'd only bring stuff she already knew; the Satie could stay in the basement, among her many boxes of unfinished projects. Rachel went on to pack a dozen aromatherapy bottles, her complete regimen of skin cosmetics and tooth shiners; make-ups and fingernail gems; bookdisks, music disks. No seminar tapes, she decided, and no wake-up console. In Seattle, she'd have nothing important to wake up to anyway.

While packing her final choices, Rachel decided to voice-call her mother, who must be at work at the family catering business, Fabulous Fare. When Helene came to the phone, Rachel made polite inquiries about her father's sanity (no better) and her mother's news (none). Helene could be so exasperating, with her relentlessly chipper exterior. Inwardly the woman was bored as a stone. Rachel could feel it, even if her mother couldn't.

Rachel carefully explained that she and Brent had been invited to visit an old friend in Washington West, which her old-fashioned mother insisted on referring to as Seattle.

"You're leaving your husband to go to Seattle?" Ma's voice sounded horrified.

"No, of course not. My friend Marguerite invited me and I thought it seemed like a good change of scene, especially now with Jeremy under so much pressure with work—you know, dealing with the huntids."

Helene shrugged. "Bugs come, bugs go. Let me tell you, living in New York means living with roaches. You remember. Bugs aren't the part that worries me, honey, it's Hickory Helms and his little disciple, President Stevie."

"Whatever, Mom. I'm sure everything's going to work out. Anyway, I wanted to let you know that Brent and I will be away until Labor Day Week."

"And your son is okay with this? Seattle is far away, Rachel. Is my grandson a child who likes change? If I remember correctly, this is the kid who, when he loses a tooth, insists on keeping it a month before he gives it up to the tooth fairy. Am I right?"

"You're right, Mom. But he's very fond of Marguerite's son, Gilavael. Plus I have everything all arranged." Rachel unpacked one of her aromatherapy bottles, "Stress," and sprayed herself all over the back of her neck, then replaced the bottle in her suitcase.

"Everything arranged. I see, like not being with your husband during his time of trial?" Helene sounded like she was charging up her car battery for a lecture at 60 miles an hour.

"Ma, if you must know, I admit that I have a strategy in making these plans. Here's a hint: Absence makes the heart grow fonder."

Helene sighed heavily.

"Jeremy and I have been together almost every day since we moved to Capital City." *Oh golly, a mistake to say this.* Rachel's parents had been furious when she dropped out of college to follow Jeremy (A goy, yet!) to Capital City when he got his first job with the government and, eventually, marry him. Helene still complained that they lived so far from New York—how careless of Rachel to bring up the subject. She held her breath.

Helene said, "Leaving him, huh? That's one hell of a way to show you care. Still," she paused, "it might work. But there's one thing I hope you'll think about while you're in Seattle. Did it ever occur to you that the big problem in your marriage is how you're too quick to figure everything out? It's like you're always doing three things at once.

"You're too efficient, Rachel. You're so efficient you're losing yourself."

"Um-hmm. Thanks for the advice, Ma." Rachel said, reaching for a tissue. *I hope you're happy now. And you wonder why I don't call you more often?*

"Listen, Baby. I've got to get back to the store. Send me a hologram-card, okay?"

After the call, Rachel was tempted to add a few boxes of Kleenex to her suitcase. Oh yes, so long as she was feeling rotten, this was the perfect time to leave a goodbye message to Heather. An e-mail, not a call, because she didn't want to have to look at Heather's selfish Barbie-like face ever again.

"I'm going to have to break our Runner's Club date for the rest of the summer," she typed. "Sorry. Going to Washington West with Brent to visit a friend. When I get back, I'll call you, I suppose. ;-)" Before she pushed SEND, Rachel reviewed her message and changed "a friend" to "a very good friend." Not that Heather could be expected to appreciate the nuance.

Evening improved Rachel's mood, however. For their *bon voyage* dinner, Jeremy took her to The Watergate. Admittedly paying for a heli-cab to D.C. and back was an extravagance, but driving would have taken six hours. Rachel loved to travel in whirlybirds; Jeremy actually put his arm around her as they snuggled inside.

God, that was one of her favorite things a man could ever do for her—made her feel both protected and nurtured. With Jeremy, there was an extra element of pleasure because his arm culminated in those long, thin fingers; she could feel intelligence pulsate out of them right into her, like a kind of energy transfusion. The bustling of the day, her horrible talk with Helene, all Rachel's worries about this trip seemed to vanish as soon as the cab lifted off. She was in a state of romantic bliss even before they alighted on the roof of the historic hotel.

President Nixon would never have recognized the restaurant in the apartment building that wrapped around the Potomac river, a stately mid-sized skyscraper. Since his day, it had been refurbished in a gold metallic hue that went with the rest of the glittering city. These days D.C., the pride of Capitol City, was either marble monuments like museums, or sleek silver-and-glass office buildings, or other shades of burnished metal.

For this dinner, Rachel had chosen a sizzling dress; it had a fashionable pop-up top that made her breasts nearly perpendicular. The silky black fabric was gorgeously alive with polka dots in marigold, aqua, lilac and pink. Jeremy liked it. She could tell by how he looked at her, especially the very tight skirt with no colorful polka dots, only sleek blackness that clung to the curves of her body.

At times like this, Rachel was glad she worked out a couple of hours each day. She had earned the right to eat whatever she liked, whatever the calorie count. Jeremy ordered his usual uninteresting selection from the menu—the man talked like a poet, thought like a professor, and chose his food like an eight-year old. Tonight he chose Watergate's famous cloned steak, with crispy fries and onion rings. When it arrived, Rachel had to admit that the onions were perfect round circles, crunchy and practically greaseless. After she ate one off his plate, he offered her one of his precision-cut five-inch fries, pencil thin. It tasted as fabulous as it looked. She nibbled hers seductively, slowly working her way down its length.

Jeremy also indulged in a glass of some fancy red wine, which seemed to give him a pleasant buzz. Rachel never drank liquor, even wine, because of her alcoholic gene. The thought of drinking summoned up a picture of her brother Walt, with his perpetual alcoholic stupor. No, she drank Flegets, a new golden-hued anti-cola with the freshness of just-mown grass and an under-taste of gardenias.

Rachel ordered a fondue, mostly Fontina and cream, simmered to a perfect warm gooiness. The enormous platter came with exquisite steamed vegetables: miniature cauliflowers; huge, tender artichoke hearts; baby beets in several shades of gold; white and green asparagus. When she offered Jeremy the longest asparagus stalk, he took it; the first moist bite made his mouth glisten.

Rachel drew in her lips for a minute and squashed them against each other, sensuously. *"My lips feel so lonely,"* she wanted to say. But that wouldn't work with him. "So, Jeremy, don't you have anything romantic to say about my going out of town?"

He looked deep into her eyes, then stared down at his plate, concentrating.

"Love's not time's fool," he said, finally.

She stared back, scrunching up her face with a quizzical expression. He reached across the table to unfurrow her, stroking her skin quickly with the tips of his fingers. "Shakespeare," he whispered, then started again:

> Love's not Time's fool, though rosy lips and cheeks
> Within his bending sickle's compass come;
> Love alters not with his brief hours and weeks,
> But bears it out even to the edge of doom,
> If this be error, and upon me prov'd,
> I never writ, nor no man ever loved.

Rachel's eyes teared up.

"I'm not an original man," Jeremy said apologetically.

"You're just the only man I know who memorized a million of Shakespeare's sonnets, plus all that other poetry." Rachel wished that she and Jeremy could throw everything off the table, fling off their clothes, and make love right there in the middle of the restaurant.

No use shocking the patrons, though. Besides, the food was too good to waste; it was absolutely glorious. She looked glorious. Mentally she started taking photographs to remember Jeremy by, like how his slate-blue eyes twinkled above his straight lower eyelids.

It was his voice she'd remember, even more than his face—that wonderful deep voice. In the years before Brent was born, they would sing together a lot. His voice still sang in her memory, a better hologram than the fanciest photo you could buy.

For dessert, they shared a slice of 10-layer fudge cake, with computer-perfect gradations of chocolate ganache: The bottom layers were sandwiched with rich, buttery dark chocolate; upwards the cake filling lightened, so by the top layers it became a fluffy, creamy mocha. This amazing cake tempted you to take it apart, forkful by glorious forkful, and savor all its variations on the theme of chocolate.

After the last bite, Rachel said solemnly, "Thanks, Jeremy. I'll never forget this evening."

He smiled in agreement.

"I'll miss you so much." The words escaped on their own. Rachel hadn't meant them to. Quickly excusing herself, she made it to the Ladies Room before hot tears squirted out of her eyes.

Except for that one small lapse, it was a perfect evening for Rachel, especially since, once home, it was only a matter of minutes before her husband seduced her.

Jeremy hid his eczema rash under a super-soft undershirt made of pima cotton. Such a gentlemanly gesture! Otherwise, they were both magnificently naked. He even tried a position they hadn't done for ages, where he held her against the wall.

"Hold on, Rachel," he said after a while. "I'm not as young as I used to be the last time we did this. Is it all right with you if we move back to the bed?"

For answer, she tenderly cupped his muscular butt in her hands, as if to say, "Of course, you hot man."

Unfortunately, by the time Rachel was positioned on the bed, his seduction had lost its heat; the man seemed to be pumping, pumping forever. Jeremy was giving it all he had, no complaints there, but Rachel began to feel like she was connected to some kind of machine that would never stop, like an old-fashioned washer, stuck forever in the agitation cycle.

Bad thought. He was making love to her, not just fucking, and Rachel had every reason to be grateful. Still, her mind started wandering to the image of herself pumping on a swing, never able to get up too high. By an effort of will, not to mention good manners, Rachel called herself back for the ending. It was worth it. She loved how Jeremy's face scrunched up while he throbbed within her; she loved the moment of utter vulnerability when he pulled out—it seemed to balance the strength he brought her the rest of the time (not that she would ever tell him any of this).

The other part, which she decided she *would* tell him eventually, when she could find the right words, was how the biggest pleasure for her when they had sex wasn't physical at all. In some strange way, she felt the energy of his love join with hers. It was like nothing else in her world. She lived to receive the special kind of intensity that came from him then—what was it, anyway? The power of a quiet man's love, perhaps.

Admittedly tonight hadn't been their greatest sex ever. But at least, Rachel concluded, it was something. Maybe her leaving for a while would cause him to take her more seriously. *Gravitas* in her absence if not her presence—that was better than nothing.

III. Ignoring the Huntids

Chapter 21
Pressure to Affiliate

"Welcome to Seattle, the best of Washington West," said a talking hologram on the wall at the airport. The visuals showed an unimpressive collection of skyscrapers and Mt. Rainier, lit up with a pink glow; the voice-over for the display came from one of those annoying dubbers whose cheerleader tones would have cloyed on first hearing.

Rachel and Brent were doomed to hear the false enthusiasm repeat every 30 seconds, like a sped-up cuckoo clock, while Marguerite reclaimed their luggage. "Trust me," she had told Rachel. "You don't want to go to the luggage area—too much pushing and shoving. Wait here. Gil and I will be back in a flash." Rachel accepted the offer gratefully, even though listening to Miss Congeniality turned out to be no bargain.

Supposedly American transportation was considered the envy of the world. Rachel remembered that some politician had uttered this ludicrous piece of propaganda a couple of years ago, after which the rest of the country collectively threw back its head and howled with laughter. Transportation wasn't what it was cracked up to be. Sure America had high-tech galore. The problem was how that high-tech stuff interfaced with everything else.

Rachel shook her head remembering their journey today. Although their cross-country flight took 45 minutes, security check at their airport back home took three hours. Another four had been consumed on the gridlocked highway to *get* to her neighborhood airport. And even after Rachel's plane arrived, it took another hour in the sky for clearance from air traffic control.

Rachel laughed, remembering the highlight of her journey, the actual flight. Much as she loved to fly, modern airways had way-too-friendly skies. In this 2,000-seater were more people's emotions than Rachel usually had to deal with for a whole week. And Channel 4's classic TV commercials were broadcast over a huge

3-D screen; today's travelers had to have their entertainment. For Rachel, however, a little of Channel 4's highly-rated *Nostalgia Vision* went an awfully long way.

During the flight Rachel was far more interested in looking for huntids. Anxiously peering through the window, she hadn't seen any. From the sky, houses barely registered as blips, but at least she could tell that the checkerboard designs of agri-businesses looked fine, not devastated by huntids.

People talked about huntids constantly, on board the plane and now over TV. Come to think of it, Rachel saw an alarming number of TV sets where she waited in the airport lobby. They were scattered about liberally, easier to spot than toilets or flight information robots. Without moving from the place where Marguerite was going to meet them, Rachel counted 84 TV screens, big and small, blaring away.

Still the scene at baggage checkout was undoubtedly worse. Rachel imagined her fellow travelers pushing through the crowd to claim their electronically scanned and sorted items. Down the chute would tumble pagers, camcorders, laptops, portable VR sets and quadri-phonic boomboxes, suitcases, entertainment chests, cosmetic bags, medicine chests, even personal robots.

Baggage security wasn't a problem, at least. Every item was stamped with your datamate and had to pass a match scan. Rachel had given her datamate over to Marguerite when, half an hour ago? Now her valiant friend was contending with the grabbing, the shoving, not to mention the whining of kids who were starved for entertainment and hyper from airplane candy.

Marguerite nearly danced when she returned with Gilavael and a cart full of luggage. "We're almost out of the woods. And we're going to have so much fun once we get out of here. Follow me. I'll show you my favorite shortcut out of the airport."

As they scooted through a long, out-of-the-way corridor, Marguerite explained, "I had to learn the ins and outs of Seattle Airport because Gregory travels so much." Modest of her, Rachel thought. Even if she never made more than one trip to pick up her husband, Marguerite would have found the best way. That's how she operated.

Now she was guiding the four of them through a service elevator, then down a long unmarked hallway. Soon they emerged into an enormous state-of-the-art garage, big as a football field, packed solid with cars. Marguerite clicked a kind of gizmo Rachel had never seen before. One car lit up.

"Ours," Marguerite said cheerfully.

She scooted everyone inside their ancient black Honda Hybrid. Before Rachel could offer to pay for parking, Marguerite swiped her own datamate through the meter. By the time Rachel had fastened her seatbelt and settled the kids into their seats, Marguerite had packed all 12 of Rachel's parcels into the trunk. With a whir of the motor, they were off, onto the highway. A mere three hours later, they pulled into Marguerite's home, with its spectacular view of the Cascade Mountains.

As Marguerite made tea for two, Rachel admired her signature style of dressing, layer upon layer of clothes in solid colors, unusual shades, as if she were a painting. Right now she was wearing an aqua turtleneck, a cerulean sweater and a pale yellow scarf that matched her silk leggings. Atop that sartorial crayon box, Marguerite's eyes glimmered bright green; her long straight eyebrows reminded Rachel of a sable paintbrush, pressed against paper until the bristles fanned out.

She looks the way she always did, Rachel thought, as they sat sipping herbal tea, except that lines like spider webs now framed Marguerite's eyes; they circled the lower half of each eye in a near-perfect circle. *Oddly beautiful, in a way* (though in her place Rachel would have had the wrinkles zapped into oblivion, pronto, with a Health Elective).

Rachel needed the cheer of this little tea party. Minutes before she'd called Jeremy to let him know that she and Brent arrived safely. Despite his charming smile, he looked preoccupied. "Remember to have a good time," he said, "And I'll call you in a week."

So much for spontaneous endearments. "You mean Wednesday will be our phone date?" Rachel asked, still hoping that virtual Valentines would pop out of his mouth.

"Sure. And why don't you have Brent call me for a quick chat every morning when he wakes up? He's old enough to use a screen phone by himself."

"That sounds good. And I'll join in at the end, right?"

"You could, but aren't you the one who told me how the latest parenting theories tell us to make kids independent, especially with technology?"

That came from a seminar Rachel had taken years ago. Interesting that it made an impression on Jeremy—maybe because it fit with his usual preference for family interactions, which was "Two's company, three's a crowd." Well, she'd let him win this time. He'd talk solo to Brent, solo to her, but when the three of them were reunited in Capitol City, she'd make family dynamics her number one priority.

"Okay," she told Jeremy. Still, she felt hurt at being left out of the phone calls between father and son. Before hanging up, she couldn't bring herself to give a real smile. But apparently in his exhausted state Jeremy couldn't tell the difference.

Anyway, she was with Marguerite now, and this bright pink beverage tasted gloriously of no-cal honey and mysterious aromatic herbs. The boys were off playing. During the drive to Marguerite's, their initial monosyllables had turned to wisecracks, then questions. Now Brent and Gil were talking with their old rhythms of give and take, talk and twirl.

Brent's obvious happiness wasn't all that cheered Rachel as she contemplated her new surroundings. Marguerite asked to hear her news, and she seemed to genuinely want to hear the deep stuff. So Rachel went into more detail than she had on the phone, describing all the flavors and colors of hermetically sealed life in the '20s in Capitol City.

The way Marguerite listened was immensely comforting, especially compared to how Jeremy listened lately. These days, she wanted to grab his shoulders and shake him to make him pay attention, even when, technically, he *was* paying attention. Marguerite, by contrast, listened without limits.

Marguerite also had a kind of contagious curiosity. If someone had come into the room to test IQ points, no doubt Rachel would have scored higher than usual. Marguerite was so smart, she almost made the air crackle.

"Want to move over to the couch?" she asked.

Rachel followed her. The couch faced a fireplace and, above it, a TV screen. "Your furniture is gorgeous," she told Marguerite.

"Thanks. It's just one of my hobbies."

"You *made* that furniture?"

"It started as a redwood carpentry class," Marguerite said. "You know, here in Washington West, logging and reforestation have been issues for a hundred years. About the time our boys were born, Seattle loggers finally began to use a new technology. They planted a tree with a kind of speeded-up growth, a designer form of redwood. It's the only bio-engineering I ever approved of. Just last year, the first generation of these trees came to maturity. When the wood came on the market, I took a class. And then you know me—busy, busy, busy."

"So you actually *made* these end tables?"

Marguerite nodded.

"And the sofa?"

"Back when I lived near you, I took an upholstering seminar, remember?"

"But how did you find lamps to match them so perfectly? Did you take a class in shopping too?"

"No. Lamps aren't that hard to make. I told you about my glassblowing when we moved to Atlanta and Gil started school. While I was making the furniture, I thought it would be fun to work on shades to go with the funny little art pieces you see on the shelf here. For the base, I used more of that redwood."

Rachel realized that envy must be leaking out of her ears like Brent's former lime-green cold because Marguerite gave a sudden, forced laugh. She said, "Don't worry, Rachel. I bought the wiring. And, believe me, if they didn't have good robots to help you at the hardware warehouse, I would have been lost."

"Mom, when's dinner gonna be ready?" Gil's voice preceded him into the living room. When he stood facing Marguerite, his curved nose was the image of his mother's.

"Why do you call his hair *red*?" Brent had asked, back when he and Gil were toddlers. "His hair isn't red. It's orange."

Still was. Rachel fought off the urge to ruffle that shiny, natural red hair the way she did Brent's curls.

"I guess it's getting to be time for dinner, huh?" Marguerite smiled at Gil indulgently.

"Mom wouldn't remember to eat if I didn't remind her," Gil told Brent.

"Now that's an exaggeration." Marguerite turned to Rachel. "Luckily, when we moved from Arizona we invested in a pretty smart house, so when we cook here it doesn't take long. We have 50 menus to choose from. What do you want, Western, Mexican, Chinese..."

Rachel selected Chinese, then shrimp with broccoli.

Everyone walked into the kitchen, where Marguerite gave a voice command to the console. "Brent, should we have that with rice or noodles?"

"Noodles."

Marguerite looked at him appraisingly. "I thought so."

"Noodles" she commanded. All four of them watched admiringly while the Stove Wizard lowered several cubes into the microwave and turned on its own power. A digital timer with tangerine-colored lights began to count backwards from 10 minutes. Marguerite was the first to turn away; she asked the boys to set the table while she threw a salad together.

"This will be a very traditional Chinese salad, I suppose," Rachel said teasingly. "Can I help?"

"Not this time. On the first day, you're treated as the honored guest. It's all downhill from there. By the end of your visit, I might even ask you to wash the windows."

"Ooh, you're tough," said Rachel, working her calf muscles from different angles while Marguerite used the sink's germicide and anti-parasite spray attachment on the veggies. One more wash and she had a pile of food that looked like a still life. Smiling, she plied her knife on the celery, cucumbers, red and green peppers. Geometric shapes appeared on her cutting board, then were flung into an exquisite ceramic salad bowl. "No, I didn't make this one. Look, for the dressing, what do you think about toasted sesame oil with rice vinegar and fresh cilantro?"

Rachel nodded. She was, admittedly, struggling. The effortless beauty of Marguerite's salad, the furniture, the squeaky clean house, the fact that Gil said Marguerite could actually forget to eat . . . . On this visit, she was planning to forget all about the huntids. Maybe jealousy would be something else she'd have to forget.

"Earth to Rachel. Come in Rachel." Marguerite was smiling ear to ear. "It was so perfect that Brent wanted noodles. You too, right?"

"Sure, but—"

"Perfect because just last Friday at the Center—that's the place I told you about, run by my teacher, John."

Rachel didn't remember Marguerite's mentioning any of this before, but she nodded politely.

"He was talking about the spiritual vibrations of wheat and rice. You know how you were talking about isolation? Well, it fits perfectly."

"What fits?"

"Grains are the staff of life, John says. But they're also natural balancers, like how a staff helps someone to walk on difficult ground. Well, rice is the traditional grain of the East, where *togetherness* is taught as a primary cultural value."

"You mean like the tradition in India of extended families?"

"That and the importance of consideration everywhere in the East."

"Okay, I'm with you, except how does togetherness relate to rice?"

"What do most people from the us-cultures eat as their staple? It's rice. Every grain of rice stands as a separate thing and, energetically, it teaches, 'You're an individual, no matter what.'"

"Okay, so what does wheat teach?"

"The lesson of gluten, Rachel, is what we need in a me-culture, where *individualism* is our pride and joy. You know, we've encouraged individualism so much that people feel isolated."

"Yes, I seem to have heard about that."

"So I wasn't surprised that you and Brent preferred noodles over rice. Wheat foods are about togetherness."

"Like communion bread?"

"That's a perfect example. When society constantly teaches, "Be separate," and the message gets to you, why compound it by eating rice?"

"So this teacher of yours says that isolated people choose noodles and bread so we'll have better luck making friends?"

"Exactly—and I think Brent feels some of the same separateness that you do, Rachel, just that he's not as aware of it."

"I wouldn't be surprised," Rachel said. "By the way, what do you do here to plug in socially?" Rachel eyed the perfect salad. "Those summer weeks can stretch on and on. Not to offend you and Gil, of course." Foot in mouth again. Marguerite didn't seem offended, though.

"Not to worry," she said, smiling. "I'll show you my favorite places and my favorite people, too."

She picked up the salad bowl. "Help me carry in the drinks, would you?"

Next morning, Rachel woke early, still on East coast time. Staying in bed past six o'clock seemed like torture so she tiptoed downstairs to turn on TV. Better to catch a familiar face or two from the Oprah network.

Rachel made herself a mug of plain boiling water (it wasn't hard to get Marguerite's smart stove to do that much). Down went her drink on a sweet little end table. In went Rachel, sinking deeply into the couch's plush, plum velvet upholstery. Up went her feet, onto a little redwood coffee table. Rachel chose ab crunches for her first exercise and voice-commanded a program.

John Denver was being interviewed, telling viewers all about his latest bestseller (Number 34, he said modestly), *Your Body of Choice.* Denver was cloned from a long-dead, classic pop singer; to Rachel, he seemed a pale imitation. His seminars didn't appeal to her either.

More interesting to her was his interviewer LaRhonda McGinty, who wore a fascinating powder blue leotard and tights that actually seemed to be made out of summer-weight cashmere. Rachel didn't listen closely at first, because she was daydreaming about ordering this outfit for herself with the TV's Interactive Order button. Jeremy would drool, she thought. She hoped. Hey, who was she kidding? He was, in every sense, a thousand miles away.

Back to her ab crunches and the show, then. Denver was beaming and telling Ms. powder-blue cashmere that she was absolutely right.

"Now, John Denver, I have to ask you about the vote in Congress yesterday. Do you manage to keep up with the news while you're on this book tour?"

"You bet," said the revered seminar star. "It's a test of my program. A balanced body-mind can handle the news without ever getting overwhelmed."

LaRhonda said, "Then you know that yesterday America was stunned at the failure of the Bi-Partisan Non-Religious Interference Act. How about you?"

He shrugged, smiling blandly.

Facing the camera, she explained, "This bill was sponsored by the Speaker of the House. Basically, it told President Tucker that he wasn't allowed to use his office to proselytize religion. But the argument about separation of church and state turned into a floor fight. The speaker had hoped for enough votes to withstand a veto from President Tucker, but—

"LaRhonda, I think the expression is that the Non-Religious Act didn't have a prayer." The seminar star looked so placidly amused that Rachel wanted to smack him.

"Come on," said LaRhonda, "weren't you shocked that The Righteous won on this bill?"

"Majority rules," he said. "The House has 435 seats, and 331 of the members wore their beads when they came to the floor. With that many reps dressed up as The Righteous, how could you expect the bill to pass? Besides that, most of the others wore crosses to show they were with the Traditionals."

"How can you sound so matter of fact about this?" LaRhonda's voice softened. "You're not wearing religious symbols, any more than I am. Don't you worry that you're part of a dying breed?"

"Certainly not," said the seminar leader. "I don't believe in worry. You can read all about it in my new book, *Your Body of Choice.* Download it like that!" He snapped his fingers.

"Come on," LaRhonda persisted indignantly. "You mean to say that your book will take away all the pressure to affiliate during these so-called 'Broken Times?' 'Cause I sure feel it, even if you don't."

Hearing that phrase, Rachel felt an empty space in her gut. LaRhonda's eyes sparkled, as did John Denver's. Yet Rachel had the sudden feeling that, regardless of how they looked or what they said, inwardly both of them were just going through the motions of this interview. Instead of speaking from real conviction, they were more interested in showing themselves off at flattering camera angles. And these were the people on *her* side. *Heaven help us!* Rachel thought.

Chapter 22
Allergic to Butterflies

"Rachel," Marguerite's voice, a forceful whisper, floated down the stairs. "I don't mind if you watch TV but could you turn it down? I'm trying to meditate."

"Sure. Is this better?"

After a few more minutes, Rachel turned off the TV in disgust, but not before she learned that yesterday the Supreme Court had decided politicians could defend their "constitutional right to express their religion." LaRhonda showed a vidclip of Chief Justice Clarence Thomas saying so ... while he performed a dance of The Righteous.

Religious sanity, already a contradiction in terms, might be endangered. That didn't mean Rachel had to watch it on TV and call it entertainment. Instead she took her indignation out for a walk. Along two sides of her two-story, cherry-colored house, Marguerite had created a garden with row upon row of raised flower beds and a maze of sprinkler hoses. Tulips stood at attention, flaunting their designer shades of pastel pink, chartreuse, and periwinkle.

As a gardener Rachel didn't trust tulips. Even when she planted seeds that were engineered to bloom for months, for her they drooped. Marguerite's garden was another story. Each blossom stood erect, and when it finally wilted no doubt another perfect flower would pop up to take its place. Was the technical term overplanting? Marguerite would know. In fact she'd probably taught gardening techniques to farmers in some starving third world village. Her friend's alarming set of accomplishments included plenty that Rachel didn't yet know.

Give me a break, she thought, and looked out towards the mountains on the right. On the left, the limpid waters of Puget Sound made her catch her breath. *It's so beautiful*, Rachel thought. *Just look at those evergreens.* They gave Seattle its signature look of abundant greenery. She liked that.

Rachel liked it here so much, in fact, that she stood stock still and let the peace of the place wash over her. Deep breaths of air smelled fresher than anything at home, even the country. In the serene light of the early morning, when she gazed up at the sky, clouds looked downright sculpted, more 3-D than the best movie she'd ever seen. And when she looked down, to her relief, Rachel didn't notice a single huntid or any other insect.

After Rachel's walk, the morning continued to be perfect. A leisurely breakfast was followed by Gil's performing—he made everyone listen to his piano scales. Then Brent showed off, picking up the kid-sized violin that Rachel had packed just in case. Back home he refused to practice; this trip was going to be good for him.

Marguerite took videos of the boys; then she and Rachel went to the computer room to make a vid-clip which Marguerite forwarded to friends. Rachel sent personalized variations of it to her list of 50 closest e-buds, including her mother, Heather and Jeremy. She was glad Marguerite stayed with her—sending individualized messages was so mechanical it took only half a yawn of brain space.

"You've never asked about the kind of meditation I do," Marguerite said.

"Tell me," said Rachel, leaving the "Get it out of your system already" unspoken.

"Even if John had never taught me anything else, I'd be grateful for the One Minute Blessing."

"John Denver?"

"No, my teacher, John Wilcox. You know how to meditate, right?"

Rachel shrugged. "There are millions of ways to meditate. Which kind are you talking about?"

"First you check in with your body, so you can correct anything not in balance. Grounding energy from the earth is a very underused resource, you know. You pull in what you need through the soles of your feet. Then you balance your mind and feelings in the same way. Afterwards you ask God to connect you with the life force of everyone on earth. "

"That's a One Minute Blessing? It sure sounds longer."

"It could take a few minutes unless you're crystal clear."

"Interesting," Rachel said, hoping to end the conversation.

Marguerite persisted, "But the really cool part of the blessing comes after it's done, because you feel connected to everyone. John says, it's only fair to give the world back a One-Minute Blessing each day."

"Like the prayers the Traditionals repeat like robots? I'm starting to worry about you."

Marguerite laughed. "This kind of blessing means tuning in—unconditional love, not trying to change anyone. When you connect in that way you can really feel your place in the world." She paused. "All the painful separateness in our society, that's an illusion."

"Some illusion! I'd call it the story of my life."

"A lot of people are in the same boat as you, Rachel. The irony is how technology supposedly makes us more connected. In reality, it does just the opposite."

"The global village, huh? Virtual community with nonstop skin-phones and TVs and computers."

Marguerite said, "Funny thing about that—are you done by the way?"

Rachel rose and shook out her shoulders, swinging her arms from side to side. "I'm telling you, the global village is an utter fake. Aside from my family, I wouldn't trade all the e-friends I just messaged for one real-life friend like you. Even in person, how many people really connect any more unless they've been brainwashed by some kind of cult? No wonder people join groups like The Righteous."

Marguerite stood next to her and copied the exercise. "Good stretch."

Rachel enjoyed the sight of them walking side by side, waving their arms like windmills.

"I couldn't agree with you more," Marguerite said, stopping. "Technology only connects us mechanically; it doesn't open up the human side. John says technology is only a metaphor for what we can do with our consciousness. And by 'we,' I mean you, too, if you want to."

Rachel felt uncomfortable. Had Marguerite changed so much in four years, since the innocent days when their children were babies? "I'm on vacation from seminars, okay?"

"Sure. Let's take the kids and go play."

Marguerite took them to Seattle's antique Space Needle and the magnificent Children's Museum. Brent behaved well, except when Gil led them to the Butterfly Garden. Within this high-security walled-off area of the museum were thousands of exotic butterflies and rare trees, nurtured in the atmosphere of a tropical climate. No huntids, Rachel noticed to her relief. Of course! This exhibit was climate- and plant-controlled, with nary a speck of dust.

Gilavael chattered on as if he owned the room. The butterflies were so tame, he bragged, that all you had to do was stand still and they would perch on you. Sure enough, they alighted on Rachel, Marguerite and Brent. But almost immediately Brent started flapping his arms until the butterflies flew off.

Gil said, "What's *wrong* with you. Are you allergic to butterflies?"

Brent ignored him.

"Stop squirming," Gil yelled.

All the nearby butterflies flew off as Rachel and Marguerite tried to get Brent to stand still. The crowd shrank back, studiously ignoring the incident while creating a two-foot space around them. Rachel's face flushed with embarrassment.

Brent seemed oblivious as he twirled his fingers in the air, spooking any butterflies within range. Finally Gil screamed, "You're scaring all the butterflies away, dumbo."

"Butterflies aren't as much fun as the huntids." Brent yelled. "Huntids are worth standing still for. They're fun to play with, but butterflies are stupid."

A gasp rippled through the crowd. Rachel saw several women fingering their beads and crosses.

"We're getting out of here, Buster," Rachel said, grabbing Brent and pulling him out of the room. Marguerite and Gil would have to catch up later.

"When Gilavael comes out, apologize," she scolded when they were alone. "You were rude. And you are not to talk about huntids in public. Understand?"

"What's the big deal, Mom?"

"Lots of people are scared of huntids, honey. Didn't you notice their reactions, the way they clutched their beads?"

"Well I'm not scared of The Righteous, although they're a lot scarier than huntids."

"Come on, Brent. We're visitors here. We do not have permission to offend anyone. *Anyone!* " Rachel shook her head. "Did you notice you also offended the Traditionals?"

"What's *their* problem?"

"According to Rev. Pilgrim, the huntids are sacred. I think I heard her call them 'taahny creechures,'" Rachel said, mimicking Stacey Pilgrim's cupped hands and saccharine smile. "Traditionals are so darned reverent about huntids, they think playing with them is blasphemy."

Brent giggled. Rachel fluffed his hair, then cradled his face in her hands and looked him in the eyes.

"I know it seems ridiculous, honey, but you have to treat the Traditionals with respect or you're insulting their religion. And the other thing is, I don't think that you appreciate how many people are scared of the huntids, whatever their religion."

"Why?" Brent broke away from her grasp but he was still listening.

"I don't know. Even I'm scared in some way, although I can't tell you exactly why. So let's just consider it a matter of good manners. You are not to talk about huntids in public. And when Gil comes back, I expect you to apologize."

Which he did, and the rest of the day flowed smoothly, especially when Rachel bought them lunch at a restaurant specializing in dramatic food presentations. Her enormous stuffed prawns were delicious; the boys' bio-engineered baked potatoes were football-sized and they competed to see who could stir in more butter and sour cream. Marguerite, who ate less than a quarter of her gigantic Caesar salad, was clearly not a big eater; Rachel decided she not to take this personally.

"My one special treat, just like yesterday was your treat with company manners," a happy Rachel told Marguerite. The boys were getting along famously, their argument forgotten.

"Looks like our normal weather is back," Marguerite said the next morning, making a face. "But I'd like to take you for a walk after I clean the house."

Although the drizzle didn't look inviting, Rachel's body craved exercise and so she agreed eagerly. While the boys played a game about astronauts, Rachel vacuumed and polished furniture.

Marguerite cleaned things Rachel didn't even notice needed cleaning, like the spotless tiles in the guest bathroom which weren't shiny enough for Marguerite, and dust on the 10-foot ceiling. *Ceiling dust should only be my biggest problem in life,* Rachel thought as Marguerite hooked up the vacuum's snake attachment. Mentally she composed a letter to Jeremy describing Marguerite's heroic cleaning efforts, but knew she wouldn't send it. She was not going to contact her husband before he called on Wednesday.

Marguerite was in a funny, distant mood when they left. Maybe that's how she always was as the anti-grime warrior. As the four of them walked to her car, Marguerite reached for a bottle of sunscreen. Gil put some on and offered it to Rachel. It took effort for Rachel to avoid looking as if she thought her friends were insane, rubbing smelly tan goop all over themselves.

"No thanks," Rachel said casually. "Brent and I get sun protection at the monthly Health Screening. Don't you?"

"Heavens, no!" Marguerite said. "We haven't gone for years. That official Health Screening Protection Coat is bad news. It loads the body with chemicals that numb a person's consciousness."

"I suppose you learned that from John," Rachel said, trying to sound pleasant.

"As a matter of fact, I did," Marguerite sighed. "I'll be seeing him Sunday at the weekly service. If you want, you can come. Or not," she said, after a sidelong glance at Rachel. "You don't have to decide now."

Both women were quiet as Marguerite drove down a back road to a little county playlot with old-fashioned swings, a huge slide and several colorful plastic climbing mazes. Nobody else was there, even though the drizzle had stopped. It wasn't a beautiful day, but it was comfortably warm and the boys raced off to the swings.

"Like they were shot out of a cannon," Rachel said, smiling. "This was an inspired idea."

"I hoped they'd like it, and I wanted to talk with you alone." Marguerite gestured at a narrow clearing in the trees that circled the playlot.

"Will the boys be okay by themselves?"

"Sure," Marguerite said. "This is a safe place. I've been leaving Gilavael here to play since he was six years old. Even though he's too young for a skin-phone, he has a Pocket Pal if he needs to call us."

Rachel nodded, trying not to seem overprotective. Marguerite called the boys over, explained the walk, reminded Brent and Gil how to use the Pocket Pal and pointed out where they'd left their water bottles. "You're on your own for an hour, like astronauts on a new planet," she concluded, and they ran off bouncier than ever as Rachel followed Marguerite into a wooded area.

Their silence seemed ominous. Suspense made Rachel's stomach churn as she walked. To relax, she pressed her palms together and did some isometrics.

"Marguerite, what is it?" Rachel said, finally.

"Oh, I've been worrying," Marguerite said. "I was watching the news last night, after everyone was asleep. There's a lot going on."

"I heard about the Whatsie Bill going down in Congress."

"The Bi-Partisan Non-Religious Interference Act? That's part of it. Did you know, all of President Tucker's new cabinet officials have been cleared and confirmed."

"Well, wasn't that record time?" Rachel said sarcastically. "How nice for him. So what else is new?"

"Last night, Cooper Hackenworth—"

"Our so-called Minister of Intelligence?"

"Right, the one who always matches his prayer beads and suspenders, only they always clash."

"Marguerite, you have such an eye! I never noticed."

"Thanks. Anyway, Hackenworth gave a Press Conference to announce new evidence that the huntids are a result of biological warfare, although he refused to give any details. He ordered the American people—"

"Ordered? That's a pretty strong word, isn't it?"

"I think so. He ordered Americans to resume killing all the huntids, because they were the work of terrorists. Apparently, a couple days ago Rev. Pilgrim gave a press conference in which she said there could be dire consequences from harming even one huntid. 'The deaths will be on Hickory Helm's head unless he changes his position,' is how she put it in the vid-clip Hackenworth showed."

"Come now," Rachel snorted. "Since when does somebody in the President's cabinet defend a religious leader like Helms?"

"Religious leader? President? Is there a difference any more?" Marguerite sounded weary. "Anyway, Hackenworth said Pilgrim scares people, and something about how it was every American's constitutional right to kill huntids. Only everybody ought to use a fly swatter, not their hands, or they could catch something called Huntid Disease. Supposedly it comes from touching huntids."

"Big deal," Rachel said, laughing. "Brent's already had Huntid Disease."

"Really?"

"Gilavael hasn't?"

"No. What happened?"

"A cold that came out of his ears instead of his nose. Weird green-colored mucus. Some of his friends got it, too, and their colds came out of different places for them—like their eyes and mouth."

"That does sound strange."

"Gross, actually, but no big deal. You know what it took to cure his case of big scary Huntid Disease? One tiny shot of Superbiotics from Health Services."

"I may not be crazy about going to Health Services, but even I wouldn't call going there 'death'." Marguerite said, smiling for the first time all day.

Rachel said, "Besides, my husband knows that guy Hackenworth. He talks big because he's power-crazy. Don't let him scare you. So what else happened in this Press Conference? Or did he just give his little message about sanitation?"

"A reporter asked about Huntid Extermination Day. According to Hackenworth, our plans are to coordinate pesticide air bombs with other governments' efforts all over North and South America. Europe, Africa, Australia, too."

"That sounds scary—like a war against bugs."

"That's how he was trying to make it sound. He said we should plan in advance and be prepared to stay indoors for 24 hours, pack plenty of food and bottled water, games for the kiddies."

The path forked and Marguerite asked, "Do you want to go through more forest or around a little lake?"

"Lake, of course. I always choose water." Sarcastically Rachel added, "So that's all it took to get you so upset?"

"No, actually. There's more. Economists are predicting recession. Last night I was doing the family investments—"

"You do that?"

"Why not? Every couple has one financial whiz and someone who's just the opposite."

"That's me," Rachel said with a small giggle. "In my family, Jeremy does all the money stuff. In your family, you're the financial brain, huh?"

"Well, I have trouble sleeping more than three hours a night, so usually I do our investments around one in the morning. Last night on the Internet, pundits were making dire predictions about what's going to happen to the stock market before Huntid Extermination Day. One sight bite was really scary because the man seemed so very sure. Of course, he was also wearing the beads of The Righteous."

"Know what I think?" Rachel said, shaking her head. "They're Looney Tunes. Nothing's going to happen to the stock market. Here's the lake. Let's rest a while."

Stepping onto the grass, she jumped, feeling huntids around her ankles. They looked pretty—a twinkling green-and-purple frosting on the weedy grass as far as the eye could see. *Squeamishness is a choice,* she thought, remembering that she was a woman who could pick up worms and squish them onto fishhooks. "I don't think huntids will be that big a deal in the long run, do you?"

Marguerite shrugged. She began picking up stones and skipping them across the water. Every skip was perfect.

"How'd you do that?" said Rachel, scooped up a handful of stones. When the first sank immediately, she dropped the rest. "Marguerite, I'm going to have to get jealous of you."

"Jealousy would be your problem, not mine." Marguerite said, as her skin-phone rang. Within seconds, Rachel sensed her friend's heart racing and she saw Marguerite turn as still and cold as a stone.

Chapter 23
Doing a Good Job

"Are you sure?" Marguerite said into her skin-phone. Lifting it towards her ear, she stood motionless, listening intently. Rachel saw her bite her lip. "Stay with him until we come back," she said firmly. Turning off her skin-phone, Marguerite broke into a run toward the playlot, motioning Rachel to follow.

"What is it?" Rachel asked, falling into step beside her.

"Gil says Brent fell down and can't get up. We'll see when we get there."

Even running, it took them a good 10 minutes to reach the boys. The whole way, Rachel screamed Brent's name inside, imploring him to be okay.

He lay on the plastic foam at the bottom of the slide. Gil stood beside him, crying.

Marguerite ran straight to Gil. "What happened wasn't your fault, understand?"

Rachel leaned over Brent to cradle him in her arms. Marguerite stopped her. "Let me examine him before you move him. Remember, I was an EMT for a couple of years after college. Just hold his hand, okay?"

"You were an emergency medical tech?" Rachel said. She was dizzy, and Brent's hand felt clammy and lifeless.

"He's still breathing," Marguerite said, listening to Brent's heart. She sat up, reaching for his wrist. "Only did EMT for a couple of years but it still comes in handy." She looked up. "His pulse is slow, Rachel, but he's very much alive. Gil, did he fall on his head?"

"We weren't doing anything tricky," Gil said, looking away. "It was normal sliding."

"Tell us about it," said his mother.

Gil's face tightened, holding back tears. "We were playing astronaut, going down the slide fast for liftoff. We'd slide down, then climb up. Well, it was my turn to slide down. I was at the top when I saw him like he is now. I told him to get out of the way, and when he didn't move I yelled at him. I thought he was playing a trick on me. When he didn't answer, I got scared. I didn't want to bump him, so I climbed backwards down the stairs. And then I called you."

Rachel put her arm around Gil. "It was smart of you to give up your slide so you wouldn't bump into him," she said tearfully. Turning to Marguerite, she asked, "What do you think?"

Marguerite's hands moved rapidly as she systematically tested Brent's body—feet, legs, arms and head. "All the joints seem fine. I think we can move him."

"Hadn't I better call an ambulance?"

"I can get us there faster. Let's take him ourselves."

"If you say so," Rachel said. Marguerite was already carrying Brent to the car.

Realizing that she felt like a tag-along puppy, Rachel blurted out, "Let me carry my son."

Hearing the steel in Rachel's voice. Marguerite handed her Brent's limp body.

Carrying him, Rachel kept reaching out to make contact but he was gone. Never before had her son been unconscious; somehow he felt farther away than when he was sleeping. Where had Brent's spirit gone? Would it ever come back?

Rachel's body felt like it moved in slow motion but her mind wouldn't slow down. *How often did I call him an impossible little pest? How many times was I sarcastic? I even used to make fun of him to Jeremy. If something serious happens, can I ever forgive myself?*

She felt hollow, as if nothing but determination kept her upright. Brent hung limply in her arms. She held him tighter, close to her heart.

Jeremy's face came up instantly when she called from the hospital's pay phone, but he looked less than pleased to see her.

"Rachel, please don't get in the habit of calling me at work. We're still very busy here."

"I know you don't want me calling you about every little thing," Rachel said, shaken. "I'm at Health Services. Brent had an accident and he's in the hospital."

Jeremy's smoky blue eyes bored into her. "What happened?"

"He fell off a slide at a playlot."

"Concussion?"

"I don't think so," Rachel said, pushing away her guilt for leaving Brent unsupervised. She wasn't accepting any more guilt—Marguerite had called her on it a dozen times already and her last words had been: "Rachel, Brent needs a mother, not a drama queen."

"Are you going to tell me what happened?" Jeremy didn't seem to sense any guilt in her voice. What did she feel from *him*? Just his usual X-ray intelligence. And she felt a gray kind of loneliness, sad and flat.

She covered the feeling by talking: "Brent landed on his tush. But instead of getting up, he passed out. We rushed him here, and the doctors have been examining him for a couple of hours. One finally called us in to look at him. Nothing's broken—he's just lying there like he's in some kind of coma."

"Don't they have any clue what's going on?"

"Actually they do—the doctor said it fits the profile of Huntid Disease."

Jeremy gripped the edge of his desk, then crossed his arms and began rubbing his shoulders. He stopped abruptly, only to clutch the desk again. "That's ridiculous. I've never heard of anyone coming down with Huntid Disease. What are the robots telling you?"

"We haven't been dealing with robots because this isn't a routine visit," Rachel said in a small voice. "Dr. Chai looked it up on the diagnostic computer and printed out a statement to show me. Huntid Disease is not the same thing that Brent and half the scouts at day camp had—that's called Huntid Inflammation. It comes on like a cold, with green mucus dripping out of the ears or nose or mouth or eyes. Usually it goes away fast with a shot of Superbiotics."

"What's Huntid Disease then?"

"It's so rare that fewer than a hundred people in the country have ever come down with it. All of them went through the inflammation stage first. It seemed to heal but later they went into comas."

"Anyone die from it?"

"No, but a couple of those patients are still in comas."

"What do the doctors do? Just let their patients lie there until they wake up?"

His anger was rising along with his voice. Rachel started to shake inside, but she took care to look and sound calm. "Pretty much, Jeremy. Brent is on an IV. He's in a single room in a pediatric unit. It's nice, as far as hospitals go."

"Don't they know anything?" Jeremy's voice sounded accusatory, and he looked at Rachel as if she was someone he barely knew. Drawing a sharp breath, Rachel realized that she had expected better from him. Comfort, perhaps; certainly warmth and concern. Not this cold, impersonal interrogation. She recognized that she'd hoped this might bring them closer, that maybe he'd offer to get on a plane to be with her and Brent.

"No, we're all idiots here," she said bitterly. "I won't bother you again unless there's something you need to know."

"Come on, Sunflower, I was just asking," he said, this time in his old familiar Jeremy voice. "Let me call some people who may be up on this stuff. I'll call back tonight and tell you what I find out, and you can tell me how he's doing. Sound good?"

"Okay, Jeremy. Thanks for doing the research. Goodbye," Rachel said.

Jeremy made a gesture as though wrapping his arms around her for a hug. He said, "Sounds like you're doing a good job, Sweetheart."

Too little, too late, she thought sadly.

That night, Jeremy was no better informed. None of his contacts could tell him anything new about Huntid Disease. Rachel had nothing to add either. She felt a million miles away from his polite attempts at small talk, and she carefully avoided telling him that Marguerite had arranged for her to have a personal healing session with John. If she liked it, said Marguerite, he could do some distance healing on Brent via videophone. Rachel had no intention of telling Jeremy about the experiment—it was expensive and, she knew, far too offbeat to suit Jeremy.

"Rachel, are you sure you're telling me everything?" His voice brought her back to earth with a thud. "You seem to be taking all this so well, and I know it can't be easy."

You've got that right, Rachel thought, but where did she start? The worst was the cold, numb feeling, the grayness, the sense that Jeremy simply didn't care. Courageous though Rachel could be, she couldn't confront her husband with that; it might only drive him farther away. It was as if their marriage was in a coma, too, maybe one worse than Brent's.

"I remember you once said that I have a tendency to over-dramatize," she replied with a faint sigh. "I've been working on that, and I have a feeling that Brent is going to be just fine." She gave him her prettiest smile. "Let's talk again Wednesday, unless one of us has some real news before then."

"Love you," Jeremy said.

Rachel blew him a kiss as she pushed the Fade button. *What the hell,* she thought. *You've got to keep the flame of hope alive.*

Chapter 24
The Healing

Skeptical though Rachel was about seeing John, it would give her something to do besides calling Health Services, which she began at dawn, visiting Brent's bedside electronically. What a strangely inhuman way it was to visit her son—voicing a number, giving a code, seeing him over the private room's telescreen. It showed Brent in his hospital bed, an IV drip in his lightly muscled eight-year-old arm and strange wires from various monitors crisscrossing his blue hospital gown. Only his blond hair looked familiar, curly as ever. His eyes were closed.

Yesterday Marguerite had advised her, "Talk to him, even if he seems a million miles away."

Rachel did, sitting on the living room sofa in front of the family telescreen. Maybe it really was good for Brent in some mysterious way, hearing the voice of his mother. She told him the reasons she loved him, and that she'd love him even if there were no reasons. Even the annoying things she used to scold him for were praised now, with tears running down her cheeks. By the hour, she told the motionless form in the bed his favorite family stories, the stories he loved.

"Brent, do you remember the first time you climbed out of your crib? When you landed on the floor, you caught your arm between those two bars and you started crying. When I came to help, you said, 'It hurts.' I'll never forget the pride in your voice. Sure your arm hurt, but you knew it was a victory. That's my brave son!"

"Remember when we bought your big boy bed and you ran toward the mirror at the back wall of the furniture store? I kept wondering who you thought that other little boy was, running toward you without moving away, until you crashed right into the mirror."

"Hey Brent, do you remember when you were three and I left you alone in the bedroom? You unscrewed all the knobs to my bureau and threw them on the floor. When I yelled, 'Why did you do that?' you turned to me with an enormous grin and said, 'Because me clever.'

"You *are* clever, Babycakes. You're the smartest little boy I ever saw."

Sometimes Rachel felt numb with worry but, no matter what, she kept on sending healing thoughts to Brent. She kept asking him to he pull himself together and wake up. Afterwards she'd wait a while, just in case it might magically happen. No such luck.

When Rachel didn't want breakfast, Marguerite brought her tea: a handmade teapot on a beautiful tray, with a little honey pot on the side. In a cheerful voice, she said, "It's really a good thing, their allowing telescreen-only visits until Brent's better. This way you can see him all you want. No hospital smells, either."

Marguerite and Gil hung around all morning, staying close to Rachel but never intruding. At ten o'clock Marguerite suggested gently that Rachel call The Spiritual Center if she still wanted an appointment. Rachel expected Marguerite to make the appointment. It had been her idea. But ever the contrarian, she insisted that Rachel do it herself. Her heart pounding, Rachel voiced in the number. If John Wilcox was half the healer Marguerite said he was, he would prove it during this session; then Rachel could have him work on Brent. Meanwhile Marguerite puttered around, rearranging the chairs in the dining nook—eavesdropping, obviously.

"The Spiritual Center," said a pleasant looking, middle-aged woman. "I'm Consuela. How can I help you?"

Rachel explained that Marguerite told her to ask for an emergency session with John for herself, and that maybe afterwards she might request a session for her son Brent, who was in a coma because of Huntid Disease.

Consuela's brown eyes turned very bright. "Could you be here by one o'clock today?" she asked.

"I don't know," Rachel started to say when Marguerite stage whispered across the room, "Sure you can. Take my car."

Consuela gave Rachel directions, concluding, "If the parking lot on the Center's property is full, there's plenty of on-street parking. Just avoid parking near the houses on either side or they might tow you."

"Your neighbors don't like what you're doing, huh?"

"It just a traffic problem," Consuela said, extra pleasantly. "If you owned one of the mansions around here, you might not appreciate all the people who come by. For us, it's different." Consuela gave a conspiratorial smile. Awkwardly Rachel smiled back.

John's house, at the end of the block, was some place! It stood out, not like a sore thumb, more like a big purple one with red nail polish. From the street it was obvious that the mansion's parking lot was filled, so she parked around the corner.

It was fun walking back to the house. This was an exquisite waterfront neighborhood overlooking Puget Sound. Rachel could almost smell the old money, which reminded her of her party girl days. She passed one mansion after another, half-hidden behind their tidy hedges. Gardens bloomed on every lawn: Roses, dahlias, peonies, and all sorts of engineered flowers, like long-blossoming lilacs.

Behind another row of gorgeous mansions stood the Puget Sound shoreline. Across the sparkling water, mountains lined up side by side. Olympic Mountains. Their tops were faceted like diamonds, turned surreally huge and smoky blue. Even in August, the chiseled peaks had snow. Ancient was how they felt to Rachel, definitely a balm to the soul.

Turning away from the mountains to walk toward The Spiritual Center, however, seemed like going from the sublime to the ridiculous. The place had no sign. Not that it needed one to stand out in this neighborhood. The big gravel parking lot to the left was one tip-off. Rachel counted eight cars, one a shiny new Hyper-thrust Jaguar, the rest old clunkers like Marguerite's. The building itself had two stories and a balcony, just like the other houses on the block; however, a whole extra wing of the Center had been built onto the right.

The blue paint on this box-shaped hideosity didn't begin to match the rest of the house, which was pale yellow. *I'll bet the neighbors just love this,* Rachel thought, taking in the lavender curtains, pink trim and the bright red front door.

She sighed. Even if John was an utter, hopeless, retro-hippie fake, this visit would be entertaining, definitely something to take her mind off worrying about Brent. On the path to the door, Rachel passed a few straggly rosebushes in one corner—John's sad excuse for a flower garden. Then she walked by a huge vegetable patch, with neat rows of blooming plants, what you'd expect to find in the country, not someone's front yard, for crying out loud.

When Rachel finally reached the front door, it was closed. Then she saw a little sign with an arrow, steering her toward the side of the house. *Their grand entrance must be the kitchen door,* she thought. Sure enough. A hanging assortment of bells jingled as she entered.

The kitchen was huge and empty, sparkling clean, with a lot of blond plasti-wood setting off a blue-and-white floor. She walked through a hallway into an enormous room. In one corner stood the oak desk she'd seen on the phone, with a standard-sized phone-screen angled against a wall. The same woman Rachel had spoken with earlier, Consuela, was doing something on a computer. She turned briefly and smiled, then went back to work, which left Rachel to self-consciously walk across the long room to meet her.

Before John's group got hold of this mansion, the long rectangular room must have been the living room and dining room combined. *They must have ripped out a wall when they added the hideosity wing,* Rachel thought. Now the place was set up with rows of chairs, auditorium style. She counted the rows as she walked— 27—before she reached Consuela's desk. Some reception room! It was as friendly as a tomb. Even before she reached Consuela, Rachel decided this place had to be nuts. Otherwise what would explain their having a supposedly public reception area without even the courtesy of some cheap quadriphonic Muzak?

"You must be Rachel." Consuela smiled. Her antique desk was made of real oak. She looked deeper into Rachel's eyes than Rachel wished to be seen right now, thank you. Rachel blinked and lifted her datamate out of her purse.

"Oh, you won't need that," Consuela said.

"How about paying?"

"You can pay on the way out. If I'm not here, just leave a check on the desk."

A check? Rachel guessed she had some with her. How old-fashioned, though, not to pay the bill with her skin-phone. The Center's lack of disclaimers was even more shocking but, hey, not *her* problem.

"Whenever you're ready, you can go on up." Consuela gestured toward the stairs. "Second floor. Knock on the door. John should be waiting for you."

Rachel nodded and curved her lips upward into a sort of smile.

While she walked up the two flights of stairs, her heart was pounding wildly. *Come on,* she told herself, *it's just an appointment with some healer, who could be a total phony, a partial phony, or something else. The real question is, should I open the door or will he use some fancy schmancy telepathy to figure out that I'm here.*

Just as she raised her hand to knock, the door opened. A tall redhead walked out, passed Rachel, and descended the stairs. Rachel found herself staring at John, a short man, only a head taller than her five foot two. His far-set brown eyes riveted her: Soft and sunny, tender and earthy, all at the same time. Connecting to his eyes made time seem to stop.

She was the first to look down. John's nose was small and beneath them were big, curved cheeks, surprisingly chubby since the rest of him seemed as solid as a football player. Wide jaws showed a hint of untamed beard, and his full lips were crimson, curved to form an impersonal smile, as though he didn't know who she was. Rachel found this annoying even though common sense argued, why should he? They'd only just met.

Still it did annoy her, she realized. His arm gestured for her to come into the attic room. The door squeaked as he shut it. They sat on folding chairs next to a large picture window. *Impersonality. That was what bothered her.* John's perfectly nice little smile reminded her of being at a delicatessen when your number came up. The man behind the counter would say, "Next," and you'd feel about as special as the pre-cut slices of cold cuts in the refrigerator case.

"Right, you're Rachel, Marguerite Bauman's friend. Tell me, what can I do for you?"

"I'm auditioning you. Marguerite thinks maybe you can help my son."

"Fair enough. Well, is there anything you would like me to know about your health before you go on the table."

"Not really," Rachel answered, looking away. "I guess I should tell you I'm skeptical about healers. If you can look into people's bodies and auras, the way Marguerite says you can, you shouldn't need any other hints from me. Oh, do I keep my clothes on?"

"Please, all but your shoes and socks."

She complied, tucking each sock neatly into its shoe, then lining the shoes up like straight little soldiers.

"Up you go then."

Rachel was wearing her favorite blue jeans and a yellow silk blouse. She lifted herself onto a cushy massage table and slipped between aqua sheets with fussy little flowers in a repeating pattern. "*Here goes nothing,*" she thought.

John leaned over the table to catch her eye. He said, "I always begin with a prayer. Are you affiliated with any particular religion?"

"Not really," Rachel said.

"I'll go with my standard version, then. Archangel Michael, Rachel and I stand before you and almighty God. I call in her Guides and my Guides, and ask you to direct us all to Your highest good."

As Rachel lay on her back, she could see John's hands poised motionless several feet above her head. Suddenly he smiled. "There we go. Your Guides just gave me clearance." His hands began waving over her body in motions that made no sense whatsoever.

"What are you doing?"

"Oh, you're the sort that wants to know? Some don't."

"Sure I want to know. You mean you've started healing something already?"

"Parasites, lady. Yellow and green crawly things down your abdominal area. Some red ones in the back, over your behind. I'm stirring things up. Then I'll blow them away. . . with some help from my friends.

Omigod! "Is this about huntids? Maybe I was exposed . . . ."

"Not at all. Huntids are no problem."

Rachel looked at John quizzically. He kept moving his hands. "Parasites, though, they're a common problem. You're lucky to be rid of them so easily. Be more careful in future about the water you drink. Even when you rinse your toothbrush, make sure it's filtered water, okay? Quiet now."

John closed his eyes, opened them, scooped up something from the air near Rachel's stomach, then closed his eyes again, and blew. "Thanks," he said. To whom, his invisible Guides? After a moment's pause, he started making more motions, moving his hands downward as if stroking the air around Rachel's throat.

"Well," she said, "According to one seminar I took, every physical ailment means something psychological, too. Do you think my having parasites shows any particular weakness?"

John chuckled. His downward strokes shifted to the air above her ribcage. "Well, right now I'm pulling out some old globs of fear locked into your intestines. But that's not related to parasites, necessarily.

"I don't specialize in finding emotions, the way you would, Rachel. A feeling, like this fear you're releasing, must be majorly obvious for me to find it. You know, I'm set up to be a spiritual teacher and physical healer, not an empath like you. The main thing we've got to work on this session is some chronic—"

"Hold on. What do you mean, an empath like me?"

"You didn't know? You're not skilled yet, obviously. But you have what it takes to be a first-rate emotional empath."

"How can you say a thing like that?"

"It shows like neon signs all over your aura, my dear. Your gift involves noticing feelings. Anyone's feelings. In fact, about 80% of the strong emotions you go through on any given day—guess what? They don't belong to you at all."

"Whose are they, then?"

"Other people's. You can learn to sort it out. That's called becoming a skilled empath."

"Ridiculous," Rachel said, sitting bolt upright. "Sometimes I think I'm the most selfish person I know. Now I'm scared to death about Brent and worried about my husband, but that's only because we're going through an official crisis. Usually when people I'm close to feel bad, I'm clueless until they tell me. As for my having close friends. . . ."

She glared at John. "If you must know, being so insensitive is something I don't like about myself. Supposing I was an empath, wouldn't I naturally be just the opposite? For instance, I have this friend, Heather. When she found out her ex-husband was HIV positive, she went through horrible feelings of abandonment. But did I notice? Noooo. I thought Heather was being her usual bubble-headed self. I didn't notice a thing until she told me she found the H on his butt. Rotten George's, I mean. Some empath!"

John pushed her down with one finger. He started stroking the air again, about six inches off her ribs.

"Even an empath won't know how others feel until she learns to listen."

Rachel pouted. "Who listens, nowadays?"

John kept working in mysterious silence.

"Well? Supposing I *did* want to get skilled at being an empath, what would I do?"

"Apprentice here at the Center. We have some very skilled mentors for emotional empaths—like Consuela who made your appointment today."

A hotshot empath? And she's dumpy and working as a receptionist? Empath must be quite the career path. "Anyway, John, you were telling me about some chronic thingie you're pulling out ...."

"Right." His hands were moving strangely now, as if grabbing energy out by the handful and pulling it upward through his fists, like long spaghetti strings. "You said before you're not involved in any religion. This session is confidential so don't be afraid to tell me."

"Was that supposed to be a question? What makes you think I'm involved in some religion?"

John kept silent, slowly moving his hands. He was working above her breasts now, which made Rachel self-conscious. She continued, "Both my parents are Jewish, but I'm not into that and my husband isn't anything, either. He comes from a long line of Catholics."

More silence.

"Jeremy, my husband, calls me a Seminar Slave—if you know what that means."

John shifted to working over her right arm, pulling and pulling. Rachel felt a faint tingling under her skin, which was impossible.

"What was there about my aura that made you ask about religion? If you tell me I have some mark on my aura that says I've got to sign up as one of The Righteous, or one of those soppy Traditionals, I'm gonna lose my cookies right on this table."

"You brought cookies?"

"You know, throw up."

"No, nothing like that," John said. He was working over her left arm now. "I'm just surprised, that's all. Usually when I see this type of neurological strain it's from someone who's a heavy duty. Constantly doing dances of The Righteous, working the beads, a real heroic self-multiplier."

"Well, I do multi-task a lot."

"I'll say!"

"What's wrong with that? You've got to keep your body toned, at least if you're a woman. And you've got to keep your mind occupied, especially if your life is boring. Which mine is—good but boring. It's not like I'm some V-R addict. Wow, when they come to see you, their bodies must really be messed up."

Silence.

"Well, aren't they?"

John said, "Numb more than anything, but these days most people have chronic neurological disturbance of one kind or another."

"I'll have to tell Jeremy that. My husband. He's always saying the big problem of the modern age is weakness of our immune systems. You don't think so, huh?"

"Both are problems. Strain to the nerves makes immunity weak. Turn over, please, so I can work on your back."

John wasn't any big talker, to put it mildly. In response to Rachel's questions, he explained his idea that constant multi-tasking, especially doing four or more activities at once, put stress on subtle parts of the mind-body system. Knots, he called it. He was unwinding some of those knots in Rachel. He said it would help her calm down.

"Maybe I'm worried about my family right now, but that doesn't make me tense."

"You empaths are so funny," John said. "Since your lens for seeing the world is mostly emotional, you typically won't notice when you're tense on a physical level. IMHO, when you came to this table today your body was strung so tight, it was ready to snap."

"I'm that out of touch?"

"You'd notice the tension emotionally, not physically. Ever feel as though emotions are bombarding you from every direction? Sometimes it could be a mental commentary, like you have a sportscaster in your head, giving you a blow by blow of the rugby match."

"How about making wisecracks?"

"Could be. Or it might show up as one feeling coming back over and over, like a song on replay. Know what I mean?"

"I guess so. Sure. Could this healing of yours make a difference?"

"Should. You can help things along by changing your habits. Try doing just one or two things at a time. Not half a dozen, kiddo. All right? Now roll over and rest for a few minutes before getting up. You're done."

Rachel took her sweet time on the table before getting up, which was unusual. She resisted the impulse to exercise as she lay there, supposedly relaxing. When a few songs started to run through her head, she turned them off and got up, slowly and purposefully. Rays of gold sunlight came through the window, delighting her. She put on her yellow socks and swirl-patterned sneakers, then said, "Thank you, John. That was relaxing, I think."

"Don't think too much." He moved to give her a hug.

Rachel bent forward so he got no more than her arms and the tops of her breasts. Ginger-colored hair tumbled straight and soft over his forehead.

John pulled back as quickly as she did. Someone knocked at the door. "It's my next appointment," he said.

"But wait. I want to talk to you about working on my son."

"Just check with Consuela downstairs," he said, smiling. "We already set aside a session for him at three o'clock, in case you wanted it."

Chapter 25
Brent's Turn

"Hey, Marguerite, it's me, calling from my skin-phone. John was great."

"Well, that's a relief. Are you going to have him work on Brent?"

"It's all set. I've been walking around the neighborhood, killing time 'till three o'clock. What have you and Gil been doing?"

"For a while we worked on his algebra. Then, it's such a beautiful day, I took him hiking back at the playground. We took the trail to the lake."

"Gilavael still feels guilty, doesn't he? You wanted to take him there so he could go back to the scene of the crime—which wasn't a crime, of course. Am I right?"

Marguerite laughed softly. "You're something, Rachel."

"I'll call you right after John works on Brent, before I drive home."

"That's okay, we can share notes when you're back. Starting at three, I'll tune in and Gilavael will too, probably. Usually he thinks spiritual exercises aren't especially relevant to real life. Brent's accident could turn out to be very motivating for my fidgety little boy."

"Hold on, Marguerite. When you tune in, does that mean you and Gil will see exactly what happens to Brent, like on a telescreen?"

"No, because I'm not an appliance. I have my unique set of gifts, like Gil or like you. On the inner, everyone perceives differently. That's part of the fun, when you think about it."

"Oh, get this, Marguerite. John said I could be a first-rate emotional empath. Does he say that to all the girls?"

"You'd have to ask all the girls. He didn't say it to me, I can tell you that."

Foot in mouth as usual, Rachel thought. After an awkward pause, she started to say goodbye. Marguerite talked at the same time.

"Go ahead," Rachel said.

Marguerite said, "Don't feel too sorry for me. I'm not an empath but Santa Claus didn't entirely leave me off his list. Spiritual abilities aren't one-size-fits-all—"

"Like that 'calling' Rev. Helms talks about, where either you have It or you don't, and if you don't you'll rot forever in Hell?"

"Exactly, Rachel. Welcome to disorganized religion, where you have to find the truth for yourself. Someone like John is just a facilitator."

"Well, I sure hope he can facilitate a miracle for Brent."

"Me, too. See you back home."

As she said goodbye, Rachel's eyes began to leak tears. It was like years ago when Brent was a baby, and one quick thought of him would send down her milk.

For the session with Brent, John came down from his attic room to set things up in the reception area. He said he wanted Rachel to be able to see Brent over the telescreen. Consuela was to move her work into the kitchen, where she could intercept John's next appointment, plus anyone else who wandered into The Spiritual Center.

"I appreciate your going to all this trouble," Rachel said. She and John were pulling over a couple of chairs from the auditorium-style seating. He angled their chairs in front of the reception desk, giving them both a clear view of the telescreen.

"Do I have to sit down?" Rachel asked. She preferred to stand and do some stretches, maybe inner thigh isometrics followed by ab crunches.

"How about taking a deep breath with me. Sit here."

As John pointed to the chair, Rachel felt a slight tingle. *Yes, there could be something sexy about sitting next to a man like this, on command.* Then she thought, *He has such an interesting way of holding his body, as if he's aware of every muscle.*

John said, "If you like, you can help by holding a space for Brent and me."

God, he isn't the slightest bit interested. Well, I shouldn't be either. I'm a married woman. "Sure," she said, staring straight ahead at the blank telescreen.

"Did you ever hold a space before?"

"I was trying to bluff my way through, I guess. What am I supposed to do?"

"Pay attention."

"That's it? Holding a space means you pay attention?"

He laughed. "How about I talk you through this?"

Rachel nodded. Seminar mode—she was used to this. Learning one more technique shouldn't intimidate her in the least.

John had Rachel close her eyes, then take "Vibe-raising" breaths—in through the nose and out through the mouth. He asked if she felt the energy around her body. Rachel felt nothing. Nothing but stupid. "Not really," she said. Her eyes flew open. "Listen, if I don't do this right, will it make things harder for you to help Brent?"

John looked her straight in the eye and smiled warmly. What a smile he had, with those big, muscular lips! "Anything you do is a plus. I invited you in mostly for your sake."

Rachel felt as insecure as a teenager. "I'm willing to do this," she said. "But I don't know how to feel energy around my body. Unless you're asking how much energy is *in* my body right now. I've got plenty of that."

"I bet," he said. She felt a wave of electricity shoot through her in a very personal place, then disguised it by sitting up extra straight. "Okay, so what do I do?"

"Would you like a little boost?"

"Sure."

"Here's what I'll do then. Close your eyes and keep breathing in through the nose and out through the mouth. I'm going to stand in back of you, Get Big in my consciousness, and zap you by putting my hands on your shoulders."

Rachel nodded, giving permission. She breathed as deeply as she could. *Does smelling him count? I like it, I like it*, she thought.

"What do you feel now?" he asked.

She swallowed. "Well, your hands are strong. They feel good. You're not holding too tight or anything."

"Rachel, notice my energy presence there along with you. Let go and feel. There's the sense of *you* in your body. Along with it, sense *my* being there, too."

That's what sex is all about, honey, Rachel thought. "Obviously, you're here." she said primly, opening her eyes.

"Do you give permission, during the rest of this session, to experience me and Brent along with yourself?"

"Sure."

"Then consider yourself plugged in. From now on, everything you notice will belong to one of us, or one of the angels who's helping us."

"How do I know which is which?"

"You don't have to, for now. Learning to sort that out will come later, if you study to become a skilled empath. For now, the only thing you need know is how *easy* it is to move in your consciousness. You're far better at this than you think. In fact, it's so easy for you, it's ridiculous."

"If you say so."

John sat down next to Rachel and said, "Hello, Brent. Your mother and I are here to help you. I'm John.

"We're creating one big energy space for you, mate. It includes your hospital room and our room here at The Spiritual Center. As a matter of fact, we're also speaking to your energy presence in *all* the places it is right now, not just your physical body.

"Father-Mother God, I acknowledge your presence here along with Brent and Rachel. I call in all our Guides and Angels. I call in Archangel Raphael since he specializes in healing. God, direct us all to Your highest good."

Rachel opened her eyes to peek at Brent. He lay on his hospital bed, slumped as usual, his body small and lifeless as a doll.

"Rachel," John said, "Take more vibe-raising breaths to feel how the energy volume just turned up. Remember, the secret of holding a space is to pay attention to your inner experience.

"Brent, back to you. There's a reason why we're joining with you now. Your physical body is in a bit of a coma. Come back to your body. It's time. We're joining with you first, to give you a boost. Your Mum and I are closing our eyes, now."

Rachel thought that this last remark of John's seemed to be more for her benefit than Brent's.

"We're here with you in a very big space, Brent. We're ready to learn. . . ." John kept talking but his voice shifted to the background. With a shock Rachel felt the top fall out of the sky—the way that you can be outside in the twilight, as it grows bluer and bluer until, all at once, the color goes out of the air and, suddenly, it's night.

In this kind of big, night-time space (not *sky*, but *space*), Rachel was simply being alive. Although she still had a body, it ceased to be relevant. Far more interesting were the little white sparkles of light which, somehow, she was. John was there, too, whirling around like more little sparkles. The two of them began to travel like magnets, aiming to attach themselves to the sparkles that belonged to Brent. Finding them was easy, except that the Brent sparkles were in so many places. More places than Rachel was used to inhabiting as just one person. (*Whatever that meant!*)

The sparkles of Brent were spread out all over the world and, especially thickly, in the United States. An image flashed into Rachel's mind of a strategy map with colored pins stuck into it, many, many pins. Dots of light that belonged to

Rachel and John were spreading out, searching until they made contact with every pin that was Brent.

Finally they connected to the last one. What happened next was startling, like switching on a light in a dark room. Brent recognized her and John; they hugged together like iron filings and magnets and did this simultaneously in all the pin places on the map. Rachel noticed, this made her feel wonderfully complete.

Strangely, this sense of completeness included Jeremy, too, as if he had been present all along with Brent. Her husband's presence seemed faint, only a small part of who he was—*however this could be possible,* Rachel thought—but there was no time to figure it out now. What mattered was that all four of them were together, Jeremy, John, Brent and Rachel, in a whirling pattern of energy that moved through space.

In the background, John's voice continued speaking in a calm, commanding tone. *How odd*, Rachel thought. His voice, like the room at The Healing Center where the two of them sat, reminded Rachel of a grayed-out, black-&-white computer image. Meanwhile the whirling sparks of who they really were. . .was more like a movie, full-color, 3-D and full of joy.

Then John asked her to listen for a sound. Out of the deep silence came little pulsations, like what? It sounded like crickets at dusk. Now that Rachel-Brent-John-Jeremy were listening to the sound, it shifted and grew louder, into a strong hum. A memory flashed: Rachel used to hear a hum like that as a child; how could she have forgotten? *Could I please be with it forever?* A great longing rose up in Rachel. It turned her inside out, as if she was coming into a rush of electricity, wide awake inside, her body at peace.

John's voice in the background became gentle and very quiet. "Brent, I know that you can hear us. We are calling you back into your body. All of you, body-mind-spirit, are to be collected back in *one* place. This is a command. Come back now." John's voice, though soft spoken, rang with authority.

Rachel froze for a moment. It seemed like everything stopped. When he spoke again, his voice said, "Rachel, come back to normal and feel yourself here in this room."

She did, opening her eyes. Then she closed them again because the transition made her feel dizzy.

John said, "God, if it is your will, bring Brent back now." He clapped his hands—once, hard. It broke the sound in the room.

"Brent, breathe in and out. Come back through your breath. Do it *now*."

Rachel blinked. Her heart seemed to skip a beat.

John chuckled. "Right. It's a bit of a shock, landing back in your body. You feel real to yourself, though, don't you?"

Rachel found herself giving John a flirtatious glance over her shoulder. "What did you think I felt like before, chopped liver?" She flicked her attention back to the screen. Brent opened his eyes, just as she'd seen him do a thousand mornings.

"Mom, you and Dad came to get me. And this man. I've seen him before," Brent said. He sat up, eyes dazed.

"Babycakes," Rachel said. "Look up at the telescreen. Can you see me?"

Brent stuck up his chin, blinked a few times, made eye contact. "Hi, Mom."

Rachel waved. "You've been in the hospital at Health Services, taking a kind of long nap."

"An adventure," John said, smiling.

"Whatever," Rachel said. "Brent, I'm getting in the car right away to come get you. Save a big hug for me, okay?"

"Sure, Mom," he said.

"Hello, mate," John said. "My name's John Wilcox and I'm a friend of your Mum's. Here's an idea. While you're waiting for her to come get you, there's a little button to the side of your bed, on the right. There you go. Push it. You'll bring in a nurse. Tell her you're awake now and your Mum's coming to take you home. Tell her that you want your clothes back, okay?"

Later that night, with Brent safely picked up and at Marguerite's house, it was time to call Jeremy. Rachel punched in a conference call, just like she used to do for party clients and entertainers, only now Rachel put Brent on the line in the living room, with the big family-sized screen, while she hid in the hall, using Marguerite's portable screen to secretly watch close-ups of both Jeremy and Brent, over a split screen. When Jeremy picked up the phone, and his screen went from dark to color, it reminded her of the curtain going up in a theater.

His routine hello dropped off in the middle, soon as he saw Brent. Jeremy stared, his eyes like magnets pulling into the core of his son. Then he unfolded his full smile, a rare event. With a bittersweet pang, Rachel remembered that when she first met him back in college Jeremy always used to give her that kind of smile, slowly pulling his long mouth as wide as it could go, then lifting his upper lip to reveal his slightly overlapping front teeth. Middle-aged Jeremy smiled rarely, and only curved his lips slightly. But in the early days with Rachel he used to smile so big and so often. What did she call him then? "Mr. Umbrella Mouth." Where had that smiling man gone?

He was back now, for Brent. Unlike Rachel, Brent had no sense of nostalgia; in fact, his first words on being reunited with his father were, "Hello, it's Joe's Pizza. Would you like to order a banana?"

Jeremy answered, "You crazy, old man? Why would I want to order a banana from a noodle-head like you?"

Instantly they were off and running, into their private world of Dad-and-son jokes. If Rachel had given birth to a girl instead of a boy, maybe Jeremy would have been the one who felt left out. How many times in the past had Rachel listened to their banter, thinking "Two is company, three is a crowd." This time was different. She felt so relieved they could be together.

Finally she came out of hiding and joined her men-folk at the living room phone screen. After exchanging greetings, she told Jeremy, "Huntid Disease turned out not to be that big a deal. This healer friend of Marguerite's, John Wilcox, did a session of what they call 'remote healing.' Fixed Brent right up."

"Remote healing?"

"Long-distance, from John's Spiritual Center to the hospital. I sat next to him and watched. We called Brent up on the telescreen; that's how our session started."

"What did this remote healer do, exactly?"

"I couldn't tell you." Rachel said. This was more-or-less true.

"I see," said Jeremy dryly. "Brent, you were the star of the show. Do you remember anything about your remote healing?"

"Sure." Brent's face lit up so bright, his skin looked transparent. "It felt like they came and got me. You know, I went somewhere beautiful while I was asleep. It felt real, not like a dream. There were colors there, Dad, different colors from anything in the whole wide world."

"Anything else happen, that you recall?"

"No. I sure wish I could see those colors again. Wish you could see them, too." Brent's eyes were shining. Fortunately he didn't notice his father's skeptical look. Rachel did. She narrowed her eyes. "Jeremy, you can believe in the session or not, but I was there. Something really happened. By the end, Brent opened his eyes and came out of the coma."

"Well, I suppose acknowledging his recovery could be considered more important than maintaining my perfect score as a non-believer." Jeremy laughed, unfurling his full smile. Rachel found herself smiling big, too, for her first time this phone call.

She said, "John wasn't expensive, by the way; I paid for it out of my spending money. And everybody at Health Services was very nice about letting Brent go home right away."

"They have no clue about what happened, do they?"

"Only statistics. To them this is one more mysterious case of Huntid Disease. All the pre-discharge tests on Brent were normal. That jibes with their records, because everyone else who came out of the coma has been as right as rain."

Jeremy grunted.

"They gave me soup for dinner," Brent said. "And tomorrow we're going out for ice cream. And, Dad, Marguerite said she knows a really great place to take us in the morning for fun."

Out of courtesy, Marguerite and Gil were invited to join Jeremy at the end of the call. All five of them made happy small talk together. Rachel would have said things were back to normal except for one thing. That night, before bed, after she went through her usual of stretches and said her routine prayer to God, Rachel turned into sparkles again.

If only this would last forever....

Immediately she landed in her body — part flab and part sex goddess, part healthy and part horny. Grumbling, Rachel recognized that she was back to business as usual, and promptly fell asleep.

Chapter 26
Magical Marvin's

Marguerite kept her promise, taking them out for what she mysteriously called "ice cream and an adventure." Since it was Sunday, Rachel agreed they'd go to the service at The Spiritual Center afterwards.

The prospect of an adventure seemed to impress Brent—he didn't even fight with Gil on the way there.

When the car stopped, Gil blurted out excitedly, "It's the Fremont Folk Festival." Rachel looked around. All she saw was the enormous public heliport where Marguerite had parked the black Honda Hybrid.

"Where are the taxis?" Brent asked, puzzled by this helicopter lot. The only vehicles there were cars, parked in rows that ignored the yellow, box-shaped guidelines that normally indicated 'copter parking.

"Banished by decree," Marguerite said gaily. "You'll discover that the parking lot is just as wacky as the festival."

"I love having everyone park in the wrong place," said Rachel. "It's as if a whole community decided to put square pegs in round holes."

"That's Fremont," said Gil. He pushed Brent forward onto the exit slideway, where they rode giggling as they experimented with ways to move their feet against the slowly moving transport belt.

Then Marguerite led them down a street lined with charming storefront shops. "They put on this Folk Festival every year. I think it started as a PR stunt when the Boeing Corporation moved back here and opened this public heliport parking lot—it was the first anywhere, not just Washington West."

"Big deal," Brent said.

Well, Rachel thought, *sounds like he's getting back to normal.*

"Do you even know how big this city is?" Gil asked him.

"Bet it's no bigger than Capitol City. We go all the way from Baltimore to Richmond."

"Washington West has more suburbs," Gilavael said, his red hair glinting in the morning sunlight. He counted off the names with his fingers: "Bellingham, Shoreline, Seattle, Bremerton, Takoma, Olympia, Longview."

"Well, our suburbs are better. We have the government."

"Yeah? You can keep the government."

"Boys, boys," Marguerite said. "Go play some games and meet us by the music stage." She grabbed a handful of dollar coins out of her purse and dropped them into Gil's cupped hands. Before Rachel could stop her, she handed another fistful to Brent. The boys ran off.

"You shouldn't have," Rachel protested. Then she mumbled, "You don't think there will be huntids around here, do you?"

Marguerite faced her, placing her hands on Rachel's shoulders, a stretch for such a short woman. "Lighten up about the huntids, kid. Do you think we'd have come if I thought we'd be in danger?"

That's what you said last time, Rachel groaned inwardly, trying to keep her face from reflecting her thoughts. Out of habit she started doing butt crunches to divert her annoyance. On the second crunch she remembered John's advice and stopped. She'd just have to relax and walk.

Marguerite was saying, "From what I know about huntids, they lie low. They don't alight on you unless you stand still among them. Also, huntids swarm where there's vegetation. Look around. What's here besides plastics and blacktop? Freemont sidewalks are paved with a very pretty pink shade of tacky-tile. I don't think you'll find any huntids."

Much as Rachel hated being lectured to, she supposed she deserved it.

"Besides," Marguerite continued, "What really worries you isn't huntids but Huntid Disease, right? The doctors told us that Huntid Disease is systemic. Brent's coma wasn't brought on by contact with flies in the playground. He'd been carrying the syndrome ever since that strange cold he had last summer. Besides, if anything, Brent's having had it was an honor—"

Abruptly Marguerite stopped speaking.

"What did you say?"

"Nothing. That's the stuff you can learn more about at the Center. By the way, do you really want to come to the service today? You don't have to. I could drop you and Brent at home."

"Thanks, but I'm coming. Assuming skeptics are allowed, of course." Rachel's voice trailed off as they reached the stage area. Her friend bustled through the crowd, surprisingly large for a Sunday morning, pointing them towards a space near the front.

Before them, a folksinger in a rainbow-hued, tie-dyed dress strummed an antique guitar made of real wood. It had been years since Rachel had seen one. The guitar must be very valuable; today's musical instruments, like her violin, were made of Synthe-wood.

The singer's clear soprano voice rang out with a contagious kind of freedom that made cares melt away. Rachel recognized the next song as Joni Mitchell's "Chelsea Morning."

She started to tell Marguerite, who whispered, "I know. They mostly sing classics here. Isn't it great?"

Even the makeshift stage was fascinating, and soon Rachel noticed that behind it was a sculpture of a huge cement troll eating a Volkswagen, a pre-electric. Wow!

After the singer finished, to a huge round of applause, the crowd straggled off.

"Let's stay put. Gilavael will find us. I have him trained," Marguerite said. So they sat on the pink tacky-tile street, relaxing in the warm sunshine.

"Beautiful weather," said Rachel.

"You have no idea," said Marguerite. "We come every year, rain or shine— mostly rain. This far into the concert, Gil and I are usually soaked."

"What time does it start, anyway?"

"Crack of dawn, and they play for two hours, break for one, then repeat the cycle for 12 hours straight."

"They must be nuts! And you bring your precious Gil here and let him sit dripping in the rain for hours?"

"We're nuts? Look who's talking." Both of them laughed.

Rachel started to trace the edge of one pink tile against its cement border. "Yesterday John said he thought I was an empath. Do you think that's possible?"

"I don't have to think," Marguerite said, chuckling. "It's obvious."

"Is this good?"

"Sure! If you knew other empaths, you'd see how perfectly you fit the mold."

"A mold? That certainly sounds exciting. And speaking of high praise, John compared me to Consuela, the receptionist."

"Aw, come on. What's your problem with her?"

"She seems perfectly nice, in a placid kind of way, but she's dumpy. Don't get me wrong. Just . . . if I start training as an empath, will I wind up looking, I don't know, dowdy?"

Marguerite laughed. She looked up and down Rachel's pink and orange unitard with 3-D paisleys. "Developing God-given talents shouldn't be confused with a wardrobe decision, Rachel. Is that really what's bothering you?"

"Actually, there's something else," Rachel said. "During the healing, Brent said that Jeremy was there, keeping him company. Jeremy, the biggest skeptic in the world. Makes me wonder if Brent was hallucinating."

"Which makes you doubt yourself, which makes you doubt what you experienced," said Marguerite. "Let's see. Next you'd doubt what John was doing, and yourself for being there."

"Well, yes."

"Rachel, doubts are pretzels. You start curving around with their logic and you go round and round. Pretzels are probably an esoteric Talmudic reference to getting lost."

Rachel stood up, secretly feeling proud. Perhaps becoming a Jewish mystic was genetic. "Easy for you to say, since you've never been lost in your life."

Marguerite rose. "Believe me, Rachel, I know what it's like to go through doubts."

Sometimes you can be so condescending. Just because you're older than me. Or smarter than me. I hate that. Rachel didn't say this out loud, of course.

"Look," Marguerite continued. "I can't promise that going to The Center will erase all your doubts. Doubts are healthy. I think it's great that you're willing to learn from John despite them."

"Really?"

"Sure. There's a very human beauty in that. Think about it, Rachel. What would be the beauty in spiritual growth if you had no doubts? I wouldn't exchange a thousand hellfire-sure Righteous for one Rachel. Or a thousand certified Traditionals."

Who cares about religious wackos anyway on a gorgeous day like this? Rachel thought. She and Marguerite walked to the right of the concert area. There were storefront shops on both sides of the street, and today's carnival added to the clutter. Marguerite spotted the boys in front of a shiny display made of black Fleximold gel with four holes. The boys were throwing bean bags through the holes, or trying to. Brent took a final shot, missed, made a face and turned towards them.

"Hi. This weirdo and I have been having major fun," he said, punching Gil in the arm.

"I think it's been okay," Gil said, racing around Brent's back and emerging to punch him in the arm.

"Time for our ice cream adventure, fellas," Marguerite said, leading them all to Magical Marvin's Ice Cream Adventure. Through the window they could see it was a buffet-style ice cream parlor unlike any restaurant Rachel had ever seen.

Marguerite ushered them through the door and up to a self-serve counter. "My treat," she said, handing money to the cashier who handed each of them a tray with silverware and a large bowl.

They slid their trays down the counter. It was stocked with huge tubs of different flavored ice creams with colorful names, along with neatly labeled syrups and whipped toppings plus about 50 different containers of add-ons, like jelly beans and Heath Bar mini-bites. All the containers had glo-plastic scoops in primary colors that were pretty enough to make your mouth water.

Rachel loved reading the names of the flavors—"Borgelnuskies" and "Fizzing Whizbees." Large signs on the walls showed caricatures of Magical Marvin and a slogan, "Scoop all you like but eat all you scoop." Her sundae was virtue itself: Peach, Mango and Klima Fruit flavors of ice cream, with butterscotch syrup and coconut candies.

"Do you want to eat indoors or outside?" Marguerite asked Brent. Her sundae was as small as Rachel's, and consisted of variations on the theme of chocolate: Fudge, French Silk and Mocha ice creams plus hot fudge, M&Ms and milk chocolate whipped cream. Everyone knew that chocolate desserts had double the calories of any other. Where did Marguerite put it all? Not fair!

"Outdoors," Brent said, gleefully balancing a jazzy creation of Blueberry, Bubble Gum and Creamsicle ice creams topped with what looked like a million jelly beans.

"Indoors," Gil countered. "The colors of the tables are much cooler and I like the music in here." Rachel noticed that Gil had made a mountain of different sherbet flavors. Instead of toppings, he had plunged half a dozen mini-popsicles into the mound, sticks poking up at rakish angles.

"Outdoors, then," Marguerite said. Rachel heard her whisper to Gil, "Brent is our *guest*, remember? Don't be selfish."

"Maybe Gil would like to pick our table," Rachel said, putting her free arm around him. "You've been here before, haven't you, big guy?"

"Every year," he said, striding to a table in a vivid turquoise. Its chairs were navy with turquoise-and-pink squares. Probably computer-colorized furniture, Rachel thought, like her kitchen table back home.

"Excellent view, boys," Marguerite said.

And what a view it was! Brent and Gil were soon totally immersed in their eating adventure. Rachel was just as immersed in watching the crowd. People - watching with Marguerite was far more interesting than checking out Health Services with Heather. Talking with Marguerite instead of Heather added another dimension— Marguerite was actually an adult. What was Heather was doing right now? Fat chance that she missed Rachel!

"People here seem so laid back," she said, watching parents and children at the carnival games. "Hey!" she said, almost choking on a half-spoonful of sundae. "I just realized, nobody here's using datamates."

"And nobody's being sued, either," Marguerite said calmly, spooning in more chocolate. "All Washington West is mellow, compared with your side of the country. Fremont, where we are now—well, it isn't normal by any stretch of the imagination. For me, visiting this part of town is like time travel. At the rate we're going, Fremont is how the whole country will be a decade from now. Take a good look at all the big blended families."

Marguerite was referring to groups of two or three adults, in a variety of sexes and ages, some accompanied by as many as 10 kids. Their outfits were electric and their hair, eyes, and skin often even more colorful than their clothes. Apparently people here didn't even try to match skin among family members!

"Can Gil and I play more games?" Despite Brent's enthusiasm over the ice cream, his bowl was still pretty full.

"That depends," Rachel said. "They have that slogan. What happens, Marguerite, if we don't finish all we scoop? Will Magical Marvin, personally, come out and slug us?"

"No fear of that, kiddo."

"Then go play, guys. Here's some change." This time Rachel came up with the handfuls of one's and five's.

As the boys left, a beaming Marguerite turned to Rachel. "Between your company and Brent's keeping Gil amused, this is the most relaxed folk festival I've ever had." She leaned back in her chair, smiled conspiratorially and, with a series of small bites, sculpted her ice cream into one perfectly formed oval-shaped scoop. Even her half-eaten sundae looked beautiful. How did she do that?

"Hasn't Greg come to the festival?"

"He's been here a couple of times. That's hardly restful, though, because Greg is such a big kid himself. When he teams up with Gil, I have to play Mom to both of them."

"Hey, do you remember that Inner Adult seminar we took with Neville Quinby?" Rachel asked, swirling her pastel ice creams together.

"That was a great one. I'm glad Neville became famous for that seminar. He deserved it."

Rachel started remembering how much fun they had had in the playgroup back in 2012. That had been an important time politically; their sons were born the year that "No-Flash" Stilton won the election. His first act as President was to sign Health Services into law. Both seminars and Official Holistic Medicine became free Monthly Electives. Rachel and Marguerite had taken a new seminar each month, often together. That was plenty of seminars ago, Rachel thought.

"What else did we take together?" she asked Marguerite dreamily. "Money Management?"

"Wasn't that grim? Still it was better than Mom Rejuvenation as taught by a man. What a joke!"

"Gosh, remember when we sneaked out with Carlotta from the Mom's group and we all took the masturbation course?'

"Fundamentals of Pleasuring? Thanks to Greg's travel schedule, I remember that one on a regular basis. What did you tell your husband it was about?"

"Secrets of giving a perfect manicure," Rachel laughed, then said, "I had to lie. Right before that seminar I took the one about diplomatic speech."

"I remember it. Seemed like the whole purpose was to scare you silly. Supposedly one wrong word would make your husband leave you forever."

Rachel ate faster, her ice cream now gloriously melted. "What a time that was. Remember the political fights? Remember when the media made a big thing out of federal money paying for a seminar on gay marriage?"

"Rev. Helms' big opportunity, if I remember correctly."

"That's right. He became a celebrity by leading an attack on the AMA. He got hysterical when America's official medical association let us choose any Medical Electives we wanted within our personal quota. The sex change operations really drove him nuts. Studly old Hickory didn't even like the idea of teenage girls getting breast implants—he said," Rachel snickered.

"Right!" said Marguerite. "That's when Rev. Pilgrim made the headlines because she opened up her new church to gays and transsexuals. Remember when she debated Helms on TV?"

"He turned purple. He kept screaming, 'You call your church Traditional?'"

"I can still remember his expression when she said that women had a right to abortion pills so they wouldn't have to be slaves to men like him."

Rachel imitated Stacy Pilgrim's sultry trademark drawl. "'Ah don't think yuh could pay me enough to be a wife in a Righteous family. I lahk being able to see my feet when ah'm standin' up.'

"Now here's the big question, Marguerite. If you had to choose between being a Traditional or being one of The Righteous, which would you be?"

"Not gonna happen," Marguerite said fiercely as all the laughter drained from her face. She stood up. "Let's go."

Rachel followed, puzzled. In all the years she'd known Marguerite, Rachel had never seen her so stern. Right now, her mellow friend looked like the most uptight person in Fremont.

A folk singer's sweet voice sounded in the background. "She sure sounds good," Rachel said placatingly.

"There's no time to listen. We're running late." Marguerite marched over and collected the boys. As they walked to the car, Rachel wished she could bask in the last echoes of the music. Instead, she found herself shaken from Marguerite's sudden burst of anger.

As they drove toward the Center, Rachel worried. Maybe going to the service wasn't such a hot idea. Having a real adult as a girlfriend felt so right—but if she didn't like John's service, would the full force of Marguerite's scorn be turned against *her*?

Chapter 27
Hallowed Be Thy Names

Parking spots at The Spiritual Center were all taken and no spaces were available near it. So it was well past 11 by the time they parked and walked back to John's Center.

As they neared the front door, Rachel saw an attractive blonde woman chasing a fair-haired little girl. The child was blowing saliva bubbles, which dribbled down her chin as she ran; her mother looked furious.

"It's *funny*," said the girl.

"No, it's not," said her mother.

Rachel heard this exchange several more times as she passed them.

Marguerite nudged her. "Take you back to the good old days?" Despite herself, Rachel snickered.

Inside, Gil offered to take Brent upstairs to the Sunday School room. *He's a nice kid,* Rachel thought, surprised by his thoughtfulness. She and Marguerite entered the main room. As heads turned, Rachel was mortified.

Why shouldn't I look uncomfortable? I do seminars, not religion. Even though the Center seemed innocent, it could be as bad in its own way as the Traditionals or The Righteous. Jeremy had warned her to watch out for good reason; these days, weirdos were everywhere.

John's service was in progress, but no one was speaking when Rachel and Marguerite entered and the silence made her even more uncomfortable. "They must have just finished a meditation. Hurry up. Over there," Marguerite whispered, pointing over to the side but right in the front row.

John looked handsome, Rachel had to admit. Framed by a large window, he wore blue jeans and a fudge-brown shirt that matched his eyes. Rachel realized she'd expected him to wear some kind of ceremonial garb when giving a service, not a plain shirt and jeans. His Spiritual Center felt more like a living room than a church.

"Our Father who art in heaven, hallowed be Thy name," John said. "How many times have we said The Lord's Prayer? That's what most of us were taught growing up. God's name was supposed to be said just one way, as in 'My religion has it all right. Everyone else is wrong.' Thinking like this turns God into a kind of trained dog. He only comes when you call the proper name.

"Today let's consider that God has many names and many teachers, so we might instead say 'Hallowed be Thy *names*.' By using *any* of these holy names, you can make contact with the reality of God."

For a moment, John seemed to catch Rachel's eye. She didn't know how to react. His gaze shifted, and he said, "When you talk to God, by all means, use the name that has meaning for you. But here's a secret that can mean the difference between studying about God and experiencing God: Be open to the presence of God in God's own terms, instead of expecting that you set the rules.

"In fact, I invite you to experiment by calling on God's many names. Call on Krishna, Jesus, Mary, Mohammed, Buddha, Kwan Yin, Babaji, St. Germain, Archangel Michael, Lady Athena. And the list goes on.

"Now, prayer is the usual word for making an inner phone call to God. But in practice, most people simply beg. Ask yourself, what does prayer mean anyway? Isn't it simply making contact with God?"

John caught Rachel's eye again. "*He's making contact,*" she thought. "*If I didn't know better, I'd think he was interested in me.*"

He continued, "Prayer's as simple as using your skin-phone. If you dial the name, you're plugged in, mate. Start talking.

"Your call will go through automatically, provided you're willing. Of course, it helps not to carry around false gods or mistaken beliefs that stand in your way.

"Hallowed be Thy *names*. I like that phrase, because it reminds me how *any* name of a realized being is packed with the presence of God. That's enough from me—it's your turn. Stand up and tell us about your experiences with calling God by different names."

A woman near the back raised her hand; after John nodded at her, she stood to speak. Turning, Rachel got a look at her. Marguerite whispered that her name was Danielle Green.

"I have a story," Danielle said. "When I moved to Washington West, I had come straight from New York." The New York reference clinched it. Rachel decided she liked her. Danielle was tall and lean, and her voice had freckles—a faint stutter reminiscent of Jimmy Stewart, the old movie star.

"Some of you know that scene," she continued. "You live in an apartment that's really a glorified box. None of your neighbors are friendly, and when you walk down the street, you're invisible. So it was a shock when I moved here and strangers actually looked me in the eye. You'd think I'd like that but instead I wondered if they had an ulterior motive, like converting me into the Traditionals or The Righteous. Those big crosses made me flinch.

"Ever since I was a kid, I've had a kind of friendship with Jesus. Like I visit him every day, but on the inner. And all the stuff people like Rev. Stacy would say in the name of Jesus really bothered me. One day I asked him about it. Here's what I got:

"'Let the children play with their toys.'"

Danielle sat.

"Meaning what?" John asked gently.

She stood again. "Well, duh! I realized that people need to approach God from their level. God can handle that—he understands that people call out to him the best way they can, whatever name they use. If they need symbols to touch, like ten-pounder crosses or pink plastic prayer beads, that's none of my business."

"Hallowed be Thy names, unconditionally." John said, nodding.

Danielle nodded back. "That experience was a turning point for me because it released a huge amount of anger."

"Anger? Why?"

"At the Traditionals and The Righteous for perverting what it means to me to call on Jesus. Now my attitude is more 'Live and let live.' I don't need to advertise how close I am to my inner teacher by wearing a cross. If others need to, they just come from a different place. It's not necessarily better or worse, just different. I guess you could say that I realized the name I use to talk to God is personal. Who cares if other people use the same name in ways I never would? 'Hallowed be Thy name for *me*' — that's the point."

Danielle sat and rubbed her right palm over her upper chest. Several in the room did the same, making little clockwise circles.

"What's that?" Rachel whispered to Marguerite.

Marguerite said, "When truth touches you, you can make that little gesture to rub it in. Some people think that helps you hold onto truth longer. It's because that part of your *physical* body connects to the place where your *energy* body expresses your soul."

Rachel's face must have shown how utterly weird she thought this was, because Marguerite quickly added, "The rubbing is strictly voluntary, of course."

Actually what Rachel really wanted to ask Marguerite was one of those things you never said out loud: *"What's wrong with these people? They don't even bleach their teeth."* The more Rachel looked at this crowd, the clearer it became that they didn't make the slightest attempt to look like the people on TV. Of course you could never really look *that* good, since celebrities were digitally enhanced, but at least you could wear colored contacts, pay attention to fashion....

As if to contradict her, an incredibly good looking, dark-haired man took the floor. His jaws were wide and chiseled, his skin clear and fair. Muscles rippled under his bright aqua T-shirt, curly hair peeked out the neckline—and quite possibly, all this was natural.

"What a hunk!" Rachel sighed into Marguerite's ear.

"Steve Ambrosian? He's taken," Marguerite said. "For that matter, so are you, remember?"

After John nodded to Steve, he stood. "My story dates from a near-death experience. About 10 years ago, I was walking down a street in Chicago, a gun went off and my body fell down and died.

"'How strange,' I thought. There I was, floating above my body, watching people load it into an ambulance.

"Next thing, I was falling upwards into the most beautiful light you can imagine.

"'It's so beautiful,' I thought, 'It's heaven.' Suddenly I got it. This *was* heaven. At that very moment I popped out through the end of a kind of tunnel, made of light. This light was singing, if that makes any sense to you, and the light was inside me and outside me, both at the same time. By now, I was feeling pretty good. Then I saw Jesus, right in front of me.

'What the hell are you doing here?' I asked him."

Laughter filled the room. Even Rachel laughed. Marguerite laughed so hard she had to wipe tears from her eyes.

Steve continued, "You think you've ever been embarrassed? Well, top that! Just my luck, that was my first thought. And he could hear me.

"So I told him, 'I didn't mean that, but this conversation can't be happening. I don't believe in you.'

"Jesus smiled, as if he loved me no matter what idiot thing I did—like your mom when you're an adorable baby who barfs all over her. 'If you like,' he said, 'You can talk with one of the others instead. Would you prefer Mary Baker Eddy? Joseph Smith is here, too. All of us are. Speak with anyone you'd like.'

"I said I might as well stick with him, since he's the one who showed up." Remembering the moment, Steve rolled his eyes in embarrassment.

"We had a good talk before I was sent back, but that's another story. The point I'm trying to make here is that having a conversation with Jesus taught me there *was* such a thing as a hallowed name. I had called it without even meaning to. Talk about easy! When you see famous preachers doing their thing on TV, maybe they're sweating more than they have to."

Steve sat down, as people around him made little circular rubs on their chests.

"John, I have a story from when you and I were in session. Is that okay?"

Another gorgeous specimen. "Who's this?" Rachel whispered.

"Sunil Patel," Marguerite said. "And you're still married."

John nodded for Sunil to go ahead.

"The first time we sat in session together, you told me that I had a temple before my third eye —with many fine white marble statues, a very fine temple, but still it had to go."

Rachel couldn't believe how gorgeous Sunil was. Slender and graceful, he spoke with a lilting Indian accent, his huge dark eyes framed by copious lashes, full lips, and a handsome arched nose. Since he was sitting in their row, Rachel had a great view.

"Imagine how this terrified me. Hinduism was my tradition, a tradition I loved. It was all I missed of India when I came to America for engineering school.

"But John said my old habits of worship had to go, if I wanted to make contact with God instead of illusion. I was willing but, for a week, nothing happened. Next time I saw John, I asked what I needed to do.

"He offered to help me make contact by calling on an incarnation of God, and he said I could choose whichever one I wanted. I picked Krishna since he's my chosen ideal. 'But how to bring Him?' I asked.

"'Think his name,' John told me.

"'That's it? Don't I have to do anything besides that?'"

"'Breathe,' he said, 'And stay awake.'

"Even though I felt foolish, I tried. Immediately, Lord Krishna was present— more clearly than I had ever felt him before. Mentally I prostrated myself, as I had been instructed by my guru back home. Krishna laughed and said, 'Please, rise. I have no need of worship.' As I got up, I was shivering all over. Yet I was in such a state of bliss, I could have stayed there forever.

"In the physical world, John still was with me. After a while, he said, "We have a job for you, Krishna. Sunil needs room for you in his consciousness. Tear down that temple, would you?"

"How Krishna did it —I must tell you, this amazed me—was to take out his flute and play. The melody was indescribable and it shattered the building as if it was made of rock candy. Ever since then, I've met with Krishna directly whenever I close my eyes to meditate. That's Krishna, the real thing, not... some piece of real estate."

John smiled as Sunil sat down. "Good story, Sunil, but what does it have to do with hallowing and names?"

Sunil stood, thought for a moment, and said, "You helped me to find the name *within* the name. Every one of the names for God has this potential, I suppose. It's not enough to worship God by calling out a name, as so many of us have been taught. After we call the name, to hear it answer, we need to pay attention within."

Rachel felt tears in her eyes. Sunil made having contact with God sound so easy. She wished it could be that way for her.

A short woman, barely over four feet tall, rose next. "Hi, everyone," she said cheerily. Rachel did a double take. "Shortness counts, huh?" she wisecracked to Marguerite, then remembered that Marguerite, her friend, was just under five feet tall, at which point Rachel wished she could retract her head through her unitard, like a turtle into its shell.

"Get over it," Marguerite said, elbowing her gently. "That's Beverly Goldsmith. You're missing good stuff."

She was saying, "During my NDE, like Steve, I talked with Jesus. Unlike Steve, I was glad to see him. I'd been brought up low-church Episcopalian and even though I became a religious dropout during college, I recognized Jesus right away.

"And I had plenty of questions saved up, too. We talked for a long time. Then I asked, 'Why do you allow suffering?'

"He answered me in images. First I saw a starving mother and child, like the kind of vid-clip we see on TV. That image morphed into others. I saw this same starving woman as a spirit, only in different bodies—a fat Persian woman on cushions, a Hun warlord, a Cheyenne warrior. It was a crash course in reincarnation. I understood the essence of each of this woman's lives. I could feel the perfection in her death this time around—not rejoicing, you understand, because her suffering still was horrible. Yet there was a perfection to it."

"I asked lots more questions, more than I can talk about here, except to tell you that Jesus answered every one with love, like sunshine nourishing a green plant. It was pure, unconditional love for my essence.

"Basically, I came to feel really comfortable with Jesus. Just out of curiosity I asked him, 'Is there anything that upsets you?'

"'Yes,' he said. Then all at once he revealed his wildness. It was like Aslan, the lion C. S. Lewis wrote about in *The Chronicles of Narnia.* Jesus had been treating me so tenderly, like a lion cub. Now I realized, he was also the great lion. He was wild and he could roar.

"He said, 'I do not like it when people kill in my name.' The growl in his voice was like an earthquake—it practically knocked me over. And that moment is when the doctors say I came back to life."

"Thank you, Beverly, for a powerful lesson," John said. "Killing is one activity that does not belong in the same breath as any name for God."

He paced a little, then looked back at the group. "Do all of you realize that in exactly 20 days President Tucker will begin exterminating the huntids? I invite you to counter that with a life attack. We can call upon God to keep our country alive and living as fully as possible."

Consuela raised her hand. "And the point here, John?" she said. "What, exactly, are you asking us to do?"

"What do you think we can do?"

"Call upon God's many names?"

"Exactly," John said. "Every call will be a blessing. Understand, everyone? Hallow those names by using them. Automatically you'll bring to your awareness the purest expressions of God: the ascended masters and archangels. Call them as many times a day as you like and ask to feel their peace. When you feel it, you can live it."

Hands in prayer position at his heart, John made a slight bow and closed his eyes. Many in the audience copied his gesture. Rachel made a mental note to ask Marguerite what it meant.

Music began playing on a small, inexpensive synthesizer. As people began leaving, Marguerite moved over to talk with friends, leaving Rachel to her own thoughts. *What am I feeling?* she wondered. *I'm still no a true believer, though I was moved by the stories I heard today. But they might as well be science fiction, as far as my ever having that kind of experience.*

She flexed her feet, pumping her shin muscles. The rhythm felt good and helped her to think. *Inadequate is one word for how I feel. And kind of serious.* By the time Marguerite came back, Rachel had it: Gravitas—*that's the perfect word to describe my feelings right now—solemn and seeking, a lot of angst.*

Gravitas. Who would have thought it? What a win! Rachel returned Marguerite's smile with such triumphant delight that her friend looked startled.

Lunch downstairs, why not? After Rachel agreed to stay, the boys ran down the stairs. Obviously Brent had enjoyed himself. He and Gil bounced up and down, looking like a couple of rubber balls.

Through a window, Rachel saw a couple waltzing in the backyard. They weren't kids, either, more like 50. She whispered to Marguerite, "I always thought I was a free spirit but the people here are something else."

Marguerite laughed. "No, Rachel. I wouldn't call you a free spirit, not yet. You're just eccentric."

Rachel must have looked wounded because Marguerite hastily added, "Of course, I mean that in the nicest possible way."

Still, Rachel folded her arms in front of her as they joined a long line.

"Mexican potluck," Marguerite announced. "Come on, Rachel. I know you love Mexican."

Rachel couldn't stay mad. "Does it matter that we didn't bring food?" she asked.

"No problem. There's always plenty. If you don't bring food, you pay a small donation. But you don't even have to do that because first-timers don't pay."

"The food here is great," Gil said. "You can take melted cheese off the tacos and put it on your teeth, like fangs."

"I've had Mexican food," Brent said loftily. "It's okay."

"Yeah? In Washington West, it's usually awful," Gilavael said, still enthusiastic. "But here at the Center, it's good. Watch out for the jumping beans, though. One might sneak into your food. Then you won't be able to stop wiggling around for three whole days."

"Gil!" Marguerite said sternly. "He's making that up," she told Brent, giving her son a scolding look.

When they got to the front of the line, the food looked so good that Rachel forced herself to take only a small spoonful from each dish. Brent, however, attacked the serving platters with abandon as Rachel watched. "Put most of that back," she told him more than once. "There are other people in line, you know."

As they looked for a place to eat, Rachel focused on the crowd. She felt overloaded in every way. Marguerite, on the other hand, seemed energized and excited. "I have an idea," she said. "Remember when we talked about your being an empath? Why don't you have lunch with Consuela and let her tell you about it."

Chapter 28
Empath Training

"Sit here," Marguerite said, pushing Rachel into a seat. Minutes later, Marguerite and the kids were sitting with her friends from the Center—and Rachel was facing the plump and plodding Consuela.

At first they ate in silence. Consuela didn't bother with small talk, and Rachel continued to scrutinize her as unobtrusively as possible. It wasn't as if she was ever going to sit with the woman again, so she might as well figure out what made Consuela so repulsive. . . .

While the silence stretched between them, Rachel realized that Consuela and she were almost exact physical opposites. *My eyebrows are thin; hers are thick. I have a petite chin while hers is the large economy size.*

"I guess I can take you on," Consuela said. "You'll be a challenge. But I can take you."

Rachel stared blankly.

"That's my initial assessment."

"Huh?"

"Both Marguerite and John told me you were interested in apprenticing with me."

"Really! What an honor. Can you tell me how much that would cost?" Any price could be too high for her budget.

Consuela laughed; her whole body shook like a tail-wagging puppy. "It's free."

Rachel realized she must look horrified. "Free, huh?"

"Look, Rachel, you pay by having to grow, which isn't always pleasant. But don't you think it's worthwhile?"

Growing. That struck a chord, so she began to consider exactly what Consuela was offering. Empath training wasn't taught in any seminar Rachel had ever heard of, so maybe this was a great opportunity. How else was she going to kill time while she was stuck in Washington West, away from Jeremy?

"No hidden costs? No strings?" She looked Consuela straight in the eye.

The mud-brown eyes were not golden like hers, but they looked honest. "Later, after you're a skilled empath, you might choose to return the favor."

"To you?"

"To somebody. The world could use more trained empaths."

"Oh," Rachel said. "Hey, can I get you some coffee?"

"Sure. I'd like double cream and seven sugars."

Rachel smiled and headed back to the buffet area, grateful for a little privacy as she considered Consuela's offer. *A free seminar about becoming an empath— as taught by a chubby weirdo. Well, why not?*

"Aren't you curious about my initial impressions?" Consuela asked, after a sip of coffee.

"Sure." Rachel smiled, confident.

"Let's begin with a definition. Empathy means the ability to travel in your consciousness and experience what it's like to be another person."

"Like feeling someone else's pain?"

"Maybe, but usually the people who claim to be doing that are fooling themselves. True, they feel pain. But it's their *own* pain, projected onto another person. Of course, most people aren't empaths."

"Is it rare?"

"Medium rare—about one person in twenty."

Rachel covered her disappointment. "So your assessment is that I'm this one person in twenty?"

"Yes," Consuela said. "But you won't enjoy it until you become a *skilled* empath. This has two aspects, like the two sides of a coin. First, there's the ability to turn empathy off. You do this for self-protection, like learning to use the brakes when you drive a car."

Rachel nodded.

"Then there's the ability to open empathy up—so you can have deep experience, which helps you to be of service to others; also to gain wisdom. This part of your training is a little like learning to use the accelerator on a car. I can teach you to go from zero miles per hour to ten—or to a hundred, if you dare."

What a great adventure, Rachel thought, as she said, "I see."

"Good," Consuela said. "Well, so far, the part of being an empath that you're really good at is the closing off part. My job will mainly be to open you up." Consuela seemed to relish this idea, unlike Rachel.

"So that's what I'm good at, huh? Anything else."

"Yes," said Consuela, causing Rachel to feel a delicious little flurry of excitement which she squelched in the way she'd shush Brent when he got too full of himself.

Consuela continued, "You're really good at contempt."

Rachel covered her forehead with one hand and dropped her head. Finally she wiped the tears of laugher from her eyes. Looking up she said, "You remind me of my husband. Does being an empath mean you can read my thoughts?"

"Certainly not. That would be an act of spiritual trespass. Empaths aren't mind readers, but we do read the pattern. And that pattern has nothing to do with what someone projects through expression or body language. Becoming a skilled empath means that you learn techniques for reading auras, the energy fields around people. They always tell the truth."

"Okay. So how do I sign up for this training?"

"Consider yourself signed up." Consuela gave her a penetrating look. "In fact, I have a first assignment for you to think about."

"Ooh, a Zen puzzle like 'What's the sound of one hand clapping?'" Rachel said with an expectant smile.

"It's about breathing. Most people today pay way too much attention to what they eat and way too little attention to their breath. Remember this, Rachel. Breath links you directly to God. At any moment, you can shift attention to your breath. Doing this can teach you deep things about yourself."

"From breathing?" Rachel said, disappointed. She'd been hoping for something flashier. Consuela was no Tanya Willoughby, that was certain.

"What do you think of my friends?" Marguerite asked later as they walked back to the car, and the boys chased each other down the street.

"They were okay, definitely okay," said Rachel. After a pause she added, "But didn't the women look kind of retro?"

"What do you mean?" Marguerite said, frowning. "I didn't think clothes in Washington West were so different."

"Not that, silly. The women." Rachel hesitated. Then she whispered, "Kind of flat chested?"

"Gee, thanks for noticing," Marguerite said, laughing. "A couple years ago John suggested that we have our implants removed, that's all."

"You're kidding. Why?"

"It seems more natural. The typical American woman of the 20's has breasts that are bigger than her face. Haven't you ever noticed?"

Rachel hadn't. She looked down. *Not quite, but then again, I've never had implants.* "It's only a look," she said, the expression on her own face clearly saying "Lighten up."

"Personally," Marguerite said, "I think women were better off in the days of corsets."

"No way."

"At least a woman could take her corset *off.* Today we change our bodies to match the latest fad. I don't believe in that."

"Easy for you to say. You're thin."

Marguerite stopped walking and faced her. "Because that's how I naturally am. If I were fat, so be it. Why not love the body you have?" Marguerite gave Rachel a Get over it! shove. "What percentage of each day do you think you spend obsessing over how you look?"

Rachel resumed walking toward the car. She was too practical to be interested in Marguerite's neo-feminist theories but she was curious. "How did you get rid of your implants, anyway? Did John take them out?"

"It was a Health Services elective."

"Really? They'd do that for non-medical reasons?"

"Sure—all we had to do was ask. For a lot of us, that was the last time we went to Health Services for anything."

Weird! thought Rachel as she they reached the car. *Wonder what Heather would think of these women. Well, it's less competition for me,* she concluded, smoothing her blouse as she adjusted the seat belt. *Not that I'm out to get anyone. Basically I'm a happily married woman.*

Later that evening, Rachel drove back to The Center where Consuela took her up to her room. Other than a beautiful quilt the drab room looked as if it had been furnished with consignment store markdowns. The drizzle outside didn't help. Consuela lit a big purple candle that mellowed the light from a full-spectrum lamp; then she gestured Rachel toward a worn blue armchair.

Consuela sat in the other chair, a plain wooden one that matched her desk. She sat backward, her skirt wrapped around the chair's long, curving back, her arms folded on top with her plump chin resting on her arms. Silently she surveyed her new student.

Consuela was mostly a physical empath, she said. When she switched on her gifts, she'd experience in her own body whatever was going on with the other person. So her first personal comment was about Rachel's mild hunger pangs. "They feel chronic," Consuela observed. "Why do you do that to yourself?"

Without waiting for an answer, she explained that she also felt other people's emotions go by, like movie footage, one scene after another.

"Those emotions—do you feel them in a detached kind of way? That happens to me a lot." Rachel said, thinking she was finally beginning to understand.

"What kind of detachment? Could you give an example?"

"Like sometimes when my son Brent feels happy but I feel a million miles away."

"Well, no. That's a bit of an emotional problem—just slightly."

Rachel tried to wipe the horrified expression off her face.

"But that's common," Consuela continued reassuringly. "Sometimes detachment comes from stretching yourself too thin, like doing too many things at once. Other times it's from being out of touch with yourself. See, I can tell from joining with you empathically that your biggest emotional talent is for *oneness* — it's natural for you to feel other people's emotions as intensely as if they were your own."

"But didn't you just describe your emotional knowing as a kind of detachment?"

"Sure, because empaths have different gifts."

"Maybe my husband has yours. His emotions seem detached most of the time."

"Do you have his picture? I can tell from that."

Rachel poked in her purse and pulled out her Insty-Cam. Opening up its photobank, she found a little hologram of the family, with Jeremy's head about one inch high. "Big enough? It's all I have."

"Sure." Consuela studied the photo. "You're right. He is an empath, mostly an intellectual empath. That means he can take on another person's thought process. That's a rare gift. Good for him! Besides that, he shows some emotional touch."

"Meaning what?"

"Hey, Rachel, do us both a favor. Take a deep breath."

Rachel realized her stomach was in a knot. She looked at Consuela accusingly.

Consuela laughed. "It's healthy for him to be that way. He's emotionally detached, just like you said. If he were studying with me, the first thing I'd ask him to do would be to pay attention to his inner life. Your process is just the opposite."

"Does that make us incompatible?"

"Not at all. Different kinds of empaths can get along just fine, and they can also be happily married to non-empaths."

Rachel sighed. "So what's my first lesson?"

"It's appreciating that about 90 percent of the feelings you go through on any given day don't belong to you at all. You're picking them up from other people."

"That's ridiculous." Rachel cleared her throat and added, "With all due respect."

"With all due respect," Consuela responded, "I'm not surprised that you don't notice this yet. You're used to putting most of those borrowed feelings into denial."

Rachel stiffened. Consuela continued, "Please, don't take this personally. Most unskilled empaths start out that way. For your first lesson, I'm going to teach you to meditate."

Consuela tried to teach her, at least. After a very long half hour, she suggested a break.

It was mortifying. Rachel couldn't do it, no matter what Consuela tried, and Consuela tried everything.

"This doesn't make sense," Rachel finally cried out in exasperation. "I've taken lots of seminars, lots, and I was always good at them. I've even meditated on my own, by playing a tape and imagining something uplifting. Could I be too advanced for what you're trying to teach me?"

Consuela just looked at her.

"Am I hopeless?"

"Here's the problem, and it's not a big one. You haven't done much work on the inner, have you?"

"But—" Rachel protested.

"Look, there are many kinds of meditation. What you described is like putting a fresh layer of paint on a canvas. What I mean by meditation is more like making contact with the canvas itself."

"Like peeling off different layers, you mean?"

"Maybe, probably not... ideally meditation's simple." A gap-toothed smile lit up her face. "Hey, I know what we can do. It's extreme—but you're spunky, right?"

"What do you have in mind?" Rachel asked stiffly.

"How about tomorrow we go to Adventureland West?"

IV. The Training

Chapter 29
Ups and Downs

"Roller coaster rides are just what you need," Consuela said briskly. First thing Monday morning, she had escorted a reluctant Rachel to Adventureland West, a franchise amusement park in the northern suburb of Outer Bellingham. Marguerite and the kids had come, too, but right now they were doing something fun, like the wave pool, whereas Rachel was stuck with pudgy, pleasant, stubborn little Consuela. Who was, it turned out, relentless as hell.

"There are two kinds of people in the world," Rachel tried telling her. "Some people love rides like this. Some people hate them. I'm that kind. If you're the other kind, I won't hold it against you—"

"Let's discuss this while we're in line." Then Consuela proceeded to march— positively march—toward Goofy's Classic Coaster.

"I can't believe the line's so long," Rachel said. Watching the crowd, dressed in strangely colorful leisure wear, actually seemed like a lot more fun than the ride Consuela wanted her to go on. Maybe it was just a West Coast thing, the way these teenagers wore shorts and tops in triple layers, with bright fabric bandages covering their knees. Cute look!

"Don't forget to steady yourself with a breath," Consuela said.

"What kind of a breath?"

"Good question. As the weeks go by, I'll teach you several different breaths to use for different purposes. On the coaster, take a deep breath whenever you start to feel tense. As you're doing that, pay attention to your body."

Rachel nodded, pretending to be deeply fascinated with her nostrils. Actually she found the hairstyles in front of her to be far more interesting. Heather would have enjoyed the man nearby with dreadlocks the colors of Froot Loops.

"Come in for a landing, Rachel," Consuela was saying. "What did you notice with your breath?"

"Oh, the usual," Rachel bluffed. "I'm not completely new to this, you know. I've been breathing for years."

Consuela didn't seem to get the joke.

"Seriously," Rachel said. "I may not have studied being an empath before, but I've taken lots of seminars. I know all about breathing."

"Good. So what did you notice about yourself, in the here and now."

"Nothing special."

"Rachel, I'd like you to close your eyes again, okay? Take some deep breaths."

"Here? Standing in line?" Disgusted, Rachel rolled her eyes beneath her closed eyelids where, presumably, even her snoopy teacher couldn't see.

"I'll join with you," Consuela said.

"What?" Rachel's eyes flew open. Surely Consuela wasn't making a pass, but what did she mean?

"Join you in consciousness to make your experience stronger. Now. Close. Your. Eyes. Still breathing?"

"Yes."

"Let's also call on God to make your inner experience 20 times stronger than normal. Any name of God you prefer?"

"What, like in John's sermon? Not really."

"Then how about we call on Archangel Raphael, the one in charge of healing. Yes?"

"Sure."

"Done. He's turned up the volume of your inner experience. So, how do you notice yourself? Pay attention."

Slowly Rachel said, "I feel the outline of my body. Inside there are these particles of something like white light. Weird." Her eyelids opened and she stared at Consuela. They moved forward in line.

Consuela insisted that Rachel keep her eyes closed while they went on the roller coaster. Rachel thought that missed the whole point. "Kids close their eyes because they're scared," she protested. "It's a way to escape."

"Escape to where? Your job is to pay attention inside. If you can do it, I think you'll move into a different kind of balance."

"Whatever you say." They stepped into their seats. This was an old-fashioned, wooden coaster which was perfect, since Rachel felt an old-fashioned, wooden kind of terror. *I don't do rides like this,* she wailed inwardly. Outwardly she made sure her seat belt was good and tight, though that was nothing compared to her iron grip on the handlebar.

Clattering, the rickety coaster cars moved upward. Rachel felt them pause, as if poised on the brink of a hill so high she didn't even want to think about it.

"Describe, please," Consuela said.

Through clenched teeth, Rachel mumbled, "All the dots of light are inside, like I said before. And I'm very big. Inside." Down lurched the coaster. It veered to the left, then the right, then left and right again.

"And outside?" Consuela shouted above the rattle of the coaster.

"My hands are clammy. I *am* remembering to breathe from my gut." The bumpy ride made her voice wobble. *What did this maniac expect?*

This was as scary as Rachel's worst nightmares: Bumps everywhere, bumping out of control, bumping one side, bumping another. Her poor neck. Not to mention the workout her poor breasts were getting. Bravely Rachel kept breathing from her gut and scanning inside for a sense of herself.

"It's still. It doesn't move," she said finally, feeling a kind of triumph. The car lurched to a stop.

"See, you survived. What did you learn from the ride?"

As Rachel opened her eyes, her attempt at a polite smile turned into a glower. "Can we go join the kids now?"

"Not quite yet. Know what my goal for you is, today?" Consuela asked, raising her eyebrows.

Rachel lowered hers. "Just break it to me gently."

"We're going to keep riding this roller coaster, eyes closed and attention inside... until you enjoy it. Sound like fun?"

Eventually Rachel felt she could depend on her inner sense of self to stay put, no matter which way her poor body lurched. That constant, quiet part of herself even had a kind of buzz, a silence.

All it took for Rachel to learn this was a dozen more rides.

Afterwards she and Consuela met Marguerite and the boys at a buffet restaurant called Spaghetti-land. Brent and Gil seemed fine when they went through the sauce area. Both of them wanted "Baby Meatballs." Since Marguerite looked leaner than ever in white shorts and a floppy T-shirt, Rachel was curious to see how much food she'd take. Though Rachel felt pudgy in her leopard-pattern jumpsuit, she wasn't going to deny herself. After all those coaster rides, she deserved a good meal.

She topped her pasta with a large ladle of Alfredo Sauce. Consuela took some too, slopped it on, as if her waistline was perfect—which was demonstrably untrue. Marguerite didn't choose the creamy sauce or the meatballs, just a small serving of mugwort soba noodles with a mushroom sauce so unappealing it had to be health food.

Marguerite seemed quiet. She led them to a corner table with a pretty red-and-white checked tablecloth. Rachel sat between the women and across from the boys. Monopolizing the conversation, Gil and Brent interrupted each other's stories about their favorite ride, Mickey's Spaceship, which simulated zero gravity as realistically as if you were in outer space.

"Before we go home, would you buy me an astronaut suit with Mickey Mouse on it?" Brent asked. "I saw them in the Souvenir Shoppe."

"No," Rachel said. "We're not buying souvenirs." She exchanged looks with Marguerite, whose eyes signaled emphatic agreement.

Brent didn't notice. "In Mickey's Spaceship, you feel as if you could ride forever."

"If you pee, you have to use a collection jar," Gilavael added helpfully.

"Yeah, otherwise it could hit you in the face later, flying around the ship."

"Boys, are you speaking from experience here?" Rachel asked, raising her eyebrows.

"They wouldn't even let us spit," Gil said, disgusted.

"But we had fun playing tag," Brent added.

"Bouncing off the walls is more like it," said Marguerite.

Conversation faded away. The boys slurped their pasta, strand by strand, showing off for each other. Rachel enjoyed the long-delayed pleasures of eating, having her eyes open, and being off the blankety-blank roller coaster.

Nevertheless, she started to feel a strange deadness inside her. Was she missing Jeremy? Was it relief that Brent was okay? Could it be lack of suspense now that his Huntid Disease had been cured? Something was different, but Rachel couldn't figure out what.

"Uh-uh-uh," Consuela whispered in her ear.

Rachel turned to Consuela sitting motionless in her dull brown denim dress. Didn't she ever wear anything colorful?

"Yes?"

"Rachel, what are you feeling now?" Consuela spoke softly, almost in a whisper.

For a second, Rachel was tempted to scream into her ear. Given the woman's irritating habit of being so calm, how refreshing it would be to drop a live frog down the front of her dress and watch her jump. Ever polite, however, Rachel said, "If you must know, I was missing my husband."

"Are you sure? Close your eyes, please. Go inside. I'll coach you through it."

Rachel closed her eyes, groaning inwardly.

"Steady yourself with a breath."

"Okay.

"What do you really feel?"

Rachel breathed silently for a very long time. "Tired, I guess. More tired than you would believe." Suddenly she was close to tears, a fact she found shocking.

"Now pay attention, Rachel. Ask inside, 'Who does this feeling belong to?' Then take a breath."

Rachel's eyes opened and she whispered to Consuela, "You're not going to believe this, but I think it belongs to Marguerite."

Consuela nodded.

Rachel finished her food slowly, thinking. Then she offered to swap child-watching duties with Marguerite, so that she and Consuela could have some fun together.

"Did Consuela put you up to this?" Marguerite asked.

"Not exactly. Go bungee jump or something. You're the adventurous one."

Marguerite gave her the biggest, happiest smile that Rachel had seen on anyone all day.

Chapter 30
T-Shirts

That night, after the kids went to bed, Marguerite made a pot of tea. She and Rachel sat in the dining alcove, their faces reflected in its multi-paned windows. A turquoise beeswax candle cast a gentle glow. On a SilverLux tray, one of those sparkly, never-polish silvers now advertised everywhere, was a yellow stoneware teapot inset with glass jewels that sparkled like rubies, emeralds, and amethysts. Marguerite, looking unusually refreshed and serene, poured mango-scented tea into the matching goblets.

"What a delicious way to spend an evening," Rachel said, stretching contentedly. She checked herself, practicing today's lesson at Adventureland West. Did her happy appearance match what she felt at her core? For a change, the answer was yes.

"You're so quiet," Marguerite said.

"Tell me about this gorgeous teapot. Did you make it?"

Marguerite's face crinkled into a smile. "It's a souvenir of my pottery phase—you know, after glassblowing but before furniture-making."

"You never stop, do you?"

"Story of my life," said Marguerite. Clear as a bell, Rachel heard a mixture of regret and laughter in her voice, like the bitterness of the black tea beneath its mango perfume.

They talked about their lives—their non-lives, actually, as creative people. Marguerite came closer to complaining than Rachel had heard in years. She felt stuck, she said, waiting for her next art form to materialize. She couldn't bear the waste.

"Waste?"

"For me a day when I don't create something is a waste. It's like a hole in my life, especially when it goes on day after day."

Rachel remembered her frustration with the violin and told Marguerite about failing to make the Satie recording for Jeremy. "My music-reading skills are pitiful," she concluded. "Most days, I didn't even feel like a musician any more. But, of course, I've made such a habit of worrying."

She stopped, startled by her words, and reflected on what she'd just said. *That was true!* "Don't tell Consuela, but I've been much happier since I started empath training. A lot of the stuff I used to worry about didn't belong to me at all. Being me isn't nearly as complicated as I once thought."

"So why don't you want to tell Consuela?"

"She's conceited enough, don't you think?"

Marguerite stiffened. "What makes you think so?"

"She's so sure of herself all the time. 'Steady yourself with a breath.' Like she's always in control. I don't know her as well as you do, Marguerite, but I think that control thing makes her kind of obnoxious."

"No, you don't."

"What do you mean, no I don't?"

"You don't know her as well as I do. And John says that whenever we make a judgment about someone, it puts up a wall. Eventually, you have to ask yourself, Rachel, if that isn't too high a price to pay."

"For what?"

"For a momentary feeling of superiority."

Rachel stood up, stretched, and touched her toes a few times. *Marguerite was right.* To save face she said, "I guess I just dumped on Consuela to cover up being worried about the huntids.

"Don't get me wrong, Marguerite. I'm having a fabulous time with you, and so is Brent. But part of me is always watching for kids who might fall down the way Brent did. Or have bright green mucus coming out in odd places, the first stage of Huntid Disease."

Marguerite chuckled and tilted her goblet to swallow the last drops of tea. "Rachel, tell me when you last saw sick people in public?"

"I don't know."

"I do, never. Disabilities aren't seen in America any more. Ten years ago, we had people in wheelchairs and blind people using white canes. Don't you remember seeing half the Baby Boomers wearing hearing aids?"

"Sure, and those enormous bathroom stalls with their wheelchair-accessible logos. You're right, Marguerite—all that stuff's gone. Now everyone looks perfect because of genetic alterations or microchips or laser surgery or psychoactive meds. For the small stuff, it's Superbiotics. Even band-aids are pretty, the way they come in designer colors. Back home we have the Stella McCartney 60-Color pack."

Marguerite began tracing the goblet's jewels with her pinkie. "John's the one who first called my attention to it," she said. "Nobody walks around sick any more. When Brent and his friends came down with those colds, they were taken to Health Services so fast, their moms barely noticed they were sick, right?"

"So am I crazy to be worrying about the huntids?"

"No, but I don't think huntids are the scariest thing happening now, Rachel. To me, it's the way people react to the huntids. Did you notice what people were wearing yesterday?"

Rachel thought. "I did see a guy with the most interesting dreadlocks."

"Focus, Rachel."

"Oh, of course—that layered look with the knee fringes. I don't think it will last."

Marguerite glared. "Not that, the T-shirts."

"Well, shucks, Marguerite. I've been reading people's T-shirts my whole life and so have you."

"Not like some of the new ones I saw at Adventureland—and in Fremont, too. Every group you can imagine is wearing its own T-shirt."

"Such as?"

"Such as IT'S ALL V-R and ATHIEST AND PROUD OF IT. And SAVE THE WORLD WITH HUGS AND DRUGS. I even saw one huge family yesterday where everyone wore matching shirts that said, LUTHERANS ARE NORMAL on the front and the back said, TRY IT SOME TIME."

"Come on, Marguerite. What's so sinister about that? I'd call it religious pride, maybe verging on arrogance, but no big deal."

"Rachel, if you'd been following the news the way I have, you'd know it's a backlash against The Righteous and the Traditionals. They've been saying that everyone has to show an affiliation.

"So what, everyone gets to play dress-up? Let them. This is no different from any other craze."

"We'll see," said Marguerite, loading their tea party leftovers onto the tray. "When is a T-shirt just a T-shirt? And when do religious affiliations become so important, people fight over them?"

"You call me a worrier," Rachel said, following her to the sink. "Back home I used to worry a lot about the true believers, but John—of all people—has made me mellower.

"How so?"

"Between you and me, that session with him changed me so much, it's almost a miracle. Studying with Consuela's giving me more perspective, too. And even though you had to remind me about it tonight, I *am* judging people less often. Besides, didn't John just give a sermon about everyone's right to call God by whatever name they choose? Marguerite, who'd have guessed that you could be more uptight than me?"

Soon as Rachel awoke on Wednesday, she began thinking about what she'd tell her husband that night during their weekly phone call. For starters, she'd have a feminine, gadabout story for him, because Marguerite had made plans to take them all to the marina.

It was worth the long drive. More boats than Rachel expected were parked on the waterfront in strange elevator-like gizmos. Endless rows of pleasure boats, painted outrageous colors to match their sails, stood like cars in a traffic gridlock, and the place was so open that you could stroll right up to any boat and admire its fine points. Gil and Brent were a few feet away, playing on a boardwalk-like strip that ran for miles.

In the distance they could see boats sailing on Puget Sound. Even though the bright sails looked dingy under the gray sky, Rachel thought that being out there must be fun. She said, "Some of the names on these boats are so romantic, like *Surprise, darling!*"

Marguerite said, "I like *Lighthouse Eye Candy*."

"How about this one? *Barbara IV*—do you think it's Barbara's fourth boat or named after a fourth wife called Barbara?"

Marguerite gave her an affectionate Get out! shove. "Here's the bathing area."

A beach! Rachel smiled at the sight. She noticed a playlot near it—recycled tires, colorful ladders and a large climbing maze.

"Go ahead, boys," said Marguerite. Almost immediately, they were climbing like monkeys as the women continued their walk, circling the playlot.

Marguerite said, "Know something odd? A little after midnight, I turned on TV and there was our buddy Hickory Helms. He and the other two guys sailed though their confirmation hearings so now they're official."

Rachel snorted. "Helms must be ecstatic. So proud of his new political title. Maybe we should start calling him Minister Reverend Hickory Dickory?"

"Dickory, huh?" Marguerite raised her eyebrows. "He was right in the middle of one of his fist-pounding speeches, how Satan was Lord of the Flies, pound, huntids were flies that symbolize all the evils of terrorism, pound, everyone must turn to God immediately, pound, or instead of the Second Coming, pound, all of us will be destroyed on Huntid Extermination Day." Marguerite emphasized each point by pounding her fist, an accurate if not respectful imitation of the televangelist.

Rachel rolled her eyes; her friend was at it again. Oblivious, Marguerite kept walking. Unaccountably Rachel realized that she was fighting off a powerful urge to listen to some music on her skin-phone. What in the world was she feeling that was pushing her so frantically out of the here and now?

She steadied herself with a breath. Was it fear of the huntids? Disgust with Hickory Dickory? Strangely, she was feeling closer to frustration and sorrow. Recalling an instruction from Consuela, she asked her inner self, *Who does this feeling belong to?*

Marguerite, answered an inner voice in the vicinity of her right ear. *Okaaay*, Rachel said to herself, or whoever was talking.

"So what's going on with *you*?" she asked out loud. Suddenly Marguerite's face expressed surprise mingled with a respect that Rachel never had seen before. The look was gone in an instant as Marguerite lowered her head and muttered, "When you're an artist living in the wrong time, little things like these boats remind you that nobody's interested."

"How can you say that? There are beautiful things all around us. Even these boats—look how perfectly they're painted. Some of these designs are amazingly elaborate."

"My point exactly," Marguerite said. "Computer-generated designs on boats? Give me a break. Almost everything's computerized these days. Whether I draw or make glass, or I create furniture from scratch, any kind of art I might produce— you name it—I'll guarantee you that a computer can do it better."

Rachel's frustration deepened. Venting made Marguerite feel worse, not better; kicking the mulch as they walked, she muttered, "Whoever invented fractals should go to hell." Ooh, Rachel was going about this empath stuff all wrong.

Later that afternoon, Marguerite and the boys stayed at the marina while Rachel went to the Center for her next empath lesson.

Consuela was sitting backward on the desk chair, placid as ever, her wide nose and plump cheeks unimproved by make-up. She wore an olive green jumpsuit — another unflattering outfit from her apparently unlimited collection. Strangely her bedroom had a soft kind of silence that almost made up for the woman's complete lack of glamour. *Could Consuela simply be more interested in creating beauty* around *herself than* on *herself?* Virtuous though the choice might be, Rachel found it hard to respect anyone who looked that unattractive.

Outwardly dutiful, though, Rachel reported on her mixed progress so far. Going within herself was easy, when she remembered to do it. Consciously using her breath as an ally did bring more clarity, and questioning where her feelings originated and why was fascinating. "But after I ask a question, I hear the answer inside my ear. Is that crazy or what?"

"You're clair*audient*, that's all," said Consuela. "If you were clair*voyant* like me you might see lights. Another empath might notice a smell or have an underlying sense of spiritual truth. Each empath has specialties. Clairaudience is fine."

"Why should I trust it? What if I'm being tricked?"

"See me settle into this chair? You do it."

Although Consuela's answer seemed evasive, Rachel obediently went through the motions, rocking sideways and nestling into her armchair.

"That symbolizes what you can do in your silence," said Consuela. "Settle into awareness of yourself—let deep breaths move you along. After your guidance shows up through one sense, like hearing, ask for confirmation through a second channel. Try it now."

Closing her eyes, Rachel realized that she felt downright radiant. Once she relaxed into the feeling, and realized it came from Consuela, she asked what it meant. In response, she heard the words *spiritual peace.* Breathing slowly and evenly, Rachel asked to feel it more clearly—asked as gently as a feather touch. Bam! She felt emotionally huge.

"That's the presence of angels. Easy, huh?" Consuela said. Seeing Rachel's awe she explained, "For a backup to your clairaudience, you just used your clairsentience. That means subtle knowing through touch."

Angels! Rachel didn't settle any deeper into her chair. Instead she leaned back as far as she could go, shaking her head in amazement against the worn, cushy fabric.

"How'd it go?" Marguerite asked. After she and the boys met Rachel at the marina, they had begun the drive home.

"Not bad," Rachel said. "How'd it go for you guys?"

"We had fun, Mom," Brent said. "We went back to the boats and listened to the different sounds they made in the water and touched some of them, too. Ms. Marguerite said it was okay."

"We might even have pretended that a few of the boats were ours," Marguerite said, winking.

From the back seat, Gilavael said, "It was a real pirate adventure. There were even bullies who made us put on their necklaces."

"That part was real," said Marguerite, her voice icy.

"What?" This was no longer small talk, Rachel thought.

Marguerite explained, "Some Righteous kids asked us why weren't wearing beads, said they needed to see our affiliation. After I told them we didn't have any beads, they treated us like charity cases and gave us some."

"We said no, Mom," added Brent, sounding disgusted. "But they wouldn't listen. So we took off their stupid necklaces and threw them back."

Rachel turned and quietly assessed both kids. They didn't look upset. They were playing with Twist-a-Lanyard, a computerized craft that was this summer's must-have item. Poking one of the colorful plastic threads would make all four of the threads start weaving a pattern. Pulling two threads at once made the lanyard unravel, and jerking a thread sideways turned off the toy. If it hadn't been for the crick in Rachel's neck, watching it would have been fun.

When she turned around, Marguerite whispered, "It gets better. The Righteous were getting ready to force more beads on us when a couple of Traditionals told them to stop. The Righteous guys left but then a second bunch of Traditionals arrived—they seem to run in packs—and asked if we wanted to hear the good news about Salvation."

"I said to go away," Gil said.

"We all did," Marguerite added, her carefully controlled rage showing only in her eyes. "They told us we were fair game because we weren't wearing anything to show affiliation. Can you believe it?"

Back at Marguerite's, they ate lunch quietly. Particles of worry got into their food like sand into picnic sandwiches, so Rachel worked a 3-D puzzle with the boys after lunch. The idea was to give Marguerite some time alone but Rachel surprised herself by having so much fun she felt energized. Bouncing downstairs like a kid, she found Marguerite sitting glumly on the couch.

"You still worried about all those T-shirts?"

Marguerite sighed. "There were new ones today. The T-shirt wars must be escalating."

"Tell me. I could use a little comic relief."

"PROUD TO BE PRESBY'S. What else? SEMINARS MAKE YOU SMART. Oh yes, I saw buttons that read, SCIENCE PROVES ALL OF YOU ARE STUPID.

"That's a way to communicate, I suppose. Wonder which came first, the Science buttons or the Seminar shirts."

"Then there were the people being Jewish."

"Oy vey!"

"I was shocked, Rachel. Women and men out on the street wearing yarmulkes isn't traditional, is it? Some of them wore T-shirts, too—they were printed, ALL SABBATH, ALL THE TIME.

"I'm almost tempted to call my mother and ask what they're doing in New York."

"Why don't you?"

"Right, that's all I need do to calm myself down—talk to Helene. When do you think this circus will end?"

"After August 29, if we're all dead from insecticide poisoning."

"No way!"

Marguerite lifted one of her glass paperweights and fingered it. "I called Gregory while you were upstairs and told him what's been happening."

"Was he shocked?"

"Let's just put it this way. Although he's usually a little stingy, as you may remember, he offered to fly Gil and me out to stay with him in Columbia City. He says it's not bad, and that at least everybody there wears the same necklaces."

"Boring!" Rachel said disdainfully. "I think it's the funniest fad in years. Every day is like Halloween."

A song started running through Rachel's head right before her call to Jeremy, *You've got to keep the flame of hope alive.* She was hopeful, and she'd worked hard getting ready for this phone date.

Her hair was perfect, and she'd spent a long time on her make-up. She wore a clingy maroon velvet dress with a plunging neckline. On impulse, in case it might show over the phone, Rachel had brushed a little glitter into her cleavage. Then she and Marguerite collected every candle in the house, surrounding her with their light.

Jeremy picked up before the second ring. He was there. *See,* she told herself, *he cares.* To break the ice, she told him what had happened at the marina when the pirates turned into Righteous and Traditionals. Conveniently, she omitted the part about her empath training, which she intended to keep secret until she was such a hotshot empath that even Jeremy would be impressed.

Instead of laughing at the idea of Brent and Gil all decked out in Righteous necklaces, Jeremy's face got the familiar craggy look that she privately called "Mr. Mt. Rushmore."

"Rachel, you sound like you think it's a joke."

"Jeremy, if you can't laugh, you might as well be dead. Come on! Where else except funky old Washington West are people wearing such silly T-shirts?"

"Everywhere—you haven't been surfing the Net much, have you? It's all over TV, too." The sweetness in Jeremy's bass voice disappeared; he sounded shrill. Rachel cringed inside, like a child being yelled at by daddy.

"Everyone's selling T-shirts and souvenirs with affiliation messages. They're even in vending machines."

"In sleepy Capitol City? You're kidding!"

When he scowled, Rachel made sure that her cleavage showed, then flashed a lighthearted grin. "You're telling me that our do-nothing neighbors are walking around in those hysterical shirts?"

"Every one of them."

"It's just another phase. . . wait a minute. You've actually been watching TV? What a riot! When did that start?"

"I started watching the news."

"How ironic! And I've been too busy to watch. We've had a good time, Jeremy, except for missing you. I wish you could be with us."

"I saw Rich Davis on TV today," said Jeremy, as if he hadn't heard her. "I know Rich. He was just confirmed as Secretary of Communication and he gave a fascinating speech comparing T-shirts to truth in advertising. He said there's no such thing as objective journalism."

"Maybe he's got a point," Rachel said, with a subtle little shimmy.

"Then you'd have been thrilled with his logic. The observer influences what he observes, he said. He even dragged in Heisenberg's Uncertainty Principle—as if he knew a quark from a quack. Rachel, he claimed that, in addition to having personal biases, every pundit and member of the press has a reputation that's like a brand name. So, in his opinion, it should be a law that they wear a symbol of affiliation whenever they're on TV, the way supermarket foods carry a nutrition label."

Rachel laughed her most feminine laugh. "Like what? Let's see. Rachel is Jewish from her mom and dad, so she needs a yarmulke. Her Seminar Slave grandma influenced her, so she'd better add a few seminar buttons. Then there's the influence of big brother Walter, who isn't hooked on government-rationed drugs but does mighty fine with alcohol. Maybe I could wear a little beer can bracelet. And since Rachel would prefer to be a Seminar Slave but is currently between gurus, maybe her logo should be a big question mark! I'd like to wear it all, but where will I find the room?"

A laugh lit up Jeremy's eyes, though he didn't smile. Nevertheless, throughout most of this conversation, he'd sucked his lips in so far, they practically disappeared. So Rachel felt encouraged that, for the moment, he looked as though he had lips.

"Nothing so sophisticated," he said. "Rich's slogan, as I recall, was 'Wear what you believe.' He said that all responsible Americans should wear a simple Righteous necklace like his. Or a T-shirt or a five-pounder cross, if you were unfortunate enough to have a less enlightened view of reality."

Rachel realized that her jaws were clenched. To loosen them up, she considered a few butt crunches but John had said multi-tasking was straining her nerves. On the other hand, Consuela had told her to steady herself with a breath whenever she started to get upset. *Geesh, she thought, it's beginning to feel like I'm playing Simon Sez.*

"Jeremy," she said finally, breaking the silence. "You're not scratching any more. Is your skin better?"

He looked almost sullen, for Jeremy. "The eczema was starting to show on my hands and neck, and the itch was keeping me up nights. So finally I went to Health Services and now I'm one of their big success stories. Isn't that just dandy?"

"Oh, Jeremy, I know you don't like to going there but I'm glad you feel better."

"Feel better! I'm in charge of the biggest extermination project this country has ever seen. Not only don't I believe in it, I think it's dangerous and scientifically indefensible. May I also mention immoral and 100 percent politically motivated? Everyone at work now has to show group spirit by wearing this asinine T-shirt."

"That's awful. What does it look like?"

"Hang on. I'll show you."

He returned holding a green shirt on which fluorescent violet letters read SCIENCE WILL STOP THE HUNTIDS."

She laughed. He caught her eye, laughing along with her. "At least it says something positive, Jeremy," she said.

"Swell. You know how much I love dressing exactly like everyone else."

"Does the back of the shirt read, 'Nyah, nyah, nyah'?"

"Let's see." He dodged behind the shirt, as playful as if he were teasing Brent. "Nope. Darn."

"There's just one problem," said Rachel. "Does anybody actually look good in lime green?"

"None of us, that's for sure. But they don't call it *lime green* anymore, Rachel. They're calling it *huntid green*."

"Yuck! Can we come home soon?"

"Two weeks," Jeremy said, looking grim. "Precisely two weeks plus four days—not that I'm counting."

That had romantic possibilities, thought Rachel. She wanted to feel as if they were in a war movie, he on a heroic mission, she as the irresistible love interest, maybe a cross between Greer Garson as Mrs. Miniver and Donna Reed, making Jimmy Stewart tremble with desire when he talked to her on the telephone in *It's a Wonderful Life*. Unfortunately her husband didn't seem to have any tenderness whatsoever—at the end of their conversation, all he said was, "Take care of yourself."

Still, it could have been worse, Rachel decided. In a grim, gossipy way, she couldn't wait to turn on the news.

What *were* people wearing?

Chapter 31
Holding a Space

Maybe there was a brighter side to those worrisome huntids. At least TV should be exciting, for a change.

Sure enough, to Rachel's enjoyment, every star on every program was showing affiliation—with T-shirts, five-pounder crosses or glass bead rosaries. Unlike Marguerite or Jeremy, Rachel followed fashion, so this latest fad didn't scare her so much as give her a good gossipy thrill.

By breakfast-time Thursday, Rachel had already spent hours celebrity watching. After the kids went outdoors to play, she invited Marguerite to watch with her.

Marguerite, however, didn't share Rachel's glee. "Look, this isn't new to me. I watched this... this spectacle... for several days before I mentioned it."

"Come on, Marguerite, it's fun seeing The Righteous get some real competition." Rachel clicked onto The Oprah Network. Dr. Andrew Weil was in the middle of his regular Longevity Show. His T-shirt combined a peace sign with the slogan, HEALTH IS WEALTH. SEMINARS MANIFEST BOTH.

Rachel flicked a peace sign at him as if America's most famous doctor could see her through the screen. "What a great way to learn about the personal lives of celebrities!" she told Marguerite. "It's real, not stuff from their press agents."

Marguerite didn't look so sure, so Rachel added, "Come on, aren't you secretly curious about what they'll wear? Let's click on Dave and Donna."

"What people wear isn't a personal statement anymore, Rachel. These T-shirts are ominous. Can't you see that?"

The phone rang. Marguerite seemed glad to flee to her bedroom; it had a big screen-phone where she could talk privately. Well, she could just take her grouchy mood with her!

Later that day, Marguerite did manage a smile. It was when Rachel asked to borrow the car for a session with John.

Back on the healing table, Rachel felt far less nervous than she had the first time. She found John a lot more attractive too, and peeked at him while he closed his eyes for the attunement prayer. Afterwards she avoided staring at his ginger hair or crimson lips but was entirely too aware of his irresistible smell. *Get a grip, girl,* she told herself. To break the silence, she asked, "How'd you get started doing this energy stuff?"

John kept moving his hands above her body, like in the earlier session. Eventually he answered, "Back in Sydney, I used to be a car mechanic. Went on a hunting trip with some of my buddies, took a tumble on a loose rock and passed out. Docs called it a concussion. They said I'd be good as new. When I came back, I had some marbles I didn't have before."

"Really," she said. "I wonder if. . ."

"What's this?" he said, with a start. " A sword coming out of your back? Oh, one of your own people stabbed you from behind, then pulled out the sword. All you guys were dressed like in The Three Musketeers. What do you think that's about?"

"Are you talking about a past life? Don't tell me you believe in reincarnation."

"Sure I do. First time anyone mentioned it, my reaction was, 'Of course, I know about that. How couldn't we all have many lives? What a relief that somebody's finally reminded me.'"

Evidently Rachel looked appalled because he added, "Don't worry. You don't have to believe in reincarnation for this session to help you. What matters is that God is present within you, here and now."

"But *you* believe in past lives?

"Lady, I don't have to believe. Stored-up junk from them comes out in healing sessions. That's what's happening to you right now."

"Something from a hundred years ago is coming out now?"

"A deep wound is moving out. I'd say it has been carried in your aura ever since this particular incarnation."

"How creepy!"

John threaded his fingers through the air over Rachel's upper body. He left plenty of space between his hands and her chest; she wondered if he always kept a professional distance from attractive women.

He said, "Emotion locked into the scar is the real injury. Emotions are always involved when we've been hurt. This one—do you want to find the emotional scar so you can complete the healing?"

"Sure."

"Then ask inside, 'What feeling was stuck inside me when I was stabbed?'"

Rachel shook her head. "That's obvious. I mean, my feeling would have to be suspicion. So are you saying this memory from a past life has made me paranoid now?"

"Slow down, Rachel. Injuries aren't obvious. You've been carrying this wound around for a long time—can't you spare a few minutes to explore it?"

"I suppose."

"Ask inside, then. Close your eyes, take a few deep breaths and ask, 'What feeling have I been carrying related to this injury?'"

Yellow. Slimy. Shame.

She said, "Our soldiers found out something about me, something that made them suspicious. We had sworn an oath of loyalty, but their mistrust overcame everything else and they murdered me rather than discuss it. Oh my God, I can't believe I just said this. How could I know?"

John instructed, "Breathe deeply. Ask inside, 'What else do I feel?'"

"I'm at the scene of my death. My spirit has flown out of my body and I'm looking down at it from above; I can see it as clearly as a movie. Six men are standing around my body. They're silent. Next to me is my best friend, and he's the murderer. He slumps over, as if all the life has gone out of him, and he looks at the bloody sword in his hand."

"Oh no," Rachel said, stopping.

"Take a few breaths now and be strong. What else do you notice?"

"His face is sorrowful, but his eyes don't belong in it. They're not sad, they're burning with rage. He reminds me of one of The Righteous. No wonder Rev. Helms scares the shit out of me."

"Rachel, does this man say anything?"

"He seems intensely proud of what he's done. He's killed me because of religion. How peculiar." Rachel paused. "And now I'm daydreaming about what I did after my body died."

"I'd call that re-experiencing, not daydreaming," John said dryly. "Go on."

"My spirit has turned away from the murderers and my physical body. Being in my light body, I feel wonderfully free—and relieved not to be connected to the body on the ground. I'm just looking at it, seeing my uniform soak up blood. And I can see how handsome I was, with big bushy eyebrows and jet black hair. I feel a detached kind of pity for this man who died so young and full of promise."

"Ask to know more. Your soul remembers all your past lives so it will have the answer. What had you done to arouse suspicion from the other soldiers?"

"I can know that?" She breathed into the silence, repeating her question inside. "Oh! It's about my having an empath's heart and spiritual hearing—whatever that means."

Rachel took another deep breath, requesting clarification. "I see now. I had an angel who came to me whenever I fought, and I made the mistake of telling my friend. He told the others in our regiment, and they freaked out. To them, anything spiritual had to bear the mark of the Church. You had to use the right language, too, or else you were considered a tool of the Devil."

"What else?" asked John. He moved his hands faster in a spiral pattern around her ribcage.

"This is so strange..."

"Go on," he said. "You're doing great, moving this old stuff out."

"You know what convinced them they had to kill me? Even though their minds were closed, their hearts could feel the warmth of my spirit—and it was so different from them that they decided I must be dangerous."

"Good work. Take a breath now, Rachel, and remember one last thing. Earlier you said you felt shame. I want you to remember why."

With a breath, Rachel moved back into the soldier's body; as the sword was pulled out, blood began spurting from the wound.

"John," Rachel cried. "I heard my murderer's last words. He said, "Get Thee behind me, Satan."

Rachel lay on the massage table, back in her own body. Icy tears slid down her face.

Finally, in a flat voice, she said, "Now I understand the emotional scar. When I died, I knew I had done no harm—yet I also knew that this deeply pious man, someone I loved and trusted, believed me to be so evil that he had to kill me. At the instant of my death, I believed him."

She wept for a long time.

"Pay attention to that," John said finally, in an incredibly tender voice. "It's a story I've heard many times. There's always a reason when people with gifts like yours don't use them. Now that you've found out the reason, Rachel, you can really move forward."

He moved his arms more slowly, then stopped. "You're done, by the way."

"Well, something agrees with you," Consuela told Rachel as they started their Tuesday lesson. It was true; much as Rachel hated to admit it, she'd been feeling a lot clearer since her last session with John. She'd practiced self-awareness every day; now she was ready to learn something new.

Unfortunately, the afternoon was gray, Consuela's outfit was gray (a terrible color choice with those muddy brown eyes, Rachel thought), and Rachel herself was fending off the grumps. Back home, Jeremy had the glory of an important job, even if he hated it. But what did Rachel have? At most, this was it—learning how to read auras from the inside out. But what would this bring her besides another useless certificate for her collection?

"Hey, wake up, Rachel." With a deftness Rachel never would have expected, Consuela jumped up, stood behind Rachel, grabbed her armchair and started rocking it. Was the woman a maniac? As Rachel looked around to see what was going on, Consuela scrambled back to her chair, mischief all over her face.

"Decide right now," she said. "Do you want to be here? Yes or no?"

Rachel nodded a yes, feeling both guilty and impressed.

"Okay," Consuela said. "Our goal for today is for you to learn how to turn your empathy on. That means holding a space."

"That's it? Hold a space?"

"You can do it now, because you've started to become self-aware. Holding a space means that you extend your awareness to include another person. To pay that kind of attention, you've got to be in the here and now. No pretending, understand?"

"Not exactly," Rachel said, thrusting out her chin. "I thought becoming an empath meant you'd teach me to *do* something to people. Just paying attention seems too plain vanilla."

"Every time you hold a space for someone you help that person to heal and grow. Besides, an empath's gift is a terrible thing to waste."

Somewhere deep inside, Rachel heard Consuela add, *"Especially now, as America moves into a crisis over the huntids, we're going to need all our spiritual healers. Why else would I bother working with you?"* But surely placid, chubby Consuela couldn't be thinking something like that.

Or could she? As Consuela reviewed the rules for holding a space, Rachel cheered herself up by scrutinizing her teacher's face. Consuela's upper lip was even fuller than her lower one. The right shade of matte pink lipstick could correct that, Rachel noted.

Consuela was saying, "First you explore what it's like to be you, for a frame of reference. Second, you think of the name of an archangel or ascended master, because connecting to them keeps other people's stuff from sticking to you. Ask God to be of service. Then all you have to do is direct your attention towards the other person."

"That's it?"

"Don't be fooled by how simple this technique sounds, Rachel. Keep awake, open your heart, and you just might learn something."

Obediently she practiced holding a space with Consuela. *Click*. Rachel felt weird, as if she was more in her body, and it was a thicker body that moved more slowly than Rachel's usual bio-rhythms.

After a few more breaths, another *click*. Rachel now felt as if part of her was used to living inside a deep sky. This velvety blackness seemed connected with her breath, moving in and out, slowly, and hugely. In Consuela's serene space, it seemed that the most startling kind of thing that could happen to her would be playing peek-a-boo with a star—because any of the glowing stars was a version of That, a part of her God-filled self.

Whoa! The thought popped Rachel's awareness back inside her own body.

They discussed the big contrast between how Rachel normally felt when awake versus how it felt to travel into Consuela's aura. "One obvious difference," her teacher said matter-of-factly, "is those sunscreen treatments you get from Health Services. They numb you out. They have tranquilizers in them, you know, not just sunscreen."

"What?" Rachel squeaked.

"Health treatments keep people in line. Most Americans are numbed out and don't even know it."

"How can you say that?"

"John thinks President Stilton had this in mind when he started Health Services. He realized he could use health screenings to tranquilize the American people."

"Of all the pathetically paranoid ideas!" Rachel sputtered. "Some sedation! Everywhere you go, people are fidgeting like crazy. The Righteous do. Even I do. If that's being sedated, I shudder to think what uncontrollable loonies we'd be otherwise."

"Personalities have layers," Consuela said calmly. "When our innermost layers are numbed, energy finds a way to express itself. Usually it turns fidgety, because it's not integrated with the rest of the person."

Rachel pondered this. "Just supposing this were true, how long would it take for the sunscreen treatments on Brent and me to wear off? I mean, if we didn't go back to Health Services."

Consuela's face took on a look Rachel couldn't decipher, so she kept on talking. "Come to think of it, I haven't gone to my monthlies since Brent and I came here. Back home, my friend Heather used to remind me. It was the highlight of my month, between all the coloring choices and the electives. I loved watching people and—"

"Just stop going," Consuela blurted out. "Who knows how long it will take? Better late than never."

"Let's see," Rachel said, hiding the anger she was beginning to feel. "I can stop getting protected from cancer because that's better than walking around like a twitchy zombie. Gee, thanks for the tip."

Consuela simply shrugged.

Rachel thought, *I used to look forward to my monthlies more than anything—except sex with Jeremy. And Health Services you could depend on, at least.*

Consuela said, "Sunscreen still comes in a bottle, you know. Isn't it possible that Health Services had an ulterior motive for going into the sunscreen business?"

"That's ridiculous. John's just saying that because Health Services are competition. Hey, I didn't mind paying for healing Brent or my sessions with him. I walked out of that last session feeling about 10 pounds lighter. He's a fabulous healer.

"But don't you think I could get the same results from Health Services acupuncture? Or Reiki? Maybe the docs with Official Holistic Medicine aren't as talented as John, so you'd need three of their sessions to do what John could do in one, but it's all the same, basically."

Consuela gave her a sharp look. "Is it?"

"What do you mean?"

"They're fake."

"How can you say that? Back home I used to have the greatest time—"

"Then call it entertainment, Rachel. As healing, it's fake. Those OHM doctors take a weekend workshop to become so-called acupuncturists. How can that prepare them to replace traditional practitioners? Real acupuncturists handed down their art, generation after generation, until it was practically part of their DNA."

"OHM doctors are licensed, Consuela."

"Great, they're officially okay, like all that bio-engineered food they sell us— genetically modified broccoli grown over sewage. Give me a break, Rachel. You think our bodies can't tell the stuff's energetically dead? Our government-sponsored 'alternative medicine' is just as bad as our fake food, whether it's aromatherapy or chiropractic or whatever. You know what President Stilton's health policy did? Put most of the genuine practitioners out of business."

"How can you say that?"

"It's obvious if you'll only read auras, which everyone can learn to do, and which *you're* learning to do as part of becoming a skilled empath. Fake and real look the same on the outside. Don't you get it, Rachel? Energetically most of the people you meet are only half alive."

"I had no idea," Rachel said in a small voice.

"Oh, come on. Now you're going to tell me that you didn't know John's sessions are illegal."

"Why didn't you warn me?" Rachel asked Marguerite as soon as the kids were in bed and they could talk. Sitting in the dining alcove after dinner, they cross-stitched small decorative pillows. Rachel's, a surprise for Jeremy, had a series of overlapping hearts in shades of pink so sweet they were almost edible. But Rachel felt anything but pink as she blurted out Consuela's allegations.

Marguerite looked up as she worked gold thread into her pillow. "Nobody's going to raid the joint—unless you decide *you* have to," she said.

Rachel met her eyes. Finally she turned away and went back to cross-stitching.

"Look," Marguerite said. "It's not as if the police are waiting to bust John's Center."

"I still can't believe you'd take me to see somebody illegal."

Marguerite shook her head. "It's 2020. We depend on our government and the media to keep us safe—to such an extent that we're like cows trained to avoid an electric fence. After a few shocks, cows won't dare to go out of their comfort zone. We're just the same. After the government teamed up with the AMA to start OHM, most alternative healers went out of business because establishment people do exactly what you do, Rachel. They go every month for their cheap imitation from Health Services and think they're getting the deal of the century."

"Okay," Rachel said. "But let me ask you this. Could I be put in jail for seeing John if somebody else blew the whistle?"

"Nah, I think the worst that could happen would be that John would have to pay a fine. You'd probably get a lecture about how you were wasting your money."

"You don't think they'd put John in jail?"

"I sincerely doubt it," Marguerite said coldly. "That would make him seem much too important. All this stuff is downplayed—even the law against healers has been kept out of the news, which is why you never knew about it. In all the years I've studied with John, I've never heard of a healer being arrested. Have you?"

Rachel stood up, calmed herself with a few leg lifts, then said. "Here's what I'm gonna do, Marguerite. I won't hassle John. And I'll keep studying with Consuela until I can read auras more clearly. Then I can decide for myself what is true and what's fake."

Marguerite said nothing but looked relieved.

Thoughtfully Rachel added, "I don't think I blame you or Consuela, because if you'd told me everything, Brent would still be in a coma and I would have learned zilch. Now I have a chance to make up my own mind. And I'm already sure that the government has no right to secretly pass a law that tells me who I can or can't choose for a healer."

She walked over to Marguerite and gave her a hug. "You know what's the most disturbing part for me? Ever since 911, I've worried about terrorists. Even though I'd never tell this to Jeremy, sometimes I've even wondered if the huntids are some kind of biological weapon. But with all my fears about terrorists, it never occurred to me before that, in their own way, our own politicians could be worse."

Chapter 32
A Sweet Little Ritual

Brent didn't want to go to bed. So what else was new?

No way would she let him dawdle tonight, Rachel thought. It was Wednesday, and in a couple of hours she had a phone date with Jeremy.

Most nights, the mom and son bedtime ritual was the sweetest part of Rachel's life in Washington West. But tonight, even if she hadn't felt rushed, Rachel couldn't expect much of a soulful dialogue. She had to wash his hair, which he hated. But what else could the silly boy expect? He and Gil had played space monsters in the back yard all afternoon, which they thought meant coating themselves with mud. When they made their triumphant return for dinner, grimy as could be, she and Marguerite had laughed until they were weak. The boys liked that; the idea of a major clean-up didn't please them as much.

Now Rachel scrubbed her reluctant bather. Stretched out on his back in the tub, her big boy was growing so tall. She scrubbed him until the bathwater turned brown and Brent returned to his normal hue; then she asked him to scoot down and dip the back of his head into the water.

"That's okay, Mom, I don't need a shampoo," he said, as his blond-and-mud curls fanned out like seaweed.

Carefully, Rachel sloshed water onto the back of his hair, then lathered it with Squeaky Clean shampoo. He'd loved this brand since babyhood, because when it sudsed up you could play simple tunes with the lather. Rachel did this now to distract him; he'd always hated having his hair washed.

"Don't rub my ears, okay?"

The only way to survive a shampoo with Brent was to keep scrubbing and ignore his comments.

"The water's going into my ears, Mom."

"Yeah, but you're tilting your neck at a weird angle. Just lie back—the water's shallow."

"It's too hot."

"You know I'll use fresh water to rinse. Here, I'll make it cooler. Is that better?"

"Yeah, but leave my ears alone."

Rachel steadied herself with a breath, then asked quietly, "Brent, have your ears been more sensitive since you had that huntid attack?"

"Mom, it was just a cold. You've asked me that a million times. The answer is still no."

As she began rinsing his hair, he tucked in his chin and tilted his head as far away from the water as possible. Was there ever a more exasperating little boy?

"Would you please put your head back in the water? It would be easier to get the shampoo off, you know."

"I'm not going any deeper. Get my ears wet if you have to. But *touch* them, don't rub them."

Getting seriously frustrated, Rachel decided to see if empathy could help. *Click*. She felt Brent's discomfort, including how stiffly he held his neck. Brent wasn't just being stubborn about having his hair washed, he genuinely hated it. Feeling this made Rachel remember the vividness of her own body's likes and dislikes when a little girl. What a gift! She'd have to thank Consuela. Then Rachel wondered, *What else can I learn about how it feels to be Brent right now?*

Click. Beneath the tension in his strong little body, it felt as if his heart was throbbing with joy at being alive—and with his perception, no wonder. Everything in the bathroom looked bigger and brighter. Tiny particles of air seemed to dance. Even hearing was different—intense silence within and all the noises around him with their volumes turned up.

Coming back to herself with a pang of sadness, Rachel realized how different Brent was from her as a child. He wasn't just 30+ years younger, he took for granted a kind of joy she had never known.

"It must be fun, being you," she told him.

Was she just imagining that her voice sounded different? The difference was, this time her words matched what she felt—unlike her normal way of speaking, which was to try out one parenting ploy after another. Rachel continued to think about this as she got Brent ready for bed. When she tucked him in, she looked at Brent thoughtfully and he seemed to be curious about her, too. Then he hugged her with unusual enthusiasm, more like a baby gorilla than a well-behaved boy. *Being an empath could make all my relationships more real*, she thought, feeling gratitude and wonder.

But talking to her husband couldn't have been more the opposite of Brent's child-like joy. Soon as she saw Jeremy's face on-screen, Rachel realized you didn't have to be an empath to tell how awful he felt. His job these days must be a nightmare. No empathic holding a space for *him* right now: Consuela had taught Rachel to avoid overload. If she exhausted herself, she'd be no good to either of them.

Instead, Rachel could still act like the good wife and cheer him up. So she smiled into the phone-screen in the way that accented her dimples. "Wait a sec, Jeremy," she said flirtatiously, and ran off-screen.

"This was supposed to be a surprise," she called to him, grabbing her cross-stitch project. Running back to the telescreen, she pushed the zoom button, and showed him every stitch, larger than life.

Suddenly, Rachel realized that she was embarrassed by this staged show-and-tell. This wasn't the first time she had play-acted in front of her husband. On some level, she was constantly vamping for Jeremy, trying to connect him with his sensuality. When it worked, both enjoyed the payoff. But it wouldn't happen tonight, and not just because Jeremy was on the opposite side of the country. *He looks so exhausted, he couldn't make love if his life depended on it.*

At least he felt like talking, complaining about the preparations for Huntid Extermination Day and his difficulty in deciding which insecticide to use, although much of what he said was too technical for Rachel to grasp.

"So what's new with you?" he finally asked.

Rachel felt torn. She didn't want to keep secrets from her husband. But could he possibly understand what she'd been learning with John and Consuela? Integrity was especially important for an empath—Consuela had instructed her, "Always tell at least one little piece of your truth, if only to leave the door open." Jeremy had been telling her what was important to him. Shouldn't she do the same?

"On a lighter note," Rachel said, "I've started a little project."

"Yeah?"

"I'm learning how to become an empath."

"That's nice," Jeremy replied casually.

But this isn't just another hobby, Rachel wanted to say. She tried again, adding a flirtatious giggle to her voice. "The other day, I even relived part of a past life."

Jeremy groaned. "Would you please explain something? Why does everyone who fools around with past lives only remember being somebody famous, like Cleopatra or Marie Antoinette? What a load of malarkey!"

"Are you going to let me answer?"

"Sure." Jeremy shook his head, an extra-wide frown accentuating his already wide forehead.

"I asked the exact same question, and John had two explanations. First of all, when we remember past lives, we recall the most important ones, the experiences that can help us now. Considering that each of us has at least 10,000 past lives— if you include the animal ones—"

"Sure," said Jeremy. "And let's not forget being Pokemon or Winnie the Pooh."

"Anyway" Rachel continued, "with all those lives, there are bound to be some that were pretty colorful. Are you ready to hear the second reason?" Hiding behind her sexiest smile, Rachel gave Jeremy a searching look. Clearly he wasn't buying any of this.

"Jeremy, are you even listening?"

He heard that, stretching his long lips into a reluctant smile.

"I'm not asking you to believe this, Jeremy, but haven't you noticed how often people identify with seminar givers, politicians and movie stars?"

He nodded.

"My teacher says it has always been that way, not with stars but with people who were famous or powerful in their time. It's as if, when President Tucker is a major political personality, people say you look just like him."

"God forbid, as you're so fond of saying."

"There's a reason, Jeremy. Tucker's image works like a brand name because it sticks to your mind. Subconsciously you might remember yourself as being *like* President Tucker, or actually being him. That wouldn't be a clear past life recall, even though it has an element of truth. If it came up in a healing session, a good therapist would help you to correct the mistake. During these sessions you have to be careful not to jump to conclusions."

"I'll remember that," Jeremy said, smiling dismissively. "Hey, Beautiful, kiss Brent for me and tell him I've been enjoying his morning calls. You and I will talk in a week.

"One more phone call next week and we'll come home to you," Rachel said reassuringly.

"One phone call and a hell of a weekend," Jeremy said, very carefully blowing her a kiss.

Rachel wasn't sure what to make of that kiss, with its strange intensity. After the phone clicked off she burst into tears.

Chapter 33
Breaking Habits

At breakfast the next day, a waffle was easing its slow, delightful way through Rachel's mouth when Marguerite almost made her choke.

"Do you plan to nibble around the edges of Empath Training or are you ready to gulp the whole thing down and get on with your life?"

Rachel questioned back with her eyebrows.

"Tomorrow, I'm taking Gil camping with John and the gang," said Marguerite. "Wanna come?" The Center had arranged a last-minute weekend camping retreat, and Marguerite was sure a lot of her friends would be there. "I see myself there with Gilavael," she concluded. "You're free to stay home with Brent, of course, but it might be fun. John's never had one of these before."

Rachel paused long enough to consider the alternative—alone all weekend with no car. "Hey," she said, "that's great! I won't be the only newbie for a change." *And maybe it won't be too weird for words,* she added mentally.

Efficient as always, Marguerite kept a ready-packed box of camping gear in her garage. Rachel would use Greg's sleeping bag. One phone call netted a sleeping bag for Brent and second tent for the boys. Marguerite ordered food from a favorite mega-market, which delivered it before dinnertime. Rachel didn't have to do anything except pack a few clothes, then help load the car so they'd be ready to start first thing tomorrow.

Brent was excited. Since Scout camp had been his only exposure to rustic living, he asked to "camp out" in Gilavael's room that night and the boys turned Gil's bed into a tent by draping it with sheets and sleeping on the floor beneath it. Marguerite entertained them for a while, using a flashlight to send shadows of mysterious creatures scampering across the bedroom walls. By midnight, the boys were still roaring their best imitation of wild animals. *The real thing should only be half as much fun,* Rachel thought, when she entered their raucous bedroom.

"Lights out now!" she bellowed above the din, hiding her grin until she had left the room.

Something strange thing happened on the way to Rolling River National Forest the next morning—Rachel couldn't figure out how to occupy herself during the four-hour drive. The boys chatted gleefully in the back seat, but no fascinating discourse was forthcoming from the driver's seat, except for an occasional "Look at that!"

Usually by the time Marguerite said this, the moment's picturesque object had just disappeared from view, so instead of inspiring Rachel, the tour-guide comments had the same effect as if Marguerite had said, "Nyah, nyah, you'll never see as well as I do." Rachel knew this was true. And it seemed like a perfect symbol for her current life that the fascinating scenes she passed never came in focus until it was too late.

Meanwhile, her purist friend refused to play music to disguise the silence, the car was unbearably stuffy, and Rachel couldn't distract herself with isometrics because she was heeding John's advice about multi-tasking.

Rachel stroked the sleeves of her aqua pantsuit, admiring the way the rainbow-colored sequins had been attached with robotic precision. The fabric shimmied whenever she took a deep breath, not that anyone here would notice.

Rachel sighed. John would be at the retreat. Yesterday Marguerite had talked about how much she looked forward to being with him and her friends from the Center. Rachel paraded them before her imagination, part fantasy, part Daffy Duck cartoon. Steve Ambrosian would be there, maybe also the Indian-bloodstream guy with the near death experience. Cute but unavailable men—in that regard, not unlike Rachel's own darling husband. Or John.

She began critiquing John: the way he behaved like Mr. Popularity when he gave his sermons—not phony exactly, but irritatingly remote—when suddenly a strange thought popped into her head.

Judgment is a habit that can be broken. She heard the words as clearly as though the relentless Consuela were sitting right inside her head.

Weird! Rachel tossed her luxuriant curls, then decided a more effective way to clear her mind might be prayer breathing. Consuela had taught her how to alternate the use of her nostrils by pushing her fingertips against the flanges of her nose, allowing one side at a time to breathe out, then in.

Once this got this underway, she was supposed to add a prayer. At the moment, all Rachel could come up with was, *I feel stuck in every possible way.* The lament began reverberating inside her like a mantra.

Don't poison yourself; turn the thought into a prayer, urged an inner voice. She didn't know if this came from her own Higher Self, from Consuela, or another source altogether. But her breath deepened and she found herself imploring God to break her habit of making judgments.

"All you had to do was ask," Marguerite said out of the blue. She opened the car windows; then the boys began chirping like birds. Rachel looked around, amazed. Were these people all nuts? Or were they in cahoots with God?

Don't stop. Breathe and pay attention to what you're feeling, she heard. She did, and minutes later told Marguerite, "I'm worried about the people from John's Center. Do you think they'll like me?"

"Just be you," she said.

Rachel sat wide eyed, enjoying the view and the presence of her three companions—four, maybe, if she counted God, too. This was turning out to be some trip.

After Marguerite guided their car to the campground, they all jumped out and stretched, sucking in the fresh air.

"What do we do first?" Rachel asked.

"Admire this," Marguerite said, leading them to the nearby river bank. Silently, they watched how the fast-moving waters of Rolling River crashed through huge boulders. The sky was big, the air so sweet that Rachel thought she would never get enough of it.

"It's lovely," she said at last. "But don't we have things to do?"

Marguerite sighed and turned back to the car. "Let's put up the tents," she said. Her antique tent had pegs and stakes but she got it up in less than 10 minutes as Rachel and the kids watched in fascination.

"Kids, you've gotta work, too," Marguerite commanded when she saw everyone else standing around. Gil was asked to set up the kid's tent. Ceremoniously, he laid this shiny new pop-up on a flat patch of ground. Modern tents were only as big as a book these days, Rachel realized. But of course these days downloadable novels were flashy affairs, wrapped in such promo products as T-shirts and packaged with an audio version of the novel, the video of it, often a matching computer game. Even cheap books could take several minutes to unwrap and, in some cases, releasing a novel from its surrounding goodies was the best part of buying it.

By contrast this book-sized tent contained only one thing, glistening aquamarine Steel-Cloth. Gilavael turned it over, pushed a button, and stepped back fast. Out whooshed a circular tent almost six feet high. Rachel followed the kids inside.

"Be sure to close the door all the way," she told them, pressing the flap's Velcro seal to reinforce the arched shape of the door.

"Come on," teased Gil. "You afraid we're gonna let the bugs in?"

"Now that you mentioned it, I am," she retorted, her delight in the tent gone. "Come on, boys. We've still got work to do."

Marguerite asked Brent and Gil to gather sticks for the orientation campfire; Rachel's assignment was unpacking the car. When she carried her sleeping bag into the tent she'd share with Marguerite, Rachel observed the way huntids swarmed thickly all over the grass in a constantly moving greenish layer. Instead of coming just up to her ankles, as they had at the lake when Brent fell ill, these buzzing creatures came halfway up her calves.

Thousands of disgusting creepies wherever she went! Stifling a scream, she joined Marguerite, who was setting up their water purification equipment. Taking care not to frighten the kids, Rachel whispered, "Did you notice the huntids? How dangerous do you think they are?"

"So you finally saw them."

"Well, how do we protect ourselves?"

"Rachel, you don't have to handle the huntids as if they're a problem. All you have to do is accept them. You know what makes huntids land on a person, don't you?"

Mechanically Rachel recited what she'd heard a million times on TV. "Huntids only alight when you go where they already are and you stand as still as a statue."

"Exactly. John says to think of them like the presence of God—they're always available, but if you want action you have to get quiet inside."

Rachel snorted. "Now that's flattering. Versions of God with lime-green bodies and day-glow wings in that impossible shade of purple!"

As she toted over the duffel bag with her clothes and towels, plus a bag of groceries and several pillows, one of the pillows fell to the ground, "Shit," she said. "Shoe," she corrected herself, looking in the direction of the boys; they were so busy playing they still hadn't left to gather wood for the campfire. "Shoe, shoe, shoe."

"Rachel, lighten up," Marguerite said, laughing. "You're carrying three loads in your arms—no wonder you're dropping stuff."

She called to the boys. "You have a new assignment. Help Ms. Murphy unload the car." As they hopped to it, Marguerite arranged things inside the tent, muttering how silly it was that people constantly over-packed. "Nothing personal," she insisted to Rachel, who was crouched over the foot of her sleeping bag arranging her clothes on a pink plastic Porta-Shelf. "Taking on too much is a universal disease these days, like multi-tasking. Wouldn't it be great if we could cure it, once and for all?"

"Who says I want to be cured?" Rachel said. "If I wasn't carrying 20 things at once, I don't know what I'd do. I *have* to carry a lot. Always, always, always."

Marguerite's lack of response left Rachel's words echoing in her head disconcertingly. Maybe it wasn't always necessary to load up. She remembered an affirmation from Alan Cohen, a popular Seminar Star: "I always have enough time for what God wants me to do." Rachel added a memo to her skin-phone Do List: "Reconsider multi-tasking. Again."

But Rachel didn't stay discouraged. Brent came over and pulled her out of the tent. "Mom, let me show you someplace neat."

She waved to Marguerite, who was apparently in deep communion with her own duffel and Porta-Shelf.

Brent led Rachel through a patch of woods across from the river bank. Huntids swarmed, but she got better at ignoring them, partly because of the gorgeous wildflowers that grew here. Rachel noticed some she'd never seen before. Her favorite was a spiky flower with bright orange blossoms. Even the dandelions looked exotic, tipped with squared edges.

"They look like they just got a haircut," Brent said.

"I should have brought your magnifying glass from back home," said Rachel. "Hey, I've got an idea." She pulled Brent over to a couple of tree stumps. "Sit down. Let's take out our ears and use them like a magnifying glass."

Following her example, he closed his eyes. Rachel heard the sound of rushing water, plus some kind of insect singing into the silence. It pulsated the way a hummingbird might hover in the air.

"What do you think?" Rachel asked him, happily.

"It sounds great, Mom. And most grownups wouldn't do anything this far out, you know?"

When she opened her eyes, he was smiling at her affectionately—and his head was covered with huntids, like a green-and-purple halo.

Revolted, she flinched. Then she made the mistake of looking at her own arm. It was covered with huntids, too.

"Don't worry, Mom," Brent said, comfortingly. "Move around, that's all."

Rachel followed his advice. If he wasn't upset, why should she be? "You're the expert on moving around," she told him. "The day you eat an entire meal sitting down, I'll know you've grown up."

Walking back to the tents, Rachel realized that breaking the habit of cynicism wasn't all she'd have to do on this trip. *I'm going to make a new habit and stop being scared of these huntids,* she promised herself.

The group of John's campers was lingering over dinner when Steve Ambrosian rang a miniature brass gong.

"Group meeting starts in ten minutes," he announced, pointing to a large grassy area near the river bank. Lucky they had enough space, thought Rachel; John's group must be over 300.

As a veteran seminar-taker, Rachel knew the advantage of a good seat so she quickly staked out a tree stump for Brent and shoved a rock next to it for herself. An uncomfortable rock, it turned out, but that was camping.

As the group assembled, Rachel noticed very few children besides Brent and Gil. Most grownups seemed to know each other, hugging and chattering away. At this rate, it could take hours before any meeting began.

Rachel watched as Steve, apparently the evening's emcee, surveyed the group. John sat next to him, eyes closed. Rachel, focusing on Steve, decided he was a professional charmer. Maybe he turned his mellowness on and off; she certainly didn't think it was an accident that he happened to be wearing a perfectly pressed, spotless $400 pima cotton T-shirt. Sweeping his eyes over the group, he spoke in a voice loud enough to be heard above the chit-chat, "Enjoy that campfire because I don't think we'll bother with them other nights. In weather like this, we don't need it, do we?"

Rachel made a concerted effort not to stare at the rippling biceps that emerged through his cream-colored T-shirt. He was saying, now in a slightly louder voice, "John thought we should gather around every night about this time, so listen for this gong after dinner, okay?"

Danielle stood up, a striking figure in the hazy evening light. "John asked me to sing through a blessing when we have group meetings." Self-consciously she added, "It's improvised, as you may know." Then she closed her eyes and opened up her voice.

The wordless song called to parts of Rachel she didn't even know existed. When it ended, she had tears in her eyes. Nobody applauded. Instead, the group's silence dropped down with a whoosh, as though they had all taken an express elevator 50 stories down. Attention shifted to John. He hadn't said a word yet.

Rachel realized that he was sitting exactly opposite her. His steady gaze left her feeling flustered. She began picking up pebbles and stacking them by the stump where Brent sat. When she looked up again, she was prepared to give John a casual glance. Unfortunately he missed it. He was looking at a plump woman in jeans and a baggy sweatshirt featuring a hologram of the earth.

See, it was nothing special, she thought. *He's just looking around the circle.* Still, Rachel's eyes felt hot and her body self-consciously busty, as if she were back in High School again—when she had a crush on Muhammad Jabbar, the class poet.

"Thanks for coming, everybody," John said. "Welcome to a weekend that is going to rejuvenate you. It couldn't come at a better time. Extermination Day is just one week from tomorrow and our job is to make ourselves ready." He paused, letting silence fall again, like a thick curtain over a stage.

Finally he spoke again: "Consuela, please give everyone the background on our situation."

"You bet," she said, rising to her feet with that solid, planted look she always had. Although Consuela had been sitting next to John, Rachel hadn't noticed her. Maybe it was that outfit she was wearing—awful, as if olive green could begin to. . . . *No*, Rachel thought, *I don't have to do this.*

"John predicted the huntids," Consuela said. "He was doing his One-Minute Blessing for the world. How many of you do that spiritual exercise every morning? Let's see your hands."

Although Marguerite raised her hand, many people did not, to Rachel's relief. "The One-Minute Blessing connects you with ideas for helping people in the world outside yourself," Consuela explained. "Sometimes you receive information that you never expected. John was doing a One-Minute Blessing several years ago when he first learned about the huntids."

John's gorgeous smile revealed bright, even teeth. *He beats Ambrosian,* Rachel decided. In the background, she heard Consuela say:

"The huntids have to do with consciousness, among other things. As you may know, there's a relationship between human consciousness and all life forms on the planet. Take so-called endangered species. There's always a circumstantial cause why certain animals cease to exist, but what's the underlying reason?

"John says it's because old abilities of human consciousness become obsolete. It's that simple. For instance, a lot of the old wilderness survival skills haven't been needed for centuries. When they ceased to be necessary, we lost passenger pigeons and bison. But when humanity develops new faculties of consciousness, that can cause new species to evolve.

"When John did his One-Minute Blessing near the turn of the millennium, he discovered a child born with telepathic abilities that hadn't been found before. Over the years he noticed more of them being born."

"What kind of telepathy, Consuela?" someone called from the crowd.

She said. "People with this kind of telepathy can shift their awareness to other life forms and copy their faculties of consciousness. Then they can communicate that knowledge to other life forms— moving *them* forward in consciousness."

The crowd was listening intently. Personally, Rachel didn't get what all the fuss was about.

Consuela continued, "I think most of you know about the Hundredth Monkey Effect. About 40 years ago, researchers who were studying wild monkeys discovered that when the hundredth monkey on one particular island developed a new skill—opening up coconuts by banging them on rocks, say, all the other monkeys on that island immediately acquired that same skill.

"Amazingly, so did monkeys on other islands. Even though they had no direct contact with the first group of monkeys, they copied their learning. This proves that the consciousness of a specie is interconnected. Once *enough* members of a tribe learn a skill, *all* members can access it."

Consuela paused to let that sink in. With Rachel, it didn't sink very far. Unless someone could convince her that people were more like monkeys than they appeared, her private reaction to this big news was a big "So what?"

Smiling, Consuela said, "In a similar way, some very advanced souls have been incarnating on earth during the last 20 years. You could call them Light Holders. Although their numbers have been growing slowly, it wasn't until last March that John noticed the Hundredth Monkey Effect with *them*. Enough of these telepathic Light Holders have been born to reach that critical number of 100."

"They're like flashlight people," John said, standing up. "They have big heads with a lot of glow—their auras, mind you, not their faces. Physically they look like anybody else."

"You don't call them huntids, did you?" came a voice from the crowd.

"Not exactly," he said. "I call 'em 'Big Heads,' actually."

The group laughed, but the laughter sounded nervous to Rachel.

John gestured to Consuela, as if saying, "Go on, you're the talker, not me."

Consuela nodded, clearing her throat. "First, one of these Light Holders was born, and the next year a couple more, and so forth. When Light Holder number 100 arrived last March, human consciousness changed irrevocably, John says. It's as though all of humanity instantly gained the ability to telepathically travel in spirit like the Light Holders.

"Coincidentally or not, on that same day, some flies began to mutate into a new life form. John noticed that, too, during one of his One-Minute Blessings. Months later, these flies were sighted and called the huntids.

"Right?" said Consuela, turning to John in a way that Rachel thought could have been coquettish, except that the woman was so singularly unattractive. *Stop that*, she told herself, and made her breathing pattern change and deepen. Watching for flirtation, judging about attractiveness—that needed to go in the pile of her old habits.

Breathwork could change the pattern. So she began by checking her breath, with her palm placed beneath her nose. Both nostrils were working at once, which corresponded to both sides of her brain being engaged. She was definitely becoming aware of her own consciousness, even if she was no Big Head!

Consuela had paused. Now she said to John, "I feel doubt coming from some members of the group. John, could you explain more about the Light Holders?"

A loud voice broke in. Rachel recognized it as coming from Steve Ambrosian. He said, "Hey, man. How about you just plug us all into that Light Holder consciousness?"

"Well, how about this, mates?" John smiled at Steve, then swept the group with twinkling eyes. "It happens that one of those original hundred Light Holders is here with us tonight. Maybe he'd like to connect us to his kind of consciousness. What do you say, Brent Murphy?"

Rachel's mouth fell open as John gestured, introducing her son to the group. All of a sudden, Rachel realized that, by virtue of sitting next to her in the huge campground circle, Brent was also sitting directly opposite John. Rachel saw their eyes lock. She was torn between protectiveness, hoping that John wasn't doing some kind of hypnotism on her baby, versus a feeling of humiliation. She'd had no clue he was telepathic—and a "Light Holder" at that. What did that make her, some kind of psychic moron?

Then Rachel felt communication flow between Brent and John as they stared at each other in silence across the circle. But when Rachel joined her gaze to theirs, trying to push her way in, she felt like she smashed against a force field with a powerful and slow gravity all its own. Was she making this up? Could she be hearing a whooshing sound, as if she were standing next to a waterfall?

Meanwhile, some 300 heads turned to stare at her boy. A couple of people smiled benevolently at Rachel as if to congratulate her on being his mother. Marguerite's expression seemed to say, "Ta da! I have produced them." This was getting way too weird, thought Rachel.

Brent finally got his mouth into gear. "Sure, if you want," he told John. "I can bring them with me."

Then Brent turned to the group. "Okay, let's start with the river." He pointed to the water. "Close your eyes and pretend to jump right into the water."

He paused as if he could hear the crowd's unspoken doubts. Rachel's emotions were racing in every direction; whatever else happened, she didn't want anyone laughing at him.

Brent's voice grew stronger. "Moving with your mind is like finding a secret passageway in a house. You know where it is. Then you just push the button and go in, okay? Remember, your way of going in could be different from mine. Mostly I listen. But you could go in by looking. Or else you can kind of touch it with your eyes. All your senses are connected, you know, when you go deep enough into consciousness."

Even with her eyes closed, Rachel could feel a look of mischief come over Brent's face. He said, "When you're in that secret passage, it doesn't matter whether you crawl through on your belly or slide in on your butt. Just go."

He paused. Rachel wondered if he was listening telepathically to John. Brent continued, "Another way could be to say something like this, inside: '*I* am here and I hold you in my heart right now.'

"Anyway, come into the river. Once you've thought you'd like to go there, you gotta trust that you're there—because you are, in your consciousness. You can stand up and move around just like normal. Okay? I know you can do it, everybody. Close your eyes and ask to be part of the river."

What happened next, at least for Rachel, was a whoosh not unlike riding on her dear old friend, the roller coaster at Adventureland West. She turned into pure energy. It was a pattern of light that vibrated at hummingbird speed. Listening inwardly, she felt free and loose and big and cold and . . . .

After a while, she noticed things that stopped the flow of her energy. *I was being the river*, she thought. *Now I can shift to explore the rocks in the river.* It seemed like the most natural thing in the world to do, as she slipped the fine light particles of her consciousness into the rocks. Their presence felt very old, thick with memories, as if holding impressions of everything that had ever touched her and the material aspect felt solid, heavy and slow. It was not unlike being pregnant, she realized.

Laughing, Rachel felt her mind give a kind of yawn that opened her up bigger and set her off shifting again. Her energy took on a dancing motion. Joy was in it—excitement and change. Breathing out of both nostrils, she woke up within her own wakefulness. *What's this?* she asked, inside.

Oh, I'm joining with huntids in the river, came the answer. Her individual consciousness moved as part of a group that swirled together, every member of the group awake, loud and clear.

Suddenly she heard Brent's voice calling her. He said, "Okay, everybody. You're there. Now comes the tough part. You have to make yourself leave. To do that, think your name three times. That will help you to put your consciousness back inside your own body."

Rachel sighed, but she did as she was told. *Click.* Immediately the tiny particles of her light began moving to a faster rhythm.

"Go ahead, you can do it." That was Brent, her baby, talking to the whole group, his voice full of command.

"Do it," he urged, inside her head. "Open your eyes right now, even if you don't want to."

One more push. Rachel opened her eyes. She looked around. It seemed like everyone else's face wore the same dazed expression as hers.

There was a lot of staring, especially at Brent. Rachel sure did her share. *For heaven's sake, why didn't you tell me?* she shouted at him through her eyes.

I did, Mom, only you weren't listening. But I knew that some day you'd be interested. His eyes softened and she heard him say, *Mom, don't worry about my teaching other people. I still love you the best.*

"Good job, Brent," John said. "Let's all take a break. Back in ten, everyone."

People started talking excitedly to their neighbors. Not Rachel, she was too stunned. John said, "You're off to a good start, everyone. Let's have a show of hands. How many of you feel that you connected with the huntids?"

Rachel's hand went up slowly. Soon everyone's hand was raised.

"One more question. Huntids weren't what you thought they would be, were they?"

The shock of this registered on her, and she saw an equal amazement reflected on many of the faces around the circle.

John beamed. "All right, everyone. Lesson two is tomorrow, ten o'clock. Same place. Be here."

Chapter 34
Relating to Animals

"John told everyone Brent was a Big Head," was Rachel's first thought the next morning, setting the tone for a grumpy day. She went looking for him, planning to give him a piece of her mind, and spotted him walking to the campfire with Steve.

"John, we have to talk. In private."

Turning, his face lit up with that beautiful smile, he spoke Rachel's name with enough warmth to melt any logic she had left. Steve dodged out of the way; he saw her anger, even if John didn't. No matter, she knew exactly what she wanted to say, and she didn't miss a beat.

"John," she said, crowding him a little. "Why did you single out Brent in front of everyone? Why didn't you didn't ask my permission before you revealed his connection to the huntids? You humiliated me by making me learn about it in public. I'm his mother, remember?"

Rachel was furious. She also noticed that John smelled great early in the morning, sweet and strong, very male—not that she'd let that make any difference.

He said, "Rachel, I thought you knew all about Brent's abilities. Don't you remember what happened when we brought him back from the coma?"

Rachel rocked back on her heels to glare up at John. "Do you really think bringing my son out of a coma is such an everyday experience that I'd notice something like that? You're the big expert on healing, not me. But who gave you permission to reveal something so personal about my son in public?"

In the morning light, his hair glowed like splinters of sunlight tinted golden brown. He said, "Sorry, Rachel, but I assumed you'd put two and two together. I've found 112 children born on the same vibration as Brent, these wonderful new light travelers. All of them have gone into the same kind of coma Brent did, and most of them have come back—"

"Most of them?"

"The last time I checked in consciousness, three hadn't. But they'll be back eventually."

"Exactly how do you know that? And why didn't you tell me?"

He held up his hand like a traffic cop. "Slow down, Rachel. I'll answer any questions you like but, please, one at a time."

Rachel stiffened as she felt a wave of electricity pass through her. Where was it coming from?

"Can we get together after the large-group meeting, around at 11:30? My car's a blue Electra, parked about half a mile up the road," he said with a gesture. "My tent's there, too—a turquoise bubble tent. Why don't we meet there, by the tent?"

Rachel didn't know what to say: It was as if her lips had vanished clean out of her face. She nodded and turned away; soon her angry walk turned into her normal gait, hips swaying gracefully, as though John hadn't just shattered her poise. But she was still breathing in short, angry gasps as she joined the campfire. Marguerite had saved her a place near the kids.

The entire group had assembled by the time John ambled up to his favorite tree stump. People stared at Brent with a kind of admiration that Rachel found unsettling. From the look of things, at least John didn't share in the hero-worship. Businesslike, he swept the circle with his eyes until conversation stopped. He looked so fresh this morning that his aura might have been made out of gold—not that Rachel could see his aura.

"I want to be extremely clear about something today, something important." He paused, smiling. Rachel made a polite grimace about half the size of a real smile, which meant "Oh yeah?"

"Many of you are concerned because the huntids are due for extermination a week from today," John said, raising his voice slightly. "As you now know, their purpose is to elevate humans to a higher state of consciousness. I'm training you to learn from them while you still can, just as other teachers like me around the country are training *their* groups. On Extermination Day, all of us will be able to share any final information the huntids choose to give us."

Was Rachel really hearing this? She remembered the day when a friend called to tell her that the World Trade Center had just been demolished. This was just as surreal, in a different way.

He concluded simply, We're calling it a Wave of Oneness and you can be volunteer Lightworkers."

Steve Ambrosian asked, "What are we Lightworkers going to *do* to the huntids, exactly?"

"First we'll join in consciousness with as many people as possible. Then all of us will join with the huntids and ask them to leave, instead of driving them out by force."

Steve's voice was husky. "You think we can do this?"

"I'm betting on it, mates."

"But then why not do it now? Or the day *before* the government drops all the chemicals?"

"Good question," John said. "My colleagues and I have met in spirit—in our light bodies. We believe the timing will be best if we all act simultaneously. The world's attention will be focused on Extermination Day, so this will be a time of maximum power. In a vision, my colleagues and I were shown that we can succeed."

"What if we don't?" Consuela asked quietly.

"Then humanity will be no better off than before the huntids arrived," John said. "Plus, of course, we'll have to deal with all the toxins from the extermination."

He paused, letting that sink in.

Someone Rachel didn't recognize called out, "So you don't believe in a Rapture?"

"No, Hank, " John answered. "But I do believe that without help from the huntids, and a huge awakening on our part, humanity will have an enormous problem handling the chemicals sprayed next Saturday."

He cleared his throat. "The purpose of our meeting today is to sort Lightworkers into study groups."

Somebody grumbled "Right, we'll study toxins." Other smart-alecks babbled in the background. Rachel found their behavior incredibly rude—obviously these people had never been to a real seminar. Not that she treated John with excessive reverence, but at least she had manners.

John told the crowd that everyone present had at least one gift comparable to Brent's Light Holder ability. Now it was time to get serious about using these gifts to move consciousness.

"Hold on," Steve interrupted. "I don't want to get too serious."

Acknowledging the comment with a faint smile, John continued, "The theory behind what we're about to do is contained in an ancient saying, 'As above so below.' What does that statement mean to you?"

An unfashionably wrinkled woman said, "Like the world outside us reacts to the world within us?"

A man with long hair and a cleft chin said, "How about ordinary coincidence? Things happen to us in life because of what's spiritually happening on the inside."

"Good points, Melanie, Ezekiel." John was too patient, Rachel thought. He needed to act more like a real seminar teacher. These days, teachers took command of their audience, selling their programs is if they were on infomercials. Why did John ask all these questions? He'd never make it as a celebrity.

In fact, nothing about John made him look like a professional seminar giver, all of whom had the razzle-dazzle of entertainers. Rachel couldn't help noticing how handsome he looked in that plaid shirt and worn jeans, but he didn't send out one speck of razzle dazzle.

"Each human being has a special gift of consciousness," John explained. "That's on the inner. On the outer, everyone could be compared to some kind of animal with a comparable gift." A short woman, whose hair was a shade of platinum not seen in nature, waved at him frantically. "Susie?" he said.

"Wow!" she blurted out, "Just like totem animals. Isn't that idea part of Native American wisdom?"

"Could be," John said. "Everyone has a pet animal, or might—if they thought about it.

People in the group began chattering, and Rachel heard her neighbors say, "That's Grandpa and his hunting dogs!"

"My Aunt Taylor used to keep 17 cats."

"Dad always said he could relate to being a turtle. Whenever Mom would ask him to fix things around the house, he had this turtle cap he'd put on."

"One at a time," John said.

He called on the singer Danielle, who said, "One time when I was down on my luck, I rented an attic apartment in California City. The woman who lived there before me was into owls—I mean, really into owls. She had owl figurines and paintings all over the place, and when she moved out, she left owl stickers decorating the walls. I had to scrape them off—42 of them. I counted. Promise me, John, you're not going to turn us into weirdos like that woman."

Everyone laughed, even Rachel.

"At different times in history, " John said, "people have psychically related to different animals. Native American tribes, long ago, could align with animals of every size, including large ones like buffaloes and bears. By 2000, Americans mostly related to domesticated animals, cats or dogs. Now, because of the accelerated growth of consciousness, there's a different group for most people to psychically align with."

He paused. "Let me warn you, these animals aren't necessarily cute."

"Shucks, John, just break it to us," said Steve.

"Arthropods," John said. "You know, nature's original hardbodies."

"Insects?" Susie said, looking appalled.

"Yes," John said. "But I'm also talking about spiders and centipedes."

Rachel chuckled inwardly. If only her entomologist husband could hear this, maybe he'd finally accept New Age wisdom.

Arthropods were among the wisest animals on earth, said John, as well as the most socially sophisticated. In today's world also they stood out due to being one of the few life forms that had not been genetically altered. Finally, insects and related species were among the oldest surviving creatures on earth.

Marguerite spoke up. "Their bones are on the outside, John. Exoskeletons, I think it's called. As an artist, that's what intrigues me the most."

Rachel looked down at her hands, white and soft, with turquoise Perma-nails. Bones on the inside, please and thank you very much.

Marguerite was saying, "John, is it your idea that people today identify with insects because our brains—not our bones but our brains—are now on the surface?"

"As usual, Marguerite, you're way ahead of most of us," he said. "Inside on the outside—that parallels how humans have evolved in the computer age. Brains come first, not brawn. As leaders of the human race, you've taken that process one step farther by allowing consciousness to come to the fore. Wearing your skeleton on the outside, as it were, you're starting to experience consciousness as the essential fact of who you are."

"Amen," Susie said loudly.

Ugh, that Susie! Then Rachel remembered something Consuela had said: "It's your choice. Either judge people or learn from them. You can't do both." Rachel promised herself to explore Susie at a deeper level some day. Rachel needed to because, frankly, Susie drove her nuts. But John was talking again.

Chapter 35
Assignments

"Animal affiliations may sound like an abstract theory," John said in a quiet voice. "What do you say we put it to the test as I describe the main types?"

"Hey, that means you," Steve said in his booming voice. Like Rachel, he'd apparently noticed how few people were paying attention to John. Instead they chatted with their neighbors. "Whatever you're talking about now," Steve continued, "Don't miss this. Come on, guys."

"I think you'll recognize the name of your specialty when I describe it," John continued serenely. "When you feel called to a group, go stand with the leader I'll be assigning to it. I've shown them techniques that will help you deepen your talent, and joining all our talents together can help us on August 29th—"

"What are we planning to do, protest the Extermination?" Susie interrupted. Rachel took a long, patient breath, hoping it would help.

"All in good time, Susie," John said, giving her a wink. "First let's sort ourselves into groups. Cockroaches come first. Your gift is that you know how to stay grounded. This weekend you'll practice going into meditation, connecting with an archangel or ascended master, and then with the huntids. You'll learn to bring the huntids' enormous energy back down to earth."

Could that be me, a big grounder? Rachel wondered. *Hardly, that's what men are for!* She smoothed the glowing violet sleeves on her form-fitting blouse, a perfect contrast to the summer-weight jeans that emphasized her flat belly. (Not that anyone here would notice.)

Some people from the circle headed to a grassy area nearby as a man named Lance Gilmore was named the leader. With his hefty body, placid face and short blond hair, Rachel thought he looked like a good ol' boy from Virginia. "He moves pretty slow for a cockroach," she wisecracked to Marguerite.

"Ah, but nobody's chasing him now," Marguerite said.

"Next, Ants," John announced. "You're the technicians. In everyday life, you're meticulous about details. Your job here is to hold a psychic space complex enough to include everyone—and I do mean everyone."

The meticulous part sounded just like Jeremy, thought Rachel. Sure enough, she spotted a few nerdy men and women, their foreheads furrowing as they walked over to John. Sunil, the Indian guy with the gorgeous hands, was chosen to head this group. No wonder she had been drawn to him, Rachel thought; if her attraction to Jeremy was any clue, she was a sucker for focused, techie types.

"Spiders come next," John said. "You're the artists."

"How can you call us spiders?" inquired a young woman with a god-awful assortment of tattoos and body-piercing jewelry. A classic look, perhaps, Rachel thought, but definitely unflattering. "I thought that artists like me are walk-ins from the Pleiades."

"Could be, Penelope." John said, not unkindly. "But let's be practical. We're not into space travel here, except for the kind that all of us can do in consciousness, with our feet planted solidly on Mother Earth.

"As I was saying, Spiders are driven by the need to create, and our success depends on your creativity. During the Wave of Oneness, we'll need you to join in consciousness with people, then figure out creative—but non-coercive—telepathic messages to wake them up."

Marguerite sure liked that idea. Her heart opened up with such intense relief, Rachel could feel it three seats away. "I'm not alone—that's what I have to remember"—this phrase from Marguerite popped into Rachel's head, and tears came to her eyes. Reaching across Brent and Gil, she squeezed her friend's shoulder. In return she saw a look that was soft and utterly vulnerable, unlike any expression Rachel had seen her wear before.

That glimpse into Marguerite's vulnerability kept Rachel from feeling jealous later, when Marguerite was assigned leadership of the Spider group.

"Termites, you're creators, too. But you create destruction—against rot, stagnation, and ignorance. No doubt you already know who you are, because you've been rebels from day one. Your willingness to join in the Wave will be extremely important, because you'll attract so many others like you. Stand by that dead tree."

Chuckles were heard when Steve Ambrosian was named the head of this group. Rachel saw him roll his eyes, pretending to be surprised. Gilavael joined him immediately, kicking his shoe into the dirt with fiendish enthusiasm. Yep, this was the group for them.

"Your job will be to join with people and shine your light of consciousness at whatever doesn't belong," John told them. "Fear, pain, hypocrisy and rage aren't the core truths of human experience. You'll need to turn up the energy until patterns like these become intolerable."

"We'll love it to death," Steve promised, while Gil just hollered, "Yeah!"

"Bees are the visionaries." John continued. "This is a rare gift, as specialties go, but all of you can understand it. Think of the instinct to reach into the heart of a flower. Bees are the nectar seekers and the honey makers. They will not be stopped in their search for the truth, and they can see in every direction."

He named himself as head of this group. Only two men joined him, both uninteresting-looking men. *Must be worker bees,* Rachel decided. *Not attractive enough to mate with a queen. Except, of course, for their handsome Fearless Leader,* she joked to herself.

Her mind wandered as John named other small groups. She couldn't relate to being a Centipede, Silkworm or Ladybug, whatever, so she tuned out while these groups gathered, although she never failed to notice the better bodied among them. Not many people were still seated, and Rachel began to fear that she was nothing special.

Finally, John turned to Consuela. "Butterflies, I think you know who you are. You're empaths, the nectar drinkers. You can hold a space for two or ten or a hundred. Train well, because you'll be among the leaders when we have our Wave of Oneness. Consuela, you'll facilitate, of course."

Rachel felt her chest fill with pride, and she raised her head a bit as she walked over to Consuela's group. Wow, she was a Butterfly! Consuela looked happy, too. Wonder if there would be any potential friends in their group.

The next two groups were Fireflies and Beetles. After that, John said, "Finally I must name those who relate to the huntids, those masters of intelligence. They can think like all of you already in groups and also like animal specialties not represented here. Huntids can think like any creature or plant on the face of the earth.

"If they traveled to life beyond earth, they could do the same there. As you know, we are privileged to have one in our midst, Brent Murphy. I'll be training him along with my group. Or maybe he'll train me."

"Hold on," said Steve Ambrosian. "You haven't mentioned ordinary houseflies. We had flies long before we had huntids, didn't we? They must count for something."

John said, "Good question. Fly consciousness is the most prevalent in America today. It specializes in gathering information and in sociability. It's a higher vibration of intelligence than, say, pigeons, but I don't think anyone with that consciousness is attracted to the teachings at The Spiritual Center."

"How about mosquitoes?" Susie asked. She was in Rachel's group, unfortunately. Rachel suppressed a groan. Was she going to monopolize their meetings all weekend?

"We don't have any of them with us, either," John said. "What would you guess they do, Susie?"

"They suck your blood," she said, doing a pretty fair imitation of Count Dracula.

"Close," he said. "The Mosquito pattern involves hovering around people, which makes them feel important, then feeding off their energy. That's Rev. Helms' style. And can you think of someone else in public life today with a similar pattern?"

"President Tucker?" asked a teenage girl from the Ant group.

"No," John replied, "Although he's a good example of Fly consciousness. Think of someone enough like Helms to be his identical twin."

"Reverend Pilgrim?" asked Susie.

"Bingo!" said John. "Now, go work with your group."

Chapter 27
Where's My Answer?

As she followed Consuela to their practice area, Rachel replayed how John had set up the groups. It made her furious. He had announced only the names of leaders, not members. And "Go where you feel called" sounded like one big cop-out for organizing people. Didn't he believe the Wave of Oneness was important? Now she wished she had said, "What if you don't know where to go?"

Instantly his image flashed into her consciousness. "You don't know?" he asked, amused.

"Well I do, but what if not everyone does?"

"Then they can come and ask me," he said.

As the daydream—or whatever it was—faded, Rachel stomped along the dirt path. Yeah, she was disgusted with the man but she also sensed a delicious excitement. Think of the secrets she might learn from him and Consuela.

Naturally John had named her honcho—Consuela was clearly the teacher's pet.

After leading them to a small clearing near the river and welcoming everyone, she said, "This will be our meeting place for the weekend, and these three large rocks can be your landmark."

Insufferably bossy, Rachel thought. *As if I can't find my own landmark.*

"Let's start with introductions," Consuela said. "Say what is most important for you to tell us about yourself."

"You go first," said (who else?) Susie.

"I'm Consuela, and over the past few years I've worked with all of you." She gave them a huge smile, then nodded at a medium-handsome man. Rachel found him a little un-muscular for her taste but he did have huge dark eyes and a graceful arched nose. Rachel had noticed him the first time she went to the Center.

"Gregory Lee," he said. "I'm grateful that I've had several years to prepare for whatever we're about to do, because I'm still very much a student."

"Priscilla McKenzie" said another voice. "I like being an empath so far; it does wonders for my sense of humor." The poor woman was 40 if she was a day, Rachel thought, and in urgent need of weight reduction surgery. Oops, she was judging people again. She took a breath and it dawned on her that Priscilla actually looked nice.

Next was Evangeline Jones, a thin woman wrapped in opulent brown-and-gold kente cloth—which only accentuated her drab personality. Several more women and the group's only man besides Gregory introduced themselves, as did a shy girl who looked about 14.

Altogether there were 11 in the Butterfly Group, including Rachel, and none of the women looked like what she would call friend material. Maybe it was time for her to deep breathe some more.

The ultra-platinum blonde spoke up next. "I'm Sioux-Z," she said, spelling it. "Nobody in my family comes from a Native American bloodstream but I like to play with logic. When I'm not studying with John and Consuela, I'm a math major. I didn't see why I should be a boring Susie when I could have a name like Sioux-Z. It's on my license plate, too." Her smile was enormous—big mouth, big teeth, like Julia Roberts—but pushy instead of vulnerable.

I am not going to judge this woman for being on the aggressive side, Rachel told herself. *I will not judge the color of her hair or her name. For one thing, if she's a skilled empath, she'll be onto me in a flash!*

Everyone nodded at Sioux-Z; but when Rachel heard someone mutter the word "creative," she deep-breathed so hard that she almost snorted. Were John's other groups this depressing?

Consuela gave her a sharp look. "Now for that quiet one at the end of the line. Rachel?"

"Yes, I'm Rachel," she said, smiling sweetly at Consuela, then at everyone else. Why say more? Better to impress them with an air of mystery. Fortunately she had just checked the time on her skin-phone. "I just remembered that I have an appointment with John," she added with a little shimmy. "I'll be back as soon as I can. Byeeeeee."

It was a long schlep to John's tent, it turned out, but Rachel didn't mind. Walking parallel to the Rolling River for 15 minutes gave her great views of the countryside. The air had freshness that a can of "Country Air" could never rival, and if Rachel had been visually gifted she would have counted 50 shades of green between the campground area and the clearing with John's blue minivan and tent.

Instead Rachel ignored the colors, rehearsing what she would say to John. It would not be pretty. Privacy was going to be the heart of her complaint. Privacy was so vital in America that an amendment guaranteeing privacy had been added to the constitution. John should realize that she could sue him for telling everyone about Brent. She'd never stamped her datamate even once on a legal disclaimer, and John's status as an unlicensed healer wasn't all that legal to begin with.

Surely he'd apologize. Maybe he'd even tell her how important she was to him. She'd be tough, though. Rachel tried focusing on the apology part but instead kept hearing her own complaint run through her head again and again. No matter.

Suddenly she saw. . . what was that? Looked like a large Righteous family, maybe two, in a wooded area near the road. About 20 people, mostly kids, were doing a kind of twitchy, unsynchronized dance. As she drew closer, their hands and beads were flailing, and several were singing—though not well, at least to Rachel's ear. *Breathe, breathe,* she reminded herself. Some toddlers were restrained by a kind of leash, as if they were pets, and their mothers appeared to be frantically teaching them how to make Righteous mudras with their feet. Sudden, uncontrollable fear ran through Rachel like a lightening bolt.

Dangerous? How could they be dangerous when they seemed so utterly self-absorbed? Yes, dangerous, because they seemed so maniac. Insane asylums were supposed to be things of the past, but Rachel felt as if she had just walked right past one.

To Rachel's relief, John was standing beside his tent. But he wasn't standing exactly--he was balancing on the ground, his arms straight, with one leg stretched out behind and the other lunging forward. Even though she was approaching him from behind, he turned around.

"Saluting the sun," he said as he straightened his body and stood up.

When she looked blank, he added, "It's a traditional yoga pose. You might like to try it sometime."

"Sure. Thanks for seeing me, John. You know, I just passed a group of the Righteous. They must have been trying to earn virtue points or something." A nervous giggle escaped her; she wouldn't have felt more embarrassed if she had just broken wind. Something about that man made it so hard to her to have *gravitas*.

He shrugged. "I can feel many groups at Rolling Ridge this weekend. They mean no harm. They're just like you and me, struggling to do the best they can at a time when God has turned up the energy."

God has turned up the energy? This was such a conversation stopper that Rachel almost gaped at him like a fish. Changing the subject, she asked, "I suppose you turned around just now because you felt my presence here, not because you heard me walk over."

"Both," he said. "I've felt your presence a lot on this trip."

What did that mean? Was he making a pass? She'd better say what she'd planned: "Since you're here, who's in charge of your group and looking after my son?"

"I put Timothy in charge—the tall one with glasses."

"Oh," Rachel said, "Okay." She cleared her throat. "John, you're supposed to be sensitive, so how could you let me be the last one to know that Brent's one of the kids who are like huntids? There are invasion of privacy laws against that." She waited for his apology.

Bending his face towards her, his dark brown eyes showed real concern. "Rachel, how can you say that? In a very deep way, you were the first to know, not the last."

What a crock, she thought angrily. But she didn't need to say so because she had a very effective glare. She turned it on like a spotlight.

"Rachel" he said, "you were with me when we joined with Brent to do the soul retrieval. Don't tell me you've forgotten."

"I remember that it happened, of course."

"It happened?"

"Well, I mean, I'm still grateful to you and everything."

"Grateful? Thanks, but that's beside the point. Rachel, you were there. Don't pretend that you didn't feel what happened."

Was she supposed to have had some kind of sexual experience, moving through space with John as they went to locate Brent? "I don't know the rules for this kind of thing," she mumbled.

He laughed softly. "Rachel, sometimes it's hard for me after I join with people in consciousness; I don't know how much they do or don't remember consciously."

"What's that supposed to mean, that I'm stupid?"

John sighed and started walking in a little circle. Rachel followed. He wasn't going to get off that easily.

"Well? I want an answer, John, and not just some little telepathy cop-out from your so-called consciousness."

"How can I explain this?" he said, facing her again. He shook his right hand in front of him, opening the palm. "Say this is me." He opened his left palm with a similar gesture. "Say this is you." We go through a healing experience with your son in which we join together in consciousness." In a quick gesture, he brought his right palm over the left, making a loud clap.

Rachel jumped.

"You still with me?" he asked. She shrugged. "The experience of traveling in consciousness is like moving in a different medium—like the Rolling River over there. I get wet. You get wet." He moved his joined hands from side to side. "Afterwards we come back, dry off." He separated his hands. "Under the circumstances, would it be so necessary for me to tell you that you're wet?"

Rachel had no idea what she was feeling until she heard her next words pop out of her mouth: "You know, John, you can talk to me like you're playing Scrabble for Juniors and make me get the point. But you know what? You still hurt my feelings. I just might leave and take Brent with me."

"You're free to leave if you wish."

John sounded regretful. Jeremy, now, he would have been angry. If she could just be home with Jeremy, everything would be normal again. (Also she wouldn't be so horny that it was driving her nuts.)

She started to walk away, but stopped when tears began rolling down her cheeks. She wasn't going to wait for John to notice; instead, she turned and faced him.

"You're supposed to be the teacher," she said. "People like Marguerite have studied with you for years but I'm new to this stuff. It seems to me that a teacher should be able to tell the difference between a first-grader like me and a high school senior like Marguerite. You know what I think? You expected too much of me, and that isn't my fault."

"Finding fault won't help, I agree."

"So you agree it wasn't my fault that, when Brent was in the hospital, I was too upset to fully understand your adventure in consciousness?" As soon as she said it, a grimy feeling came over her, as though she had spoiled something. But she didn't care.

"Watch it, Rachel," John said, his smile fading. "Don't mock an exquisite experience for the sake of your ego. It could take years before it comes again and, frankly, we don't have time to play games like that right now. Take a deep breath."

She did. It felt good.

He said. "Let's go step-by-step, alright?"

She nodded.

"You acknowledge that Brent was in a coma?"

Another nod.

"You're grateful that he came back?"

"Of course, I'll always be grateful. I'm just blurry about what happened, when we traveled together. I'm new at this, John. Maybe I'll never be very good at it."

He smiled slightly, shaking his head as if trying to comfort a frightened child. "You want me to help you remember?"

Was he going to kiss her?

"Sit down," he said, pointing to a tree stump. She did.

"Close your eyes," he said. She was happy to. What was she wearing anyway? She couldn't remember. Oh yeah, the violet blouse and her good jeans.

"I'm going to hold your hand and take you there telepathically. Do I have your permission?"

"I guess so."

John sat beside her, taking her right hand in his left. It felt warm and muscular, stronger than Jeremy's. God, it felt so good to be touched by a man.

"You're awake in your body. Excellent," he said. "Now close your eyes and let go."

Beneath the darkness of closed eyes, several layers of something flashed by. The sensation of travel reminded Rachel of a control on her computer that allowed her to press a button and magnify any image tenfold, then do so again and again. One tiny apple in an orchard could be enlarged until it filled the entire screen.

What was going on here? Rachel felt a hum so thick she could fall into the sound; then she realized that she could look down and see her body, still on the stump next to John. But who she was, ah! that was much, much bigger. Enormous. She was vibrating in the silence and she knew that hum. That hum was her consciousness, it was in everything, that and nothing but joy.

I wish this would last forever. The instant this thought came, Rachel landed back in her body. John's voice came through, as if he was talking directly into her mind. "Did you feel the presence of God more clearly than usual? You can return there anytime, you know. But now we need to explore some of those animal archetypes. Are you ready?"

He took her to ant, then to termite, then caterpillar. "They're strange, especially that last one," Rachel thought back to John. "How frantic, having that hungry, wiggly body. Every time I move in a different direction, my consciousness joins with it, and I can go in so many different directions at once. Wow!"

"Learn to love it," John said. "That's you."

"Wasn't I supposed to be a butterfly?"

"Will be," he said. "Your whole group is in the process of evolving into butterflies."

Rachel felt cheated. She tried (unsuccessfully) not to whine when she replied, "Butterflies are beautiful and free. But caterpillars—"

"It's a necessary requirement," John said firmly—awfully firmly considering that he was only a voice in Rachel's awareness. "Don't knock being a caterpillar. Besides, you butterflies-in-training are just a few steps below Brent's position on the evolutionary ladder."

"I thought you were going to let me be a huntid," Rachel complained.

The silence split open and started to dance, as if lit up by thousands of whirling fireflies moving in sequence. Their entire bodies glowed, not just the lights they carried. The brightness made Rachel giddy with happiness. It felt like. . . what? As though she had never known life's disappointments. The innocence reminded her of the time when Brent was a toddler and his frustrations could be erased within seconds. There was none of the accumulated psychic crud Rachel was used to carrying around.

"Focus on the wings," John transmitted.

Instantly Rachel's attention shifted to those blurry whirring wings, the color of blooming lilacs. Categories danced through her mind, even numbers. She thought, *This is like being inside a picture made from a math formula—what's it called, a fractal?* She understood it through a process that was completely different from her ordinary thinking; she let go instead of concentrating, and the specifics effortlessly flowed into her awareness.

"You're doing fine," came John's voice. "That's being a huntid. Now, if you like, choose something you'd join with if you were a huntid."

"How about this tree stump?" Rachel flashed back. *Click.* Her awareness was filled with a 3-D image of huntids swirling. They outlined the stump's shape. Then she heard lessons about survival: how to withstand any weather, how to be just porous enough to breathe very slowly. Lesson followed lesson—there was even information encoded in the texture of the stump's nubby bark.

"How about going into the rings of the stump?" John suggested. Instantly Rachel clicked onto a different kind of learning dance. This one was about the tree's concentric growth rings, as the huntids eased Rachel through layers of time. The effortless movement brought back memories of sledding as a child; she felt so free, she never wanted to stop.

John gave her hand a little shake. That was what she felt, a shake applied to her physical hand. "I think that's enough for now," he said, out loud this time. "Take some breaths. I'm going to let go of your hand but I want you to keep your eyes closed for a bit while you adjust."

Rachel sat obediently. She was utterly serene now, so why not? She felt, in fact, as if someone had just given her a million dollars. Her eyelashes fluttered like butterfly wings when she finally opened her eyes.

"Better?" John asked.

She stared at him. What kind of a man was he, that he could give her an experience like that?

John smiled. "People who study at the Center are used to doing this whenever they like. You were right—they've done this longer than you have. But you can do as well, if you stay."

Rachel looked at him, her heart opened as big as it could go. She heard herself say:

"If I can come back and talk more with you tomorrow, I'll stay. But I want to be able to talk if there are problems. Okay?"

"My schedule's pretty full," John said, avoiding her eyes.

"Then I'll come before breakfast," she said decisively. "Okay?"

John didn't say a word.

V. The Roar

Chapter 37
Mellowing by the Minute

Rachel and Brent arrived late for lunch, since her warped sense of direction got them lost on the way to the overhang. Now all the long tables seemed full. She could see Marguerite and Gil, but their table was already crowded. *Let's worry about food first and find our seats later,* Rachel decided.

The buffet's oversized bowls looked nearly empty, but Rachel and Brent filled their plates with Greek salad, soaked almonds and a peach and kiwi salad. Walking self-consciously, Rachel saw people stare at her and her celebrity son, but the looks were friendly.

Brent spotted a table with a few empty seats, and Rachel couldn't help comparing this scene to the last meal they'd eaten outdoors with a group—that nightmarish Scout Camp lunch. Everyone here seemed connected, a refreshing improvement from V-R zombies and Righteous bead-thumpers. If anyone at her table was superficial, Rachel decided, it was probably she.

Wait. That wasn't fair; she was doing fine.

A few moments later, Gil squeezed between her and Brent, practically in her lap, as comfortable as if Rachel were his second mom. Marguerite, animatedly engaged in conversation, exchanged friendly glances with Rachel from across the room. Her beautifully toned arms were exposed in a Mondrian-style T-shirt with tiny blocks of color. *She ought to wear prints more often*, thought Rachel.

John's table was packed, but nobody was treating him like a star—more proof that he hadn't a clue how to act like a seminar leader. She shook her head in exasperation. But when he began eating a nectarine, she watched the slow bites vanish into his beautiful crimson mouth. In a kind of trance, Rachel wished she could be that nectarine.

Rachel shoved her eyes back to her plate. The vegetarian food was a treat, especially the Greek salad, aromatically dressed with plenty of pungent feta cheese.

Rachel ate daintily, flirting with her food. Nobody seemed to notice, except once Brent gave her a look, as if to say, "What gives? You don't eat this way at home."

What really mattered was that everyone here treated Rachel as a friend, with an easy conversational give and take. Deb was a lanky deep sea diver who cleaned up underwater trails in Puget Sound; Hanifa, wearing a stylish Madras-plaid unitard, introduced herself as an incorrigible Spider and a photographer by trade. Danny and Mocha Nguyen were a 50ish couple who had grown together in the way some couples do, entwining like trees. Watching them eat from each other's plates roused sorrowful comparisons to her relationship with Jeremy.

Zap those comparisons! she thought, deciding to break the pattern the way Consuela had taught her. Biting into a tomato, Rachel asked her inner self to connect with her husband and actively feel his presence.

Jeremy was so grim and gray that Rachel was tempted to push him into a happier frame of mind, but she knew better. ("Coercive" was Consuela's word for it.) Instead Rachel sent Jeremy some free-floating energy to use however his spirit wished. The energy trailed out to him like the white streak in the sky left by old-fashioned jets.

Back at Rachel's table, conversation flowed easily, and by the time she rose to recycle her leftovers, Rachel realized that every one of her seat-mates had friend potential. She'd learned something else, too—not once during the meal had she needed to use her breath to restrain the habit of judging. *Maybe the sweetness of the peaches had helped.* Nah. Truth was, Rachel was mellowing by the minute.

Afternoon training did not mellow her further, however. Their practice area consisted of a room-sized patch of dirt carpeted, like everything else at Rolling Ridge, knee-high with huntids.

At 2 p.m., Consuela called the group to order. "Kids, we have work to do. Pair up," she announced. Looking pointedly at Rachel's skin-phone, she reminded them that they had just one week to get ready for Extermination Day.

"Today, we'll practice turning up your empathy so you can experience from the inside what it means to be someone else. Everyone have a partner?" Sioux-Z marched toward Rachel, her looming smile terrifyingly wide. *Please don't let her pick me,* Rachel prayed. The only one in the group Rachel didn't like, and the pushy. . . *Oops, no judging.* What could she admire? That shiny dyed platinum hair? Oh, rats.

Outwardly, Rachel just waited. *What the hell,* she thought, returning Sioux-Z's welcoming smile.

Consuela told the couples to stand facing each other. "Close your eyes," she barked, sounding like a drill sergeant in the movies. "Now connect to your spiritual source."

Rachel 's eyes popped open to give Consuela a skeptical look. "You know how," Consuela said sternly. "Close your eyes and take deep breaths. Then think the name of an ascended master like Jesus or an archangel like Gabriel."

Rachel closed her eyes, feeling stupid. Then the thought struck her that, since the whole purpose of calling for help was to actually *receive* help, it might not matter that she felt like an idiot.

"Set your intention," commanded Consuela. "Ask inside to experience what it's like to be your partner."

Ugh, Rachel thought. There was no exercise that could make her bond with this pushy little social climber. She'd probably chosen Rachel as a partner only so she could say she was close with Brent's mother.

"Hold your partner's right hand as if initiating a handshake," said Consuela. "But don't *shake* hands. Keep your hands connected to help you bring your awareness into your partner's energy body." Reluctantly, Rachel opened her eyes long enough to find Sioux-Z's hand.

Whoosh! She was Sioux-Z, and the first thing she noticed was that her already quick mind was moving much faster. Meanwhile, her body felt vulnerable, holding her muscles and something else—organs, maybe?—with a chronic tension.

Recalling her sessions with Consuela, Rachel knew what to do next. She asked inside, "Where does this tension come from? Immediately she saw an image of a large man with a red face. Rachel's inner voice said, *You're receiving the thought form of her father. He used to beat her.*

Oh, she thought.

Rachel's guidance didn't want her to stop there. *Feel the scars,* sounded deep within her. *Hardly any pain is left. This kind one has given many prayers for forgiveness and knowledge.* Rachel felt a tracery of hair-thin scars that extended from the base of Sioux-Z's spine all the way to her throat. *She has such courage,* Rachel's guidance continued. *Ask to explore the power center of her aura.*

Rachel did. To her surprise, she felt a kind of throb, perhaps even a sob, then a sensation of pushing herself outward. *What does this mean?* she asked inside.

The answer came from her own awareness, blended with that of Archangel Gabriel. *She's bright. So she has learned to use her mind to keep away... Of course*, Rachel thought, *She's protecting her vulnerability. She pushes her mind out into the world in a sort of preemptive strike. That's why she seemed so pushy.*

"Time's up, folks." Consuela said, asking them to open their eyes and share observations with their partner.

At first, Rachel just blinked at Sioux-Z. She looked physically different now, as if a mask had fallen away, revealing the smaller person inside—someone with a softer face and nothing hidden beneath her eyes.

"Oh, Rachel, the way you fly into others at the drop of a hat! You're so much like me. I thought so the first time I saw you. That's why I wanted you for my partner," Sioux-Z told her, squeezing her arm affectionately. Rachel smiled, too, only this time she didn't have to remind her face first.

They practiced the travel technique over and over, pairing with different partners each time. It was exhausting and mind-boggling but Rachel's spirit soared. When Consuela finally dismissed them an hour before Volunteer Posts, Rachel felt so good she found herself doing the unthinkable, lingering just to hang out with Consuela.

Rachel was preparing a thank-you speech about how much she appreciated the empath training. But the words dried up as she approached Consuela, who had knelt to pick up twigs and pebbles, tossing them away from the clearing and into the woods. Rachel felt a strong and unusual emotion radiating from Consuela. It felt like… sorrow.

"Hey, kid, how ya doing?" Rachel said tentatively, kneeling beside her.

Consuela grunted in response, not even lifting up her head in acknowledgment.

"I think this is the first time I've ever felt you in a sad space," Rachel said gently. "Want to talk about it?"

"You wouldn't understand, not yet."

"Try me. I'm supposed to be an empath, remember."

Consuela sighed. "It's about looking older."

"Looking older?" Rachel studied the details of Consuela's face, puzzled.

"When I look in the mirror, one day I'll look normal. Another day I'll see bags under my eyes, my skin drying up, stuff like that. I'm not terribly vain, but it bothers me. Seeing all the young faces here today, in the sunlight, reminded me that I'm starting to look old. That's all." Still on her knees, she cleared away another assortment of pebbles.

What was there to say? Rachel didn't want to lie. And she couldn't say something like, "You weren't so hot looking to begin with." So she just picked up pebbles, too.

"It wouldn't be so bad if I could just wake up 80 years old—all my relatives lived into their 90's you know, even before modern medicine—if I had an old lady's face all at once and was done with it—that'd be fine. But instead aging sneaks up on you, line by line and hair by hair."

Rachel couldn't stand another moment of this: It was time to lighten up, so she said, "And that, my dear, is exactly why God invented cosmetic surgery."

"Not for me."

"Why, because John doesn't approve?"

"Neither do I. None of us do. With a fake face or body, you lose your authentic—"

"So this anguish you're feeling over looking older is purer and more authentic?"

Consuela's expression closed up, like a camera shutter covering a lens. She seemed to shrink inside her skin, and her mouth set into a line.

Rachel decided to persist. Consuela was honest so maybe she'd appreciate some honest advice. "Since you brought it up, Consuela, the way you dress doesn't help. All those dingy earth colors."

No reaction.

"Especially the denim!" Rachel went on heedlessly. "It's fashion suicide. I've often watched you and thought, 'Couldn't she try poly-suede?' A solid color look isn't bad, except you need to give it contrast with, say, an ice-blue scarf. I could even show you a cute way to tie it."

Consuela looked at her in a manner that was reminiscent of ice-blue something, probably a glacier. She said, "I don't need to do that. You know why? The way I dress balances my aura. If you could see it, which you can't, you'd find quite a shimmer. The way I dress, Rachel, is my business. And I'm dressing for people who have the consciousness to..."

But Rachel had turned on her heel and was heading toward her own campsite, feeling as if she'd just been slapped.

She was so angry that she decided to skip Volunteer Posts and began walking to John's tent. Her feet seemed to move by themselves: Who was she to stop them? She did wonder if anyone else would be in John's tent and decided to vibe it out as she walked. Did she feel aware of anyone in the tent with John? Barging in on that would be embarrassing.

Nothing. Maybe that meant the tent was empty. She hadn't planned to talk with him anyway. She was just out for the exercise, Rachel told herself, subtly accelerating her stroll.

As she walked, she felt the green freshness of real trees wake her up like a Health Services ozone treatment. The distant sound of the river breaking against its rocky banks altered the rhythm of her steps. In one corner of her mind, she marveled at the way so many extra campgrounds were hidden away like honeycombs. She hadn't realized how big this place was. No doubt it was the same all over the country.

There might even be as many campers as there are Seminar Slaves, she reflected.

Suddenly Rachel saw something that made her stop short. By a cookout area similar to the one at which John's group assembled, she saw a group of campers doing something bizarre. What was it exactly? Rachel padded closer, then froze, her eyes wide.

Traditionals, that's what they must be, judging by the enormous crosses—but uncannily quiet Traditionals. Many were kneeling in prayer. Were they imitating St. Francis as he might have looked if he camped in a forest? Other Traditionals stood as motionless as statues, arms outstretched. None were chanting sing-song hymns, as they did on TV. Although their eyes were wide open, not one was making eye contact with another. Weird! Rachel could feel the group's intent focus, but what were they focusing on?

Then she realized that by standing still they were attracting huntids. It must be a contest to see who could attract the most. "Tahhny creechurs," Rachel remembered Rev. Pilgrim calling them with her deep-South accent. "Blessed tahhny creechurs."

That's not my religion, thought Rachel, *but live and let live.*

Farther up the path, Rachel stumbled upon the group of Righteous she had seen the day before. The tip-off was the sight of colorful day-glo plastic moving randomly through a large field. *Like lightning bugs in daylight*, she thought, as they flapped squares of bright yellow, red, and blue—old-fashioned fly-swatters, two or three per hand! Even before she spotted their necklaces, Rachel knew these were The Righteous. Who else was so coordinated and so ambitious?

They were swatting huntids, of course. Killing 'em, too, in the name of religion.

"Sister, join us," one cried out as she passed. When she hesitated, another yelled, "Can't you hear the call?"

What would they do if she refused, she wondered. Swat her, too?

She didn't wait to find out. Turning around, she ran all the way back to her tent. She could talk to John first tomorrow anyway. With all the new experiences she was having, she needed to talk to an expert—and if she had her way, it wouldn't be that killjoy Consuela.

After dinner Rachel snatched a few minutes to call Jeremy. Crawling into her sleeping bag, she punched his phone code into her skin-phone.

"Rachel," he said, and she could hear his slow smile. It reminded her of a candy bar she once found in her car, a delicious discovery that had slipped out of her purse and was, when Rachel unwrapped it, perfectly warmed by the sun. Jeremy's voice was so seductive; he didn't seem tense for a change. "My sunflower's on the phone and it isn't even Wednesday!"

"Oh, Jeremy, I wish I could see you. Why are you at the office on a Saturday night?"

"I'm amusing myself by doing the usual assortment of calculations and computations. We only have a week before we pull this off. So why'd you call? Still my jealous baby?"

"I just missed you, Jeremy."

"Is Brent okay?"

"Sure. Not one single emergency, honest."

"Well then, tell me what you're up to."

She told him that she was on a camping trip with Marguerite, her friends, and the boys.

"How retro," Jeremy said admiringly. "Could you be turning into an outdoor freak? By the way, you are watching out for huntids, aren't you?"

"Of course. Brent and I stay away from the huntids. But outdoor freak? Hardly. I have the best manicure in all Camp Rolling Ridge." She giggled.

"So what's in it for you, Rachel? Variety?"

"Not really. This may sound silly to you but I feel as though Marguerite's friends are making me come more alive."

"You were already plenty alive." Jeremy did not sound as if he was paying her any great compliment.

Rachel wanted to tell him more. "You know how strange people are getting these days. Well, I think being awake in your consciousness can be a protection against being manipulated. If somebody like a Righteous tries to cross over the line and coerce you, I think your best protection is staying awake in yourself. That way you can feel it coming."

"We wouldn't be turning a tad paranoid, would we?"

She laughed. "I hope not. I just wish you'd learn how to protect yourself psychically. Politicians, people at work, anyone could have a hidden agenda for you when you have so much responsibility."

Rachel took his sudden grunt for encouragement. "What I've learned here is that you can just say no. When I'm a really skilled empath I'll be better, but I'm making enormous progress at fighting psychic coercion."

"Rachel, in my shoes, you'd need more than anti-coercion voodoo."

"What do you mean?"

"Yesterday we received our latest directive, courtesy of Secretary of Intelligence, Cooper Hackenworth. Remember him?"

It was Rachel's turn to grunt.

"From now on, we must wear the beads of The Righteous at work."

"Oh, goody—a fashion statement from Mr. Suspenders."

"Seriously. Otherwise we'll be replaced Monday."

"How is this possible?"

Jeremy laughed mirthlessly. "Group morale for fighting terrorism, Hackenworth calls it. He's not kidding, either. Says he has dozens of Righteous faithful signed on as contractors, and they'll be waiting in the wings Monday morning. Anyone who shows up without beads will be fired for insubordination."

"Whatever happened to separation of church and state? They can't do that, can they?"

"I could take Hackenworth to court and eventually I'd probably win. But I'd lose my job now, when it counts. My boss says to handle it like a joke. He told Wayne and me he's planning to wear the beads over a karate outfit and throw in a sheriff's badge for good measure."

"Weird. How's Wayne taking this?"

"He'll probably quit. I'd guess his wife is pressuring him; she's into the Traditionals."

"Oh, Jeremy, I wish I could be with you at a time like this. Have you decided what you'll do?"

"I'll go along with their dress code. It's the lesser of two evils."

"You sure?"

"You think I'll let some over-zealous brainwashed buddy of Hackenworth's screw up this project? I've been working hard to keep insecticide doses current with the population growth of the huntids. The lab keeps reworking their population figures, which are bizarre, probably because so many of The Righteous are killing them now, and that only makes them come back stronger."

"Your job sounds impossible," Rachel commiserated.

"No, I just I keep up with the latest figures. Every time I adjust the insecticide, I have to update links to our flying teams all over the country, which forms the basis for my counterparts' calculations in their countries. They've agreed to copy our insecticide formula so the worldwide environmental impact stays constant. Believe me, there's no way I'm going to let a little jewelry stand between me and this assignment."

Rachel asked if he'd heard of any health developments related to huntids.

"Plenty of children are getting the colds, if that's what you mean. Marty established a contact between our department and Epidemiology, and huntid colds are apparently not considered any big deal."

"So you haven't heard of other cases like Brent's?" Rachel said. Maybe she should tell Jeremy what was going on in John's group. To test the waters, she said in a neutral voice, "Some folks here think Brent is special because he had Huntid Disease."

She listened carefully to his response. Would he pull back in his usual way? "Not surprising, Rachel," he said evenly. "Maybe your seminar group can help you get through this. Sure wish I had something like that. Guess I'm too addicted to reality."

Rachel could easily imagine the Fred Astaire-like shrug Jeremy made along with that statement. Back when she was 20, she thought his stance as a perpetual skeptic was so cool. Now it just made her furious.

"Come off it, Jeremy. You could use a new idea. I don't think you've had one since you got married."

"Excuse me?"

"You heard me."

"What's the matter with you? It's not impressive enough that I'm in charge of Huntid Extermination Day? You think this is a good time for me to throw my scientifically trained mind out the window and turn into some ranting, credulous. . ."

". . . weirdo like me?" Rachel finished, yelling into her skin-phone. "You could do worse. And to think that I was feeling guilty because I wasn't there to support you, like maybe we should fly back before next Saturday."

"Do us all a favor, Rachel. Stay away until I get my job done."

"Not even call you before Extermination Day? You can't mean that, Jeremy."

"Sure do. You shouldn't even have called me tonight. I don't need any more stress."

She burst into tears. "So that's I mean to you, stress?"

"Stay away from me now," Jeremy said. "Talk out your feelings with this group you're in. Wallow away, for all I care. I don't have time for feelings right now. And don't call me. I'll call you."

"But Sweetheart...."

"I'm not your Sweetheart right now—I'm a man with a job to do and no time for this. Goodbye." She heard him slam the phone into its headset.

Rachel was still crying when Marguerite popped in to change for dinner. For her, that meant adding a scarf that picked up one of the colors on her T-shirt. Rachel watched her, quiet and sullen.

"I'm not going to dinner," she announced.

Marguerite jumped. "Jeepers creepers, I didn't even see you."

"I know," Rachel said. "Listen, I don't want to go to dinner. Would you keep an eye on Brent."

"No problem. What's the matter? Aren't you hungry?

"No. And I have some thinking to do."

"I understand. This camping trip must be like an immersion course, huh?"

After Marguerite left, Rachel walked to the river and sat on a stump. Huntids swarmed around her but they didn't alight because her back was shaking so hard as she cried.

It was hot that night. Trying to sleep, Rachel suddenly saw John, in his light body, fly into the tent. He knelt above her sleeping bag, his head just inches below the top of the tent. Rachel sat up and looked around. Marguerite wasn't there. What a relief!

Shocked and thrilled to see him, Rachel blurted, "It's about time you came."

"You pulled me, you know," John said, drawing closer. "I could feel you thinking about me."

He nodded, drawing closer, his far-set eyes chocolate brown and delectable.

"I can't believe you've never made a pass at me, John. Someone as sexy as you? What gives?"

"Let's just say my work keeps me pretty occupied."

Pathetic! she thought, sliding out of her sleeping bag. She knelt facing him in her peach-colored cotton nightie with lace trim. She could feel him smelling her jasmine perfume.

He slowly looked her up and down, pausing on the curves. She stared at him in wonder. It felt as if they were both naked.

"Rachel," he said, moving away unsteadily, "This has to stop."

Rachel woke with a jolt. Nobody was in the tent except Marguerite. Quietly Rachel unzipped the flap and slipped outside. It was that still time just before dawn when earth's fragrance filled the air; she took a deep breath. Stretching, she looked around the campground. Colorful tents stood out amid natural greens and browns. You could feel everyone sleeping peacefully.

But what was that sound? Not crickets. Not in this quickening indigo light as stars glittered faintly through thin clouds. Wings, reverberating wings. Thousands of them. The huntids had surrounded every tent like a halo. Nobody she knew had ever seen what they did at night.

Diving back into the tent, she crouched, panting, and pulled on her sleeping bag.

She didn't want to see it, either.

Chapter 38
Sunday Morning Date

As Marguerite stirred in her sleep, Rachel whispered: "Don't worry, I'm just going for a walk. I'm restless." It was the truth, although not the whole truth.

Soon Rachel had reached John's tent. "Well, here I am," she announced cheerily. "Bright and early."

She opened the velcro doorway and entered, posing for a second in her hot pink blouse, slinky red shorts, and red leather shoes worn with lace-trimmed white anklets. "Shall we talk?"

She ignored John's puzzled look and walked into the tent. It was big enough to hold several people, she thought, glancing down at an old-fashioned notebook, a tidy pile of books, a wood-finish Porta-shelf neatly packed with clothes, an ancient toiletry kit. When her eyes came to rest on John, she ogled him shamelessly.

What was she doing? She must have lifted this kind of brash behavior from some old Mae West movie—it sure as hell didn't come from any seminar. Who would give a seminar like this? Tanya on speed? Honestly, what was she thinking?

But some part of Rachel, not her thinking self, had taken over. She heard herself say, "John, haven't you ever found me attractive?"

"I've been celibate for a very long time, Rachel." He stood, pulling his sleeping bag up under his armpits. *He sleeps naked,* she thought. *Good.*

"I can't believe that. Someone so attractive? Maybe you've never met a woman who could show you what real pleasure is." Rachel blushed. Too late, the words had come out of lips that already felt moist and reckless. She stepped closer.

"Hardly." His eyes twinkled. "Consuela and I studied Tantra for several years, but that was long ago."

"I've heard about Tantra—full-body orgasms, right?" She'd have to deal later with the unnerving news about Consuela. Rachel pushed the tiny button in her mind that could send any thought into a dusty corner. And she moved closer without even thinking about it.

Wait a minute, I can't be the lover—that's a man's job. No use protesting now, she was already drowning in the testosterone richness of his scent, and her body was so juicy she felt ripe. Her mouth was on his gorgeous lips, luxuriating in their combination of muscularity and softness. When her tongue touched his, she dropped straight into the magnetic male energy that permeated his body.

John pulled her tight, crushing her breasts against the firm muscles of his chest. It felt as if they had already made love many times; she could even feel the pleasure of release shimmering through her body. He was huge but his body was so responsive that he seemed to know everything she felt. Whatever she asked, he could answer, body to body.

As one hand held her close, the other stroked her back, tracing the curve of her hips, owning her. It felt as though he was moving to the same rolling heave of passion that had flowed through Rachel.

His tongue danced with hers, but slowly, as if time went on forever. The sexual electricity made her nipples so hard they seemed more flesh than flesh. A moan of longing passed from her mouth into his and was swallowed up in the roar of who he was.

She felt him through the silky fabric of his summer-weight sleeping bag, so hard and big and sweet that she could almost taste the power of it. Then his tongue touched hers again.

Panting, she pulled back. John was breathing hard, too. As he looked into her eyes, she felt the promise of what could come. All she wanted was to drop to the floor; gravity's irresistible force was now part of the magnetic pull between them. It would be so easy to just slide into that pleasure. She could barely think now, except to think of him.

"Rachel," he said, stepping away unsteadily, one hand clutching the sleeping bag. "This has to stop."

The physical boundaries of her body snapped back, making her feel like a sweaty animal, and a foolish one, too. Shame forced her to retreat, and tears salted her lips. Her mouth tasted the salt and she trembled. How could she say anything now?

"Rachel," he said tenderly, caressing her cheek in one slow gesture of regret as she wept for those unaccepted kisses.

"Why?" she said.

"So many reasons," he said very softly, even the rhythm of his voice like a caress. She would have gone with him anywhere. She moved closer, hoping to drink in one last kiss. "But you deserve a better answer than that, Rachel. First of all, you're married. That's a sacred vow, as you know."

"Which is *my* decision," Rachel replied hotly. "I've never cheated on Jeremy. Ever. Can't I be allowed one lover after 13 years?"

John didn't look impressed.

"Look," she added. "I'm not going to discuss my marriage except to say that Jeremy and I could use more passion, okay? It will be a *good* thing, your reminding me what a man and woman can be to each other."

John stood straighter, smoothing his rumpled sleeping bag with brisk strokes. "If you say so. But I have my own promises to keep, and I take them seriously. I am utterly committed to the work I'm doing now, and for that I need my system intact. Can't you understand?"

"I understand this," she said, placing the tip of her index finger on his full upper lip and brushing it gently. When he made no response, she was stung by his coldness. She looked away so he wouldn't see the pleading in her eyes.

"Rachel," John said, gently touching her face. "I'm not saying it wouldn't have been... well, we both know what it would have been. That's beside the point. I can't."

"I won't accept your answer," she said, moving away from him. "Does your God tell you that what we could have between us isn't holy enough for you?"

He stepped back, and Rachel felt a chill. But she didn't care any more, given the reckless excitement that had forced her to pursue him. How could she turn back now? As a teacher he'd never respect her again. If she couldn't claim him now, as a lover, she'd have nothing.

"I'm warning you, Rachel," he said quietly. "Respect what we could have had if the circumstances had been different. Physical love is a door that we can shut together. If we help each other to close this door, we'll find peace. Otherwise . . ."

How she wanted to tear off that sleeping bag! What would persuade him?

"Alright," he said almost coldly. "Let me show you the real me, the one you'd have joined with energetically had we made love. Sure you want to see?"

She nodded, trying to look provocative. As Rachel would remember it later, time went into slow motion the moment she said, "Show me."

Expressions flickered across John's face, expressions he had never let her see before—sorrow, anger, resignation. Then the air crackled and a thunderous roar filled her ears. Instead of lightning, John's body itself turned into light before her eyes, and a part of Rachel's mind noted that his image seemed more cartoon than physical body. Was he letting her see him in a different reality?

This version of John wasn't human. He'd turned into an enormous bee, emitting a deafening razor-like buzz. In place of skin, he had the hard, fuzzy, almost slimy body of a bee. Hovering exactly where John had stood only seconds before, the bee's massive abdomen confronted her at eye level, its legs dangling on either side. Bee wings vibrated in the air; a stinger trailed away from its body, replacing John's legs.

Rachel turned away in terror. When she looked up again, her gaze met two gigantic compound eyes, hypnotically fathomless, each one made up of dozens of tiny eyes that stared at her with a cold insect-like detachment.

"No! God, no!" she shrieked.

And it wasn't until her breath came hard and ragged, and her heart hammered rapidly in her chest, that she realized she had run all the way back to her tent.

Chapter 39
Real Conversation

Rachel shivered as she crammed the big blue towel into her duffel. She rolled up her sleeping bag, cursing when it took three tries to push it into its case. By then, tears were dripping down her nose.

Sniffling, she wiped her face with the back of her hand and walked back and forth, tossing a messy assortment of clothes and toiletries into a pile. Rachel pulled out a bag of cookies from Marguerite's stash and, as she packed frantically, crammed Oreos into her mouth. Folding a blouse, she didn't hear Marguerite enter the tent.

"What's going on?" her friend said, looking around.

Rachel jumped. But what difference did one more shock make?

"I'm leaving. Now. And I'm taking Brent." She wasn't going to cry.

"Sweetie, what's wrong?" Marguerite walked over to her and put her hands on Rachel's shoulders, pulling her into eye contact. "Why aren't you at our morning session?"

"It's John," Rachel said, allowing Marguerite to see her tear-stained face. "He did the most horrible . . . ."

"Oh my God," said Marguerite, her hands still on Rachel's shoulders. "He showed you his insect body, didn't he."

Rachel looked at her. "You've seen it?"

"I think all of us at the Center have seen it at one time or another."

"Oh, swell. He made passes at all of you, then?"

"What?" Marguerite did a double take. Then she took a breath; meanwhile tears continued to stream down Rachel's face. "Honey, it's just a thought form. Trained actors send them out all the time, they just don't usually aim for animal images."

Supported by Marguerite's genuine concern, Rachel stopped crying so hard. After a few minutes the sobs subsided, but she was still shaken to the core.

"I know it looks weird," Marguerite said comfortingly. "But any skilled intuitive can send out a concentrated thought form. Normally you'd learn how to do that after you've studied for a couple of years. Of course, Rachel, you would get the impact of anyone's thought form in the extra-strength version because of your gift as an empath."

She felt better. It was nice that Marguerite cared enough to explain things and comforting to think there might be a rational explanation for the hole that had just been shot through her reality.

Marguerite touched Rachel lightly on the shoulder. "Sweetie, calm down. Can we talk?"

Something about Marguerite's touch felt all wrong. "We can talk," Rachel said, turning to hide her reaction, "but Brent and I are still leaving."

"How can you go now? I know what you've been through. Believe me, I shook, too, the first time I saw an insect thought form. But we need you here for this training."

Rachel shook her head. "Look," she said, meeting her friend's searching look. "I'm being responsible. I'll pack my gear and Brent's before I go, even though my first impulse was to run away and let everything go to hell."

"Exactly how did you think you would leave?" Marguerite said, annoyance creeping into her voice.

"In your car, of course. You don't mind, do you? You know everybody; you can find someone to give you and Gil a ride home tonight."

"I suppose so," Marguerite said evenly. "But the whole retreat will be over after dinner. Can't you just calm down and wait a few hours? Get real, Rachel—you're in no condition to drive. Tell me what happened."

Rachel followed Marguerite over to her sleeping bag. Bright green and folded into a perfect rectangle on a camping mattress, it did look inviting.

"Oh, Marguerite," Rachel said, sinking into its cushy softness. "He showed you the Bee body? Does he come on to everyone?"

"Not really, although some come onto him," Marguerite said, giving Rachel a shrewd look. "I did notice you seemed to have. . . a fondness for him, but I don't think that John gets sexually involved with anyone now."

"Then why did he show himself to you as a bee? Oh, Marguerite, I don't think I'll ever forget those eyes. . . ."

"Probably to make a point—moving into thought forms is part of our spiritual training. John has taught lots of us how to do it. Wanna see me turn on my Spider?" She was joking, Rachel realized, and tried to laugh.

"You've heard John explain that all of us live as part of a multi-dimensional reality," Marguerite said. "The veil of illusion on earth is turning transparent these days. Experienced students like me—and you, eventually—can shift ourselves into other frequencies; if we're spiritually awake, we can easily send out thought forms whenever we like."

"Easy for him, anyway." Rachel realized that she had not only stopped shaking, she was indulging in a very tiny grin. "I'll tell you one thing, I don't see my mom changing herself into an Ant any time soon."

"No, but she doesn't have the consciousness of a spiritual person living at today's leading edge. She doesn't need to help make history by telepathically linking with the huntids. Don't forget. We have an emergency on our hands. Extermination Day is in less than a week. Ring a bell?"

Rachel nodded.

"And that," Marguerite finished, "is exactly why I really don't think you should leave now. Or Brent."

Rachel shivered. The way Marguerite said Brent's name triggered something—what? A glance revealed nothing more than Marguerite's usual expression—the brilliant light in her eyes and that diamond-shaped face like a rock of determination. But the feeling underneath seemed totally out of synch with Marguerite's face.

Rachel closed her eyes, took a couple of breaths, and began searching for the truth. Marguerite was upset inside—absolutely frantic, in fact.

"Marguerite, you might as well tell me. What's going on?"

Marguerite tossed her head flirtatiously, "Oh, get out!"

"I'm waiting," Rachel said.

"Nothing, nothing. Really."

Rachel stared. In the silence, Rachel felt a growing discomfort beneath her friend's smooth mask. "It's Brent, isn't it?" Rachel said.

Marguerite started pacing. "I'm no good at this. Of course it's Brent. You know he's special. We need him."

As Rachel stared at Marguerite, fury gathered momentum within her. Marguerite must have felt it, too, because she said, "Go home if you must. Drive all the way to Capitol City if you have to. But leave Brent here with us until after Extermination Day."

Rachel took another deep breath. Of course! In a tight voice, she said quietly, "You don't really like me, do you?"

"What kind of question is that?"

"When you invited me here, it wasn't me you wanted, was it?"

"I don't dislike you, Rachel."

"But you don't like me either, do you? Do you?"

Marguerite averted her eyes. Rachel walked around her to make eye contact. Then she stared her down. "That phone call—John put you up to it, didn't he?"

"Not exactly."

Rachel's rage flickered like fire. "You were using me to get to Brent. Because he's so fucking special. Little Boy Huntid."

She started pacing. "It figures. All along, whenever you'd mention John and the Oneness Center, I'd have this funny feeling. I just never figured it out. It was as if you were watching Brent and me, pretending to be casual while you got us involved."

Scenes flashed before Rachel's eyes: her front-row seat at the Oneness Center on her first visit, heads turning to stare at Brent in the dining hall, how quickly Marguerite had borrowed all she needed to take them camping—through it all, Marguerite had played her and Brent like puppets.

"Tell me."

Not a sound.

Rachel walked over to her. She wanted to slap her but settled for placing her hands forcibly on Marguerite's shoulders. "Tell me."

Marguerite shook her loose. "I'll tell you. But keep your hands off me."

Folding her arms across her midriff, she stared at Rachel. "I told you that John originally learned about the huntids when he tuned in one morning for his One-Minute Blessing. In June, during another one of those minutes, he discovered that Brent was one of the rare ones, someone who could be a major player on our team. John also felt that Brent had some kind of connection to me. We talked about it, and I told him that you and I became friends when our kids were babies.

"Right, we were friends. Even though we didn't have much in common except the babies."

"This is not to say that I didn't like you, Rachel, but we live on different wavelengths, you know?

Rachel's lips trembled.

"When John and I talked, we decided I should invite you both here."

"Back up," Rachel said. "What do you mean about Brent being a major player?"

"He's one of those rare ones, Rachel. You know that. He has the vibes of a huntid. Having him with us during our Wave of Oneness would be like having an atom bomb on our side—a peaceful one."

"So you connived to get him involved in your spiritual warfare." This time, the surge of rage started at the soles of Rachel's feet and moved up her spine. "All that training Consuela gave me so generously, that was a load of crap, wasn't it? I'm no empath. You don't need me as an empath, you only need Brent."

"That's not how it played out, Rachel. You really are an empath—and extremely talented, according to Consuela."

Rachel felt the fury in her jaws as she sat just inches from Marguerite. She held herself in, pushing a fist against her lips. Her other arm felt like an iron bar against her midriff, as she tried to decide what to do.

"One more thing," she said icily. "Where does my husband fit in with this plan?"

Marguerite refused to meet her eyes.

"Tell me this minute or Brent and I take your car, get on a plane, and you never see him again."

"You're free to go, if you wish. We are spiritual people, Rachel."

"Right. Conniving but spiritual."

"Hickory Helms says that these are broken times. He got that part right, Rachel. Maybe we did plan some things behind your back, but we never meant to hurt you. You have always been free to go. In fact, there has been a lot of love mixed in all of this." Tears welled up in Marguerite's eyes, making them greener than ever.

"Just tell me about Jeremy."

"We didn't recruit you because of Jeremy, any more than we called you because you had talent as an empath and we hoped you'd work with us. It was always about Brent. But when we found out Jeremy was in charge of Extermination Day, naturally we wished he would call it off."

"So you planned to make me influence him?"

Marguerite said, "Coercion isn't our style. If you're looking for coercion, check out The Righteous or the Traditionals. I won't lie to you—of course we hoped that Jeremy would call it off. But we've never asked you to influence him, have we? Has anyone here ever said a word to you about that?"

"No, you've just been brainwashing me from a distance. How spiritual! After all these years, it's touching that you're letting me have an honest conversation.

"Here's what I want, Marguerite. Lend me your car. Brent and I will go to your house for now. I'll put our stuff in the car while you bring him here. You tell him we're going to get something at your house. When I have some time alone with him in the car, I'll sort through all the brainwashing and decide what to do."

"You can have the car," Marguerite said, looking teary.

"And tell John from me that I think you've done a great job on us. Just great."

"Oh, Rachel," Marguerite protested, bursting into tears.

So the bitch had feelings. "I'll promise you this, my darling friend. Brent and I won't go back to Capitol City without saying goodbye. Because I don't believe in sneaking around."

Marguerite nodded sorrowfully. "We never coerced you, Rachel. Look into our hearts. They're clean."

Chapter 40
Honor

On the drive to Marguerite's, Rachel saw a stranger's face in her rear view mirror, a stranger with more layers than a stale croissant. Her pink blouse and tight red shorts looked cheap now, and her skin no longer seemed to fit properly. Not only did it feel alien, it seemed as though the person inside had shriveled up. When she probed deeper, she encountered a whole series of detached emotions: sorrow, pain, rage, guilt and hopelessness.

As they drove, Rachel glimpsed huntids streaking along the highway, pulsating green-and-violet blurs that raced between the flow of traffic. These swarms were flying below window height, so there was no danger of them flying into your car. From their side windows, passengers would never notice the huntids. Driving was another matter.

Had huntids been on the roads in these numbers when Marguerite drove them up to the campground? Rachel associated huntids with fields and lawns, not black-top. Maybe they were becoming more aggressive.

One thing had changed: hundreds of cars had balloons tied to little roof-top suction cups. The grimmest balloons Rachel ever seen, in gray or maroon with slogans like "Repent now. It's your last chance."

Where the hell did stuff like that come from?

Luckily for Rachel, Marguerite's clunker of a car had a trustworthy navigational system that displayed the route, turn by turn, on a window monitor. Sensing her despair and rage, Brent avoided conversation. She needed to say something; after all, he hadn't done anything wrong.

"What's that, Brent? I didn't think you packed any games for this trip."

"I didn't, Mom. Gil lent this to me when we left. You'd approve of this one—it's called Cops 'n Robbers 'n Toons, and it improves your math skills. Every time you solve an equation, a cartoon character pops up and you chase him, competing with a bunch of cops or robbers, and—"

"I get the idea. Just keep the sound effects low, okay."

"Oh, Mom, I turned them off. I could tell you needed to think."

"You're a good boy, and very considerate." Mentally, she added, *"And if you weren't here with me now, I'd be screaming my head off. Those manipulative, sneaky bastards. My so-called friend Marguerite. My so-called honey, John, the real-life horror movie monster . . . ."*

When they arrived at Marguerite's house, Rachel pulled her duffel through the door. Brent followed her, giving her a quizzical look.

"So how come we left early?" he asked.

"Grown-up stuff. Listen, you, we've been on the road for hours. Want juice or something?"

"Sure."

"Let's raid the refrigerator." Mentally, Rachel added, *"In the unlikely event that anorexic Marguerite has any decent food here."*

In the freezer they found pineapple juice and rainbow sherbet, and soon were drinking juice floats.

"Weren't you having fun at camp?" Brent asked. "I was having a great time." He spooned up a glob of sherbet and half-sucked, half-slurped it.

"Camp was okay."

"Come on, Mom, you were looking so happy before we left."

"What do you mean?"

"Like it showed in your regular look, the one when you don't smile on purpose. You know, usually your mouth turns down at the corners. Lately it's been up all the time." Brent made a silly face, his eyes dreamy.

Although she gave him a teasing shove, Rachel's vanity was bruised. How long had her mouth drooped? She scolded herself for skipping the anti-aging calisthenics she'd acquired at a Face of Youth seminar. *Right*, she remembered, *I stopped all that because of John. Mr. One-thing-at-a-time, Mr. Enlightenment, the monster bee man. . . .*

She was interrupted by a voice of guidance: *You're done pretending, aren't you? Let yourself have the face that you have.*

That voice had become her inner teacher; she loved that voice. What it said never failed to bring her peace. But wasn't that voice John's influence? She couldn't let herself hang on to the things he'd taught her.

A spoonful of icy sherbet slid past her lips. *It isn't just that he brainwashed me into changing my life*, Rachel thought. *I fell in love with him.*

Slurp went Brent's straw against his empty glass. "You look goofy even now," Brent said.

Startled, she gave him a look she'd learned from the classic film *Clueless* and said, "Eeeuw!"

He made an equally dopey face back.

"You had enough, Mr. Wise Guy? Then clear your place."

Walking back to the sink with Brent, she rinsed their glasses and put them in the Sanitizer. "Want to go play computers? I've got some thinking to do."

"Sure" he said. "Listen, Mom, I want you to know something. I really hope we can stay here. Whoever you had a fight with, remember that you always told me 'Don't go to bed mad.'" He gave her an unexpected hug, then scampered off to Gil's room.

I've got to think, Rachel told herself. Out of habit, she turned on TV, then positioned herself the way she had in the days when she used to work out while watching TV. She hadn't done that for ages, thanks to John's stance on multi-tasking, but she remembered the moves. She'd start with three minutes of ab crunches.

The TV voices began having their usual soothing effect. Rachel was counting reps. when she saw Britney Spears. Of all people! Still the flat belly, the crop top, the gorgeous blond hair. Hey, the former teen superstar must be pushing 30. Although Britney was 10 years younger than Rachel, Rachel had always admired her.

"I just live for my daughters," she was telling the interviewer.

"Well, let's bring them on," he said. It was Dave! *Thank goodness for "The Dave and Donna Show."* He always had something spicy to say.

Rachel was doing leg lifts while three blondes pranced onto the set.

"Meet Brandi and Tiffani and Madison—14,7 and lucky 11. What do you think?" Britney gestured, inviting applause. The poor girl must be crazed from too much touring; surely she realized that the Dave 'n Donna show didn't have a studio audience.

Good old TV, dependably ridiculous! Rachel was starting to feel better.

The girls dressed just like Mom. After Britney lined up next to the youngest, they all began spinning in rapid circles like ice skaters. Their toothy smiles were aimed straight at the camera, as each girl (wasn't Mom still a girl?) pulled something out of her anklet. Then they started to dance.

They'd pulled out beads. They were doing The Dance of The Righteous. *Say it isn't so,* she thought.

Rachel clicked the remote for a close-up. Each girl was doing a different extra-points movement—drinking water from a Blessed Bottle, Christian Mudra #5, the one-handed rosary deal—and Britney was doing them all. She'd always been co-ordinated but these moves were tough and her brow was furrowed in concentration. Oh, ick—out popped a roll of flab around Britney's midriff.

Rachel couldn't take it. She flipped off the TV, pulling up her blouse and scrutinized her own midriff. Not good. She sat down, breathing as fast as if she'd been doing aerobics.

It was time to think.

On the drive to Marguerite's, she had planned to pack quickly and head for the airport. She'd only promised to stay out of pity, seeing her old friend in tears. Now Rachel wondered where, exactly, could she and Brent go?

Back home, what was there? The Righteous, with their frantic dances. The Traditionals, oozing piety from their dangling crosses. Huntids were there, same as here, with the sinister buzz of their shimmering wings. Back home you'd have the same weird feeling about them, always wondering where they'd show up next.

Huntids seemed to be everywhere; their presence on the highway today had terrified Rachel. Where would they be next, buzzing around her neighborhood supermarket? Would they swarm into Brookside Health Club? Her house?

And what about staying with Jeremy? At this point, Rachel respected him a heck of a lot more than John, but right now she didn't want to be anywhere near him. Whenever she let allowed herself to think about him, his anxiety made a black hole in her gut. And that was from just one tiny empathic impulse clear across the country!

Until Extermination Day next Saturday, Rachel didn't want to have to deal with Jeremy and his itches. He needed love, of course, and she'd been joining with his spirit every day. Unless she kept her distance from him physically, though, they'd both go crazy. To give him credit, he'd probably known it would be this way, which is why he had encouraged her to leave on a vacation with Brent.

Rachel realized she was pacing, striding between the dining nook and the table full of Marguerite's glass paperweights. She picked one up. She wanted to hurl it, break a hole in the wall, find a saner reality, where bitterness and fear didn't press upon her from every side.

Okay, girl, calm down. Get some water. You have to be the adult now.

Rachel took some calming breaths as she poured the water. Drinking it made her feel better, so she finished it and carried another glass back to the coffee table.

Okay. I'm closing my eyes. I'm going inside to find my guidance since nobody else's answers work for me now.

Inwardly Rachel saw herself at John's Oneness Center. It felt like his usual Sunday service. Everyone was praying, their eyes closed.

But this is different, she realized. *I've traveled into the future. And people are doing the Wave of Oneness.*

Is this image a symbol of what God wants me to do? If it is, please give me a sign.

Her heart felt a tug so strong it was almost physical. *I belong with these people now.*

"But I don't like them," she screamed at that inner voice, "How can I ever forgive them? They chose me for all the wrong reasons."

Breathe long and slow. Okay. Beneath her hurt pride, what was she feeling? Every time she turned her attention inside, she felt John's people meditating for peace. An image flashed of the way Brent's friend Tom used to jump into swimming pools, face scrunched up, one chubby hand pinching his nose closed. Rachel took it as a reminder to breathe and to stop rejecting her experience.

Like it or not, I belong with these people.

"Oh brother! If I never saw Marguerite again, it would be too soon," she protested bitterly.

The world needs your love now, your forgiveness. These words came to Rachel as a knowing, along with an ice blue chill that reached straight down to her toes.

She sighed and opened her eyes. The blanked-out TV screen was a reminder of just how weird people were becoming. Not just Britney Spears. Millions of people all over the country were flailing their beads and swatting huntids and trying to bring on the Rapture.

As Rachel hunted for some cookies, she looked out the window and saw swarms of huntids. Weren't they several inches higher now than before the weekend camping trip? "You win," she told her guidance, biting her lips in resignation. "I'll stay here with Brent. I'll do my bit to help. All of us could die on Extermination Day. The one thing I can count on is my choice to live with honor, one day at a time."

Making up with Marguerite wasn't all that hard. When she came home that night, her eyes were pale green from crying. Gil gave Brent a gentle punch in the arm; he, too, looked ashamed. *Both of them knew they were manipulating us. Maybe they're relieved it's not a secret any more.*

"We didn't know if you'd be here," Marguerite said, running to hug Rachel.

"Don't worry," Rachel said, accepting a restrained hug. "We'll stay for Extermination Day and do our part. No big deal."

"Okay," said Marguerite, looking her straight in the eye. *No attempt at any buddy-buddy stuff,* Rachel noticed. *It's business.*

"Hooray!" cheered the boys. They started to chase each other around the living room.

"Upstairs," Marguerite told them, pretending to use her usual stern parenting voice.

After the boys were tucked in, Rachel felt a change as she and Marguerite walked downstairs. Sitting on the couch, Marguerite asked, "Do you want to process your feelings? I'll listen." She looked frightened, brave and resigned.

Rachel said, "You sure? You know what I'm like when I'm angry? Jeremy calls me 'The Blaster.'"

"Rachel, I'm so sorry about what happened. After you left, I did a lot of thinking about how it must have been for you."

"As you said, Marguerite, we live in broken times. Old Hickory Helms did get that part right."

Marguerite lifted a quizzical eyebrow.

"Besides," Rachel said, "If I went into my feelings right now, I might never come out the other side. And we only have one week left to prepare for this thing."

"There's no time to waste, that's for sure," Marguerite said. She smiled, exhausted, the familiar tracery of lines extending out from her eyes. "Okay, you have a raincheck to have a big fight with me, any time, any place. Now, how about a cup of chrysanthemum tea?"

A few blossoms floated to the top of Rachel's cup. The pale gold liquid had a bitter, flowery taste. *"Unexpectedly soothing, though,"* she noticed.

"I am curious about one thing," she said to Marguerite. "I know my side of the story. Tell me yours. What do you really feel about me, apart from being ordered to cultivate my friendship?"

Marguerite began stirring her tea vigorously. "The truth?"

Rachel nodded, her jaw tight.

Marguerite spoke as if she was preparing to be tactful. "Partly I've enjoyed you a lot. And Brent is a delight."

"What about the rest? I can take it."

Marguerite sighed. "Rachel, sometimes being with you is like tuning into a typical American woman of the 20s. That's not someone I feel comfortable with."

"Why?"

"It's all about appearance. All the time. Who cares?"

Rachel started laughing. "That's it? That's the boogey man?"

"You have no idea how much I've wanted to shake you sometimes."

"Why *shouldn't* you care how people look, you of all people? Aren't you an artist?"

"I don't want to argue with you, Rachel. Millions of American women were raised to think the way you do. But for me—just me, okay?—life is richer when I don't obsess over the way people look."

"So you think I'm superficial?"

"That doesn't have to be bad. The surface is a valid level of life."

"Come on," Rachel said. "Becoming an empath has been a serious thing for me. It isn't just another hobby for my charm bracelet."

"Well, I guess that's true. Otherwise you wouldn't still be here." Marguerite looked at her sharply. "You know, kid, I've noticed a lot of growth in you during this visit."

Growth, huh? Coming from such a shrimp, the compliment almost made Rachel laugh. The top of Marguerite's head barely reached Rachel's chin, and *she* was making comments about growth? Mercy.

Rachel gulped down the last of her tea and thought again. "Thanks," she said. And meant it.

Chapter 41
Practice Without Making Perfect

Rachel started worrying the moment she woke on Monday. Would a Rapture happen on Extermination Day? Would the insecticide poison humans as well? And what if even the strongest chemicals failed to kill the flies? Jeremy had told her that killing huntids only made the mutants reproduce faster. What diseases and food shortages might result?

Mechanically, Rachel showered. And almost as mechanically, she questioned her inner space. She felt different today. Why?

Broadening her awareness, Rachel realized that she took for granted feeling connected to others in her community. Like the phone lines crisscrossing the nation, this automatic part of her inner landscape created a routine background noise.

Back home, she had felt connected to neighbors—although she barely knew them. All Americans, even V-R addicts and druggies, had been energetically attached, if only to find people in other groups annoying and unfriendly.

Because she was now a skilled empath, Rachel could be conscious about her psychic environment, and this morning she realized how much her background noise had changed. She could feel that The Righteous and Traditionals had intensified their zeal to expand their numbers; meanwhile people in all the other groups were breaking away from the invisible but normal web of psychic connection. Why?

Of course! With Extermination Day just around the corner, Rachel wasn't the only one feeling a life-or-death utter aloneness. That's why the psychic silence from the lack of community was now so huge. A universal fear, cold and silent, quelled the impulse to reach out to others, in the same way that, during grave illness, you'd only want to talk to your closest friends.

An entire nation in psychic pain caused the silence she felt today. And Rachel had never felt anything quite like it. If pictured physically, it would look as if today had dawned with an anti-sun, erasing the familiar shadows around things.

Tough, she told herself. *Just because you notice the problem doesn't mean you have to let it get you down. There's work to be done.*

Marguerite must have felt something similar because after breakfast on Monday, she asked the boys to play in their rooms, handed them picnic lunches and told them to stay upstairs until she called them to dinner.

"What's our assignment?" Rachel asked.

"Practice connecting with others as a spiritual exercise. John suggested we practice as much as possible."

"What kind of practice?"

"Since I'm in the Spider group, I'm to practice finding each person's creative spark and join with that."

"Most people have no creative spark."

"Then I *do* have a job! Seriously, joining with people like that can help them to find their creativity. Everybody is born with some, but the spark is dimmed by things like wrap-around TVs and V-R. You know."

"What's the best you can hope for? It's not as though they'll ever become Picassos. You gonna turn Extermination Day into another Fremont Folk Festival?"

"Rachel, awakening the creative spark makes people come alive. Unless that happens, Extermination Day will be a killing field with precious little to counterbalance it."

"I don't get it. What does creativity have to do with removing the huntids?"

"During our Wave of Oneness, I'll work with the Spiders to awaken creativity. You'll work with *your* group to awaken empathic talent. Get it? All over the world, leaders like John are showing their people how to use their spiritual gifts, which can turn them into leaders too. All this will awaken as many people as possible—teaching by example how to have genuine spiritual experience."

"You really think that could happen to enough people to make a difference?"

"Why not? All these leaders are called Lightworkers, you know. They've been preparing their people for years, just like John."

Oh sure, Rachel thought involuntarily. *How many people compared to the millions with Helms or Pilgrim? As if we could make any difference.*

"At a pre-arranged signal from the Lightworkers," Marguerite continued, "We will simultaneously join with the huntids, request that they leave and ask for their blessing."

"Oookaaayyyy," Rachel said dubiously and more than a little apprehensively. "Guess I blew it by missing our final assignment at the retreat."

"Not to worry. All we did was a final meditation in which John helped us experience a preview."

"What was that like?"

Marguerite's face glowed. She started to speak, then stopped. After a pause, she said, "John didn't tell us what we should do or feel. He wouldn't have told you either, not in words."

Marguerite's bright eyes stared at Rachel. "Whatever you may think about John and Consuela and me," she said softly, "we're not coercive. Promise."

"I understand that now," Rachel said with a rueful smile. "But I still haven't a clue about how to prepare. Will we have meetings at the Center every day?"

"No. John says it's time for each of us to discover our own connection to spirit. Besides, the Wave of Oneness isn't supposed to be some big dog-and-pony show at the Center. It's strictly personal, volunteering one by one from our homes."

"No mind melds? No structure?"

"John did suggest we practice every day. Just sit and do the things Consuela taught you, Rachel. Make sense?"

Rachel began pacing around the living room. "I guess we have a long day ahead of us." She went looking for cookies, feeling again as if yet one more time she'd been knocked over by the ocean. John should act like a seminar star and hold daily cram sessions. The man had absolutely no showmanship.

Still, Rachel practiced. She quit worrying whether it would make her perfect. From what she knew of John's methods, perfection wasn't the point—what mattered was allowing your ego to get out of the way. Easy for a simple soul like Consuela but not so easy for Rachel.

Just for today, she'd practice and let go of any results. Sitting on the living-room sofa, Rachel closed her eyes and prepared to connect with her mother. Blood relatives were supposed to be easiest, though painful experience had taught Rachel not to expect anything to be easy when it came to Helene .

Yet it *was* easy to connect with Helene—stunningly quick, too. Rachel thought her name three times, took a few deep breaths, and bam! Her awareness slipped inside her mother's petite size-two body. *Back out*, Rachel warned herself, and eased out just enough to give herself a comfortable distance.

What is it like, being Helene? The minute she asked, Rachel felt a new texture of life—a less reactive nervous system; life experienced in far more detail; a slow, steady pace. *Cockroach consciousness,* Rachel noted. *No wonder I never thought my mother appreciated me. She's great at being grounded, but doesn't know any other way to be.*

After a few more breaths, she picked up Helene's immediate mood: Resigned to plodding through the days, forever accompanied by melancholy self-talk. *If that's what it means to grow old, I'm not going there*—the thought bounced Rachel back into her own body as surely as if she had been yanked on a bungee cord. *Oops, judgment strikes again.*

Rachel made herself a cup of tea, barely noticing its flavor. Maybe she should do her research alone in her room, the way Marguerite did. Or she could turn on the TV and take a break.

No. Time to do more research. Fun or not, it was her duty. In a week, she'd never have to do it again.

By the end of the day, and many tea breaks later, Rachel had made contact with a dozen relatives, including her father. Benny, it turned out, was a Spider. That could have been fun, but Alzheimer's had taken over most of his mind. Having half of her consciousness float in the ethers felt awful to Rachel, though her dad didn't care. Although he was consciously disconnected from his awareness, Rachel could feel clearly who he was; his artistic gift explained why she had always felt closer to him than to anyone else in the family.

Research on Eric, the brother who ran the family catering business, revealed him as another Cockroach, a lot like their mother, except that his body was male, young and busy—and unbearably tense.

The day's scariest mission was connecting to her alcoholic brother Walt. It felt like stepping into a dense fog. The one thing that made this bearable for Rachel was noticing how he operated as a Termite. Deep down, the rebel in him relished being a drunk; he had fun smashing people's expectations. He'd shock people, make them flip through their masks, and bring up deep, denied feelings. His Termite self watched this . . . and laughed.

When Rachel's disturbing but revealing merge with Walt finally ended, she considered its implications. What a revelation that the old, familiar discomfort she'd always felt with him wasn't a weakness in her! It was Walt's life work.

"Why are you letting them do this?" Rachel asked Tuesday, after overhearing Marguerite phone in an order for the V-R version of Monopoly. Usually, neither of the children was allowed to game in virtual reality.

"John's suggestion."

"He wants to rot their brains?"

"Don't think so. You know how hard we're working; he doesn't want our kids to do that and he said play is the best way to keep them fresh. We'll need their clarity Saturday."

"Okay," Rachel said. "I don't suppose they'll become addicts in a day."

"Not even two," Marguerite said. "I got a two-day rental so we could work without being interrupted. They deserve the treat."

She and Marguerite didn't talk much Tuesday, except for when Marguerite tested homeopathic cell salts on Rachel's aura, and told her to take silica every two hours for fatigue.

"But I don't feel tired," Rachel protested.

"It's your synapses that would feel tired. I'm taking it too," Marguerite said in her no-nonsense voice.

"What the hell," Rachel said, popping the sugary pills.

Today, Rachel would practice on her friends. She visited e-buddies, a peculiar challenge because she had only the most perfunctory relationships with them. It was good practice though, her inner voice told her.

By four, stretched thin, Rachel decided to treat herself to a visit with Heather. She had avoided thinking about her dippy, selfish friend since their quarrel, so she was pleasantly surprised to feel such affection for her. Heather's familiar presence, intensified by the spiritual connection, made Rachel feel more alive, as if her body had become more authentic and more present.

Interesting, she thought. *That's from the experience of love, not just Heather. And one more reason to forgive while you can.*

Once Rachel put aside her grudges, Heather was easy to forgive. Just the thought of her dimples and old-fashioned hairstyle evoked a presence as comfortable as a worn pair of shoes. Recognizing her consciousness was a cinch—Cockroach at its finest. How Rachel must have needed Heather in the days before she could ground herself.

To Rachel's astonishment, Heather made solid inner contact, so Rachel improvised and had a conversation with her, all on the inner, about holding a space and how Heather could help on Extermination Day. When Heather said, "Of course I'll help," Rachel realized that her old friend had more to her than Rachel had ever guessed.

Good job, she heard John say. *That's exactly what to do when you find others who are interested. Never coerce, simply invite. Millions on earth, especially loved ones, would help if they knew how.*

Time was running out, so early Wednesday morning Rachel connected to Heather's kids, both of whom she had known from infancy. Plump little Ashley, a Cockroach like her mom, had no interest in joining the project, but big sister Kayla sure did. Beneath those straight, suffer-no-fools eyebrows, Kayla's consciousness showed the distinctive Ant vibe. And she was thrilled to be helping. Given her flair for technical work, Kayla would connect well to other Ants.

Rachel knew what she should do next, even though she'd never done it before. *Courage*, she heard Consuela say. Without another doubt, she called on Sunil, the leader of the Ant group. Her heart opened up as if she was starting up another huge crush, and for a minute she froze. She never wanted to go through something like that again.

That's just the opening of your heart. Don't make it personal, her inner voice warned. This time she understood.

Keeping her heart space open and unafraid, she talked to Sunil as simply as if they were on a telephone. "I have a new recruit for you," she said.

"Demographics? Bio? It would help me connect."

"She's an eight-year-old girl, maybe nine now. A no-shit type, with Cockroach mother and sister. No father." Another deep breath. "Of course she has a father. And," she tuned in, "he's a Termite, but he's in his own private hell, poor guy." So much for Rotten George; Rachel actually felt compassion for him.

"Let me patch you through," she told Sunil, and kept her heart space open until she felt them connect.

Wow! she thought. *It's like a conference call. Who knew I could do that? I'm as proud as if I'd just given birth to a chicken.*

This idea made Rachel laugh out loud and popped her out of her meditative state. Opening her eyes, she felt so good that she snatched an ice cream bar instead of settling for one more virtuous cup of tea. After that, she ran around the block a few times. Millions of huntids swarmed on the ground, stretching to the horizon in every direction, but Rachel laughed companionably at them as she ran. Maybe everything would work out after all.

Thursday, the boys attended a marathon 12-hour party given for kids connected to the Center. When she and Marguerite dropped them off, Rachel recognized the hostess as Evangeline Jones.

"Nice of you to do this." Rachel said. Evangeline's home looked both elegant and, at least until the party got underway, orderly.

"I figured I might as well support my fellow Butterflies," Evangeline said. "My husband even took the day off from work so he could help."

"Do you feel prepared? For Saturday?"

"Guess so."

"Not me," said Rachel.

"Well, you came to this late. But you're a powerful empath," Evangeline assured her.

"Thanks. You're lucky to have your husband around. Wish I could say the same."

Ah, Jeremy. Who wasn't even speaking to her.

Back on the sofa, Rachel focused on her neighborhood. First she checked in with the family of the V-R addict from scout camp—all she needed to find him in consciousness was his first name, Harrison.

Man oh man, not a care in the world! A Fly. His mother had been a Fly, too, before her mental pulse went flat.

Next Rachel checked in with Brent's friend, Tom Smith, the boy fascinated by his own bodily fluids. Definitely a Bee, and wide awake. When he volunteered, Rachel connected him up with John.

Then Rachel turned to his mom, Jessica, expecting a treat. It was easy to imagine her as Rachel had last seen her, in that ridiculously adorable Tweety Bird T-shirt. But she was strangely difficult to tune into. Why?

The question catapulted Rachel into Jessica's body. It was taller than her own, and moved with the steadiness typical of someone with Cockroach vibes. But it felt as though Jessica had steel bands around her head and neck. *What's going on here?* Rachel took a deep breath before asking Archangel Gabriel to help her go deeper.

An image flashed of Jessica was wearing the beads of The Righteous. At this moment she was doing both the dance and one of the hand mudras. Jessica, once the pillar of her Episcopal church. Sensible, salt-of-the earth Jessica. "How could you?" Rachel asked.

No answer. From a great distance, Rachel sensed the thought: "Only The Righteous are allowed to speak to me now."

Rachel tried connecting again, this time through the heart. After all, it was Jessica's generous heart that Rachel had loved most. Nothing.

"Why" Rachel asked her inner guidance.

Fear.

If Jessica could be frightened into joining The Righteous, everyone could, Rachel thought.

Not everyone. Nor will all these last-minute conversions amount to much. The voice sounded like a mix of John, Gabriel and her own cynical self.

Did she dare depend upon that voice? And what if The Righteous were correct? In that case, Rachel would soon burn in everlasting Hell. So many people believed. What, ten billion people by now?

She didn't have time to analyze her doubts. Instead, she took some deep breaths, blinked, and fixed dinner for herself and Marguerite, who hated to cook.

After Marguerite returned to her room, Rachel sneaked a few handfuls of candy into a dish. She hadn't wanted to take it in front of her thin friend. Cramming her mouth full of chocolate buttercreams, she placed the rest on the coffee table.

This will be your reward.

She smiled, then reached out for Jeremy. The scariest part was that he might reject her—not just categorically, the way Jessica had but personally, the way he had the last time.

Rachel breathed long, slow and deep, then she got Big by calling on Archangel Gabriel. Setting her intention to connect, she thought Jeremy's name three times and connected in record time. He was at work, of course.

She missed him so, it was actually thrilling to join with his energy. Although her awareness focused mostly in the extra-wide space of Jeremy's forehead, she pushed down to feel the full length of his body, definitely male and well muscled, and those slender legs and long thin feet. Startled, she realized that the cute belly he'd acquired over the last couple of years had a reason. It held his sensitive system steady, especially as he toughed out the overwhelming pressures of directing Extermination Day.

It was not her only discovery. As she held him in this long-distance embrace, dancing cheek-to-cheek with his consciousness, she explored his Ant-like technician's intellect and his steady but endlessly alert mind. She savored the range of his emotions; her spirit saluted his beauty. For an instant, she even let herself curl up inside his soul the way she had in the days when they made love.

But quickly she pulled away. She knew better than to bring a personal closeness that could alter Jeremy's energy. It was compressed now, coiled, ready to spring. Rachel stayed long enough to realize that, apart from the tension around him, he remained unchanged.

And she discovered something else, something that shocked her. As an empath, Rachel had grown used to joining her consciousness with other people. But joining with Jeremy was different. He was as familiar to Rachel as her own self, and just as dear to her.

Jeremy was her husband; she had consciously chosen him to be flesh of her flesh. Unlike any other person on earth, she had lived with him, built a home with him. He had chosen her, too. Clearly, he was the love of her life—maybe not the romance, but the love. Even if their marriage seemed broken beyond repair, love joined them, as it had for 13 years.

Rachel lost count of how many hours she sat in Washington West while her consciousness lingered in Capitol City. She didn't count time, any more than she tried to play tricks with her awareness. She was content to support Jeremy as he focused on his work; she brought an impersonal clarity, knowing that she must not distract him, not even to tell him how much she loved him.

Or to say, perhaps, goodbye.

Around nine o'clock, the boys returned from the party and Rachel became aware of her surroundings. Taking a few deep breaths, she opened her eyes.

"I'll get it. You don't need to come down," she hollered to Marguerite.

Cherishing both boys, she put them to bed. Then she ate the rest of her candy, piece by piece. Some day her life would return to normal, and she'd go for months at a time without weeping. But now she cried for Jeremy—for them both—until there were no tears left.

Chapter 42
TV Pep Talks

On Friday a volunteer called, offering to take the kids for the day so she and Marguerite could have uninterrupted time to practice. Only after hanging up did Rachel realize this was her empath buddy Sioux-Z.

"I'll have 'em all back by five," Sioux-Z told her while she loaded the boys into her kid-packed van.

"Aren't you practicing too?"

"I've contacted everybody I know on the inner, so why not take a day off?"

Rachel nodded—without jealousy, she noted, a refreshing change. *I need more time than Sioux-Z does, that's all. Empathy's not a competition.*

"Well, aren't we mellow," Marguerite said as the van left. When Rachel gave her a quizzical look, Marguerite pinched Rachel's cheek. "Zee tight and angry dimple, eet 'as deesappeered," she said in a funny, phony French accent.

Marguerite wasn't even an empath—did Rachel's old habits of jealous and judging show to everyone? Rachel felt a retroactive blush wash through her. It was only after they came indoors that she realized they'd been brushing huntids off themselves the entire time they'd been outside.

"Marguerite, has that happened before? Aren't the huntids alighting faster than they used to?"

"You bet. And if we don't like it, imagine how The Righteous feel."

"No doubt they're swatting more, too. Poor things—The Righteous, I mean."

"Seriously, I wonder how The Righteous are handling this population explosion." Propelled by shameless curiosity, they headed straight for the TV.

The Pilgrim Channel came up first, catching the Reverend in close-up. Marguerite shut off the sound. "Think we can hear her better this way?"

Rachel nodded. "Classic Mosquito energy. You can almost hear the buzz. No wonder she has such a huge following."

The lack of sound made it easier to watch Pilgrim's expression. The camera focused on her mesmerizing lips, glossy with a vibrant magenta that flattered her big brown eyes, then slowly moved down to focus on her trademark gold ten-pounder. This one, however, wasn't just gold. It sparkled with green and purple jewels.

"That's a new touch," Rachel said. "Think they're real?"

"She could afford it," Marguerite said, flipping on the sound.

"So that's it, my children: a little hymn singing, a lot of prayer. This is how I urge you to prepare for Huntid Extermination Day." She paused. "Stay with your own kind, of course. When the Rapture comes, you want to be as far as possible from the wailing and gnashing of teeth."

She rolled her eyes toward heaven, sighed, and met the camera's eye.

"Remember, if you see huntids, to thank them for coming as harbingers of Our Lord. I will record no more messages until I see you in Heaven," she said with a tiny wistful wave.

"This sermon will repeat until the Glorious Day." Fade to the trumpet solo as her image disappeared.

Marguerite and Rachel stared at each other.

After a one-second respite, the trumpets began again, this time with the African-bloodstream spiritual, "I've got a robe, you've got a robe."

"To our faithful Traditionals watching, my farewell message is also a message of welcome. Let us pray," Stacy Pilgrim said grandly.

"I think we get the general idea," Marguerite observed.

Rachel nodded. "Let's catch Hickory Dickory."

When they clicked to The Helms Channel, the show was so packed with performers in sparkly costumes that Rachel was reminded of a circus. Righteous performers were doing the Dance, flailing their beads.

"All celebrities, you'll notice," Marguerite said.

She was right. Rachel realized that the young faces she'd been unable to place were current rock stars. But next to them was megastar Tom Cruise, and he was dancing. *He was lots more fun in the classic* Risky Business, thought Rachel.

"Must have converted from Scientology—no wonder they wanted him up front," said Marguerite. "He was more fun in *Risky Business*, but of course then he was 40 years younger."

Rachel counted 21 major stars, plus dozens of old-timers who made Cruise look like a kid by comparison, stars like the eternally wrinkle-free Pat Boone and Jay Leno, who winked way too often while performing his mudras.

Startled, she realized that not one Seminar Star was present. That went beyond weird. You could count on seeing dozens of them wherever celebrities flocked.

On second thought, maybe it wasn't so weird. John wouldn't be caught dead on a show like this. Even Tanya Willoughby, Queen of Pinkness, might consider it beneath her.

"Look!" said Marguerite, magnifying an area off to the side where some of the latest clones waited. Clones were a huge fad now, produced from molecular fragments left on physical objects touched by the famous. Lady Diana, Martin Luther King, all the Kennedys, the Dalai Lama—Rachel had seen them all. But not on TV, not doing the dance of The Righteous, uh-uh.

"Have they no shame?" Rachel said, pointing to the Dalai Lama clone, who wore extra sets of beads garlanded around his neck and flailed the major necklace so deftly, you'd swear he'd been one of The Righteous forever.

"One does wonder how much Helms paid for the merchandising rights," Marguerite muttered wryly.

The camera zoomed to the rear of the performance area, where President Tucker and his cabinet waited on another stage. "The one with the violet suspenders used to work with Jeremy, and was he ever a pain," said Rachel excitedly. "Doesn't he look like a Hackenworth?"

"Yeah. Hey, I don't believe this."As a brass band played "God Bless America," Helms was lowered to the stage from a red-white-and-blue hot air balloon.

"How'd they do that? The landing must have been speeded up with computers," said Rachel.

"You've got to admire the man's technology," Marguerite said.

Helms signaled the band to stop. "Welcome, my fellow Americans. I have come with a symbol of glory for us all." He was grinning from ear to ear. "Victory is upon us now, as we usher in the fabulous 10 to the 10th. Our latest estimates show we are nearly there. My friends, if only a couple thousand of you added one more dance or mudra by tomorrow, we could reach 10 billion. Show the world your faith. Say *yes* to the Rapture. *Yes* to the presence. *Yes* to the multitudes."

"The multitudes?" Rachel echoed.

Twirling his fingers with breathtaking speed, dancing, and drinking from his Blessed Bottle, Helms was performing like a one man band. "We are here in the flesh," he almost sang. "We are victorious. Are you watching us from your car or your V-R console, from home or work? If you can see us, move with us now. Demonstrate that you are one of The Righteous."

"Look at that," Marguerite said, her voice dangerously quiet. Did you hear that glitch in his voice just then? Let's see if I'm right." She clicked the close-up button, magnifying Helms' face.

"Look," said Marguerite. A vein throbbed in the minister's forehead, a cheek pulsated faintly and Rachel could swear the bags under his eyes twitched.

"When you're an artist, sometimes you notice things that other people don't."

"You're amazing. No wonder they aren't showing his usual close-ups."

It was as if someone had overheard her comment, for suddenly Helms stood completely still, his muscular body in repose except for the outstretched hands still rhythmically moving his beads. A gigantic close-up of him stretched eerily across the TV screen. Marguerite adjusted the picture to focus on the program's tight close-up without magnifying it on her home equipment. Helms held his face in an image of tight serenity as he smiled for the camera.

"I am The Way," he said, only it didn't sound right. His voice came out in an almost bleating stutter.

"The man sounds like a machine-gun," said Rachel. "Why has everyone behind him stopped moving? Are they shocked to hear him like that?"

After a pause he began again: "I am-amamam the Wayayay. I am the Wayyyy and the Tru-tru-truth. And the Light, the Light. Noone will c-c-c-c-come unto the Fa-Fa-Father but through me."

Marguerite shut off the TV. "I can't stand to watch it."

"What do you think is going on?"

"Whatever it is, I don't think it's good. You're the empath—find out!"

Rachel nodded. Without another word, she closed her eyes, gave her standard prayer and joined with Archangel Gabriel. "I don't wanna do this," a part of her was saying. Nonetheless she breathed her way into the consciousness of Hickory Helms.

"It feels like I'm jitterbugging," she told Marguerite. "God, this is scary. One part of me is here, another part is there, and another part is way out in left field. It's like joining with my dad, except my dad was divided into only a couple of pieces. I'm sorry, but Helms is cracking up. Absolutely nutso. I'm outta here."

Rachel breathed hard to ground herself. What a relief to come back into her body! She opened her eyes, hugged herself, and stroked her arms up and down to make sure she was real.

"And he's the leading spiritual leader of the Western World," snorted Marguerite. "Tomorrow should be interesting."

Chapter 43
The Wave of Oneness

Huntid Extermination Day would deploy simultaneously all over America. The night before, emergency messages started appearing on every clock, watch, appliance, skin-phone and computer. A warning message was repeated constantly on TV and radio. If you were outdoors, you found the same message on your car's directional system and on your Digitized Datamate. Most everyday machines had long ago been hardwired to transmit government programming, although Rachel hadn't realized it until now. It gave her the heebie-jeebies.

The emergency message that started Rachel's day was broadcast over the antique clock radio that clicked on, as planned, at four a.m.

> This is a message from the Emergency Broadcasting System.
> Security procedures are in effect all day.
> Be smart. Stay indoors after 7 a.m.
> Infractions are punishable by law.
> For your safety, stay indoors until you hear the all-clear signal.
> We repeat, stay indoors.

Oh, please—as if anyone was stupid enough to go for a jog on Extermination Day.

They ate breakfast by candlelight, and Rachel reminded the boys that the Wave of Oneness would start two hours before the blast. Everyone ate chocolate-chip pancakes except Marguerite, who could barely finish a cup of coffee.

"Gil? Brent? What would you like to do while you're cooped up indoors?" Rachel asked.

Giving an earnest look in Rachel's direction, Marguerite added, "Don't feel any pressure to stay with us, boys. Go play if you want to, but don't use the computer. It's important that you not interrupt us until we come upstairs to get you, okay?"

"Why no computer?" asked Gil.

"Emergency warnings every five minutes—it'll be obnoxious."

Rachel added. "And they're doing it to TV, radio, phones, everything. The government wants to make sure everybody stays indoors. It may not be safe outside."

Gil's perpetual cocky grin tumbled right off his face and Brent looked serious. "Can we sit here with you if we're quiet?" he asked. "I need to be part of this." His handsome little face looked so solemn that Rachel wanted to kiss him, but she couldn't in front of everybody. Instead, she pulled up a chair so he could sit opposite her. Marguerite pulled up another for Gil so that the four of them made a neat little square in the living room. It was almost five o'clock.

"Everyone use the bathroom?" Rachel asked.

Gil rolled his eyes at her. Rachel closed hers and began to breathe.

She felt . . . okay, not spectacularly clear and definitely not heroic. But at least she was awake, determined to do her share as a spiritual warrior.

The cold fear in her belly was totally understandable, Rachel decided. She shifted her attention to the others. Gil wasn't settled yet, but Marguerite's presence was already on full force—intelligent, inquiring, airy. Rachel could tell that she was hard at work connecting with others.

John had said that during the Wave of Oneness, people from The Spiritual Center would be working along with Lightworkers from around the world. Their mission was to telepathically gather the largest groups possible, starting at five a.m., long before official security procedures were to begin and planes would start dumping insecticide all over the world. Nobody really knew how long it would take to kill the huntids, but the Lightworkers had scheduled a meeting in consciousness at 7:30, when everyone in John's group would bring their attention to the huntids and ask them to leave in peace.

Some plan, Rachel sighed. Exactly how would the Lightworkers negotiate? Could she do her share? And what difference would any of their efforts make if the huntids refused to go?

Show time. Rachel breathed deeply, sending awareness of her body all the way to her toenails. Every volunteer had to figure out how to move her own energy. John had supplied no set prayers; you'd find more instructions on a bottle of shampoo.

That independence meant Rachel had to find her own confidence, too. A month ago, she would have squirmed, multi-tasked, run to the TV or her computer buddies, pestered Jeremy—anything but find her own way.

Now, thanks to Consuela and John, she had some idea of how to be effective. Taking a deep breath, she thought, *Archangel Gabriel, here I am, ready to connect and be of service. Guide me.*

She felt herself tumble into a slow, dark place that felt like tunneling into the earth: mustiness seeped all around her, and a dampness like mud. Then she felt herself start to vibrate fast as part of a tiny winged body. Vibrating with her were others, all of them huntids.

Well, that was one way to join with a group, she thought, ignoring the fact that the huntids had found her instead of vice-versa. Flexing her psychic muscles, Rachel prepared to take her awareness somewhere else. Where? Jeremy first.

Finding him was easy. Unfortunately, being with him was no picnic. Rachel experienced such cold calm and determination, it felt as if he'd turned into an ice cube. She sent him a blessing, surrounded him in golden light for three minutes, and moved on.

Next? Rachel joined with Heather, Kayla, Tom and everyone back home who responded during her days of research. She reminded each to connect with as many people as possible, then to join with the huntids a half hour after Security Procedures started.

So far, so good.

Next Rachel checked in with people who hadn't responded, in case they were ready now—as if Helene could have managed that overnight! Well, at least she'd had a chance to tell her mother goodbye; nobody knew for sure who would survive Extermination Day. Between the mega-doses of insecticide and the unpredictable huntids, anything could happen.

Rachel began feeling queasy. Then she felt a sensation like labor pains, but without the pain—a kind of uncontrollable shudder working its way through her body. Her mind raced: *What if the huntids refused to go?*

Rachel had seen with her own eyes how fast they had multiplied. They were so smart, they'd even got used to being with people who were in motion. Already the lilac-winged flies were everywhere except on TV, an exception only because TV studios were indoors, and so far huntids had stayed outside.

But what if this attempt to kill them made them angry? Could extermination procedures backfire and cause huntids to swarm through the air thicker than ever? What if they started to take up space indoors as well as outdoors? Imagine huntids inside her car, or filling Marguerite's living room. How many huntids could fit into Rachel's bedroom, the bathroom, onto their plates during meals? What would it feel like, having huntids fly into her nostrils when she tried to breathe?

Break the fear pattern. Now. The inner voice shook her out of the daydream.

Who owns this fear, anyway? That was a productive question. Taking a deep breath, Rachel followed up by asking to join with the group of people whose fear was strongest right now. Zap! She was with the Rev. Hickory Helms and his huge crowd in Madison Square Garden. The place was jammed with members of The Righteous praying, twirling, kneeling, sipping holy water. What was that called, drinking a mudra?

Rachel began to feel dizzy as the frenzy of The Righteous began seeping into her. It reached up the back of her neck and out through the downy hair on her arms. She forced herself to breathe deeper, stretching her grounding cord down from her tailbone straight to the center of the earth. Grounding was so difficult now that it felt like flying into mud. But still she persisted, gathering force through sheer determination. She had to be strong.

It worked. Soon as she felt like herself again, Rachel moved in on Helms. Since she was in her light body, this happened as effortlessly as clicking the zoom feature on a TV. He was twirling a full set of turquoise beads from each wrist—like a Latter Day drum majorette. Another necklace, salmon pink, jiggled from his neck while his head rotated, one circle clockwise followed by one circle counterclockwise, again and again. At the same time, his feet moved constantly in The Dance of The Righteous.

"Why are you so scared? Aren't you supposed to have all the answers?" Rachel felt herself ask Helms. Ordinarily, she wouldn't have dreamed of approaching any-one at his level of celebrity, but limits disappeared when you traveled in your light body, and questions were expressed as quickly as thought. This question hung in the air, and she could tell that Helms heard it.

Instead of answering, though, he pulled at her to join with his group's aware-ness, sucking her into his black-hole consciousness like a Supervac. Rachel's body parts seemed to be shooting off in different directions, and she longed desperately for sleep. It was the deepest exhaustion she had ever known, so deep she could barely keep her inner eyes open. She must lie down, must rest. . . .

Next thing she knew, Brent, in his light body, was giving her a hug so intense it almost knocked her over.

"Come on, Mom," he yelled inside her head, dragging her by the arm until they arrived at the Rolling River campground. Light bodies could go anywhere.

Her son had just rescued her from oblivion and Rachel wanted to thank him. Instead, mom fashion, she found herself scolding him.

"Brent, we can't be here now. We're supposed to be working."

"Lighten up, Mom, we can go wherever we want. One of John's most important rules is either have fun or don't play. Where do you want to go? We can take turns."

She chose the Seattle zoo, so they could join with both animals and animal empaths. A tiny group, but fascinating. Brent's turn, he picked musicians. "They're great at moving consciousness," he told her. "That's what music's about."

He must have been right because this group was mostly of Spiders and Butterflies. It was easy to get them to join the Lightworkers. Rachel thanked them, then explained that she and Brent had to go round up more volunteers.

"My turn," she told Brent, her confidence growing. "I'm ready to join the Traditionals. You?"

At once they were in a huge church in South Africa. People should have been sleeping halfway around the world, but Stacey Pilgrim was wide awake, kneeling at the altar and moaning with terror. She had a roomful of followers to keep her company who seemed just as terrified.

"Brent, isn't this awful? They're in such pain."

"Nah, Mom, that's just how they pray."

Rachel realized he was right. "When you believe in a scary God, I guess your prayers wind up scary," she said.

Feel the beauty of it, her inner voice cautioned. *This is your chance to understand.* Another deep breath. These people were giving their prayers all they had. It wasn't Rachel's way, any more than their version of God matched hers. Still, there was great beauty here, and pathos, too. Hearing the lamentations of the Traditionals made Rachel remember what Jeremy had once said: "All of us stumble through life." These people were stumbling forward the best they could.

"Should we join with them, Brent? Or will they drag us down?" Rachel asked, using the easy wordless communication between two people awake in their light bodies. Talking this way seemed easy and natural.

To her surprise, John's voice answered. So he was with them, too! "Send energy into the earth from your tailbone to stay grounded. Open up the top of your head to allow light to come from your source. Good. *Now* it will be safe to connect."

And they did. John's message was a relief. Although his voice had appeared from nowhere, it felt comfortable joining with him. It also felt as though he and Rachel had never had that last embarrassing conversation. Okay by her!

Breathing deeper, Rachel realized that John had brought a huge group with him—not just The Spiritual Center crew, but similar groups from the rest of the world. *How many are we now?* She heard a number: 144,000. Who would ever have guessed that an unpublicized movement of Lightworkers could attract such numbers?

It's too good to be true, Rachel thought. Never once had she seen anyone like John on TV. What he taught was no seminar, just people learning how to move in spirit. Without enough clout to establish themselves as a religion, without buildings or colleges or TV shows, how could they make a difference? And nobodies wouldn't seem important enough for the huntids to bother listening to them.

Rachel realized that she didn't even know what, exactly, she needed to say to the huntids an hour from now. Was her sense of time right, at least? She opened one eye to peek at her skin-phone.

Click. Her light body tumbled into her physical body and landed on Marguerite's sofa. Rachel surveyed the room, noticing how still the boys and Marguerite sat in the early morning light. They could have been asleep. Dreaming. Or deluding themselves.

According to her skin-phone, it was 6:45. In 15 minutes, airplanes would start dropping payloads of poison. In 45 minutes, the Lightworkers would stop gathering people and attempt telepathic diplomacy with the huntids.

Rachel closed her eyes. *No matter what happens, I must stay centered in my truth.*

Her truth? Where did that come from? She surveyed her body from the outside in. Nice curves, good hair, attractive. Muscle tone a little off, maybe, since she'd stopped working out more than an hour a day. *Go deeper*, she told herself. *Okay*, she thought, setting the direction by taking a series of deep breaths.

I still flunk *gravitas*, went her assessment. As an empath I don't even connect to my mother and never did. Can't even connect solidly to my husband, who may actually need my support at a time like this.

Go deeper and get Big, urged her guidance. More breaths, deeper breaths. Something new was happening. It took several seconds for Rachel to realize what. She was connecting with America's consciousness—the country had its own light body, just as she had her personal one. And now Rachel saw from above a panorama of America's enormous cities, as if they were lights floating in a sky supercharged with electricity. She was being shown that people could draw on this energy if they needed help awakening their awareness.

But could she and the others persuade anyone to choose to do this? She hadn't even been able to interest her own mother in waking up. Rachel felt herself weeping, although her eyes shed no visible tears. She shook her head. "You figure it out, God. I give up."

How long she sat in black despair, she never knew. John's voice startled her. "Wake up, empath. We need you."

Rachel roused herself.

"The job is getting done," John said, "but we still need your help. Take some deep breaths and check your grounding, then come back to the group."

Feeling part of a group again took some getting used to. But the connection seemed stronger this time, and the number of Lightworkers had grown a lot, too. Paradoxically Rachel felt more awake in herself when she was part of a larger group.

"Brent, where are you?" Once called, he quickly appeared in the buzzing silence.

"Mom," he said. "Where do you want to join next?"

"Where do you think we should go?"

"Well, we're joined to about five million people so far, with more every minute. I think it would be great if you'd quit worrying about messing up. If all the Lightworkers go where our hearts take us, we'll have the whole world covered as easy as pie."

He had a point.

"So where to, Mom?"

To her surprise, Rachel wanted to go as far away as possible. To Australia, John's country. Why not?

"Australia," she told Brent. Breathing deep, she made contact with a new fear. Australia was big and, to her, unknown. Still she knew what to do: One deep breath, a prayer, and she let go as if riding a roller coaster.

Gee, this place *was* different. She tried to find words for it. Individual people varied: some brittle, some healthy, some deeply alive in spirit. The difference wasn't about individuals but the utterly different climate and energy. Of all the earth's populated continents, Australia seemed the most pristine.

Intoxicating! She savored this electrically different way of being human as if it were a rare wine.

In the distance, Rachel heard a trumpet call. Archangel Gabriel!

She had called on him so often. Now he was here in person. He—or she or it—was a big golden presence about 20 feet high, with a voice that echoed inside her. Once Rachel decided to think of the presence as male, she became more comfortable, realizing that she had heard his distinctive voice before, in her guidance, as a kind of golden echo. No wonder he sounded familiar.

"Listen!" rang his voice.

Rachel responded as though she grew ears within her ears. Empathically she reached out to Brent and the rest of the Lightworkers. In the silence, she could hear a resonance of deep listening.

"Lightworkers," called Archangel Gabriel, "It's time for us to join with the huntids." His voice filled her with such electricity that the soles of her physical feet started to tingle. Would they sound familiar or scary to the Traditionals? She barely had time to wonder before she arrived in the midst of an entirely new sound.

Huntids—it must be that Rachel had entered their collective presence. Although she was used to hearing their wings make a twinkling sound, now it shifted into a deep, satisfying roar, like ocean waves curling onto a beach.

There is something very alien about this roar of the huntids, Rachel thought. *They feel a million miles away from being human.*

"Duh!" Brent said, next to her ear.

"Duh yourself!" Rachel flashed back to him. She was getting good at this telepathy stuff.

Movement within the huntids shifted now, from sound to light. They were dancing, Rachel realized, and she willed herself to watch as though being here with them was no more dangerous than watching a video. As they swirled in different patterns, their green and violet lights became a slow-moving blur. Soon the patterns seemed to be coming out of Rachel's own forehead. Were the huntids outside her or inside? There was no time to answer, because they began to speak.

"Listen," they said. "Wake up, everyone, and listen. We have been sent here as messengers of God. Before we leave, you can allow us to be a force within your own consciousness, if you choose."

How could anyone not say yes? There was so much joy in the offer. Tears of relief trickled from the outer corners of her eyes.

Yet she felt resistance, too. For instance, an active push of not-listening came from the part of her that was with the Traditionals. Their fear seemed to grow, if anything.

"Tell them, Pilgrim," the huntids commanded.

"Tell them," trumpeted Archangel Gabriel.

Stacey Pilgrim's face flashed before Rachel's awareness. The Traditional minister was wide-eyed with terror. Yet she did as she was told. Rachel felt thousands, then millions, of new people listen as if they sat on the edge of their seats. Rachel breathed with them, slowly and deeply. Within seconds, the first members of the group relaxed; then the rest of the Traditionals woke up and joined in the roar of the huntids.

Group after group was invited to join them. And each group moved like part of a parade, except that instead of marching, their energy bodies rose and hovered in the air.

Resplendent in robes of golden light, the Old Testament's Moses, Aaron, and Miriam joined the Lightworkers, bringing huge numbers of Jews. After a start of recognition, they came quickly into the dancing light. There were plenty of wise-cracks, Rachel noted, but that was her people. She felt an almost visceral relief that her family and ancestors had agreed to awaken in spirit. Even Helene was there, Rachel realized. Even both her brothers.

"Feel the family, Brent?"

He did, she could tell. His recognition brought a sense of completion, then peace, to her bones and her blood.

Next the roar of the huntids shifted to form the word "Allah," and millions of Arabs awoke. Rachel felt the impact of their training in the Muslim habit of prayer, five times each day, facing Mecca. These people moved in spirit like trained dancers. Would they choose to join or would they turn away? She felt hesitation.

Suddenly a kind of frustrated rage pushed out through Rachel's pores, and with a pop, the whole group lifted and breathed into the roar. Peace reverberated throughout the nation of Islam.

And so it went, wave upon wave, with sects of Christians, Hindus and Buddhists, plus religions Rachel never had heard of. Agnostics awoke; so did Atheists, who, to Rachel's surprise, turned out to be the most articulate. When called, they told Gabriel that they would not surrender their independence.

"Nobody is asking you to," Gabriel said. "In fact, let me be the first to help you remove the false ideas that have been forced upon you in the name of religion."

Thought forms flew into the atmosphere. To Rachel, they felt like a different bandwidth of air, like whatever stuff ghosts would be made of. It was fascinating to see brittle broken crosses, tortured images of the crucified Jesus, stern-looking shadows of authority figures Rachel didn't even recognize. All these two-dimensional images turned into particles of light that whirled faster and faster, then dispersed.

"You only wanted the truth," Gabriel told the Atheists. "The truth is that God is proud of you, because you refused to settle for less."

Rachel felt Gabriel's invitation go out to her and the other Lightworkers to extend compassion to such courageous and honest people. She made herself available and layers of bitterness and pain rolled through her, into the pulsating light, until Atheists began merging with the group of awakened souls. Then it was done. The roar of the huntids resumed, full and free.

Moments later, she could feel the huntids getting ready for something. The air held expectancy, like the start of a Fourth of July fireworks.

One question troubled her. "John?" she called. Instantly she felt his presence and an image of his far-set eyes appeared amid the twinkling patterns of huntids. "What order did all this happen in? Why did the Jews come first and Atheists last? It may be a dumb question, but it'll bother me forever if I don't find out."

John said, "If your mind were omniscient, like God's, you'd have seen everyone awaken at the same time. It's like flowers blooming in time-lapse photography—if you were God, you'd see the entire garden blossom simultaneously. Being human, you had to sort out the events in a human way, as a space-time sequence."

"You mean my mind made up one sequence, whereas others might make up a completely different one?"

"Right you are, Rachel." His voice faded as she relaxed into the swirling lights and the roar.

The huntids danced faster, now. The whir of their wings moved into high gear, which rattled Rachel right down to the cells of her physical body.

"We're all being transformed. Feel it," John's voice said as whatever was happening gave off a high-pitched burning smell and a flash of indigo light.

"It's familiar," she said, "It's like having a high fever, like. . . ."

John laughed. "That's the work of Archangel Michael. And Kali. And Hades. We call it by many names but it's all purification. What happened is that Archangel Gabriel has just upped the energy one more notch."

This cellular rearranging felt good in such an odd way—*Fascinating*, Rachel thought—much the way she felt after getting your back cracked by a first-rate chiropractor. Despite the new kind of balance she felt as a result, however, Rachel sensed that a small part of her was not quite right. It annoyed her like an itch in a place she couldn't reach, and she wondered what it was.

Instantly she was back with Rev. Helms and The Righteous. They had been so busy with moving and praying, they hadn't heard the roar. Most were impossibly tense, and many of their individual energy fields were grotesquely distorted. It had happened to Helms, and now that the fire of purification burned more brightly, many more of The Righteous couldn't bear the intensity. Rachel responded to their pain and tried to help by breathing some of it through her system, but it didn't work. Their agony was so unbearable, The Righteous were literally falling apart. Sighing, Rachel asked to return to the part of the big group that carried John's vibration.

"What more can I do?" she asked.

"Our work is done." John told her, "Don't worry. Each person is his own re-sponsibility, and all is put right in the end."

Rachel relaxed. Immediately she felt her light body being fine-tuned in the Wave of Oneness. The process felt as comfortable as if she were sitting in a movie the-ater. Yawning, she let her light body expand and contract until she shimmered as part of a sky full of stars.

John had it right again; worry felt impossible now, exactly the opposite of what she had expected. She'd braced herself to join with angry insects and calm them down, to take on their fears and let them pass through her. Instead, Rachel real-ized, the huntids never had any of the fear, pain, or rage indigenous to life on earth.

We're used to those heavy emotions as part of our lives, like dealing with grav-ity, she reflected. Isn't that how earth is set up? Fear keeps us focused on our physical bodies. The threat of pain, memories of pain—the eternal-seeming na-ture of pain itself—all contribute to the illusion in which we believe that we are our bodies, isolated and alone. But when we stop protecting ourselves, and can accept life from the depths of who we are, then human consciousness becomes huge.

Being with the huntids made it easy for Rachel to realize this. What she saw and felt when connected to them shifted her consciousness beyond what she'd ever experienced on her own.

These tiny creatures were like angels—except that Rachel expected angels to have big wings, not tiny transparent ones. And she thought of angels as carrying messages about things like compassion, mercy, and tenderness. Could it be, she wondered, that we've clothed angels in human emotions, just as our paintings have given them human faces? Huntids were neither human nor earthly. Feelings didn't enter into their experience. Or sexuality. Or so much else that she was used to.

Surrounded by huntids, Rachel settled into deep space, breathing it in like the most delicious ambrosia imaginable. Concentrated fields of knowledge shifted into her awareness, making tiny clicks like the tumblers of a safe. Millions of human souls, when joined with the huntids, had been the combination that opened the lock.

Which reminded her that there was something else she needed to do.

Wait, she told the huntids beating around her in swirls of light. *Wait*, she said to the countless human souls, pulsating along with her. *Some of us are here to serve as empaths. Teach us the part of this that we can remember with human emotions.*

Peace. PEACE. The lesson was peace. Rachel felt herself hover in time, as though one human breath could be suspended indefinitely and in that pause hold all time, all space, the fulfillment of all desires.

Peace.

Then, with a sigh, she knew that the Wave was ending. As her awareness started to shift toward her physical body, she promised herself that from now on she'd remember as much as she could for as long as she could. She wasn't just Rachel any more; she lived in each of the others—these patterns of light that were now separating rapidly into individual identities.

Falling downward, Rachel followed the golden cord that led back to her physical body. She breathed long and deeply, until she felt energy fill every part of her. Within her envelope of skin, Rachel looked at the blackness behind her closed eyes; it became a big sky full of stars.

"*Thank you,*" she thought again and again, thanks to the huntids and to God.

Sirens played in the air, sounding as inconsequential as kazoos. Rachel's eyes opened. Marguerite's eyes met hers, but Rachel didn't want to look into them yet. So she shut her eyes again.

"That must be the all clear," said Marguerite.

"Big deal," Gil said.

"Anyone else want to stay quiet for a while?" Rachel asked. "I think whatever we have in here right now is better than anything out there."

If anyone answered, she didn't notice because, inside, the fireworks started again.

In later years, children and grandchildren would ask those who consciously joined in the Wave, "Tell me about the fireworks." Rachel, for one, never saw anything like them, before or after, even with eyes open.

Each burst started with a rocket soaring into a black sky, followed by a trail of light. She would feel her heart sigh at the glory of each one until, flying farther and higher, the rocket burst open. Sometimes a colorful lightburst would start from the back and thrust itself forward. Sometimes many colors would collapse inward and cascade into spirals. Across the sky's endless canopy, light was turned inside out and never repeated the same pattern twice.

Rachel would never forget the answering cascades, one at the top of her head, another at her brow. So much light, it seemed it could never die out.

"I felt as though it was all made just for me," Rachel would tell her grandchildren.

Chapter 44
Together

Rachel lay awake, too excited to sleep. Jeremy's project had been as successful as hers. He must be enormously relieved. She'd find out when they finally saw each other tomorrow. Back when she and Brent had flown to Marguerite's, Rachel had bought round-trip tickets, wondering even then if the world would end on Extermination Day. Now they could return to normal—whatever that was.

As far as she could tell, the huntids were gone. Never again would the whoosh of their wings startle her as she went to sleep. That sound had disrupted the sequence of silence patterns that helped her drift off. Huntids even used to insinuate themselves into her dreams. Night or day, whenever her mental computer relaxed, huntids had appeared as her screen-saver.

Lying between crisp cotton sheets, Rachel realized that she would miss the violet-winged creatures. Sure, they'd worried her—kept her forever alert, checking for them in her peripheral vision. But now the air seemed empty.

The Wave of Oneness was over. While it was going on, it seemed as if nearly everyone in the world underwent a spiritual awakening. She expected people to be talking about it for years, but so far none of the media had acknowledged it.

"How come nobody but us seems to be walking around with goofy smiles on our faces?" she had asked Marguerite. "Was the Wave all in our heads?"

"I think it was real, if that's what you mean," Marguerite said, matter-of-factly. "But most people didn't participate consciously. Before your training, you wouldn't have either."

"So you think the fireworks appeared like a dream, real at the time but not necessarily real after people woke up? I know that scientists say everyone has dreams, even those who don't remember them."

"I agree. But if I were you, I wouldn't discuss anything about the Wave with other people—not unless they bring it up. Just be grateful you were spiritually awake enough to enjoy it. We know what happened, even Dave and Donna never discuss it on PBS."

Good advice, probably. "But isn't John even going to send out a press release? How's he going to get any credit for his part in it?"

"Why should he take credit—or you, or any of us—take credit? God gets the credit for the heavy lifting, not us. And when's the last time you heard God brag?"

Replaying their conversation, Rachel turned onto her right side. Ordinarily this was position two in her get-to-sleep rite, but not tonight. As if her emotions weren't enough to keep her awake, what was going on with the visuals? Swirls of light kept flashing before her closed eyes as Rachel turned onto her back once more.

The light was real, and it was moving in front of her forehead like a swarm of huntids. Yawning on the outside, mildly freaked inside, Rachel gradually recognized that this light was a part of herself, lodged in the center of her forehead.

Could she make it go away by opening her eyes? Nothing changed: the light— no, lights—continued twinkling. They reminded Rachel of a childhood visit to the planetarium at the New York Museum of Natural History, where she was shown how the night sky looked before street lights existed. It was eerie seeing a sky full of countless stars. Sure that could happen at a planetarium, but inside her head?

Rachel shut her eyes again. If she was stuck with a light show, the eyes-closed version would be more restful.

Sinking deeper into the light, she realized that she felt a quiet version of something like joy, that tucked inside each particle of light was the presence of God.

She'd expected herself to be thinking about being reunited with her husband tomorrow, or the triumph of yesterday's Wave. Instead she was awake with this presence. Was her physical body asleep? It was certainly going through its normal sequence of night-time stretches. And she recognized the familiar pattern of sleep breathing—in, out, out; in, out, out—an easy rhythm of three-quarter time.

Her jaws clenched, then loosened. Weird to witness her body fidgeting while it slept. Weird altogether to learn that her body did so many things during what was called sleep. Even her mind slept now, although her consciousness was awake. And here was God keeping her company. No fooling.

Then the thinking part of her woke up, but all thoughts turned into songs of praise. Every melody became a hymn: "O come, O come, Emmanuel"; an old Coca-Cola jingle from her childhood," The Ash Grove," from her Girl Scout days, last sung at maybe age 13? Strange how the meaning of each song always came back to

God. That bone-familiar presence had been waiting all along. How come she'd never noticed?

And so it went, hour after hour and song after miracle song. In the darkness, Rachel felt as though she was receiving the answer to a hundred riddles. Over and again, the answer came back: God.

Around 3 a.m., the air changed. Washington West was starting to wake, and Rachel felt the shift. She began taking a more active role with the silence, playing mental hide-and-seek. There was no place she could go where God was not.

Could she be losing her sanity? Maybe this was some kind of post-contact Hunt-id Disease. Maybe other people would think she was in a coma. Forget it. She didn't want Health Services to change one thing.

I know what this really feels like she thought, as her mind drifted back to sleep. *It's as if I've been on a merry-go-round and God was the brass ring. I've had invitations to grab it before. When Brent was being born, for instance, I knew in some corner of my mind that I could grab that ring and ride with God happily ever after. But part of me said, "Not yet." I was too busy enjoying the ride. God always came back for another round, and this time I'm grabbing that ring. For keeps.*

The next morning, she and Brent were dropped off at the airport by an uncharacteristically teary, hug-hungry Marguerite. With her was a very fidgety Gil, who kept jingling the junk in his pocket. Rachel went through the motions of saying goodbye but what really caught her attention was how the lights wouldn't leave unless she specifically asked them to. Then she'd be zapped back to a movie starring her and Brent.

What a lovely secret! All it took to switch on her awareness of God was intention. Closing her eyes for a few seconds would do it, and so would a deep breath. Then she'd rediscover a lively silence that combined light, sound within sound, energy patterns, knowledge and just plain God-stuff. Wow! Adventureland West's biggest roller-coaster was nothing compared to this ride.

Because Rachel could access spiritual information just by asking, she discovered a better way to stay in touch with Marguerite. Her friend was physically out of sight, but even as Rachel boarded the plane, she could feel Marguerite's presence. She'd think Marguerite's name and there she'd be, an energy presence that Rachel could read like a book. The way Marguerite's intelligent, bustling energy stood out all around her was about as subtle as blue porcupine quills. Her quality of silence was individual, too; Rachel could listen to it for as long as she liked.

Right now, for instance, Marguerite's attention was on her husband, who was supposed to return tomorrow. She was psyched with thoughts of housecleaning and, far better, good sex.

Could I be making this up? Entering the airplane, Rachel smiled at the flight robots. She was actually beaming at robots! *No way I'm making this up*, she thought.

Brent took the window seat, Rachel sat next to him. On their side of the aisle, the seat to her right was empty and, beside them, an elderly couple was absorbed in the flight magazine. Brent stared out his window as they waited for takeoff.

Inwardly, Rachel continued to play with her awareness of Marguerite's energy, switching it on and off. She could do the same for the energy in her own body, or Brent's, whose arm seemed to melt into hers as they sat.

At this thought, he turned and met her eyes. *Finally, you're awake.* She could hear the recognition in his gaze. Well, well, so that's what life was like for Huntid Boy. The plane rolled down the runway and up they went.

As Jeremy left work to get Rachel and Brent, he was relieved he didn't have to go home first. The less he thought of home or his personal life the better. Surviving this huntid project had turned him into a champ at ignoring himself, his fears and his itches. Without his family, he moved about the empty house like a ghost haunting his own life.

Driving in Capitol City's perpetual traffic jam, he had plenty of time to review the events leading up to yesterday's triumph. Determination had seen him through as he engineered his secret rebellion, day after day. Not even Wayne had known; Jeremy didn't want to risk getting him in trouble. Besides, it gave him enormous personal satisfaction to lead a secret one-man conspiracy against the Tucker-Hackenworth-Davis political cartel.

His plan had taken shape the last time he saw Hackenworth personally—or at least sort of personally—over the phone-screen. Hackenworth had been floating mid-air over his sofa, setting off a small tickle in the back of Jeremy's mind, a tickle that led to a mental sneeze. Of course, there was something he could do to thwart the bastard! Within minutes he began formulating a plan to counter Hackenworth's mandate to exterminate the huntids.

The official order had been to blitz them, no matter how much poison it took. Even Marty and Wayne had believed high doses of insecticide would be necessary, considering both the rapid proliferation of flies and Tucker's need to eradicate them in one swift display of political power. But Jeremy was convinced that, given what he knew of the huntids, less would prove to be more. Instead of bludgeoning them with a mega-dose, he would coax them with the pesticide equivalent of homeopathy. Given the huntids' uncanny intelligence, the smallest possible dosage would work best and would also preserve public health.

Jeremy didn't do anything as obvious as starting with an infinitesimal dosage. Instead he told Marty that he'd need to calculate and recalculate the toxins based on the ever-changing projections of huntid population growth. Each day, he programmed a new variation on his pesticide formula, often changing the chemical base as well as the formula's proportions, feeding equations directly into the automated nationwide system. Translation of his work was automated, of course, and the robots that loaded the canisters didn't give a damn. HHS staffers only did a quality control check of the canisters themselves, making sure that each one weighed in properly and had its lid screwed on tight.

Two days before the canisters were to be loaded, Jeremy gave instructions for a base of inert substances dusted with five different insecticides. It looked impressive. Only if you were a harder worker than Marty had ever been would you actually scrutinize the formula, and only then would you notice that the pesticide was 1 part poison to 10 billion parts propellant.

Jeremy's slender fingers drummed on the steering wheel of his alligator-green Honda Hybrid as he waited in traffic. He remembered how guarded he was with Marty and Wayne in the control room on Saturday. He had taken care to seem confident that all the huntids would exit on schedule. Furtiveness had become such an ingrained habit that he could look Marty straight in the eye and say, "Considering that we're loaded to the max, do we even have to watch?"

While the men killed time (and Marty belted a few Breathless coffees), Jeremy made wisecracks. Holding his breath, he watched the command computer's display as National Guard planes took off from America's 65 major cities, and thousands of additional planes sprayed ex-urban areas, deserts and parks. Even the lab cages at HHS and other government agencies got automated spray dosages, timed to pour through air vents at 10:30 a.m. Eastern Standard Time. Everything was going according to plan.

Keeping a low profile, Jeremy occasionally glanced at the monitors. They displayed huntid activity levels at sample locations throughout the country, and at precisely 10:37 all levels plummeted to zero. Wayne keyed in an instruction to display the lab cages in the adjoining rooms. When the activity count showed nothing but zeroes, he grinned in the maniacal way he had adopted lately.

"We did it," he said, sounding as relieved as Jeremy felt.

"Here's a toast to us all, but especially to you, Dr. Murphy," Marty said. Jeremy even allowed himself a beer and sipped it when the mighty Rich Davis called to congratulate them.

"Let's go check Lab One," Wayne said around noon. Jeremy came along. Sure enough, the diluted formula had done its job. A thick layer of huntids, as dry and dead as autumn leaves, lay at the base of the eight-foot mesh cage.

"If we walked in that, do you think it would come up to our balls?" Wayne asked.

Jeremy shrugged, avoiding Wayne's eyes. Although his assistant seemed to be flying higher than a kite, if he looked too closely, he might notice Jeremy's sadness, mixed with the relief.

When they returned to the control room, Marty was on the phone with Hackenworth. The Secretary of Intelligence sat on his ostentatious hovering couch. He wore purple suspenders, no tie—and no beads, Jeremy noticed. Greeting him and Wayne, Hackenworth's smile was so triumphant, it made Jeremy's gut churn. Even now, Hackenworth couldn't give a sincere compliment, only a leering acknowledgment that Marty, Wayne and Jeremy—minions in his eyes—had followed orders. Wayne looked thrilled. Jeremy couldn't wait to go home.

Ever since Davis had come up with the idea of exterminating the huntids, Jeremy had lived with a grim sense of foreboding. Now that his plan had succeeded, most of his fear dissolved: America would have no toxic meltdown after Huntid Extermination Day. The huntids had gone quietly, although Wayne and Jeremy, privately had agreed that the huntids would go only if they were willing to. Otherwise their super-human intelligence would allow them to adapt in ways that would thwart any extermination procedure. But for reasons best known to them, the insects had played along with Huntid Extermination Day. They had saved Jeremy's skin; any residual itches were his problem.

This Monday morning, Jeremy's drive to Dulles airport took less than four hours—pathetic but not bad. In the car, he shook his head and muttered, "Dude, you got everything you wanted. Snap out of it. Think about Rachel. Think about Brent." Yet neither family nor success could erase the sorrow he felt. The death of the huntids was an unfathomable loss. Jeremy had always felt the creatures had something important to contribute—but no one would ever know, not now. Life was, dismally, back to normal.

Would Jeremy be waiting at the gate? As she entered the airport, Rachel looked around. Brent was wiggling like a puppy in his eagerness to see Dad. She wasn't that excited, at least visibly.

Of course, glamorous Rachel had dressed carefully for this reunion. She wore a summer-weight velvet jumpsuit from one of her favorite on-line boutiques. Its cushy pile had a 3-D design of concentric circles at different depths: violet, indigo, and baby blue. The background was Rachel's favorite cream and all the colors coordinated perfectly with her complexion, just as the computer try-on photo promised. She especially liked the way the randomly placed patterns of circles drew attention to her curves.

My heart really is open to you, she thought to Jeremy. No games. No more seminar strategies, just reality. Her awareness could now find spiritual truth with the accuracy of a laser beam.

In the waiting area, they couldn't see Jeremy. It was crowded, of course, since their super-jet from Washington West carried 2,000 passengers. Even if Jeremy had got here on time....

"Don't worry," she reassured Brent. "We'll find him."

"He's over to the left, in that corner." Brent pointed.

Rachel raised her eyebrows.

He tapped his forehead with an index finger.

Of course, he used his awareness. As she followed her son's lead, she asked to be aware of Jeremy, too.

What came through was the way Jeremy felt—like a hollow man, wearing itchy skin, as dried out as a man in his 80s, not a relative kid of 42. Nowhere could she find any trace of the musician and poet she'd married. Instead, the iceberg-like indifference Rachel had noticed during their phone calls seemed to have frozen his love for her. Deep in her chest she felt a sob when Brent elbowed her, none too gently, and said, "Mom, don't make it personal."

Then she saw Jeremy's slate-blue eyes. They snapped into focus on her, the way a word processor aligns words after you press "justify." Jeremy's multi-layered attention instantly registered her presence, then Brent's.

Rachel felt enormous love coming to her from this man. However much he had suffered, his coldness had nothing to do with her. The silence between them took on such electricity, she could hardly stand it. She wished she could rip the man's clothes off right there at the airport.

"Hey, you," she yelled, "I dressed to match your eyes."

He hugged them until the three of them dissolved into a walking wiggle machine. Then he stood at arm's length from Brent, hands on shoulders.

"I know you," he said.

Brent crouched and began drumming on his father's left leg, riffing along with the airport Muzak.

"Hey sillyhead, you think I don't need this knee any more?"

Brent giggled back at him, his loony little-boy laugh.

Jeremy's hands went to Rachel's shoulders. He pulled her close, even though physically they were still at arms' length.Despite his height, he seemed to smile straight into her eyes. "What a mysterious vision of blues! They remind me of someone I knew once in a dream."

Brent pushed himself between them. "I think that outfit makes Mom look like a dart board."

Yep, Rachel thought, hugging them both. *We're home alright.*

All she could think of that evening was how soon she could hold Jeremy's body against hers. Dinner was fast food from the fridge and microwave, with Brent doing most of the talking. He yakked about Adventureland West, the troll statue in Fremont, Magical Marvin's ice cream parlor, the computer games he played with Gil. Jeremy listened appreciatively, his eyes often sweeping over to Rachel. Every glance felt like a kiss.

"I miss the huntids. Do you, Dad?"

For a moment, Jeremy looked bereft. "Sure do."

"Me too," Rachel said, "Though part of me thought they were such pesky things at first."

After dinner, Jeremy performed Brent's bedtime ritual while Rachel unpacked. Through the bathroom door came the sounds of a long-version ceremonial bath and, amid the splashing, she heard Jeremy say tenderly, "Little lamb, who made Thee? Dost Thou know who made Thee?"

"Yoo-hoo, Daddy," said a gleeful Brent. "I hate to break this to you, but I'm a boy, not a lamb."

"True enough. Let's put it another way: I want you to grow up, of course. But do me a favor and don't do it too fast."

Rachel smiled, fetching a favorite aromatherapy potion from her bureau. It was nice to have her fragrance collection back, she thought, smoothing the oil over her throat to ease the tightness. Although she'd cried a few times from the sheer relief of being home, she still felt tired from holding back tears. The fragrance helped. Gradually, she realized that, accompanied by the familiar fragrances of rosemary, pine, lavender and roses, something new was happening.

Of course, God was available now. *Click*. Instantly her bedroom was aglow with energy—hers, Brent's and Jeremy's. Energy even bounced off a half-dead African violet sitting on a windowsill. Whether or not she and Jeremy made love tonight, God would still be with her.

Come to think of it, so was a new kind of self-awareness. She hadn't looked in the mirror once to check if she looked fat, nor had she weighed in on the bathroom scale. Instead she reveled in the way it felt to stand barefoot in a pink silk negligee, healthy and grounded and fully alive.

"Did you brush your teeth yet?" Jeremy asked, locking the door—one of their signals that a night of romance was afoot. Rachel nodded. Beads of sweat formed on her forehead. *Love jewels,* she thought. *I will not call it nerves.*

He emerged from their bathroom wearing only his slightly frayed cotton briefs. Rachel watched him sit cross-legged on the bed, touching her knee to knee. He gave his curving smile and took her hand:

> Come live with me and be my love,
> And we will all the pleasures prove,
> That vallies, groves, hills and fieldes,
> Woods or sleepie mountaine yieldes.

Rachel flashed back to her pass at John. The most outrageous of many memories, unfortunately. As guilt washed through her, she countered the thought, steadying herself by breathing through her left nostril.

"Do I deserve you?" she asked. "Tell me about this poetic man, this hero of Extermination Day." Resolved to find as strong a presence in him as she had in John, she let her awareness spread out beneath the words he had spoken and that irresistible smile.

Disconnect alert! Jeremy was putting on an act, and a good one. But underneath he was hiding something. What?

Fear moved through her, replacing the fire his poetry had just kindled.

Jeremy reached out and stroked her hair, running his sensitive hand the length of her thick brown curls. His touch felt delicious, but his silence was masking something.

A long time passed; the silence became increasingly burdensome. Rachel waited until she could stand it no longer. "Jeremy, talk to me."

He got up and started pacing.

What was going to happen, nothing? She followed him to the corner by the closet, where he stood, rubbing his hands together.

"Please, I need you to talk to me." She had her tears under control, but not her eyes.

Jeremy walked her back to the bed and sat. She saw that his eyes, too, were damp, and she touched them gently. *Please,* she beamed to him, *Don't go where I can't reach you.*

He pulled her into a hug. "It's been tough," he said, in a low voice.

"All that pressure," she said, rocking him back and forth. His pain was present now, but within the pain his love was very much alive. She thanked God and said out loud, "Would it help to tell me the things you had to do? It must have been so hard."

"Another time," he said.

"But you *do* still love me, right?" Rachel told herself that the question was for his benefit, to help him become emotionally aware of something besides pain.

It worked. He laughed and said, "That's my Rachel, the queen of subtlety."

She laughed, too.

"Since you already know I have a crush on you, could I put my ear to your chest and listen to your heart?"

He nodded, humoring her.

Placing one ear near his heart, she let her awareness explore Jeremy's aura. "So tired." That was the first layer. Then came, "It hurts to feel this lonely." And beneath that: "I'm so tired of hiding." She'd address the tired layer first.

"You were working hard. It wasn't that you stopped loving me?"

He lifted her head and kissed her—falling into her body, as he had at their very first kiss.

Then he began making love to her with his usual moves. But his plain-vanilla kisses and stroking touches amazed her by their tenderness. Rachel responded with nothing new either, save the inner recognition that no other lover had ever given her this degree of caring. Even John, with all his excitement and mystery, couldn't match Jeremy's deep caresses. Here was the man who knew her, and wanted her to know him, for as long as they lived.

"Wait," she said. Purposefully she cupped her hands, cradling his most private part as though he were her tree of life and she was Eve in the garden. "I'm ready for you," she said softly.

She felt his passion match her own. They rode past months of distance, misunderstanding, heartache and hurt. Words fell away until she felt only the strength of their bodies together.

Afterward, she brought out their familiar little blue "love towel" and they dried each other tenderly. Leaning back, he fired it into the hamper in the corner of the room as if he were an NBA star and it was a hoop.

"You always were a great shot," she said.

Epilogue

Jeremy's quiet triumph exploded on Wednesday, though the day started innocently enough. Stavros' assistant announced an all-staff meeting for Capitol City employees of Health and Human Services; all 42 techs and supervisors crammed into the conference room, eagerly expecting to hear praise lavished upon them. Looking at his colleagues, Jeremy thought he could see visions of merit bonuses shining in their eyes, and maybe modest-sized dollar signs showed in his eyes, too. Stavros' assistant, Floyd Williamson, explained he'd be giving the meeting. When he began to formally speak, he didn't smile, he scowled.

The planes never took off," was the first thing he said.

What? Instantly the room was abuzz with whispers. "You heard me. They never took off, here or anyplace else. Secretary Hackenworth has informed me that the serum was never used. It was destroyed, poured down the drain—who knows. But it sure as hell wasn't used."

Floyd continued, his voice louder than ever, "Thanks to certain covert operators from within our midst, electronic messages indicated that our planes had taken off. But the messages were bogus, which means that, in our country alone, a $12.9 million program went down the toilet."

Jeremy froze. A voice shouted, "The huntids are gone, aren't they? How do you explain that?"

Floyd's scowl grew deeper. "The fact that the huntids are gone is beside the point. As your superior, let me assure you—and I'm speaking directly to whoever arranged this—there will be an investigation. And, as they say, heads will roll."

"How could this be?" Marty asked. "Our instruments registered a successful mission. Could you mean that *some* of the planes—"

"*None* of the planes in our country took off, and flights were sabotaged all over the world. Is that clear enough for you to grasp?" Floyd had obviously taken charm lessons from Stavros.

The rest of the day was a nightmare. Jeremy was suspended, pending further inquiries. So were Marty and Wayne.

Within a month, various investigations uncovered a global conspiracy, masterminded by Wayne and carried out by Stacey Pilgrim's sect. They had infiltrated HHS and the National Guard, apparently to foil a suspected drive by The Righteous to gain government control. Wayne fled the country with his family and moved to South Africa. So did Pilgrim and 250,000 of her other warriors.

The media loved it. What else did they have to write about? No Rapture. No huntids. Tom Cruise had gone into hiding. Besides, pundits had always relished pitting Traditionals against The Righteous.

There was some other news, actually, but since the media didn't know how to play it, they played it down. Rev. Helms had died on Extermination Day, and millions of The Righteous had died with him (including Stavros).

Was it a suicide pact? The huntids' revenge? The Righteous, after all, had led the attacks against them.

"Huntids wouldn't kill anybody," Brent said, when the family discussed it at dinner

"Come on," Rachel said. "What about Huntid Disease? I loved the huntids, too, but they sure made you sick, once upon a time."

"Oh, Mom," he said. "They were cleaning me out. Like those colds, where the mucus would come out of the part of you where your talents were stuck. When I had the big sleep, it was kind of like our Wave of Oneness, only it lasted longer."

"You're kidding," Jeremy said. "Why didn't you tell us that before?"

"Why didn't you ask? Besides, Dad, you were there."

"Excuse me?"

"Part of you, anyway," Brent said. "You're a lot Bigger than you think you are, Daddy. Mom, could I have another potato pancake to go with the raspberry sauce?"

Huntids or not, someone or something killed millions of the most faithful members of The Righteous. Rumors kept Rachel's e-mails coming. One popular theory involved Health Services. Apparently clinics across the country had been offering an elective to assist The Righteous in their devotions. These shots of a new proto-steroid, like many of today's medicines, hadn't been tested extensively. According to the full-blown conspiracy idea, long-term use triggered neurological damage, basically causing Righteous brains to explode under stress. A few leaders of Health Services who were members of the Traditionals, so the story went, had knowingly pushed the drug.

Yet Rachel didn't believe that *anyone* at Health Services was smart enough to pull off a conspiracy. As she wrote to a few of her e-friends, "Those techs couldn't even give a decent make-up tattoo."

Enough people believed it, however, for Health Services to come under investigation. The government tried to hush it up, but people became so suspicious that it became chic to stop going in for your monthlies—which made Rachel something of a pioneer. While in Washington West, Rachel had stopped going, initially just to avoid the sunscreen with the tranquilizer bonus.

According to another theory, the deaths of The Righteous were prearranged by certain of The Righteous faithful in a top-secret suicide pact. Although this was a popular theory on the Net, Rachel thought it unlikely. She told Heather so during one of their occasional walk-and-talks (Rachel had made other neighborhood friends by now, but remained fond of sunny Heather, bonehead or not).

Heather agreed. She said, "You can't tell me that Helms had nothing to live for. He even had theme parks."

The theory that made the most sense to Rachel was something Jeremy told her over dinner as they wolfed down trendy Chinese-Mex cuisine.

"In my opinion," he said, "the cause of death was a neurological meltdown, brought on by progressive deterioration from prolonged multi-tasking. The drugs from Health Services only made it worse. In a sense, The Righteous killed themselves. All those never-ending movements and dances kept their nervous systems under constant strain. The performance anxiety of bringing on a Rapture was the straw that broke that particular camel's back."

"Makes sense to me," Rachel said, biting daintily into a heart-shaped taco oozing sour cream, refried beans, and chunks of mandarin orange. "Remember Helms' last TV appearance? He looked absolutely lost, poor man."

Jeremy shrugged. "You've heard the expression, 'Don't work yourself to death.' This time, it actually happened."

"Think The Righteous died in direct proportion to their zeal?" Rachel was joking, but the truth in the words sent an unexpected shudder up her spine.

"There's a certain poetic justice to that," Jeremy said. "The hypocrites like Tucker and Hackenworth, who never did the movements except in public, are the ones who've survived. At HHS, people have started calling them 'Show Righteous.'"

"I don't get it. They didn't show me a thing."

Jeremy's eyes laughed as he sucked down a bright-orange Jasmine Margarita. He said, "That's 'Show Righteous' because their devotion was all for show. Now they have life sentences as hypocrites. The true believers, who really did all the movements even when they were alone, are the ones who moved on to their reward, whatever it was."

"You know what?" Brent said, methodically picking miniature corn cobs out of his dish of Rachel's chow mein chimichanga casserole. "I think that what you believe is what you get. I think that Righteous people, like Hickory Helms, got their Rapture after all."

Like it or not, Jeremy was stuck at home while investigations dragged over the planes that never took off. In mid-November, he was cleared of conspiracy charges. Once reinstated, he quit.

Rachel became the family wage earner, setting up an outrageously successful internet-based entertainment corporation. Jeremy became a stay-at-home dad and house-husband, and he and Rachel enrolled in his first seminar, a two-year course in Tantra featuring a weekly video. He also did research on huntids. (The Monday after Huntid Extermination Day, before going to the airport, Jeremy had stolen back to his closed office and acquired a research stash of a thousand, scooping them from Lab Cage One into his briefcase.)

Rachel never saw John again, except for occasional telescreen visits. But she stayed in touch with Marguerite and other friends from The Spiritual Center, mostly Consuela.

The phone visits with Consuela began with a surprise call with her former teacher, asking for help. She was marrying Steve Ambrosian and wanted Rachel's advice on a wedding dress. Thanks to his wealth, she'd be buying a whole new wardrobe— her first new clothes in years.

"Kid, I've always been a snob about dressing up. But I'll never forget that time you gave me your opinion of my clothes." Consuela laughed, but Rachel couldn't.

"I've felt so guilty about that conversation. I meant to apologize but everything moved too fast . My advice sounded so arrogant but I didn't mean it that way, really."

"That's just how you were raised, Rachel. You've learned to be an artist at clothes and womanly wiles."

"Well, I'll never be an artist like Marguerite. Still, I know what you mean. I was only trying to give you something, because you taught me so much."

Their friendship grew, and in time they created a network of empaths working together telepathically. They gained a level of political clout that Rachel could never have predicted.

As she became more secure in her skill as an empath, Rachel phoned her mother every week. She wished she could tell Helene what she noticed during those visits, and what she learned about her father, as he drifted further into senility. But Helene never developed any interest in Rachel's spiritual life, so they talked instead about things related to shoes and ships and sealing wax, cabbages and chicken soup.

Brent never had any side effects from Huntid Disease. Nevertheless Rachel knew he was not a normal child, for which she was profoundly grateful.

President Tucker's second term passed uneventfully. Within a year of Extermination Day, the surviving Righteous had lost all political leverage. According to rumor, many of the part-time bead twirlers converted to knitting.

Afterword
On Being an Empath

In the novel you've just read (or are about to read, should you be browsing through this book back-to-front), the heroine becomes a skilled empath. What motivated me to write this story was the desire to help readers like you try out this hitherto unconventional career path.

About 1 in 20 people has a built-in, significant, trainable gift as an empath. Yet even in my fictional America of 2020, few people know about it. In real America today, almost nobody is a skilled empath. On TV (where, let's face it, we seek our role models), among the bimbos, murderers and other characters, I've found only one empath—and she's in re-runs—Counselor Deanna Troi of *Star Trek: The Next Generation.*

Being a skilled empath, like her, opens up wonderful opportunities for service to others, but the greatest significance is personal. The suffering of unskilled empaths tends to be chronic, hard to diagnose in a helpful way and immensely painful. With skill, the very same gift becomes a source of joy.

My last how-to book, *Empowered by Empathy*, gives a practical answer to the question, "What does it mean to be an empath?" *The Roar of the Huntids* attempts to supply a fictional answer. But a quick summary may prove most useful of all. So I'll attempt one here, putting empathy in a context.

It's best understood, I believe, not as the mushy-gushy emotional state most people today think empathy is but as an intuitive gift for deeper perception. Just as some people are neurophysiologically wired as *Highly Sensitive Persons* (as described in Dr. Elaine Aron's book by that same title), a smaller number of people are, from birth, set up as empaths.

All human beings can explore the three deeper levels of perception that I'll describe in the following pages, but only empaths can explore the fourth.

Body language is the first, most obvious level for reading people more deeply. It's also great fun, since there's such useful insight available through nonverbal communication. Physical posture and facial expression are sometimes at odds with what a person attempts to convey on the surface, through words.

Maybe you already know that, if you must choose between the two parts of a mixed message, the nonverbal part will be more important. If, for instance, you're attempting a heart-to-heart talk with a man who stands before you, allegedly eager to have the conversation—yet his arms are crossed over his chest—well, good luck!

Deeper Layer #1, though intriguing, is really just the beginning. In fact, if you're a Body Language enthusiast, chances are that your perception has already started to drift and shift into layers that go even deeper. Learning about them will validate your experience... and also point you in the direction for deeper study.

Layer #2 is *Face Reading*, where you seek insights at the level of the physical face. For the past 3,000 years, physiognomists have interpreted the shapes and angles of the face, most of which you've probably never noticed. Why not? However well meaning, you've been trained to see only eyes, mouth, and stereotypes, not what's really there—let alone interpret it in a nuanced and meaningful way.

My trademarked adaptation of ancient physiognomy is designed to open the heart, and it can also show you faces in a new light. Exploring physiognomy, you'll discover that cheek proportions disclose power style, eyebrows show intellectual patterns and noses reveal talents for work. And it's more accurate than you probably think it is.

The laws of heredity notwithstanding, the soul shapes the face and evolves it over a lifetime. If curious, you can learn more about the system of Face Reading Secrets ® in my birdwatcher's guide for people, *The Power of Face Reading.*

Level #3 involves noticing people in an intuitive way. One minute you'll be exploring Body Language or Face Reading and *click!*, you'll slip into something much deeper. For instance, it may dawn on you that the woman you're watching is happy or frightened or lying like crazy. You'll see/feel/know this even though her body language reveals nothing of the sort; if anything, she may be using body language to *hide* it.

Well, instead of thinking (as most people do) that this intuition means you need to justify it by learning ever more arcane quirks of nonverbal communication, consider this possibility: *What if body language serves as a mask at least as often as it reveals an inner secret?*

In my experience, this happens to be true. If you'd like to understand why, maybe it's time to go deeper and deliberately read Level #3, *auras*—the human energy field.

Auras have far more to them than the popular notion of "seeing the colors." It's a spiritual level that reveals deep human secrets. And you need not be a certified mystic to read them, merely someone who is curious and willing to learn something genuinely new.

Reading auras can help you to appreciate spiritual gifts that you've had your whole life but probably not used yet in a conscious way. Exciting thought, isn't it? Among other things, this means that your people-watching could become even more rewarding. Consider becoming an aura reader by using the 100+ techniques presented in *Aura Reading Through ALL Your Senses* or my video *Thrill Your Soul: Inspiration for Choosing Your Work and Relationships.* Or find some other way. There are many good teachers available.

Level #4 is *empathy*, where you directly experience what it is like to *be* the person you're studying. Like aura reading, true empathy is spiritual and subtle… you find yourself slipping into it as easily as Cinderella fit into her glass slipper.

Most commonly, empathy happens in terms of connecting with another person's emotions. But it turns out that other forms of empathy can bring insight into health, psychology, intellectual specialties, spirituality and more.

Last night, I took a break from getting this book to press and had two conversations that illustrate important aspects of being an empath.

In session with a client whom I'll call "June," I described and validated a number of things that had been troubling her. Because I experienced them directly, I was also able to make suggestions for getting into better balance. Most dramatically, I discovered something strangely wrong with June's physical system, an overwhelming and inappropriate presence of what I could only call "metal."

June explained that she'd been taking acupuncture treatments. Her practitioner had been attempting to balance her system by increasing the proportion of one of the five elements in traditional Chinese medicine, metal—with unfortunate results, it turned out. June had been considering changing acupuncturists; this session helped her to make a more informed choice.

In contrast to my happy client, June, later last night I encountered "Sally" during an Internet interview at a book review chat room. After Sally read my definition that a skilled empath consciously experiences other people's reality, she flamed me about how horrible this would be for "mental health" and slammed the door on her way out as she fled the chat room.

There's a certain humor here, as well as the undeniable fact that many people find empaths really scary. But a skilled empath will not intrude on you in a coercive manner. Ethics and boundaries are an indispensable part of an empath's training (and, incidentally, the first skill I teach to empaths, for the sake of sanity, is how to turn empathy off).

As for reacting with fear to the thought that you might wind up being this dreaded thing, an empath, let me break some news to you. It's too late. Fearing empathy won't do you any good.

If you've signed up for this particular privilege, you've had it since birth. Squelching it, denying it, or fearing it are all unproductive ways of using a God-given gift. The more productive alternative is learning how to use your gift with skill. I'm one teacher who could help. There are others—maybe Sally has already found her perfect teacher in the next chat room. ;-)

As for you, dear reader, if you've ever felt frightened, clueless, confused or worse due to being an unskilled empath, I can relate. And I also can help you to become a skilled empath, which is the biggest fun I know.

It's unlikely that you've been more out of touch with your empathy than this novel's heroine, Rachel Murphy, at the start of this novel. Remember what happened to her? I wrote that story just to encourage you.

Rose Rosetree
Sterling, Virginia
November 2001

Photo: Jan Kawamoto Jamil

Rose Rosetree

Rose Rosetree writes from her experience as one of America's leading intuitives. A graduate of Brandeis University, she lives with her husband and son in Sterling, Virginia.

Three of her how-to books have been selected by major book clubs and she has served as a teacher of personal development for more than three decades. This is her first novel.

Order Here from Women's Intuition Worldwide

All titles can be special ordered from quality bookstores. Or copy this order form. If more convenient, you can also order online at www.Rose-Rosetree.com

The Roar of the Huntids	**$22.95**
Empowered by Empathy:	
25 Ways to Fly in Spirit	**$18.95**
Thrill Your Soul: Inspiration for	
Choosing Your Work & Relationships	
(A how-to video, digitally mastered)	**$24.95**
The Power of Face Reading	**$18.95**
Aura Reading Through ALL Your Senses	**$14.95** _____

Shipping, per total order $4.00   _____

Sales tax (VA residents only) per item:
Empathy and Face Reading $.85, Video $1.13
Roar $1.03, Aura Reading $.67   _____

Total order . . . . _____

Address _____

Name _____   Telephone _____

[ ] I request an autographed copy, **signed for:** _____
Your satisfaction is guaranteed with WIW products. Please note, in keeping with industry standards, videos and autographed books are not returnable.

[ ] Enclosed is my check or money order, **payable to** WIW
Send to: 116 Hillsdale Drive, P.O. Box 1605, Sterling, VA 20167-1605

[ ] Please charge to my credit card number.
Call 703-404-4357
Or charge by mail. **Choose from Visa, MasterCard, or Discover Card:**
Card number: Exp. date:
Signature:

Thank you for your order.